CrowHeart

John Gist

CrowHeart

MP

Montfort Press
A Division of Andmar Press
Mills, Wyoming 82644

First Montfort Press Edition, May 1999

 Published in the United States by Montfort Press, a Division of Andmar Press, Mills, Wyoming 82644.

Library of Congress Catalog Card Number
98-068128
ISBN
0-916781-45-3

Cover photograph courtesy of Buffalo Bill Historical Center, Cody, Wyoming.

Printed in the United States of America.

To my parents and my wife,
with gratitude

Acknowledgements

I would like to thank the following for their help in creating this book:

Ray Harvey, of Laramie, Wyoming, for his advice and patience; Dr. Roy K. Bird, of Fairbanks, Alaska, for his faith in my writing; Ray O'Bannon and Daniel Sandavol of Casper, Wyoming, for their willingness to help; my wife, Wendy, for proofreading and putting up with me; and Dr. F.X. Jozwik who decided to take a chance.

For those who I forgot to mention, my deepest apologies.

The dream reveals the reality
which conception lags behind.
That is the horror of life.

Franz Kafka

Wyoming can be an unforgiving land, and, with that in mind, I believe Grandpa Tom told us the story to scare us. On Christmas Eve, my mother and Aunt Ruth woke up all twelve of us grandkids in the middle of the night. We were herded into the Grandpa's study, the study he had added onto the big house with his own hands. It was a big room, a room with a fish tank lining the entire length of one wall. On the wall opposite the fish tank, just as other men might display bowling trophies, were plaques mounted with stuffed lake-trout, German-browns, walleyes, and brookies. None of us kids feared Grandpa Tom, but we respected his space, and when we were told to sit in a semicircle in front of the Angus-hide couch, we did so quickly and without talking. The brightly colored fish, swimming in the bubbling water (saltwater fish from far away oceans — warm waters that us kids had only dreamed about, or seen in pictures, or on tv), combined with the late hour and the fact that no child had ever been allowed into the study, made us all feel like we were embarking on a journey to some undiscovered land. The room smelled of burnt cherries. The only light came from the fish tank. It reflected off the glass eyes of the mounted fish, causing them to sparkle like obsidian in sunlight. My cousin Ike, at thirteen, was the oldest of us kids. My cousin Cassandra was the youngest in the room; she, if I remember correctly, was four. I was ten at the time.

Like they did every year, the families had gathered on the ranch to celebrate Christmas. A blizzard rampaged outside, gusts of wind lambasting the house, but the study was warm and safe. We all, as instructed by my mother and Aunt Ruth, sat cross-legged on the hardwood floor. Once we were seated, the adults left the room. We were excited, thinking maybe Grandpa Tom was going to give us something special, but the excitement also held an undercurrent of fear, like maybe we were going to be told that something was dead. I don't know how long we waited there before Grandpa Tom finally entered. It seemed like a long time.

He entered the room wearing a tattered cowboy hat and a plaid bathrobe. His white hair, which he usually kept tucked up under his hat or tied at the back of his skull, fell around his shoulders. His equally white beard glowed in the fluorescent light streaming from the fish tank. We could tell by the sound of his feet slapping against the polished wood that he was barefoot. He didn't say a word. The years of riding horses had ruined his back, and, without acknowledging our presence, he hobbled over to the tank and watched the fish watching him. He moved to a cabinet and poured himself a glass of whiskey. He carried the glass to the couch and sat down. Producing a pipe and a leather pouch from a drawer in the end-table, he filled the bowl of the pipe with tobacco. After lighting up, the flames crawling from the bowl like lobsters out of a pot, he took a drink of whiskey. Then, alternately sucking from the pipe and sipping from the glass, he told us the story.

He told us about his brother, a nameless brother none of us kids had ever heard of before that night. He told us how this brother had walked into the barn one morning and doused himself with kerosene and lit the match. How the heat blackened his flesh and peeled it away from the bone. How his eyes burst. How the bared teeth grinned. How this brother had danced while he burned. Grandpa Tom told us his brother did it to cure the Crowheart of its disease. How this brother was medicine. And, he told us, if the disease, which had once threatened the land, ever came again — if one of us kids carried the sickness in our blood like a sword waiting to be unsheathed to pierce the Crowheart — his brother would return to sear the wound shut and dissolve that blade forever. He finished talking and left the room. Gray dawn crept in through the windows. At the time, I believed he was simply trying to scare us. Belief, however, changes as time and memory converge.

Years later, when Grandpa Tom had passed away and my father Gabe was running the ranch, my mother gave me a small box carved from knotty-pine. She told me that Grandpa Tom had told her to give it to me when I was a man. Inside the box was an amulet of what looked to be amber, with something black and curdled encased inside of it. The amulet came with a note: Gabriel, This is the Crowheart.

That was it; that was all it said. I was never offered any further explanation.

I have always wondered why Grandpa Tom chose to give me the amulet: between his four children, there were seven male grandchildren to choose from. I've often speculated about, but have never really known, what the amulet signifies...

Driving over the high plateau named Shirley Rim, Isaac Daniels spots a dead horse in the ditch next to the two-lane highway. The horse, golden hide pearly with dew in the early morning light, lies stiff-legged in the western wheatgrass, torso swollen to bursting, wild eyes frozen open. The black-red smear on the asphalt, as if gallons of paint had been brushed over the highway during the night, causes Isaac to step on the brake. The car skids to a stop at the edge of the road. He turns off the ignition. He steps out of the car, leaving the door open and buzzing behind him. Overhead, in the incrementally lightening and cloudless sky, three buzzards circle.

Flies, morning-wet wings drying in the increasing heat of the rising sun, take flight against a stiff breeze as Isaac walks through the knee high grass on his journey to the horse. Barbed-wire fence vibrates imperceptibly in the wind. The wooden fence posts cast thin shadows towards the west. Isaac swats a fly from his neck without registering the pain of its bite, his movements those of a somnambulist. Striding through a patch of thistles, he does not feel the pain of the plant's needles penetrating the fabric of his jeans, down into the skin of his shins. He does not see the purple blossoms bobbing in the wind.

The horse's head lies on a crumpled pillow of wild mustard. A yellow jacket crawls in and out of the horse's ear. Isaac stops, his boots inches from the horse's muzzle. He is transfixed by the glazed black eye trained steadily on the sky above, as if waiting for the circling vultures to descend.

A truck, fortified with stock racks, rattles down the highway. The truck slows down, brakes squealing, and a woman's brown face peers out of the passenger's window, long black hair flapping in the wind. The driver of the truck is ensconced in shadow. The truck rattles on, spewing a cloud of blue-gray smoke as it accelerates. Isaac does not see the truck, cannot hear it. The horse's black eye, circumscribed by a strand of white, stares at the sky with its content of buzzards and a lone cloud translucent against the backdrop of blue.

The shadows cast by fence posts gradually shorten as morning gives way to afternoon. The wind gusts through the tops of the western wheat, thistle, and wild mustard. Isaac looks down at his feet. Tiny seed husks, shook loose from the wheat, cover the tops of his boots. The paradox amuses him: seed cannot conjoin with leather — their relationship is too far removed. Isaac leans over and, between thumb and forefinger, plucks a tuft from the top of a wheat stalk. He straightens and places the tuft on the tip of his tongue. He closes his eyes, tilts his head back, and points his nose at the overhead sun. The light paints his inner eyelids the color of peaches.

Isaac takes the knife from his pants pocket and unfolds the largest blade. He looks down at the bloated corpse. A droplet of sweat crawls out of his armpit, slides over his rib cage.

Kneeling down over the horse's head, Isaac cuts the eye. He extracts it slowly and expertly from the socket and holds it in his hand. He moves to the horse's torso and punctures the swollen belly with the knife. He inhales deeply, drawing the sickening-sweet scent deep into his lungs. Inebriate with fumes, he stumbles towards the car, climbs in and shuts the door behind him.

Isaac awakes in the front seat of the car, his cotton shirt damp with perspiration, black hair pasted to his skull. After sitting up and warding off a bout of dizziness, he starts the engine and pushes buttons to roll down the windows. The warm wind eases his feelings of apprehension. Dropping the transmission into drive, he notices the horse's eye. It is resting on the passenger's seat where his head, moments earlier, had lain. He does not remember cutting the eye out of the socket. His stomach spasms.

The sound of rubber treading over the asphalt quells his panic. The mutilated horse shrinks in the rearview mirror. Isaac sees his eyes in the mirror and notices the edges of the irises are flecked with tiny specks of gold. The anomaly is new to him. He wonders why he never noticed this thing about himself before.

Remembering that he has recently made a pact with himself not to be so self-absorbed, he pushes the eye question from his mind. There are more important things to ponder than himself: Tonight, on the Crowheart, his father is throwing a party in which the new matriarch of the ranch will be presented to the family. Isaac's curiosity is piqued. Realizing he will now be late due to his selfish nap, he presses down on the accelerator until the speedometer registers eighty-five. Without considering it one way or the other, he picks the horse's eye from the seat and puts it in the glove compartment. He turns on the radio. The static is like a pit of hissing snakes in his ears.

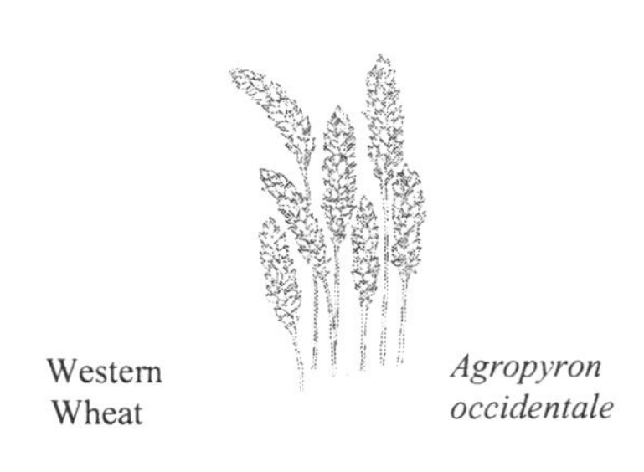

"Looks like Ike finally made it home," says Thomas Daniels, standing on the porch of the big house and pointing at the dust trail kicked up by the midnight-blue car as it lumbers over the gravel road.

Michael Daniels sits in the rocking chair on the porch, squinting from underneath the brim of his tattered straw cowboy hat. He scratches his hairy forearm with the dull edge of a pocket knife.

The screen door leading into the kitchen bursts open, is caught by the wind, and slams against the side of the house. Sarah Daniels, Michael's wife, a slight woman clad in a yellow wraparound canvass skirt and a white cotton blouse, squirts through the open doorway and scrambles to rescue the screen. "Isaac's home?" she asks no one in particular. "He made it?" Her ponytail, dishwater blonde, swings in the wind. She secures the screen door and makes her way to Thomas' side.

"Looks that way, don't it?" says Thomas. He produces a pack of cigarettes from underneath his baseball cap and tamps it on the porch railing. "Never could figure why he drives that damned New Yorker. Hell, the Old Man offered to *give* him one of the trucks."

"His way a telling us he don't want to be a rancher," mumbles Michael.

"You'd better put those away. Your father will be coming down." Sarah stands next to the railing with her right hand above her brow in a salute. "He couldn't stay away any longer. Curiosity got the better of him. I knew it would."

Thomas tucks the pack of cigarettes under his hat. "Can't blame him none. Whole thing's been eating me up like sickness. Feels like we're fixin' to meet some kind of goddamn royalty." He leans on the railing and watches the car approach. "It'll be a shame when it's all over. Kind of like Christmas morning when all of the packages have been opened and all the wrapping paper is burning in the garbage."

"Watch your tongue," says Sarah.

The New Yorker skids to a stop in the parking area, some fifty feet from the big house. A brisk wind permeates the air with a semi-audible moan; a vacant blue sky domes the land.

Michael watches from under the brim of his hat as Isaac steps out of the car. "He wouldn't have been curious if you wouldn't have told him."

"He'll be thirsty. I'd better get him something to drink." Sarah lowers her salute and waves to Isaac before turning an about-face and heading into the house.

"If I wouldn't have told him, Gabe or someone would have. It ain't like you could keep it a secret from him. He *is* our brother." Thomas takes the pack of cigarettes from under his hat, turns his back to the wind, cups the end of a cigarette with one hand, and lights the tip with a butane lighter. The smoke is tinged with the scent of cloves.

Isaac climbs the four steps leading to the porch and stands looking at his brothers as if they are strangers.

Michael and Thomas watch Isaac without speaking.

Cattle low from the pasture to the south.

Thomas grins when the tension is brittle. "Boy, I'm glad to see you. I was beginning to wonder if I just dreamed you up or something." He pokes the cigarette in his mouth and, with his hands on his hips, surveys Isaac. "You *are* real ain't you? Can't be too sure with that fancy looking car and that silk shirt. Can't be too sure."

"If you dress like a cowboy where there isn't any cows, people tend to think you're full of shit," says Isaac. "Are you new?"

Thomas laughs. The cigarette tumbles from his lips scattering sparks on the floorboards of the porch. "Well, at least you still got your old boots." He covers the distance between them in a stride and takes Isaac in a bear hug. "It's damn good to see you." He releases Isaac and stands in front of him grinning.

"It's good to see you too, runt. You been keeping out of trouble?"

"Trying not to," says Thomas, leaning over to pick up the cigarette from the floorboards.

"When did you take up smoking?"

Thomas stands erect and pokes the cigarette between his yellowed teeth. "I been at it quite a spell. Damn near two years. You just ain't been around to notice it."

"You're still too damn young," says Isaac.

Michael pushes himself out of the rocking chair, knees popping, and hobbles toward his brothers. The wind ruffles the limp brim of his hat.

"Hello, Mike," says Isaac, the wind agitating his silk shirt. "What happened to your legs?"

"Horse threw me. Nothing I won't get over." He looks Isaac in the eye. "Listen, Ike, you shouldn't have come."

"Christ on a crutch," says Thomas, "leave him be."

"Stay out of this, boy," says Michael, his eyes still trained on Isaac. "It ain't none of your concern."

"What's going on?"

"You know damn well what's going on. You remind him too much of her. He's finally getting past all that. He deserves a little peace."

"Maybe he needs some reminding," says Isaac.

"For god's sake, Ike, it's been going on seven years," says Michael.

Thomas drapes an arm over Isaac's shoulders. "Lighten up. I heard the Old Man asking about Ike just the other day. He wants him here. For the party."

Isaac accepts a plate of cheese, crackers, and sliced green apples from Sarah and sits at the kitchen table to eat. After pouring a glass of lemonade from a sweating pitcher and replacing it exactly on top of the moist ring in the center of the table, he prepares an apple, cheese, and cracker sandwich. A feeling of guilt germinates in his belly. He is alone in the kitchen, as Michael and Thomas have returned to the business of the Crowheart. Isaac wonders at the absence of Gabriel and Jedidiah: No doubt they, too, stood watch, waiting for his return, before returning themselves to the responsibilities of the day. Sarah, after ensuring his comfort with a kind word and food and drink, hastily exited the kitchen under the guise of looking after the laundry, or cleaning the windows in the dining room, or applying fresh linen to Isaac's bed..., or something, anything to stay clear of him. And where is Cassandra? He had hoped that she would be there to ease his return. Certainly, because she had recently become betrothed to Gabriel, she still resides on the Crowheart.

Isaac washes down the sandwich, the sharp cheddar sticking to the roof of his mouth and wheat cracker scratching his throat, with a swallow of lemonade. The acidic liquid burns in his belly. The thought of a glass of milk to coat his stomach makes him queasy. He feels filthy; he decides to take a bath. Maybe washing the road slime from his body, the traces of horse blood from under his fingernails, will change his mood.

The Daniels house is void of showerheads. Each of the four bathrooms is equipped with a medicine cabinet, sink, mirror, toilet, towel closet, and antique porcelain bathtub with brass lion's paws for legs. Oaken floors. The air in the bathrooms is infused with the scent of moldering wood.

Isaac opts for the bathroom connected to what used to be Clytie's bedroom. He turns on the water in the tub (the water is too hot for touch but Isaac knows the porcelain will cool it rapidly) and watches the steam rise. The vapor incites the scent of decay which finds its way into Isaac's nostrils as he undresses. It is a scent familiar and forgotten with the years of university dormitories and tiled, sterile lavatories. As Isaac dips a toe in the bath water (the water scalds his toe and he yanks his foot upwards compromising his balance), the commingling scents unleashes a flash flood of nostalgia. Images reel:

Clytie's exposed cleavage moist with sweat; the heart of an elk on a bed of red pine needles in the forest, a nefarious grin protruding from beneath a black veil, a bed stained with menstrual blood; a table laden with roast of veal, mashed potatoes, gravy, Brussel sprouts, and carafes brimming with red wine; a baby grand piano situated on top of a bearskin rug; pages of poetry and the St. Vitus' dance in flames; the sunken skull of the one who dared to put the magnum to his temple; snow falling over the windless prairie; an apple tree in blossom....

Isaac loses his balance. He grips the rim of the tub as his head cascades towards the water.

"Goddamn, you ain't nothing but skin and bones. You got a tapeworm or does that university got you picking at peas and carrots? I ain't shitting you, Ike. Looks like you're about to keel over, can't even stand up proper. Ribs are poking out, and you're the color of milk-fed calf meat. You need to get outside some. Exercise."

At the sound of the voice, Isaac regains his composure, his balance, and stands rigid. Back turned to the voice he says, "Gabe? Show a little respect."

"Tommy told me about Mike. Just wanted to tell you not to sweat it. Feels it's his duty and all. Figures that with the Old Man taking on years and all, he's the big cheese. He don't really mean it."

"Can't it wait?" asks Isaac. His back still turned to his brother, he realizes his hands are cupped over his genitals; he allows them to fall to his sides.

"Sorry. Are you okay? Doc Watson'll be at the party tonight if you ain't feeling up to par."

"I'm fine, Gabe. I'm dandy. Now will you get the hell out of here and give me some peace?"

"Fine. Have it your way. Just relax. It ain't like I never seen you without your clothes on before."

Isaac listens to the door close. He looks over his shoulder to make sure he is alone before lowering himself into the tub. He listens to droplets dripping from the faucet into the pool of hot water. He looks at the beams of sunlight flowing through the lone window, beams slashed by the Venetian blinds, beams slashing the floor with strips of honey colored light. The scent of the moldering wood transports him back to the days of his youth, the grime of experience washed clean by the cooling water in the bath. For the moment he is a child again, *capricious in his mother's love, at ease, confident in his relationship with existence*. The moment is irreconcilably marred by the realization of remembering. His mother, like his youth, is only a memory: intangible, vacuous. The recognition of time creeps through his veins like hemlock. For Isaac, the division between youth and what comes after is as distinct as the barred walls of a prison cell. Sentenced to life, memory is only an adulterated dream of the inmate. The moment, because the center cannot hold, collapses in on itself.

Isaac empties the tub. After the last of the water swirls down the drain, he stands and takes a towel from the rack on the wall next to the toilet. He wraps the towel around his dripping torso and walks out of the bathroom into the room where his mother died. He lies down on the bed. The barred walls of the prison cell disintegrate and Isaac, once again, remembers: The image of *Clytie sitting on the bed clad in her favorite silk nightgown, her bosom expanding and contracting as she breathes, her dark eyes beckoning him closer, the nighttime, the candlelight glistening*. He remembers the *small, open space between her lips and the thought of her tongue warm-wet as she pats the bed at her side, her long fingers splayed, her nails painted blood-red, motioning him to sit next to her*. He fancies Clytie's voice whispering in his ear, *"Be careful never to equate love with truth. The two are mutually exclusive and to force them into coexistence is like placing traditional enemies on the same reservation. It's mean-spirited and inhuman to couple them. Do you understand?"* Isaac's voice is that of his youth, *"Yes." "Do you promise?" "Yes." "Good. Now give me a hug and a kiss to seal the pledge."*

Isaac's legs jut stiff on the bed. There is a knock on the bedroom door. The remembrance of *Clytie, vibrant with the scent of magnolia on her neck, in her hair, the taste of brandy on her lips,* evaporates. He opens his eyes and remembers Clytie's emptiness on the night of her death.

The knocking continues. "Ike, you in there?" the voice of Cassandra, Gabriel's fiancé, penetrates the door. "Sorry if I woke you up. Sarah said you'd come home, and I just couldn't wait a moment longer to see you. Are you in there?"

Flushed with shame, Isaac rewraps the towel around his torso and sits up. "Yeah, I'm here."

The bedroom door opens and Cassandra steps through. She is dressed in black spandex shorts and a white tank top. She is barefoot. Her hair, auburn, is tied into a ponytail high up on the back of her head. Her sun-browned skin is moist with perspiration. "You don't know how much I've missed you," she says. She walks towards the bed. "Like I'm dying." She stands at the foot of the bed looking down at Isaac.

Isaac lays prone on the bed, his feet touching the floor. He places his hands behind his head and stares up at the ceiling.

"You look terrible," says Cassandra. She breathes heavily, as if she has been running. "You need to get some sun. You need to get some sun and eat some of Sarah's cooking. You need to get some sun, eat some of Sarah's cooking, *and* get some exercise." She moves to the side of the bed and looks down at

Isaac's feet. Leaning down, she touches his bare knee, "You've been away too long."

Isaac closes his eyes. "Do you mind?"

"Are you kidding?" Cassandra slaps Isaac's thigh. "I've seen every Daniels man in a compromising position at one time or another. Let alone the women. Anyway, you know I've always been in love with you. And yet you continue to mock me. You can at least give a girl something to fantasize about."

When Isaac looks at her, Cassandra winks a green eye. She stands above him grinning like a fox eating bumblebees.

Isaac's eyes clear. He sits up. "I need to get dressed."

Cassandra hovers above Isaac, still smiling.

"Do you mind?"

Cassandra's teeth are stained from years of chewing tobacco and smoking cigarettes. "I'm pretty busy with the preparations for the party. It kind of feels like this Rebecca woman the Old Man is so infatuated with is an art exhibit, but I was wondering if you wanted to saddle up a couple of horses and take a ride tomorrow. You know, sort of reacquaint yourself with the place. Get some exercise."

"Ask me tomorrow."

"I'm asking you now."

"Okay. Okay. I'll ride with you. Now will you please get out?"

"Great." Cassandra leans over and slaps Isaac's thigh. She looks once more to the floor before standing erect. "We'll take an afternoon ride. I'm sure we'll both be wanting to sleep off hangovers." She turns and walks out of the room, leaving the door ajar.

Isaac stands and closes the door, then returns to the bed. He crawls under the covers and shuts his eyes, attempting to return to the realm of waking dreams. The song of a kildeer outside the window pierces his mind like the sharpened tine of a spur. He cannot concentrate. Curling into a fetal position, he hopes the scent of the sheets, the softness of Clytie's quilt (a quilt sewn by the hands of her mysterious ancestors), will conjure up her image in his mind. The pounding of his heart against the feather pillow, the kildeer's song ruminating, the moving shadows cast by the cottonwood branches outside the window, the scent of the moldering wood amalgamating with the sterility of the bleached sheets and pillowcase, combine and force Isaac to remain in the present. Realizing the futility of his aspirations, he sits up and clicks on the antique radio perched on the maple night stand next to the bed. Honky-tonk-blues. He returns to the fetal position and listens to the familiar song, a song which he knows but cannot name. Before the song ends, Isaac sleeps without dreaming. A rivulet of drool flows from the corner of his mouth onto the starched pillowcase.

He awakes in darkness. Shafts of moonlight fall through the window like ephemeral snow. Laughter rises from below. Isaac's skin shines with sweat. He notices his suitcase sitting next to the bed and is seized with the apprehension that the horse's eye in the glove box may have been discovered. The thought violates him. He scrambles to the floor, lifts the suitcase onto the bed, opens it, and quickly dresses himself in an old pair of jeans and a silk shirt with mother-of-pearl buttons. He retrieves his boots from the bathroom, pulls on a pair of socks, and pushes his feet into the boots. Sitting on the bed facing the lone window, he gathers his wits by staring at the crescent moon and listening to another forgotten honky-tonk tune streaming from the radio.

"Don't be feeding Tommy anymore of that champagne," roars Jedidiah from the head of the long table. "He's too damn young to be getting drunk. He's got lessons in the morning, and Sarah won't want him grinning at his books like some kind of goddamn idiot."

The long table sits underneath an electric chandelier in the center of the dining room. The polished hardwood floor reflects the light cast down from above. On either end of the room, flames flicker orange in stately fireplaces. The room is large; the hanging portraits of Daniels ancestors are concealed in shadow.

There are ten chairs set around the cherrywood table (chairs with arms and legs fashioned from elk antlers), whose backs and seats are padded with red leather. Nine of the chairs are occupied. The tabletop is laden with silver serving trays, silver ice buckets chilling bottles of champagne, crystal goblets, china dishes, and polished silverware with lion head handles. The scent of roasted lamb, garlic, gravy, yams, warm bread, and pipe tobacco mingle in the air.

The members of the party are casually dressed, the men in blue jeans and button up cotton shirts, the women in skirts and blouses. For all the light in the room — the electric chandelier, the firelight — there is an anachronistic quality of darkness, as if the walls and the oil paintings are at once embarrassed and annoyed by the boisterous illumination.

Sitting to the right of Jedidiah is a girl of no more than twenty with hair the color of old axle-grease. She has almond shaped eyes whose pupils are the density of 8-balls, an aquiline nose, and skin the burnt tone of raw iron-ore. A gold band with a large diamond encircles Rebecca's left ring finger and ricochets light cast down from the chandelier. She sits rigidly in her antler chair looking down at the slice of lamb on her plate. At regular intervals, she raises her eyes to her goblet of champagne, reaches, with her right hand, to lift it and takes a drink.

Jedidiah, aware of his fiancé's discomfiture, promptly refills her goblet whenever the opportunity arises.

When Jedidiah escorted Rebecca to the dinner, whisking her into the dining room with a flourish that made it look as if she glided across the polished floor, uneasiness spread like a fast moving virus into every corner of the room. And the only available antidote, after crackling introductions around the table, was the rapid uncorking of champagne so that for a few moments the room sounded like an Independence Day celebration. Toasts were made; bottles were emptied; people began eating. Eventually, the tension that, upon Rebecca's entrance, had cascaded into the room, slunk into the dark corners, bullied by the alcohol, and created eddies of lurking dubiosity.

When Isaac enters the room a different brand of tension enters with him. Those seated at the table, aided by alcohol, compensate and adjust by employing exaggerated modes of nonchalance.

"Ike," yells Thomas. "Ike. Everybody's drinking champagne."

Isaac smiles at Thomas. He approaches the empty chair opposite Rebecca and sits down. He avoids eye contact. "You ever hear of calling people to dinner?"

"I told them to let you sleep," replies Jedidiah, his lips slick with lamb grease. He sets his fork on his plate and slaps Isaac on the shoulder. "You had us worried. Up there sweating and shivering and going on about some horse and your mother and a fire. None of which made any sense. Probably would've hauled you into town if Old Doc Watson wasn't here to convince me otherwise. 'Completely worn down,' he said. University seems to be getting the better of you."

Doc Watson, a hoary-headed octogenarian, sits at the far end of the long table chiming his fork on his plate and nodding his head. "Yes, sir," he says in a dusty voice, "you gave everybody quite a jolt lying in *that bed* twitching and sweating and moaning a cart full of nonsense." He places his fork on the table next to his plate and picks at the growth on the side of his nose, just under the rim of his glasses. "Everybody thought they was in for a repeat. Lucky I was here to calm them all down." Retrieving the fork, he stabs a cherry tomato in his salad bowl and pops it into his mouth. "Sweetest damn tomatoes I ever ate. These come from the greenhouse, Sarah?"

"Yes," says Sarah, returning from the kitchen with two bottles of champagne. "Tommy and I grew them. They came off the vine just this morning." She places the bottles in a silver bucket of ice and sits down next to Gabriel to resume her meal.

"My compliments. When you get right down to it these are probably even better than the ones Ike used to grow when he was coming up." He stabs another tomato, pops it into his mouth, and captures Isaac in his sights. "What do they have you doing down there in the academy that has you so tuckered out?"

"Just working on my thesis. You know how that goes."

"No, I don't know how that goes. I'm a Medical Doctor. M.D. Didn't write no thesis."

Isaac catches Rebecca's dark eyes and smiles. "Well, Doc, it's studying, and I can only hope you know about that."

"Oh," grunts Doc Watson, now focusing his full attention on the slab of lamb on his plate. "Well slow down some, boy." He locates a knife under the rim of his plate and picks it up. "There isn't any sense in running yourself ragged, now is there? You won't be no good to anybody then."

Rebecca averts her eyes to her plate.

"I'll bet he's been staying out too late cavorting with the coeds," says Cassandra. She sits at the center of the long table opposite Gabriel. "That's what's been wearing him down. You have to be careful, Ike. The fairer sex like to weaken their prey before the kill."

Sitting to the right of Doc Watson is Wade Ksaslmkqe, a man older than Jedidiah and the unofficial foreman of the ranch. He is the son of a Basque immigrant, a man who rarely speaks in the presence of others. "Whatever he's been doing, it ain't no good. He should've stayed on the Crowheart where he belongs."

"I agree," says Michael. He is sitting next to Cassandra and looks at Jedidiah as he speaks. "Down there in Laramie. Studying history." The words drop from his mouth with a forced air of sagacity. "That kind of crap is poison to a man raised out in the open under a clear blue sky. Nothing but slow poison."

Isaac, too, looks towards Jedidiah as he speaks. "Skies aren't always blue around here, Mike. I remember weeks on end when there was nothing but gray."

Sarah stands up and walks toward the kitchen.

"Can't you two stand on the same side of the fence for once?" asks Gabriel, hoping to rekindle the collective nonchalance. "All you ever do is bicker. You were best buds when we were kids." He looks across the table at Cassandra. His eyes shine. "I always wondered what the hell happened."

"Yeah," slurs Thomas. "What happened?"

Cassandra watches Rebecca watching Isaac. "Ike, are you dating?"

"Really haven't got the time for a social life," says Isaac. He glances at Rebecca who shifts her eyes to her plate. "You know, with teaching and seminars and research."

Michael turns his head to watch Sarah emerge from the kitchen. "Ike never set much store in dating, did you? Didn't ever seem too interested in girls."

"Leave him be," says Jedidiah.

"Maybe he just hasn't found the right one yet," says Cassandra.

"Maybe there is no right one," retorts Michael.

"Leave him alone," says Gabriel.

"Yeah," mumbles Thomas. "Leave him be, Mike."

Isaac says nothing. He eats.

Sarah, returning from the kitchen, places a large cake on the center of the table. She stands looking at the cake with her hands on her hips. "Stop it. All of you. This is a festive occasion."

"Mike's jealous," says Thomas.

"I said stop it, Tommy," admonishes Sarah.

Jedidiah empties a bottle of champagne into Rebecca's goblet. "I found one."

"Pardon?" says Cassandra.

"He says he found the right one," puts in Doc Watson, buttering a yam.

"Found the right what?" asks Gabriel.

"Found the right girl," says Jedidiah. "I found the right girl, and, by god, this *is* a celebration, and I *will* tolerate *no* more petty bullshit tonight. No more bullshit. Show some respect to your new mother."

The eddies of dubiosity couched in the dark corners of the room take current; a befuddled silence envelops the table. Everyone pretends to be interested in the food on their plates. Sarah, realizing that without something petty to talk about the party is doomed, sits down in her chair opposite of Michael and says, "I think the dogs have worms again. They're thin as bone and they've been scooting around on their hind ends."

Michael, taking up where he left off, says, "Ike's skinny as rope, too. Maybe he's got -" He is silenced by a glare from Sarah.

After a few moments of listening to pitch pockets explode in the fireplaces, and, as if taking cue from Sarah, Cassandra says, "Ike and I are going riding tomorrow. Maybe Rebecca would like to ride with us? Jed, have you shown Rebecca the grandeur of the Crowheart yet?"

"No," says Jedidiah, "I haven't. Rebecca was a surprise, a gift to the family. Wouldn't have done much good to be parading her around the ranch." He smooths his dangling mustache while refilling Rebecca's goblet from a fresh bottle of champagne. "Anyway, you know I can't ride with my back the way it is."

"Do you ride?" asks Cassandra.

Rebecca waits until her goblet is full and then takes a drink. "No. I've always been afraid of horses."

"An Indian that's afraid of horses," guffaws Doc Watson. "Now I've heard it all." The irony amuses him to the point of chortling his upper denture loose, and, in the move to clap his hand over his mouth, his goblet is upset, spilling champagne over the polished tabletop.

Sarah, snatching the cloth napkin from her lap, springs from her seat to clean up the spill.

A round of laughter circles the table.

Gabriel says, "That's alright, Rebecca. We'll saddle up old Clementine for you. She's as gentle a horse you'll ever come across. Fact is, she *enjoys* being rode. She likes to take a look around herself."

"Good idea," says Jedidiah. "See what happens when you cut out the bullshit? Good ideas start popping up like dandelions."

"What do you say, Rebecca?" asks Cassandra. "Want to face your fear?"

Rebecca glances at Isaac and smiles. She looks Cassandra in the eye and says, "Why not?"

"Good. We won't have a thing to worry about with Ike watching over us." It is as if Cassandra has been waiting for events to synchronize into this moment; she is elated. "Isn't that right, Ike?" There is no response. "Ike?" repeats Cassandra.

"What?"

"You'll watch over us?"

"Sure."

After refilling Doc Watson's goblet, Sarah returns to her chair. "Do you think that's such a good idea? Doc Watson says he's exhausted."

"I'll be alright," says Isaac. "I'm going to turn in early and rest up. So, if you'll excuse me, I'll see you all in the morning. Thanks for a great dinner, Sarah." He pushes his chair from the table and stands. "It was a pleasure meeting you, Rebecca."

"Goodnight," says Rebecca.

"Can I go?" slurs Thomas. "Can I ride with you?"

"We'll see," says Jedidiah. "Goodnight, Ike. It's good to have you home."

After Isaac has exited the room, Sarah says, "He hardly touched his food."

"He'll be alright," says Gabriel. "The fresh air will do him good."

"Better check him for worms," says Michael. "Damn things spread like disease you know."

"Quiet," says Sarah.

"He'll be alright," says Cassandra. "Rebecca and I will see to it."

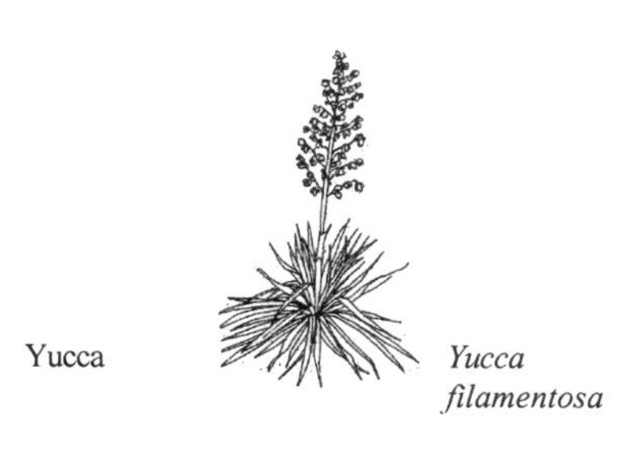

Light of morning filters weightlessly through the bedroom window. The sounds of morning birds register in Isaac's consciousness. He opens his eyes. He is disoriented. He believes he is in the dank bed of his apartment, in Laramie, a few blocks from the University of Wyoming. But the belief deteriorates as the knowledge of the house of his childhood, thick with the residue of memory, sifts into his mind. Morning scents of coffee, bacon, toast, and eggs rise up from the kitchen. For an indeterminate amount of time — a moment, a minute, a half hour — Isaac remembers an era in which the wonderment peculiar to youth, the unconditional love of existence, vibrates with the simplicity of a harmonic convergence. A rumbling in the belly shatters the emanation.

Isaac sits up. He glances to his side, half expecting to see the figure of Clytie curled next to him and breathing rhythmically with sleep. Realizing that he is not in Clytie's bed at all but in *his* bed, the bed of his youth, he lays back down and pulls the bleached sheets up under his hairless chin. A familiar feeling of despair, a crystalline sense of the finality of Clytie's death, stifles his hunger. Out of the deluge of self pity — sinking with the weight of never being able to see Clytie again, never being able to touch her — and without provocation, leaps the image of Rebecca, the sound of her voice, the dark splash of her hair and eyes. The sorrow subsides, vanishes as if ingested into the acid of a Herculean stomach. Hunger mercifully returns.

Due to the varying schedules in the Daniel's household, breakfast is served in the kitchen, rather than the dining room which is reserved for special occasions. The Daniels men come and go while Sarah, up before the sun, cooks each the breakfast of his choice. Michael, unfailingly the first man to enter the kitchen each day at around five a.m., eats the same breakfast without variation: three eggs from the henhouse fried over-easy, four links of elk sausage (or, if the elk hunt proved fruitless the previous year, a rarity, a slab of fried venison coated in spiced flour), two slices of wheat bread smeared with choke cherry jelly (canned by Sarah), and three mugs of black coffee. Gabriel enters the kitchen between 6:30 and 10 a.m.; his tastes are whimsical and eclectic: biscuits and gravy, cold cereal with fruit and milk, eggs and sausage, steak and eggs, oatmeal and toast, hash browns smothered in chili and topped with cheese and chopped onion — all this and more finds its way into Gabriel's revolving menu. Jedidiah, like clockwork, enters the kitchen at 7 a.m., consumes two bagels with lochs and sliced tomato and washes it down with two mugs of coffee replete with sugar and cream. Thomas, whom Sarah will spend the shank of the morning with going over GED lessons (with Jedidiah's permission, he has quit high school and does not care for breakfast), slugs a glass of orange juice and then and only then fills his coffee cup, adding plenty of cream. Of these breakfast patrons, Sarah looks forward to serving Gabriel the most; the variations in his menu allow her some small freedom from the prison of routine which encompasses her days.

After the men have eaten, Sarah washes the dishes and feeds the scraps to the dogs. She does this before sitting down at the freshly wiped table to eat an apple or an apricot and drink a cup of steaming tea.

When Isaac, disheveled, enters the kitchen, it is just after 8:30 a.m. He finds Cassandra sitting at the table, wearing a blue flannel bathrobe. Her face is fully made up with eyeshadow, rouge, and burnt-red lipstick. Her auburn hair is wrapped in a towel. "There he is," she says. "A good morning to you, Ike. Did you sleep well?"

"I can't remember."

Sarah stands at the double sinks polishing silverware from the previous night. She wears a denim dress that falls to her knees and a red plaid apron tied at the small of her back. Her dirty-blonde hair is woven into a French braid. At the sound of Isaac's voice, she turns around and, continuing to polish a silver spoon, says, "Good morning. What would you like for breakfast?" Her blue eyes grin.

"Good morning," says Isaac. He shuffles towards the coffeepot on the counter. "Whatever's easiest. Did you already throw the scraps to the dogs?"

"It never ceases to amaze me," says Cassandra.

"What's that?" asks Isaac.

Cassandra sips from her coffee mug. "Sarah gets up in the dark every morning and cooks breakfast for every male in the house. And yet she has never once offered to cook breakfast for me. Not once in all of these years."

"The men work," joins Sarah, wiping her hands on her apron.

"It's as if she enjoys being subservient to men. I can't understand it."

"Something smells good," says Isaac. He balances the mug of coffee between hands on his way to the table.

"Gabe had biscuits and gravy this morning. He was up and out of here earlier than usual," says Sarah. "There's still some left."

"That sounds good," says Isaac. "You always made the best gravy."

"I could fix something else. Eggs and bacon? There's some elk steak in the refrigerator."

Although the thought of an elk steak with eggs and fried potatoes produces a near unslakable craving in Isaac, he says, "Biscuits and gravy will be fine."

"Well," says Cassandra, her green eyes shining in the morning light, a smile twitching at the corners of her painted lips, "what about Ike?"

Sarah takes a plate down from the cupboard. She opens the oven and removes two large buttermilk biscuits. "What about him?" She slices the biscuits in half on the plate.

"He doesn't work."

"He's a guest, Cassy." Sarah ladles white gravy (laden with hunks of sausage) over the biscuits from a kettle on top of the stove. "I kept everything warm. I know you like my gravy."

"He's family," says Cassandra. She nudges Isaac's calf under the table with her bare toes. "Would you dish me up some of those vittles, sweet-sister-to-be?"

"You're perfectly capable of serving yourself."

Sarah carries the plate to the table and places it in front of Isaac. "Anyway, you're not a guest in this house. You're a fixture." She pats Isaac on the shoulder. "I'll get you some silverware and a napkin."

Isaac looks at Cassandra, his eyes puffy with sleep. He pushes his chair from the table and stands. "I'll get another plate since Cassy obviously won't get one for herself."

"I'll get it," says Sarah, scuttling towards the stove. "You sit down and eat, Ike. You need the nutrition."

Rebecca enters the kitchen wearing spanking new Wranglers, a corduroy shirt, and shiny cowboy boots. A blue bandana encircles her neck. "Good morning."

Isaac stands rigid. He is halfway between the stove and the kitchen table. Sunlight cuts through the kitchen windows casting a nimbus of light around his skull.

"Good morning," says Sarah.

Rebecca stands in Isaac's shadow.

"Top of the morning to you," says Cassandra. "I can see you're ready to ride."

Sarah carries a plate to the table and slides it in front of Cassandra.

"Thanks," says Cassandra, "but it looks like Rebecca's ready to go. I've got to get dressed." She slides out of her chair and stands. "Don't worry, Sarah, I'll eat an apple or something. Anyway, I've packed a gourmet lunch for later in the day. When we get to the lake."

As Cassandra walks between Isaac and Rebecca, she says, "I'll be back. Don't you dare do a thing without me."

"Good morning," Isaac says to Rebecca. He returns to the table and sits in a wire backed chair. "Is Tommy going to ride with us?"

"No. He's sick from last night," says Sarah. "Jed informed me that he would be going over his lessons this afternoon." She pours Rebecca a cup of coffee and places it on the table in front of Cassandra's untouched plate. "Now, you two eat. There's no sense in all of this food going to the dogs."

"Sarah?" queries Isaac.

"Yes?"

"Will you post a letter for me? I wrote it last night on Tommy's computer."

"Sure thing."

The Wyoming spring bears its own brand of Etruscan yearnings. Mounted on horses, riding over the greening hills and the barren canyons of the Crowheart, the three of them — Isaac, Cassandra, and Rebecca — witness the promulgation of nature recreating itself. The humans, a segment of that same nature, cannot deny the instinctual longings within themselves, instincts goaded by the witnessing. Boulders, deposited by a glacier time immemorial, flash with vitality.

Cassandra, mounted on top of a two-year-old dappled quarter horse named Daisy, leads the group. The animal is a gift from Gabriel, given on the eve of his proposal. Isaac rides behind Cassandra on a spunky roan gelding name Rastus. Rebecca brings up the rear, straddled on Clementine, the old gray mare who, despite her age, flicks her muzzle and snorts against the bit while farting in the mid-morning breeze.

A tumbling conglomeration (gnats, horseflies, deerflies) pesters the group, prompting the horses to swish their tails and twitch their ears in the futile effort to disparage the swarm. The occasional clap of a hand against bare skin punctuates the rhythmic clomping of the horse hooves against the earth. From the belabored mounts a musky scent rises and is swept northeast by the breeze. They ride without speaking; they listen to the snorts and farts of their steeds, the bumble of insects, the methodical hooves navigating through patches of prickly-pear without missing a beat. Underneath it all, below perception, the breeze flowing over the land echoes a familiar static peculiar to the high plains.

The landscape dwarfs the riders. They head west, the earth rising towards the San Pedro Mountains which rise blue-gray against the horizon. The prairie, dotted with sagebrush, greasewood, lone junipers, scrub pine, boulders and cacti, roll outward from the mountains like waves on a turgid lake. Cirrus clouds coat the blue bowl of sky, moving inconspicuously to the northeast. Patches of color — reds, yellows, and blues — attract bees. Rebecca spots a hummingbird hovering in a shade cast by a wind gnarled pine. The green breast and the invisibly beating wings prompt her to speak, but, without knowing why, she stifles the urge and rides on.

By early afternoon the air is hot, and the troop is still more than two hours from the lake. The gradual increase in elevation (as they steer towards a mountain valley which, from the distance, looks like a gash from a serrated knife) does little in the way of decreasing the temperature. Isaac suggests they find some shade and stop to eat. Cassandra refuses. Isaac objects. Cassandra, in turn, ignores him. Rebecca offers no opinion. They ride on.

The scent of horse sweat mingles with the sage tinctured breeze and flows in and out of Isaac's lungs. He cannot stop thinking about Rebecca. The scene back at the corral in which

Cassandra instructed Rebecca on the proper method of saddling and mounting Clementine loops through his mind: *Cassandra's dusky voice a ceaseless crooning, her hands continuously touching Rebecca's shoulders, the black hair, the small of her back, while Rebecca remained in indiscreet proximity, as if she was enthralled by an initiation ritual that transcended the bounds of herd sensibilities, as if taboo had been elevated into law, while Isaac stood transfixed, caressing Rastus just under one eye, aroused as Cassandra and Rebecca hefted the saddle onto Clementine's dipped back, and, the saddle now secure, the girls pausing, smiling gnostically, and Cassandra's fingers brushing the tip of Rebecca's breast as her arm arced downward to her side, and Cassandra then helping Rebecca to mount the horse, her hand lingering at Rebecca's thigh, and jealousy, so long asleep in Isaac's heart, stirring, and meadowlarks singing for the blue day, and one of the geldings in the corral pissing a thick golden stream into the dung at his feet, and Rebecca and Cassandra sniggering like titillated schoolgirls, and the jealousy, alien and unwanted, embarrassing Isaac to the extent of reevaluating his interpretation and concluding that he had been witnessing a form of female bonding outside the realm of his experience.*

As he moves across the high plains, through increasing heat and heavy sunshine, the scene continues to loop. Emotions and logic at odds, Isaac feels like a tightrope walker equipped with a drum stick for a balancing rod. He regains a semblance of composure when Cassandra, pointing towards a capacious mound of boulders, speaks out, forcing him to concentrate on the present, rather than a memory — a memory which grows increasingly distorted, and yet tantalizing, with each successive loop.

"The lake's on the other side. There'll be trees and shade."

Rebecca claps her heels to Clementine's sagging flanks. The horse canters past Isaac and Rastus. She reins the horse to a walk beside Cassandra.

"How did all those rocks get piled there?" asks Rebecca. She watches a marmot standing on its hind legs atop a boulder halfway up the mountain of rocks. "Did men do this?"

Cassandra laughs. "Why would men pile rocks out here?"

"I don't know. They didn't pile themselves."

"Terminal moraine," says Isaac.

Rebecca twists her torso and looks back at Isaac. "What?"

"Terminal moraine."

"A glacier," says Cassandra. "A glacier uprooted all of these rocks and piled them here." She reaches over and pats Rebecca on the thigh. She points to the San Pedros in the distance. "See that valley?"

Rebecca squints and nods.

"A glacier carved it. Maybe the glacier wanted to cleave the earth in two but this is all the farther it got. After centuries at grinding away at the stone, the sun gathered her forces and melted the glacier like the big ice cube that it was. So much for trying to break the earth asunder." Cassandra looks at Rebecca and smiles. "There's a little lake on the other side. It's all that remains of the glacier's attempt, except for the valley and that mountain of rocks."

Rebecca watches the marmot watching her. "I'll bet it's beautiful."

"Yes," says Cassandra. "Beautiful."

The riders dismount. Cassandra and Isaac hobble the horses. They drape saddlebags over their shoulders. Cassandra leads the way over the mountain of rocks and is followed by Rebecca. Isaac brings up the rear. The trek is littered with rocks loosened by the expansion and contraction of water that turns to ice, that turns to water, that turns to ice, according to the whims of the season. Perspiration forms on the climbers' brows and is evaporated by the breeze. Clouds form overhead.

Cassandra, picking her way deftly through the rocks, suddenly stops. Looking up, she sees the vapor trail of a jet slashed across the sky. She listens for the sound of engines but hears only the echoing static of the breeze. Without turning around, head tilted back staring up at a cloud that resembles a descending angel, she says, "I forgot to warn you about the snakes."

Rebecca, unaccustomed to cowboy boots, and feet therefore aching, travels slowly, hunched forward, using her hands for balance as if she has miraculously devolved into an ape. "What? Snakes?" she says, negotiating herself around a large boulder. "I hope we see some."

Isaac hears the voices of the women descending from above but cannot decipher the meaning of the words. His thoughts are pyretic; the corral memory loops through his mind out of sequence: *golden stream of urine flowing into manure, a hand touching black hair, meadow larks' song, the scent of horse sweat, fingers brushing the tip of a breast, heat, horse eye, sun.* Eyes focused on booted feet, he climbs the mountain of rocks slowly, unconcerned with progress.

"Be careful," says Cassandra, before resuming the climb. "They're poisonous you know."

Rebecca leans against a boulder of granite to catch her breath. "Few people actually die. Children and old people. Unless you're allergic."

A whinny rises. Both Rebecca and Cassandra turn to look down at the horses some seventy-five feet below. Clementine whinnies once more and sproings up and down in her hobbles.

"She's feeling a bit frisky," says Cassandra. "Happy to be freed from her cage for a day."

When Isaac turns to look down at the horses, he reels with vertigo and momentarily imagines himself under himself careening haphazardly down the mountain of rocks and into the abyss of his demise. The urge to jump, intensified by Clementine's hopping and neighing — to relinquish control and martyr himself in the name of gravity — to tumble down the mountain of rocks under the blue sky — cascades over him and ruins his balance.

"Or maybe she's pissed that she's in shackles," says Rebecca.

Eyes the color and consistency of tar pits.

Cassandra turns forward and continues to climb. "Maybe. I guess we'll never know."

Isaac gloms onto the words and attempts to extract meaning. He understands. "It's too early," his voice scrapes his ears. Recouping balance, he repeats triumphantly, "It's too early."

"Too early for what?" asks Cassandra, climbing.

Something in Isaac's voice stops Rebecca in her tracks. She turns and looks down. "Are you okay?"

"Too early for snakes to be spread out from the den," says Isaac. Rebecca's voice, the care that must be leaking from her dark eyes, pulls him upwards like a trout lured by a fisherman's fly. "I'm fine. Hungry. Let's get to the other side so we can eat."

"That's it," yells Cassandra, gesturing with outstretched arms to the sky. "That's what Clementine's all worked up about."

With tilted heads, they watch three dots circling above them against the backdrop of a swollen, ash-gray cloud.

"Those eagles see something dying," continues Cassandra. She shades her eyes with an extended hand perched across her brow. "Clementine's so old she can sense that sort of thing from a long way off. It worries her."

Isaac says, "I'm starving. If we don't eat pretty goddamn soon, those eagles are going to be watching us."

After achieving the summit of the rocks, the group begins the descent to the horseshoe-shaped hollow below.

"Isn't it beautiful?" asks Cassandra, rhetorically, picking her way among loose stones and gravel, descending warily. "It's always reminded me of a fairy-tale."

The horseshoe opens westward, beckoning water down from the mountains, containing the small lake in the center of its outstretched arms. The glacier, thrusting and receding slowly in methodical geological time, impressed an indelible fingerprint on the land — the mountain of rocks, a fingerprint possessing all the uniqueness and fecundity of an animated being.

Rebecca, remembering the fairy-tales of her childhood (stories designed to strike the fear of retribution into the hearts of the immature), steps on a flat piece of shale, an anomaly in the terrain of granite, basalt, and quartz. It shifts precariously with her weight. Attempting to break the fall, to recover balance, she jabs her arms forward, hands colliding with the coarse surface of a granite boulder. Her left palm is scraped raw.

Hearing the sound of tumbling debris, Cassandra turns and ascends the mountain of rocks. She reaches Rebecca the same time as Isaac and kneels down to inspect the wound.

"Why doesn't anything grow up here?" asks Rebecca, not, evidently, too distracted by her injury. She stands with her palm held outward, upward, at waist level.

"I don't know," says Isaac, standing in back of Rebecca, head hovering over her shoulder, yearning to witness the flow of blood. "Seed has trouble taking root, I guess." As he speaks, an ash-gray cloud clips the sun.

Mindful not to upset Rebecca's or, for that matter, the kneeling Cassandra's, balance, Isaac moves on past the women and continues his descent under the shadow of the cloud.

"You'll live," says Cassandra. She studies Rebecca's palm as if she is divining the future from the lacerated skin. A pearl of blood forms on Rebecca's pinky. Cassandra inserts the pinky into her mouth and sucks. She removes the finger, and the blood is gone. "Just a couple of pin pricks." She stands. "I'll doctor it up when we get to the bottom." Turning her head, she watches Isaac descending. "Look at the flowers around the lake."

Rebecca places her uninjured hand on Cassandra's shoulder. Cassandra, slightly below Rebecca due to her position on the incline, turns her head and looks Rebecca in the eye.

"Thank you," says Rebecca.

"Don't thank me. The flowers bloom whether I'm here to see them or not."

"Do they?" asks Rebecca.

By the time the women reach the hollow, the cloud has passed, and the sun shines. Isaac sits in the center of a circle of aspens, near the eastern shore of the lake. The contents of his saddlebag are spread out on the ground in front of him like a surgeon's tools. Sitting cross-legged on the sandy soil, he selects the largest green apple from the stack of six and takes a bite. The women sit Indian-style facing both Isaac and one another. The apples designate the core of the circle.

"Where's the first-aid kit?" asks Cassandra.

Isaac points at a rectangular box near Rebecca's folded legs. He takes another bite out of the apple.

Rebecca picks up the plastic box, opens it, and inventories the contents.

Cassandra and Isaac watch as Rebecca chooses a sterile wipe from the box. She tears the aluminum wrapper with her teeth and dabs at her scraped palm. A breeze trickles down from the valley and swirls in the tops of the aspens. Isaac fancies that he can hear a musical note, shrill to the point of silence, as if the trees are receptors for a gargantuan pipe organ, in a far off cave in the San Pedros — perhaps an organ with a single key. For Cassandra, the hollow is as quiet as a star on an arctic night.

The moment Rebecca finishes administering to her wound (her hand swathed in a cotton gauze held fast by adhesive tape), Isaac jumps to his feet and begins searching for appropriate chunks of granite and quartz from which to build a fire pit; he works with energy, a man tweaking with purpose. As he searches, carrying boulders the size of tether balls and placing them in a circle near the stack of apples, Cassandra stands, walks over to Rebecca, kneels down behind her, and begins massaging her shoulders. Rebecca tenses with the first touch, but, as Cassandra's fingers knead her knotted muscles, she succumbs by closing her eyes and tilting her aquiline nose in the direction of the sun; she listens to the breeze and the lapping of the water on the shore of the lake.

"I love this place," says Cassandra.

"It feels good," says Rebecca, her face streaked by the moving shadows of the aspen branches. "It feels like I've been here before."

Because the deadfall is damp with spring rains, Isaac, the fire pit complete, snaps dry branches from standing aspens. He avoids looking at the women. He attempts to will himself *not to wonder at the words they are exchanging*, for, although Cassandra's whispers are so much gibberish to him (the intoxicated rants of the Sybil), he knows that Rebecca is able to interpret the sounds and lend them meaning. Realizing the words are not meant for his consumption, he snaps twigs into exact lengths, kindling for the flames which will cook the food.

The lake, glacial sediment staining the water gunbarrel-gray, laps at the few pockets of reeds that take sustenance from the barren shores. It is a small lake without fish.

"When I was a teenager," says Cassandra, "Francis, Jed's brother, brought me out here for the first time. We rode double on a big bay stallion called Hanover." A new cloud disseminates the sunlight, casting a shadow over the trees, boulders, and the waters of the hollow. "We rode out here, climbed over the rocks just like we did today and ate lunch. Grapes and cheese and bread and wine. It was a hot day, July fourteenth — everything happens to me in July — and I wasn't used to wine, but I didn't feel drunk. I didn't know how to feel drunk, and somehow I was more aware than I ever have been..."

Listening with closed eyes, Rebecca, the tension in her neck banished by Cassandra's fingers tips, watches the scene unfold with the words.

"... and the sun was all over everything, a honey glaze, and the heat was like a drug. Halfway through the second bottle of wine, Francis — we were sitting almost in this exact spot, no, over by that rock next to that tree (Rebecca does not open her eyes) — kissed me. He just leaned over and kissed me right on the mouth. The birds were singing and the insects buzzing and the water sloshing against the shore just like it is now, and I started throbbing in rhythm with it all, and I didn't know that I could feel that way, didn't know if I *should* feel that way. I'd never kissed a man before."

In Rebecca's ears the sound of the breeze and the water is complemented by birds and insects.

Cassandra massages between Rebecca's shoulder blades, her hands keeping time with her words. "After another glass of wine he took off his clothes. I was afraid and thrilled, my heart pounding in my stomach. I'd never seen one before, not like that. He pushed me to my knees and then he was in my mouth and I'd never tasted anything so good, so real."

Isaac snaps twigs.

"And then he took my clothes off, and we made love, and it lasted forever. We only stopped because of the rain."

Rebecca opens her eyes and suddenly turns and looks at Cassandra. "How old were you?"

"I'm sorry." Cassandra removes her hands from Rebecca. "I don't know why I told you that. It just came out."

"How old were you?"

"Thirteen."

"How old was he?"

"Thirty something."

"He raped you," says Rebecca. She stands.

Cassandra stands, green eyes flaring. "No he did not. Don't ever say that." Her eyes fall to the ground. "I'm sorry I told you. I don't know why."

"It's okay. You didn't know."

"It just came out." Cassandra lifts her eyes to Rebecca's. "You can't ever tell."

"I know," says Rebecca.

"Never," says Cassandra. "Our secret."

"I know." She changes the subject, "Tell me about Ike's mother. Jed refuses to talk about her."

"She was beautiful," says Cassandra, welcoming the change. "The family rarely mentions her. It was like when she died, they wanted her memory to die with her. She's buried on the rise above the corrals."

"How'd she die?"

"It was strange. The family went to Disneyland and when they came back she was sick. Ike took it the worst. He left the Crowheart."

"What did she die of?"

"Fever, I guess." Cassandra looks to the undulating water of the lake. "Or a broken heart. She and Jed didn't share a bed for years. She shut herself up in her room like she didn't believe in the world."

Rebecca puts her arm around Cassandra's shoulders. "Sounds mysterious."

"Yes," says Cassandra. "Sometimes I think about her, but then I realize I didn't really know who she was. The way everybody acts, she may as well have been a dream. Except for Ike. Ike believed in her."

"Somehow, I do too," says Rebecca.

Preparations complete, Isaac builds a twig tepee in the middle of the fire pit. He locates a blank sheet of paper in a saddlebag and wads it up. After inserting the wad inside the tepee, he produces a butane lighter from his pants pocket, and, down on all fours, he ignites the lighter and touches the flame to the paper. The paper burns. The twigs take the heat until, suddenly, a fit of gluttony erupts, and the tepee blooms. Isaac places incrementally larger twigs into the pit.

Side by side, Cassandra and Rebecca watch the fire grow through Isaac's nurturing. The sound of water slapping against the shoreline adds a fertile back-beat to the moan of the increasing wind. The metallic-gray surface of the lake moves in concordance with the air. An armada of clouds approaches from the southwest.

Isaac kneels next to the fire and watches the bed of embers thicken in the pit. Segments of sun, falling between passing clouds to bathe him in light before the next penumbra, combine with both the wind and the sound of the water and enable him to maintain a sense of passing time. When the embers are of almost sufficient depth (Isaac's role in the hollow has changed: he is now the keeper of the flame, the provider of sustenance), he, using a Bowie knife from the saddlebag, chops three thin, green branches from one of the aspens and whittles points onto the tips. He cuts New York steaks, still rigid from the freezer, into cubes. He slices onions. He washes mushrooms in the lake.

Cassandra and Rebecca crouch by the fire, heads bowed towards the thickening embers.

Isaac skewers meat cubes onto one stick, onion chunks onto the second, and whole mushrooms onto the third. Using rocks as props, he lowers or heightens each skewer to its proper distance from the heat — meat nearest, onions further, mushrooms furthest. After stoking the fire, he leans back on his haunches and waits.

The scent and sizzle of animal fat dripping into the flames prompts Cassandra into action. After rummaging through her saddlebag, she returns to the fire pit bearing spices. She sprinkles garlic powder, black pepper, and sage onto the meat. She taps sweet basil onto the vegetables. Her mission accomplished, she lines the jars of spices into a row near the pit and then moves to the far side of Isaac, opposite Rebecca, and crouches.

"Smells great," says Rebecca, relieved to be apart from Cassandra.

Isaac rotates each skewer a quarter of a turn. "Got to give Cassy most of the credit." He, like the others, is experiencing the full extent of his hunger. "She packed it all."

"True. But everyone knows that men are superior when it comes to cooking in the great-outdoors." Cassandra, on hands and knees, crawls over the sandy ground to the saddlebags. "However, everyone also knows that women are superior when it comes to remembering details." She produces a jug of wine from the saddlebag and says, "Anyone care for a drink?"

Rebecca, eyes transfixed on the configuration of heat in the fire pit, looks up and is met by Cassandra's wry smile.

"Did you remember a corkscrew?" asks Isaac.

"Don't be a fool," says Cassandra, still looking at Rebecca. A cloud passes, revealing the sun. "I didn't forget a thing." She fishes in the saddlebag and produces a corkscrew.

Satiated with charred meat, vegetables, and the unwavering sunshine (for the armada of clouds floated away during the course of the meal, leaving the sun alone in the sky), Isaac sits near the fire pit whittling toothpicks with his pocket knife. Rebecca lies on her back watching the tops of the aspens vacillate against the backdrop of blue; she hopes for the flutter of wings, the ruffle of feathers, a robin landing on one of the branches. Cassandra sinks the bit of the corkscrew into a second bottle of wine.

"Jesus Christ," says Rebecca. She twists a braid of black hair around the index finger of her wounded hand. "I can't remember anything tasting so good."

The blade of the pocket knife (the same blade that cut the horse's eye from the socket, *the horse ritual fading further from Isaac's memory like the revelatory dream from the mind of a waking alcoholic*) pares slivers of wood from a twig.

The pop of the cork being freed from the mouth of the bottle brings a grin to Cassandra's lips. "I must agree. Once in a lifetime. Seems a shame to wash away the remnants of burnt flesh with sour grapes, but so is the way of humanity." Lifting the bottle towards the sun, she cries out, "In remembrance!" Red wine spills from the corners of her mouth as she drinks.

Rebecca sits up to take the bottle. She, too, raises the bottle towards the sun before taking a swallow. Holding the bottle in her wounded hand, she crawls towards Isaac like a three-legged dog. She taps him on the shoulder with the bottom of the jug.

"Jesus has nothing to do with it," he says and places both the pocket knife and the twig on the ground. He takes the bottle. He drinks.

Smoke rises from the fire.

"What?" asks Cassandra.

Isaac, after another swig, begins pouring wine from the bottle into the center of the fire pit.

"What the hell are you doing?" yells Cassandra. She reaches Isaac in a series of lurches and grabs the wine from across the flames. An intermingling of smoke and steam invades her eyes, momentarily blinding her. She sits cross-legged, the bottle nestled between her legs, and rubs her eyes with balled fists. "Goddamnit. There's only one bottle left."

"Libations," says Isaac. Taking up the knife and the twig, he resumes whittling.

Attempting to disguise the fact that she is pleased by Cassandra's anger, Rebecca says, "Libations? What are you talking about?"

Isaac pauses. He looks at Rebecca.

Rebecca is struck with the sensation that Isaac cannot see her, that he is looking at something *behind* her.

Her vision returning, Cassandra says, "You've been away at school too long to say something like that." She takes a drink and passes the wine to Rebecca. "All she meant was that it's a special day. You know, Ike, like the first time you kissed a girl."

A feeling of guilt pulses through Isaac. "Sorry." He has whittled the twig to a nub. "I was just thinking out loud. Didn't mean anything by it. Too much wine."

"Don't worry about it," says Rebecca, passing the bottle to Isaac.

Isaac puts down the knife and takes the wine without looking Rebecca in the eye. After a swallow, he passes the bottle to Cassandra, avoiding her eyes as well.

"Speaking of first kisses," says Cassandra, "how did you meet the Old Man... I mean Jed?"

Rebecca trains her gaze on the smouldering fire pit. "He's a friend of my father's."

At the mention of his father's name, Isaac takes up the knife and begins shaving the sliver of wood he holds between his fingers. The blade slips off of the twig, biting into the flesh of his forefinger. "Shit."

"You okay?" Rebecca crawls over to Isaac and takes his wounded hand in her own. Blood drips from the cut onto the gauze bandage wrapped around her palm.

"It's nothing," says Isaac.

Cassandra darts into action. She grabs the first-aid kit, extracts a cotton ball and a vial of hydrogen-peroxide, cleanses Isaac's wound, applies iodine and a band-aid. "I don't know if you remember this, but I think it was me that gave you your first kiss," she says. "Other than your mother."

Isaac is silent. He stares at his bandaged finger.

Rebecca gets to her feet and edges away from Cassandra and Isaac. She turns and walks towards the lake.

"Remember?" asks Cassandra. She takes up the bottle.

Isaac, staring at his finger, shakes his head.

"Well, we were really young. We were fishing for brookies over at Baterman's Creek, caught a whole bucket full of them, and it was hot and we kissed." She takes a drink. "I've been in love with you ever since."

Isaac looks from his finger into Cassandra's eyes, a skewed expression convulsing his face.

The sound of laughter and churning water dissolves the impasse between Isaac and Cassandra.

Isaac stands. "Jesus!" he yells. "That water's got to be freezing." He jogs towards the lake.

"And you've been breaking my heart ever since you son-of-a-bitch," whispers Cassandra. She takes a drink of wine. She lays down on the sandy soil next to the fire pit.

Rebecca stands knee deep in the lake laughing loudly. "Jesus has nothing to do with it!" She laughs again and watches Isaac approach.

Paul,

Since you've always come off as a sort of Lizard King, you need to answer the question: Why didn't Eva and I hear the shots? The question plagues me each time I wake up, morning, noon, or night. Waking up in the same bed as I did that night — amid the same stench of rotten socks, banal beer, and stale cigarettes — the question surfaces like a phantom, and I cannot answer. The few people that I keep in touch with (you being one of them) implore me to move out of this place, get a clean start, but, every time I consider it, I am inflicted with a dull nausea which persists until I abandon the idea. Until lately. Rebecca came into the picture and everything changed. There are certain instances in each human life (being a Lizard King, you understand me) which obliterate any conception of a future that may have once been entertained. One can either ignore these instances, although, once given the tangibility of logical thought, they're as persistent as mutating viruses, or place the event in the realm of the sacred, though to do so is to chance the stigmatization of the fool or, worse yet, the insane. Most humans ignore these events for the "pragmatic" reason that to acknowledge them as important is to cast oneself into uncharted seas. They are afraid. And rightly so. The era of the explorer has come and gone. We live in a time of cowards and criminals. Stability, material stability, is the catcall of the masses, the seducer of women and the bane of would-be men. America is ruled by a race of Pharisees whose stinking spirits infect the herd by employing fleas on rats, so that one day even the animals (like the domestic dog and cat) will prefer living in the comforts of zoos. We are a country of captives drugged with vague notions of freedom and justice — notions no longer real.

Why didn't we hear the shots? I realize we've discussed it innumerable times and concluded that the whiskey and the dope muted Eva's and my senses to the tragedy unfolding in the living room. We slept the dreamless slumber of the inebriate.

The only logical answer — the same answer Detective Alious and his associates were forced to draw after employing the sophisticated techniques of investigation and interrogation common among police forces today. The logical answer.

Logic, of course, is a man-made construct and cannot be expected to take the full spectrum of what happened that night into account. Since I have never written about the shootings, allow me to do so now in the hopes that something in my memory will fail to concur with yours. If our reflections do not mesh, then we will have a place to begin to try to understand. I am not reconstructing that night in order to relive it like some sort of ghoul. In point of fact, somewhere along the way, human tragedy lost its significance for me — that peculiar Greek sensibility is too far removed to affect me any longer. I just want to lay the entire matter to rest. Rebecca, whom I will write to you about later (I have to keep you interested one way or another), after the next piece of the puzzle has fallen into place, has altered my predilections of the future. As such, the past, a concept I have attempted to disdain by scrutinizing History for all of these years, must be brought into configuration, so that my present is synchronous with what came before and what will come after. Forgive my prattle, Paul, but this is important to me. You are the only one left who can help.

Sometimes I close my eyes and try to envision it all, but there is nothing but darkness, as if that night did not transpire in real-time. When we used to talk about them — Tom , Jeff, the dead — I couldn't help but think about those old friends as characters in a novel, men whose meaning had to be interpreted through words rather than experience. Memorizing the events that surrounded the shootings from the insulating halls of the academy, it was as if I had never known them at all — never ate with them, drank with them, played with them. Only recently, and this is a mixed blessing, has a visual memory returned. A phantasmagorical vision at best, but, nevertheless, a vision that places me in the continuum of time. I can breathe again.

I exist: I can remember the way my mother looked at me moments before she died. She was trying to communicate something to me, send me a message encoded in maternal piety. I fear that I will never be able to decode her message (and that is what I must do), unless I am able to return to the night of the shootings. The past is panoramic, and, when I turn around to view it, I find the terrain unfamiliar. I can intimate the past only from the vantage point of the present, and, when I turn to retrace my steps, the only recognizable landmark is the night of the shootings. I have spent too many years with my head buried in the sand of history books — convalescing in the spent life of the other. That night, for now, is my only reference to myself.

The images are blurred with a few notable exceptions, the sequence of events a ramshackle on which I attempt to impose order: *Jeff came into the room where Eva and I lay sleeping on a filthy mattress imbued with the scent* (the vision invokes other sensations as well) *of cheap perfume, and he shook me awake without turning on the lights, dark like used oil, and he said, "Tom shot me in the ass." His voice was monotone, businesslike, and I told him to leave me alone because we drank that shit-*

load of whiskey, and an insipid ache throbbed my brain, and I thought he was playing a deranged joke on me, and I didn't want anything to do with it. Jeff obediently left the room, and narcotic sleep engulfed me. When he returned (I'll never know what went through his mind in the interim between visits — he can't remember; his mind is blank), *he flipped on the light switch and walked around to my side of the bed and shook me awake once more. He said: "Tom shot me in the ass." I was angry, and I opened my eyes to glare at him, my sight dull with sleep, and he was holding his palm towards me, offering his palm, and it was dripping blood. He looked down on me with those transparent blue eyes of his, and he seemed unconcerned, his face as expressionless as a lab technician performing an experiment to which he already knows the results. And it occurred to me that maybe he really had been shot, but his expression, standing there in his jockey shorts with his paunch hanging forward like a sagging breast, cast doubt in my mind.*

Here is where my sense of linearity vanishes. Although I venture to place the events sequentially, I cannot be certain that my equations are valid — I have no method of testing them but this. It probably makes no difference. Framed by the realization that Jeff had been shot, finding myself in a holding cell splattered with dried blood (black blood) waiting to be questioned by Detective Alious and his cronies, I must assume that the events in between, in actuality, did occur. If I am mistaken, you are obligated in correcting me.

As far as I am able to ascertain: *I jumped out of bed wearing only a pair of plaid boxer shorts, and Jeff just stood there watching me watching him before placing his hand over the wound on his ass to quell the flow of blood. Eva, lying naked on her stomach on top of our quilt, the lion head quilt, called out the name Joe and turned over on her back, while Jeff, although he had just been shot with a .44 magnum and was in danger of bleeding to death, stared at Eva's body in a way that Adam must have stared at Eve after the Fall* (Jeff was a virgin at the time, and the sight of Eva laying on the golden quilt, her legs spread casually open, must have been a godsend), *so I took him by the shoulders and led him into the bathroom.*

I've told you before that my actions that night were without thought; I worked through instinct. In retrospect, I guess I led Jeff into the bathroom and sat him on the open toilet seat because of all the blood he was spilling all over the carpets. Eva, as you know, was (is?) a stickler for cleanliness, and, when a man is with a woman he loves for any length of time, she influences him down to his very nature. I'm sure Eva has told you that I never had sex with her in all of those months. We slept in the same bed, ate at the same table, used the same razor and soap, and I never slept with her. Not even a kiss. Platonic. I don't know why. She thought something was wrong with me. Impotence. That's why she is with you today. But that is all tangential at best.

At rest on the toilet, Jeff looked at me with an emollient expression because the responsibility of saving himself had been lifted, and he was content to play out the scene as the innocent victim. *Intuition instructed me that Jeff would live, and I told him as much, I was sure of it, and he just looked at me with a bemused glean in his eye. He asked me for a cigarette, so I trotted back into the bedroom and grabbed Eva's pack, which was sitting on the milk crate we used for a night stand, along with a book of matches, and I stood above her for a moment, watching her sleep, and I wanted her because of the downy light purring at the center of her, a woman completely, a being unto itself— she was beauty and the urge to touch her hair, to smell her, thrust me towards her, but, as my hand descended, I heard the floor board creak behind me, and the thought of Tom brandishing the pistol, glazed eyes of a homicidal maniac, surged through my mind causing me to whirl on the balls of my feet to face him, to protect Eva, but it was only Jeff standing behind me, his hand on his ass, his eyes cast down on Eva with the beguiled expression of a mooncalf watching a meteor shower, the blood from his wound pooling on the carpet at his feet. My adrenaline lost potency and was replaced by vexation. I guided Jeff back into the bathroom and sat him down on the toilet. I told him to stay there while I phoned for help. He grinned at me and took the pack of cigarettes and matches out of my clutched hand. He lit a cigarette, threw the match in the sink, and said, "Tom's dead. Paul might still be alive. You'd better check on him first." The words streamed out of his mouth — words like jazz notes from a coronet — and he sat there grinning at me, and, once again, I came under the impression that I was being duped.* It's obvious now that Jeff was merely in shock and had little inkling of his behavior. I suppose he very well could have been raving which would have made the situation more difficult, if less strange.

I stood in the hallway between the bathroom and the living room waiting for my eyes to adjust to the darkness. The scent of death entered through my mouth and nose, and I noticed the silver light of the moon embossing the carpet at the end of the hallway, and, for the first time, I was convinced that I was not being put-on. The presence of death crept through my limbs like poison oak. The aroma of freshly spilled blood is unlike any other: sweet, fertile, and foreboding all at once. It is easy to understand the quickening pulse and salivation of the predator as she anticipates the kill. Fresh blood smells appetizing. Do you remember? Warm and nourishing and vital. When the predator laps up the blood of its prey, it laps up the spirit of its prey as to sustain its own sinew and soul. These instincts are all but dead in humanity, the purity tainted. We have hidden too long behind the Plow and the Staff. I long for the glory of the hunt, the pride of the Spirit Eaters. And I ramble.

It is my guess that it was the rhythm of life fading into death (like a tide going out) which demanded that I round the corner and step into the living room. *I could not. I stood there in the night-dark hallway, magnetized between two poles, a puppet without a master.* I must have looked rather ridiculous to Jeff, *feeling him grinning behind me, watching me from his position on the stool, his lifeblood leaking out, while I stood there unable to move in the shadows — a ghost afraid of itself. Something was snuffling about in the living room, and the sound of it prompted me forward because I thought it was you lying on the carpet gargling blood. So I stepped into the half-light cast by the street lamp outside* (it wasn't moonlight at all but the same color as moonlight, the same texture) *leaning through the undraped picture window, but the thing moving wasn't human; it was a dog, Tom's Blue Heeler, Tadpole, brought down from the Crowheart, rooting around in the corner, smacking her jaws.*

As I watched my mother convulsing with death, something convulsed and died within me. Like a rabbit who has seen the preponderance of its warren rendered to pieces by ferrets, who has seen the viscera of its own kind scattered across the cold earth and gnawed on by the enemy, my life was transformed from one of innocence to one of impending doom. The inevitability of death does not sit well in souls such as mine. The concept is square and will not fit into any of the concentric circles of my being.

And yet, *I felt no fear walking towards the dog (she seemed comforted by my presence, wagging her stump tail, her ears erect), so I knelt down to pet her and stumbled and fell to my knees. Groping in the light that fell through the picture window like a phosphorescent haze, my hand sunk into a spongy, warm lump. I leaned down to investigate and was greeted by what was left of Tom's face staring up at me like a bucket of guts. My hand gripped a warm hunk of brain matter. Half his skull was missing, and his face was limp on the floor like a latex Halloween mask discarded after the holiday — one eye missing, the other open and shrieking. Mesmerized, I looked into the eye, was drawn into it. There was no time, no space, and only the sound of Tadpole lapping up her master's brains brought me out of that something-beyond-words.* Each time I am able to glom onto the image of Tom's shrieking eye, it gyrates and implodes like a black hole. The image resonates as key, because, after that moment, logic was restored — Apollonian order reestablishing time and space, drawing meaning out of the abyss: In the beginning was the Word, and the Word was Death. It seems obvious now why Western Civilization has comprehended time in a linear fashion. The life of the body is a linear progression; just take a look at the riddle of the Sphinx. *Tom was dead. The next logical step was to check on you. As I crawled over to your body, a feeling of trickery came over me once again, and I thought it was all a macabre guise, Tom's makeup job impeccable, and that at any moment you, unscathed, would sit up grinning like a vampire in his coffin. And then I saw the smile pulling at the corners of your mouth and your hands folded on your chest, as if in funeral rehearsal, and I thought 'they took it too far, so I felt your neck, found a pulse, and was on the verge of exposing you all as frauds, when an opportunity for revenge presented itself to me. I dialed 911 and informed the attendant there had been an attempted murder-suicide, and we needed an ambulance. I told him (her?) the details as if by rote. The joke would be on you. I returned to the bathroom to check on Jeff, but the bathroom was empty. I found him in the bedroom standing above Eva, his hand on his ass, blood gushing through his fingers, so I guided him by the shoulders back to the bathroom, sat him on the stool (the toilet water looked like cheap burgundy), and told him to stay, just as you would command a dog.*

At that point, societal relativism won the day. Things moved quickly — a VCR on fast forward. The sirens sounded, the ambulance shot by our apartment complex and turned around a few blocks down, while I, in boxer shorts, ran outside into the cool darkness to flag them down. Inside the apartment, one of the cops, a uniform, kept yelling "Get that damn dog out of here!" Do you remember? Somebody drug Tadpole (who was merely abiding by her instincts) downstairs and shut her in the furnace room where she stayed for a day without food or water. In the kitchen, another cop found the quarter pound of smoke we just bought from Bernie. I saw her eyeing it, but nobody ever said a word; the bag disappeared and was never heard from again. Eva, in my bathrobe, stood in the living room the entire time staring down at Tom's corpse while sporting a coquettish expression like an angel courting misery. Jeff and you were carted away in the ambulance, Tom (I suppose) to the morgue, Eva and I to the cop-shop.

The cop-shop. Questions without answers. Why would he do it? I don't know. Why didn't you hear it? I don't know. A love triangle? I don't know. Homosexual relationships? I don't know; I doubt it. Why did you pick up the gun and put it in your bedroom closet? *The stainless steel barrel was unblemished, no blood, no brains, the rubber grips warm in my hand.* Did I? Where was the gun when you picked it up? Here, draw us a picture. I can't. I don't know. Could Jeff have done it? Paul? Eva? I don't know. Why didn't he shoot you? Why didn't he murder Eva? I don't know. Why didn't you hear the shots? I don't know. I don't know. I don't know...

Eva and I saw Jeff once before he died. There was an decrepit black man in traction in the bed next to him who kept repeating the same thing over and over, incanting: "It hurts so bad. So bad. Bad. Please excuse me if I scream." Jeff was unconscious. You were unconscious. They told us that you were lucky that the bullet had been under-loaded, or you would be dead. Everything smelled like lemon-scented bleach. We came back to ICU a few hours later, and they told us Jeff didn't make it. Too much blood had spilled out of him. They told us you would recover in time.

Did you recover, Paul?

We rented a motel room and waited for Eva's parents to fly in from Seattle. We ate Thanksgiving dinner at Denny's. I concocted theories: Bernie the dope man snuck in and did it. A thief. A serial killer. I spun questions: How did Tom find the .44 and the bullets? I had them hidden in my room, you know. Why didn't I wake up while he was rummaging through my things? Why didn't we hear the shots? There were three live bullets left in the cylinder. Why didn't he shoot Eva and I? Why did he do it all?

I want to be whole again, Paul. I need to make meaning out of that night. Rebecca has reawakened my desire to create. I need to interpret that night so as to be done with it.

Tell Eva I say hello.

Write back soon,
Isaac

Avens

Geum quellyon

The rattlesnake lays coiled between two large stones, one granite, the other basalt. Rebecca, climbing up the mountain of rocks on her journey back to the horses, steps on the snake. Senses dulled by the magnified heat of the sun on the stones and its scales, the snake bites Rebecca without rattling. The fangs puncture the skin on Rebecca's calf, just missing the shin. The pain provokes a childhood memory in which Rebecca fell on the broken shard of a Coke bottle, gashed open the skin on her calf, and was rushed to the emergency room. To deaden the nerves before scrubbing the wound, a young intern with slanted eyes and thick whiskers pierced her leg with a long hypodermic needle. The memory flashes like sulphur and is gone. Rebecca stands looking down at the snake, the flicking tongue, the ominously still rattles in the center of the coil.

"I'm bit," says Rebecca.

Cassandra picks her way among the boulders, her thoughts wandering through the residue of wine and lost virginity. The words "I'm bit" ricochet before lodging in her mind. Delaying her ascent, she turns and looks down at Rebecca some fifty-feet below. She watches as Isaac, below Rebecca, skips up the mountain of rocks, scoops a stone from the ground with his right hand, leaps to Rebecca's side and sidearms the stone like a shortstop turning a double-play. Her warning earlier in the day concerning snakes and danger has been elevated into prophecy-fulfilled. She is filled with dread. She descends.

The snake wriggles inertly between the chunk of granite and the hunk of basalt, the dry rattle (which began only after the snake was unconscious) of its tail losing tempo.

"Did it go all the way through?" asks Isaac.

"I don't know," says Rebecca. She adds in passing, "That was amazing. Right in the head. Is it dead?"

Isaac picks up a slab of shale. "It will be." He slams the slab onto the snake, and the rock explodes like brittle metal. He takes another slab and slams it down. The rattling fades like the end of a song. Snake scales stuck to shards of stone twinkle with sunlight.

Cassandra reaches Rebecca. She drops the saddlebag from her shoulder and crouches. She rolls up Rebecca's denim pant leg and finds only smooth skin. She rolls up the other pant leg. Two pinpricks of red stare out from Rebecca's calf. "Shit."

"Let's get her back down to the hollow," says Isaac.

Cassandra stands up and drapes Rebecca's right arm around her own neck and shoulders. "Just be easy, Sweetie. I'll take care of you."

"You should have seen it," says Rebecca. "He hit it square in the head with that rock. It was just about to strike again and then the rock came out of nowhere and smashed its head against that boulder. I've never seen anything like it."

Isaac picks up Rebecca's saddlebag. "You'll be alright." Realizing the impossibility of making the descent back into the hollow three-abreast, he is content to bring up the rear. "Unless you're allergic. I doubt you have to worry about it."

Rebecca laughs. "What, are Injuns immune? I'm always the last to know."

Cassandra's decision to return to the horses came when a windstorm erupted out of the southwest and blasted through the hollow, like the side of hell had been ripped opened, absorbing all sound in its wake and scattering sparks from the fire pit in random concussions. Words useless in the cacophonous air, she covered the fire pit with the rocks that defined it.

It struck Rebecca as curious (as she stood surveying the hollow, somehow enthralled by the suddenness of the storm) that the brown aspen leaves on the ground were seemingly unaffected by the onslaught of wind. Unwilling to pursue the meaning of the anomaly, she helped Cassandra in containing the fire.

Isaac stood ankle deep in the lake watching whitecaps churn on the surface of the water. He lifted his arms from his sides and leaned into the stiff air.

The fire extinguished, Cassandra and Rebecca, hair alive with wind, packed the saddlebags without speaking.

After lowering his arms, Isaac bowed his head into the wind. He performed an about-face and left the water behind him.

At Isaac's approach, Rebecca's mouth widened and then collapsed, her lips pursing into an "O" and then an "o". Her voice was lost in the wind.

Cassandra stood, draped the saddlebag over her shoulder, and gestured with her unencumbered arm to the others. Isaac and Rebecca stood dumbfounded. Cassandra took Rebecca by the hand and led her forward. Isaac picked up the remaining saddlebag from the ground and, several paces behind the women, began the journey back to the horses.

The wind has waned from torrent to trickle by the time Cassandra climbs halfway up the mountain of rocks. Greenish-black clouds dominate the southwestern horizon. The words "I'm bit" enter her ears and ricochet through her mind, unable to find lodging. As her body continues upward, her thoughts remain below, in the hollow, attempting to identify and capture the exact moment between virginity and sexuality so that it can bound in space and time and kept in the dungeons of her heart. Unsuccessful, as she was, in designating Francis Daniels a place in the strata of her memory (unable to place him in the layered confine of angel-of-liberation or demon-who-brands), the return to the hollow reawakened in her a need to ensign which for years had laid dormant. When she turns around and looks for the source of the words below her and finds Rebecca standing as if stricken by the stony gaze of Medusa, she is thrilled with dread. The battle unfolding inside of her is neither won nor lost. She begins the descent.

The words "I'm bit" enter Isaac and bastion him against the onslaught of free association which began upon his return to the Crowheart. Rebecca's words, inflectionless yet ripe with meaning, are interpreted by Isaac as a cry of distress. He leaps up the mountain to slay the serpent. The quest a success, the snake convulsing lifeless between two rocks, Isaac is anything but happy. He stands above the slain monster like a present-day Beowulf.

"Did it go all the way through?"

"I don't know."

Having achieved the halfway point on the mountain of rocks, Isaac stopped, turned around, and looked down into the hollow. The same greenish-black clouds surged from the southwest. Air laden with humidity. Isaac became aware that everything — the mountain of rocks, the green leaves on the aspens, the white bark, the surface of the lake, the loamy shoreline — was glossed with a gray film coating the land like a shroud. He searched for signs of life — a marmot, a bird, a snake, a dragon, a monster — and there was nothing. Nothing except Cassandra and Rebecca in the hollow, the trees bending in the wind. He watched Cassandra sitting with her back against an aspen, cradling Rebecca's skull in the crook of an elbow, Rebecca's body prone between Cassandra's legs. He heard humming, but, when he focused his hearing, it was gone, and there was nothing but the wail of the wind wisping across the lake and into the trees.

Because he believed that he was invisible, believed that he was as gray as the mountain of rocks and thus conjoined with it, Isaac stood still and watched as Cassandra stroked Rebecca's brow. He watched with Cassandra's words reverberating in his ears.

"Fly, fool," she says. "Fly. It's not your place to stay with her. It wouldn't be right." She speaks while holding his hand. She guides him towards the mountain of rocks.

Isaac stood leaning into the gusting wind, pondering Cassandra's words. He watched as Cassandra stroked Rebecca's black hair; he watched as Cassandra leaned forward and whispered something into Rebecca's ear; he watched as Cassandra leaned forward once again and kissed Rebecca on the forehead. Isaac smiled because the mysteriousness of the universe was not only intact, but virile; he would never know what words were exchanged between the two women in the hollow as he stood looking down on them from the mountain of rocks; he did not want to know; for the moment, he delighted in the absence of meaning.

When the wind ebbed, Isaac toppled forward. After recovering his balance, he glided up the mountain of rocks, his feet sure on the precarious rubble, and gained the summit. Purging the urge to look back, to look down into the hollow one last time, Isaac vaulted down the far side of the mountain towards the hobbled horses. He was intent on rescuing Rebecca from the venom. The advancing storm obliterated from his view by the mountain of rocks, he mounted Rastus and galloped off in the pursuit of medicine.

Cassandra opens the pocket knife left behind by Isaac and cuts Rebecca's pant leg. "They say this isn't the best method, but I can't find any way around it."

"Can't you just roll it up?" Rebecca sits with her back touching the white bark of an aspen. She watches the diminishing figure of Isaac as he makes his way towards the base of the mountain of rocks.

"I'm going to suck it out." The sight of Rebecca's calf, swelling with the darkening poison, inspires Cassandra as she examines the fang marks. The words are cast out quickly, without regard for audience. "Are you supposed to slice it crossways or up and down? If you're going to kill yourself, they say you should slice lengthways into the blood vessels. I suppose it works both ways. Anyway," the tip of the knife severs flesh, "it will get the blood flowing and that's what we're after." She cuts a one inch incision and, with a fluid flick of the wrist, withdraws the blade from the skin. She plunges the point once more forward and slices a slit across the remaining fang mark. "There. Good."

Rebecca cannot bear the sight of the operation. She follows the slow ascent of the speck that must be Isaac and attempts to focus on the sound of the wind gusting through the trees. Water sloshing against the shoreline vanquishes her concentration. She looks down at the widening bruise on her bleeding calf.

"Have you ever tried to kill yourself?" asks Rebecca.

Cassandra looks up from the operation to meet Rebecca's eyes. "What?"

"You said that to commit suicide properly you have to cut a certain way."

"Oh." After tucking a few strands of auburn hair behind an ear, Cassandra leans down and sucks the wound. She spits a mouthful of blood onto the sandy soil. The blood balls up like so many roly-polies. She looks up at Rebecca, her lips a red gash. "No. I'm too stubborn for that." Midway down for another suck, she stops and looks back up at Rebecca. "If I would have tried, I wouldn't be here now." She leans down and sucks the wound.

"I wish we wouldn't have put out the fire," says Rebecca. A gust of wind thrashes the tops of the trees. "It feels like rain." A growing sensation of sickness tendrils outward from her belly.

Cassandra spits another mouthful of blood onto the sand. "It'll pass." On hands and knees, she crawls to the saddlebag and returns with the first-aid kit. "Let me get you fixed up and then I'll stoke up the fire. Wouldn't want you getting pneumonia on top of everything else." After disinfecting and bandaging the wound, she moves to the aspen and props herself next to Rebecca. "Let me rest a minute." She scans the mountain for Isaac, but he is nowhere to be seen. "Ike will be back before you know it. Everything's going to work out just the way we want it to."

Cassandra pats her thigh. Rebecca lays down between Cassandra's legs, positioning her head in the crook of Cassandra's elbow.

Rebecca's head reels. "It was a wonderful day."

"I guess." Cassandra strokes Rebecca's brow. "It won't be one we'll forget any time soon, that's for goddamn sure."

Rebecca closes her eyes. She takes in the heat emanating from Cassandras's body. "Cassy?" she whispers.

Cassandra hums. The tune is familiar to Rebecca.

"Cassy?" whispers Rebecca again, all the while savoring the song. She waits in languid anticipation for the tear welling up in her eye to succumb to gravity and fall. The tear is warm on her cheek.

The wind stops.

Cassandra, stricken with a sudden vestige of piety, stops humming. She leans down and, just as a fresh gust of wind enters the hollow crashing through the trees, whispers something into Rebecca's ear. Thinking her words have been heard, she kisses Rebecca on the forehead. She wipes a forearm across her bloody lips. "I better get a fire started. I smell rain."

"Cassy?"

"Yeah?"

"Before you go, can I tell you something?"

"I'm not going anywhere, honey. I'm just going to start a fire so we can keep you warm."

"But can I tell you something?"

"Sure."

Rebecca speaks with her eyes clenched shut. "I don't love Jed. I don't love him at all. I respect him. I admire him. But I don't love him."

"Big deal" says Cassandra. After pushing Rebecca into a sitting position, she gets to her feet. "That's it? Don't take yourself so seriously." She looks down on Rebecca with a bemused expression. "Do you think I'm in love with Gabe?"

Rebecca leans her back against the aspen. "But you love him, right?"

"That's what *I* just asked *you*," says Cassandra.

"I don't love Jed *at all*."

"Then who do you love?"

"I don't know." Rebecca looks at her bandaged calf.

Cassandra's laughter, like the wind, rips through the hollow. "Never name your love, sister. That's the right idea. Never name your love." She walks away. "I better get the fire going. You're getting delirious."

A large droplet of rain hits Rebecca on top of the head. She leans her head back against the aspen. Rain falls steadily. She fancies she can hear the sound of pounding hooves. She is sick with venom.

Isaac telephones the Crowheart two days before the wedding. When Thomas answers, Isaac asks to speak to Sarah. From Isaac's perspective, not only does Sarah possess a sympathetic ear where he is concerned, but he also feels she will be able to intuit his silent objections to the marriage as well. Isaac's aversion to the nuptials will remain unarticulated simply because he will not allow it the manifestation of words; to do so would be to incriminate himself, would bring his failures and shame into the light of conscious thought. In the interest of self-preservation, Isaac cannot bear the feelings, which are bedeviled by his subconscious, to be interpreted in the realm of logic.

Grateful for the isolating quality of phone lines, Isaac informs Sarah that he has been suffering from a combination of writer's block and lethargy, has fallen seriously behind in his classes, and petered to a standstill on his thesis — in short, is flirting with being deemed incompetent by professor and peer alike. The only remedy, as he sees it, is to utilize the upcoming spring break (which happens to coincide with the week of the wedding) to get the situation under control. There is simply no other way.

"Couldn't you at least drive up on the day of the wedding?" asks Sarah. From the modulation of Isaac's voice, or rather the lack of modulation, she apprehends that she is waging a losing battle. Out of a sense of propriety, she continues to try to change his mind, "You could drive back the morning after. You'd only lose about a day and a half."

"No," says Isaac. "I can't afford any sort of diversion." He knows that few will dare to question the validity of a adequately obtuse excuse, even when their instincts instruct them that it is nothing more than an elaborate fib. "If I don't get control of this thing everything I've worked for since I left will vaporize like it never happened at all." Isaac spins the story confident in its obfuscatory nature; the excuse is designed to ward off inquiry from virtually any angle. "I want to be there for the Old Man, but I just can't. I hope you'll explain it to everybody. I hope you understand." He banks on the probability that Sarah will be reluctant (though he assumes her instincts throb with indignation at the lie) to challenge the excuse. To criticize the excuse would be equivalent to branding Isaac a liar, which, in turn, would leave him no recourse but to lash out. "I think I'll even go so far as unplugging the phone so I won't be disturbed. It's that serious. Bad timing all the way around. What can you do?"

"Nothing, I guess," says Sarah. "Everybody will be disappointed."

"I know. I'll make it up to the Old Man. You'll see."

Sarah stands at the kitchen sink, a dingy towel slung over one shoulder, one hand on her hip, the other hand holding the telephone. She stares through the window at the cottonwood branches; they are restless with breeze. The line goes dead, but Sarah does not notice the dial tone in her ear. Her mind is focused on concocting schemes to embellish Isaac's story.

Isaac hangs up the phone. He sits down at the kitchen table. Throughout the conversation, he paced through the apartment with the cordless phone nestled between his neck and shoulder. He had walked from the kitchen, to the living room, to the bathroom, to the bedroom, and back to the kitchen again. Now, hunched at the table, his face cradled in his palms, Isaac would not be capable of answering questions concerning the objects in his apartment: Is there a soap-scum ring in the bathtub? Hard water stains in the toilet? Is the computer on or off? Is the African violet on the table in bloom or, for that matter, even alive? Is the bed made? Are there dirty dishes in the kitchen sink? Is the television on?

He would be powerless to answer.

Somewhere in the night, physicality lost significance as he imagined the wedding between Rebecca and his father. He fancied Rebecca in an off-white wedding gown (Clytie's wedding gown) mouthing absurd oaths in front of an absurd altar erected in an absurd old schoolhouse — a barn converted into a schoolhouse converted into a makeshift church. Foolishness. Blasphemy. He developed contingencies to abort the ceremony: Objections, kidnaping, murder, a declaration of love, an appeal to Clytie's memory.... He drank from a bottle of bourbon. He raged. He cried. The vision of Rebecca, black hair in contrast with the wedding gown, lithe muscles entwined with the Old Man's gravity ridden flesh, sweet breath mingling with decrepit air, the kiss and the ring, tortured Isaac well into the witching-hour. He drank. Physicality lost significance. Enraptured in a tragedy of his own design, Isaac curled up under the kitchen table and trembled with sleep.

Isaac hangs up the phone and sits at the kitchen table, resting his face in his palms. His head throbs with the indignation of alcohol and guilt. A rancid odor creeps out of his mouth and into his nose. Gagging, he lurches towards the bathroom hoping that the vomit will serve as a sort of exorcism. A puddle of greenish feces floats on the surface of the toilet water. Isaac pukes, the contents of his stomach sparse and red like thin tomato sauce. He pukes until tears are running out of his eyes and his stomach is empty. He flushes the toilet. The vomit and the excrement bracketing in the eye of the whirlpool, reddish-green soup, the smell of fermenting silage, causes Isaac's stomach to convulse again, forces him to crouch once more above the toilet. He heaves, but nothing comes up. He is empty, like a husk.

He makes his way to the sink and twists on the cold water. Cupping it in his palms, he splashes his face. Avoiding his reflection in the mirror, face dripping wet, he opens the medicine cabinet above the sink and takes down a bottle of blue mouthwash. He gargles. He spits. After turning off the water and patting his face dry with a hand towel that smells faintly of mildew, he replaces the bottle of mouthwash and shuts the medicine cabinet. He looks at his reflection in the mirror. It is done: Isaac will not witness his father's marriage to Rebecca.

A scalding shower washes away the last remnants of the guilt brought on by lying to Sarah. Isaac, wearing boxer shorts and a t-shirt, walks into the living room. He is puzzled by the overturned pot of pasta and red sauce on the carpet. An empty jar of prefabricated spaghetti sauce sits upright on the coffee table. The television, nestled in the entertainment center in the corner of the room, hisses static.

Isaac walks into the kitchen. He fills a pot with water and pours it into the automatic-drip coffee maker. After a short search for coffee filters, he adds coffee and turns the machine on. While waiting for the black liquid to brew, he notices that the African violet perched in the center of the kitchen table is very much alive and in full bloom. The purple blossoms glow in the morning light that pours through the kitchen window. The gurgling and hissing coffeepot causes Isaac to wonder when he last watered the plant. He walks to the kitchen table and sticks a forefinger into the pot. The plant trembles. The soil is powder dry. Two purple blossoms fall from the stem and land on the tabletop. Isaac pauses. He stares down at the disconnected flowers and feels the warmth of sunlight on his hand.

After drinking a pot and a half of black coffee, Isaac becomes manic. He waters the African violet, then fertilizes it with an aquamarine spike which he thrusts into the soil. He vacuums the living room carpet, scrubs the kitchen sink with Comet, bleaches the toilet and the bathtub. He strips the sheets from his bed, the pillowcases from his pillows, and washes them in the coin-operated washers, which are located in the basement of the building. He cleans the apartment, listening, as he does so, to the sounds of the university-managed radio station. Whirling with the beat (the vacuum his dance partner, the toilet brush his microphone) and singing lyrics to familiar songs aloud, he sterilizes his lair with bleach and ammonia. The work leaves him feeling morally eviscerate.

The apartment clean, Isaac fries himself four eggs and a pound of bacon. He carries a heaping plate into the living room and places it on the coffee table. He finds the television remote control under a couch cushion and opts to watch an NBA game while he eats. During a commercial break, he trots into the kitchen and returns with a bottle of hot pepper sauce. The grace of the athletes bobbing around on the television screen cause him feelings of inadequacy. He licks his palm. He tastes dirty. After swallowing four aspirin in front of the bathroom mirror, he decides to take another shower.

As Isaac slouches under a stream of scalding water, the dogged concern that has been stalking him throughout the day attacks: Isaac cannot escape the fact that he is a liar. *You lie to the only people in the world that give a damn about you.* The words swirl like wights through the gray matter of his brain. *You're a coward, that's why. Pathetic inclinations. Are you so deluded to think that there is something between you because she reminds you of Clytie in some little unfathomable way? Nonsense. You lie to protect your fantasies from the truth.* The argument repeats itself. Isaac, attempting to silence himself, adjusts the water temperature until it is as hot as he can stand it and scrubs himself with a loofa sponge until his skin glows pink. The hot water fades, and he stands shivering under the biting shower. Eventually, because his physical body takes precedence over his inner turmoil, the voice inside his head withers to a sepulcher whisper. Quaking with cold, he turns off the water, steps out of the shower and dries off with another towel that smells of mildew. He stands naked in front of the medicine cabinet mirror. As the steam evaporates from the surface of the mirror, Isaac realizes the only way to waylay the return of the dogged and draining voice is to concentrate on his body. He grooms himself meticulously. While shaving, guiding the disposable razor over his throat with a shaking hand, he cuts himself. The sight of blood flowing from his reflection eases his sense of doom. The sting of the styptic pencil sealing the wound lends him a sensation of poise.

After brushing his teeth and gargling with mouthwash, Isaac dresses in sweat pants and a t-shirt. He pours a glass of orange juice before heading to the computer to work on a paper which is due in a few weeks. The screen on the monitor pulses with energy. Isaac cannot concentrate; the paper, entitled *The Last Stand: Victory or Futility at Little Bighorn*, does not interest him. He switches the computer off. Deeming sleep will restore a semblance of rationality, he drinks a half a bottle of cough syrup. He lays down on the couch to watch television. He watches an old Clint Eastwood western in which Clint, a ghost, forces the townsfolk to paint all the buildings in their town red. Three men ride towards the town and stop at a sign that reads: Welcome To Hell. Isaac closes his eyes. While hoping the African violet will pull through, he falls into a dreamless slumber.

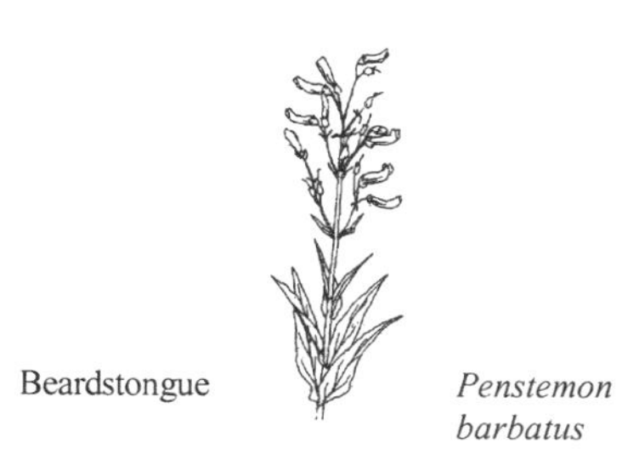

The ceremony is to take place in the old converted barn (which is now a schoolhouse for Thomas), which now resembles, at least the interior, something of a church. To the passerby who happened upon the Crowheart for one reason or another, the converted barn would not seem converted at all. Instead (excepting for the numerous intact windows), it would seem abandoned to the elements: the exterior has not been painted or stained in a number of years, giving the building the quaint yet foreboding air of the dilapidated barn popular in early American paintings. The interior, however, a single spacious room, bears the demeanor of modernity with the fluorescent lights, the buffed tile floor, and the fresh coat of white paint on the drywall. A chalkboard spans the length of the northern wall and, for the purposes of the wedding, has been veiled by white lace drapery. The long table, usually situated in the center of the room (complete with two high-backed wooden chairs, one for Thomas, the student, one for Sarah, the teacher), has been pushed to the western wall and covered with a white cloth. The computer, typically perched on top of the long table, sits on the floor, unplugged, underneath the table, and hidden by the tablecloth from view. Nine rows of chairs, eight across, with an aisle running down the center (high backed wooden chairs making up the first row, the remainder folding chairs borrowed from the Wyoming Livestock Association in Crowhaven), stand facing the chalkboard in front of a makeshift pulpit (constructed from three bales of alfalfa stacked one on top of the other, concealed by a white cloth) from which the preacher will conduct the ritual.

Rebecca, clad in a black valuer nightgown, stands at the pulpit gazing out over the empty chairs. It is the cold hour before dawn on the day she is to take her marriage vows. Flower arrangements — chrysanthemums, carnations, and Easter lilies — border the room. Vases of red roses sit on either side of the pulpit. The room is silent, except for the near-inaudible hissing of the fluorescent lights. Rebecca's mind is also silent, except for the tenuous static that abides in all living creatures. She stares, her hands on the pulpit as if expunging a sermon before it can be delivered, into the emptiness of the room, head hung low, black hair hanging over her face like a dark and tangled forest. Behind her eyes, a fire of longing (fueled by contempt) smolders.

Although the barn is devoid of any religious symbol which would legitimize its conversion into a church, a passerby appearing out of the predawn darkness to stop and peer through one of the many windows would undoubtedly classify the place as sacred. Possibly the stranger, just born out of the wilderness, would equate anything that bespoke structure and civilization as sacred, be it the Sistine Chapel or a barn converted into a schoolhouse converted into a church in the middle of an unforgiving prairie. Why else would the stranger gravitate towards the ghostly white light radiating from the barn (a light extinguished by the outer darkness like an anaerobic virus exposed to oxygen) if not for the enticement of the possibility of a miracle? The stranger would come out of the darkness and paste his face against one of the windows in order to behold the light, and this stranger alone would be able (for Rebecca cannot see herself) to discern the tears dripping out of the black maze of Rebecca's hair. This stranger alone would be able to empathize with Rebecca's consecrated despair.

A coyote's yap signals the dawn, and the apparition of the stranger vaporizes. The next yap disrupts Rebecca's meditations;

she becomes self-aware. Fearing that she is already too late for her presence in the big-house to have gone unnoticed (where did the darkness go?), she jogs down the aisle between the rows of chairs, her bare feet making slapping sounds like rubber on the tile. She turns off the fluorescent lights and walks outside. She stands a moment in the predawn light — stands between one world and the other. The cold earth against the soles of her feet causes a shiver to squiggle through her body. She yearns for the warmth of the guest room bed. She runs towards the big house.

"Seems more like we're getting ready to watch a play than a wedding," spatters Doc Watson, dentures loose in his mouth. He adjusts the thin black bow tie at his throat, waiting for either Sarah or Cassandra (seated on either side of him in the second row of chairs) to respond. "Know what I mean? You girls ever been to the theater before? I once saw a play down in Denver where this King/Warrior fellow had to sacrifice his own daughter on account of this woman who told him if he didn't all his ships would sink while he was on the way to rescue his kidnaped lover. Something like that. Famous story. Can't recall the name. Famous battle. Damn. Hate it when I can't remember things that I can see right in front of me." He slips a silver flask from his inside coat pocket, twists off the cap, and takes a slug. "It's a crying shame. I can see the girl who played the kidnaped woman. Beautiful girl." He takes another drink from the flask, twists the cap back on. "Truly beautiful. Can't remember the name of the goddamn character though. Can't remember the name of the goddamn play, but I can see it in my head." The flask momentarily disappears in the folds of Doc Watson's faded black tuxedo, then reemerges in his quaking hand. He twists off the cap and takes a long swallow. "Crying shame. You get old enough and you don't know if what you remember is real, or what you forgot is made up. Must be some sort of goddamn curse on humanity. To hell with whoever put that curse on me." After another swallow from the flask, he twists on the cap and stashes it inside his tuxedo. He places his fingertips on his upper denture and pushes them into his gums. "Damn things. First the teeth, then the mind."

Cassandra and Sarah ignore Doc Watson.

Sarah stares rigidly at the makeshift pulpit. Her dirty-blonde hair sits on the crest of her skull, wrapped in a tight bun. The collar on her green cotton dress is stiff with starch. Unaccustomed to makeup, the rouged cheeks, the earth-tone eyeshadow, and the vermillion lipstick give her the peculiar semblance of a made-over cadaver. She sits still in her chair wearing an ill-at-ease expression which suggests either an "It's tedious to be dead" emotion, or a "My shoes are too tight" sensation. (The shoes were purchased especially for the occasion.) Sarah has never been comfortable in ostentatious settings. Formality casts an unsavory shadow on the practical business of living. Pomposity, whatever the degree, inevitably leaves her short of breath and with the nagging feeling that she needs to visit a toilet.

"Damned if I can figure why *this* wedding is putting me in mind of *that* play," continues Doc Watson. He wipes his lips with the arm of his tuxedo. "Saw it years ago when I was down in Denver for some medical convention. Zeke and Mary Ann were still alive. The Crowheart was still thriving. The good ol' days. Jed hadn't even met Clytie yet." He pulls the flask from his pocket, unscrews the lid and drains it in a single motion. "I swore the second I heard that Zeke and Mary Ann got mowed down by that train that I'd always stop before crossing the tracks. Left them boys orphans. Frank and Jed were still friends. They had to be. Couldn't afford no trouble between them. Couldn't even recognize them in that wreck of a pickup. That's one promise I've never broke."

"Quit being morbid," says Cassandra. She, auburn hair hanging to her shoulders, fidgets in her chair. She wears a snap-up, blue silk, western-style shirt and a new pair of black jeans with the legs tucked into the tops of her red leather cowboy boots. “This is a grand occasion. We owe the bride and groom our best vibes if we want to see them happy.” Euphoria oozes from her body. She sniffs. “I’ve always been superstitious about weddings and funerals.” The words tumble rapidly from her chapped lips. She sniffs again and smacks her tongue against the roof of her sticky-dry mouth. “I guess most everybody is. And everybody knows you never mention death at a wedding.” Glancing at Doc Watson, she slaps him on the shoulder in mock disapproval. “We have to think good thoughts if we want the marriage to work. Just like at a funeral, you think good thoughts so the dead have an easy journey. Whoops,” she claps her hands to her mouth and sniggers, “now I’m the one doing it.”

Doc Watson offers the flask to Cassandra. “I can’t help it.” He runs his fingers through his shock of white hair. “Can’t stop thinking about it. Feels like I’ve been here before.”

Cassandra tips the flask back against her lips only to find it empty. “All weddings are like that. And funerals. The eternal return, as Ike would say. Here,” she nudges Doc Watson with the flask, “it’s empty.” She wrings her hands. “There I go again.” After standing up and surveying the room, she says, “Where the hell is everybody? Are we early? Where’s Mike and Gabe?”

“Comforting their father,” says Sarah.

“I’ve got to get out of here,” says Cassandra. “Is there time?”

“Time for what?” asks Sarah.

“Go on then,” says Doc Watson. “You’re making me nervous. Things won’t get going for a while yet.”

Cassandra walks away, the heels of her boots clicking on the shining tile.

Doc Watson sucks on the flask before realizing it is empty. “Damn.” After screwing on the cap, he tucks the flask inside his tuxedo. “Is it just me, or is it godawful hot in here?”

“It’s hot.”

When Doc Watson stands, his joints creak from the pressure. “Suppose I’ve got time to glue in my teeth and get some more bourbon?”

"Oh yes. Go on."

Doc Watson hobbles after Cassandra.

"Go on," whispers Sarah. "Please go on."

Rain begins plunging from two-tone gray clouds a half an hour before the ceremony is to begin. Hours earlier, the sky was blue as sea with only a few straggling plumes of clouds gliding through the brightness. Sparrows, meadowlarks, and the occasional gray-jay flitted through the warm air and perched on tree limbs, telephone poles, and fence posts to sing morning songs. Kildeer strutted through the fields of alfalfa and western wheat feeding on grasshoppers and moths. The air was still; the horses in the corral swished their tails to ward off biting flies. Michael, Gabriel, and Thomas, along with Wade Ksaslmque and the few ranch hands, went about the morning chores with more vigor than usual, charged by the anticipation of the day's upcoming festivities. The scent of oats poured from buckets into troughs, the sounds of dogs growling and scuffling in pseudo battle, horses chomping grain, the cock-a-doodle-do of the roosters, the smoothness of a warm egg fresh from the roost in the palm of a hand, the aroma of horse manure and the musky scent of tack in the horse barn... (sensations taken for granted due to routine), these and more were infused with a quality of newness, as if the ranch hands were city-dwellers granted a day in the country and magically invested with the knowledge and skills to carry out their assigned tasks. Even the coffee (Thomas sucked down three mugs as if it were a tabooed elixir of a fertility cult) seemed richer to the men as they sat on the porch and watched the spectacle of the eastern horizon change from salmon-pink to peach to a blue that revealed and intensified the green of the fields and the trees. With the sun looking like a flower in the sky, the men placed their mugs on the porch railing and set off to tend to their duties. There was a rarified lightness in their steps, derided only by the creaking of the porch (the insidiousness of dry-rot a familiar topic of morning grumblings) under their boots.

A childlike elation pervaded, and the hands ignored the groaning wood; it was a morning in which the considerations of decay were as absurd as nuclear fission to the Neanderthal.

Although the ceremony is not scheduled until one o'clock, guests begin arriving on the Crowheart as early as nine a.m. The younger men have shaved and dressed in skintight, black Wrangler jeans, western-style long sleeve shirts, scuffed boots and cowboy hats freshly cleaned and shaped with steam and starch. The older men, scoffing at their young counterparts' audacity, have dressed themselves in dark suits, bolo ties, shined boots, and cowboy hats taken down from the closet only for formal events. The women, with the exception of a few of the younger ones who have dressed in the fashion of their male equivalents, have attired themselves in long skirts and blouses complete with high-heeled shoes more appropriate for a posh gathering in Denver than a ranch so far from the maddening crowd. The many children, infant and prepubescent alike, have all been dressed up to mimic their parents.

The guests arrived almost exclusively in pickup trucks — trucks that tooled down the dirt road leading to the big house kicking up clouds of dust in their wakes. A few of the adolescents rode out of the prairie on horseback, proud of the scent of leather and horse sweat clinging to their clothes. Although the preponderance of the guests converged upon the Crowheart from neighboring ranches, a few made the trek from Crowhaven to the east. The ranch community is clannish, and most who are born to the land die on the land (unless death plays its trump while they happen to be abroad in Puerto Vallarta, Athens, or the Caribbean, both enjoying *and* disdaining the outside world while constantly worrying about the status of the homeland, much as children pine for the warmth and familiarity of their beds and blankets on their first extended absence from home). The rumble of incoming traffic corrupted the pastoral tranquility of the morning with the insinuation of debauchery through food and drink and frolic and the titillating assurance of dance and flirtation between the sexes. Although a handful of the guests will be stirred by the reverential gravity of the wedding, most, masquerading obeisance, will squirm in their chairs during the actual marriage. Meanwhile, the aches in their backs and buttocks, the sweat crawling down their armpits like worms, the stiffness setting into their knees, and the buzzing of flies, all will combine and hone the anticipation of the reception where reverence will be shed like an old snake skin, exposing revelry. The preacher's voice will drone on until an outbreak of visible anxiety threatens the sanctity of the marriage. Then, at the crucial moment, just prior to an implosion of the psychology of the guests, the groom (monarch of the realm), will kiss the bride (who at that moment will become a Daniel's proper and, until the falling of darkness, will be heralded as a virgin queen). That kiss will mark the end of solemnity, and, after a collective silent sigh from the audience, the festivities will begin.

Before Cassandra and Doc Watson are able to return from the big house to the makeshift temple, the clouds muster above the Crowheart and rain begins to fall. Sarah, alone in the church, mesmerized by the implications of the impending ceremony, is not aware of the large droplets drumming against the tin roof above her. The adults, ambling around inside of the big house, are alerted of the storm, with the first few drops of rain, by squeals from girls who stand on the porch in starched skirts nurturing daydreams of their own weddings: They comment on the boys frolicking around the fountain where Isaac once sought poetic inspiration. The rain thickens and the girls see their futures dashed by the odious omen of a thunderclap. Pop-eyed, they stampede into the house, sounding the alarm. A ripple of superstition (Cassandra, standing behind the locked door of the upstairs bathroom wetting the tips of her fingers under the sink and snorting the moisture into her nose, mutters, "Bloody Hell," and inspects her reflection in the mirror for traces of white powder) passes through the gathering. The old men, having grown accustomed to the unpredictable nature of weather on the high plains, are the first to shake off the sudden whisperings of local folklore concerning weddings and rain. Instead, they take up tumblers of bourbon and scotch in defiance of the gods and fate. This posturing causes a trickle down effect from age group to age group, and, in a matter of moments, the laughter and gossiping and lightness has been resuscitated. Mothers run out on the porch and scold straggling boys indoors. Herd dogs assist the mothers by nipping at the boys heels.

Sarah sits alone in the temple, staring at the makeshift pulpit. The expectations of the past, of her own wedding ceremony held seven years ago under a full July moon, collide with the present and blur the possibilities of the future. Remembrance and speculation become one. She does not hear the rain falling in droplets the size of marbles, running in rivulets down the corrugated tin roof to form puddles on the ground; she does not notice the absence of the boys' voices around the fountain outside; she does not feel the tears (emotionless tears caused by failing to blink) falling over the banks of her lower eyelids and streaming over her cheeks.

An inner reckoning moves through Sarah without the aid of an inner voice: Conflicting images drift through her mind and dissipate before eliciting emotional response: The first time she and Michael made love. It was on a mattress, in the back of his truck, on a moonless summer night filled with stars and the sound of crickets, parked next to a gargantuan stack of baled hay. The vacation in Reno, glutted with pulsing neon and gallons of whiskey and Michael's resolution that they would not gamble and continually feed at cheap buffets. The love letters before they were married, written in Michael's unpracticed and angular script, the promise of children only after Michael is the boss of the Crowheart, the frigid windtorn winters on the prairie, the violently promiscuous springs.... The images flash and tumble through Sarah's mind and leave her physically paralyzed. It is as if she has been assigned the task of reassembling a shattered egg, knowing full well the disparity of the situation. The pieces of the past and present do not fit together and yet are part of the same puzzle. She sits stunned by her incapacity to project a plausible future.

The remembrance of her own wedding begins as an overhead panoramic camera shot: Lamp oil torches on bamboo shafts, like landing lights, demarcate the boundaries of the open-air cathedral, set up in the pasture south of the big house. The full leaves on the cottonwoods are unmoving in the warm air. The wedding guests sit in rows of folding chairs watching either the backdrop of the full moon or the figures of Michael and Sarah (both dressed in white, standing in front of an altar constructed of stacked bales of hay masked by white cotton). Crickets chirp to the rhythm of the night. Coyotes yip from draws of darkness. Insects (moths and mosquitos and gnats) flutter around the flames of the torches, bewitched by the amber glow, charred by the invisible heat. A thin scent of honeysuckle and horse manure permeates the air.

The vision shifts: Sarah stands in the sitting room of the big house. Outside of the picture window the eastern horizon is tinged with the promise of a new day. It is the morning after the wedding. Michael, who got drunk to the point of oblivion during the reception, was unable to consummate the marriage; Sarah was unable to sleep.

She stands in front of the fireplace. It casts the only light in the room, save for the minuscule flicker of flames from the nubs of the three candles secured in a three-pronged wrought iron candelabra sitting on the closed lid of the baby grand piano. Being July, there is no need for a fire in the hearth, but Clytie, before departing to the sanctuary of her bedroom an hour earlier, insisted. Sarah is alone. Clad in her wedding gown, she stands on the bearskin carpet silhouetted by the blaze in the fireplace. She holds her left hand outward, slowly tilting it back and forth so that the ruby, encircled by diamonds, on her wedding ring reflects simultaneously the light cast by the fire and the candles. She thinks about Clytie who has become her mother-in-law:

Clytie, who changed out of the white dress (a dress Michael purchased and insisted that she wear for the wedding) immediately after the ceremony, wore a baby-blue cotton nightgown that fell to her ankles. She sat on the piano bench and watched Sarah. Remembrances of her own wedding so many years ago, veiled by an ashen film, dart through her mind's eye on their way to the murky labyrinths where memory cannot follow: Clytie's heart was starved for love. Her marriage to Jedidiah bound her in contractual obligation, a social contract, which, out of pride and a yearning for martyrdom, she refused to breech. The only child of a mother who was Jewish and a father who was a Canadian of Nordic descent, Clytie perceived herself as uniquely oppressed, an endangered species and, although she married Jedidiah solely in order that her parents would receive a substantial dowry from the Daniels' clan (who insisted on tradition), a dowry which would loosen the vice of poverty and allow them to live in relative comfort, to break the contractual agreement due to a lack of love would be beneath dignity. Possessed with a rare and vivacious love for flesh and spirit alike, Clytie took her vows believing she would, in time, grow to love Jedidiah. After all, they had only courted for two months before Jedidiah asked for her hand, and the entirety of the engagement spanned a mere three months. Yes, she would grow to love him with the passing of time. She did not. As the days became weeks and the weeks became months and the months became years, Clytie became embittered by her circumstance. She began asking herself rhetorical questions, because she had no one else she could ask: Is it a sin to knowingly lie while taking wedding vows if you do not believe in the god which you "sin" against? If we are so removed from the beast, so enlightened, why do women allow themselves to be impregnated by men on the basis of "social stratification"? Is love a thing in itself or merely a human construct? Is love a habit, familiarity precipitated by biological attraction?

And yet, as the years passed and Clytie became inextricably enmeshed in the irony that was her life, she became lascivious in the bedroom. She craved pregnancy and was worried that either she or Jedidiah was sterile and went to all ends to remedy the situation: herb treatments, X'ing off days on the calender as they related to her cycle, coaxing sexual energy from Jedidiah thinking the more excited he was the more potent his seed would be, attempting to convince herself through books and meditation that she was in love with her husband.... It is a dangerous predicament for a woman so naturally inclined for love to marry and have no outlet for that love. Clytie sensed hers was a precarious situation and prayed fervently, at first to any god that would listen and then to Tenyri, a Mongol god whom she became enamored with while desperately searching for a solution to her quandary. Her prayers were answered when, during the beginning of her third year of marriage, she missed her period for the first time since she was thirteen. Exalted, her prayers became more fervent and of a different disposition; she prayed that the fetus in her womb, a child that was to be named either Michael or Michaela according to Daniel's tradition, would prove to be the necessary outlet for her pent-up love. He was not. The pregnancy contorted with problems from the beginning. By the third trimester, Clytie was praying for a miscarriage. Her back ached with the persistence of disease; she was violently ill virtually everyday of the pregnancy; during the seventh month, paranoia enveloped her psyche, and she became convinced that the thing in her belly was apocalyptic in nature. Jedidiah, who at first adhered to the belief that pregnant women are prone to hysteria, eventually hired nurses to keep an around-the-clock watch on Clytie. He did this both for her sake, because he loved her, and for the sake of the unborn child, who, if born male, would be heir to the Daniels empire. By and by, Michael was pushed out of the womb and into the existential world. Clytie, from its first breath, loathed the infant. The baby was guarded against its mother by the same nurses who had guarded him while he lay in the darkness of the womb. Michael never suckled at his mother's breast; from his newborn perspective, Michael's mother was a woman in a white dress whose face changed from shift to shift. Clytie barricaded herself in a room on the north wing of the mansion. She slept without dreams. Upon waking, she sat in front of the lone window in an antique rocking chair staring out over the brown, rolling prairie that stretched out to the gray horizon. The fall wind, on certain days, sang a lyric of isolation. Clytie came to think of herself as the last of a dying breed, utterly alone except for the ghosts of her forebears who at night would whisper in a tongue which, try as she may, she could not comprehend. At the witching hour, on the night of the first blizzard of Michael's first year, Clytie awoke singing with fever. The wind, howling like a host of banshees, prompted Clytie out of bed and over to the window. She drew open the curtains and was momentarily blinded by the obfuscating snow hurtling against the windowpanes. Her eyes adjusted and she became mesmerized by the driven flakes. She fixated on a tiny spot of blackness in the cacophony of white. The black spot began to pulsate and grow, until Clytie stood transfixed by a void of shadows. She descended. When all was gone — earth and sky, color and light, existence and oblivion — Clytie was rendered. When time resumed its course, Clytie felt curiously out of place standing in front of the window staring into an impenetrable white wall. The moan of the wind sent a shiver from her groin to the top of her skull. Tingling with anticipation, she walked across the floor and exited the bedroom. She walked to Jedidiah's room, the marriage chamber, let the blue nightgown fall to the floor in a heap, unsnapped her bra, shed her panties, and climbed into bed with her husband. Jedidiah, who loved Clytie from the beginning, responded favorably to his wife's advances, hoping that the ordeal of their inexplicable estrangement had drawn to a close. In the darkness, Clytie began the harvest of the seed.

She incanted something under her breath during the course of the copulation. He, engulfed in the moist recitations of her sexuality, reached climax. The seed was planted. Clytie climbed out of the bed and walked out of the room and closed the door behind her. The blue nightgown heaped on the floor was Jedidiah's only clue that the episode had not been a dream.

Isaac was born.

And then she was pregnant again.

And this time the pregnancy did not fill her with loathing or joy but indifference as Jed, laboring under the misconception that Clytie's love for Isaac stemmed from her love for him, crept into her room during the cover of night, and, while she lay demented with sleep and wine, he, luminous as a spectre in the moon-filled room, flesh white as froth, stripped her panties and planted seed again. When she awoke to the windswept day, she designated the episode as a disturbing dream.

Gabriel was born nine months later. When the sun would set, Clytie began locking the bedroom door.

Sarah reassembles Clytie through the structuring of pieces gleaned from old photographs, fragments of speech gathered over the years, Clytie's room (which is as undisturbed as a mausoleum), memory and inference. She remembers Clytie's knowing glance, but the design of that glance becomes clear only now as she sits alone in the converted schoolhouse waiting for Rebecca and Jedidiah to be married:

Clytie stood up from the piano bench and looked Sarah in the eye. She glided toward the fireplace, the light-blue nightgown flowing behind her. The gown reflected the light cast by both the hearth and the candles, like starlight off glacial snow in the stillness of an arctic night. Halfway to the fireplace (to Sarah), she changed direction and moved toward the window. She opened the window and stood with the dawn in her eyes, caressing the swell of her exposed bosom with the fingertips of her right hand. Her jet black hair moved with the summer breeze. A horse neighed from the corral.

In the next instant, Clytie stood in front of Sarah. All motion had ceased. *The shadows snaking along the waxed wooden floor, and walls, and piano, were frozen. Clytie's arm was outstretched, stiff, and from her fingers dangled a leather thong weighted by a pendant. The dull glean of tarnished silver, the tribal rendition of some cyclopean eye, the pendant pregnant with untranslated meaning, filled Sarah with apprehension. The leather thong looked as if it had been soaked in grease. "Take it," said Clytie, and pulled her eyes from the pendant to look at Sarah. "A wedding gift."*

Sarah watched Clytie's lips, and they did not move as she spoke; her jaw was as taught as a statue's. "Go on," coaxed the voice, "take it." Sarah looked into Clytie's eyes and fell under the impression that she was observing an oil painting, a scene pulled from antiquity into the present. "Take it and remember that you are woman and that it is woman and not man who can create beyond herself. Man can only penetrate the mystery. Woman is the mystery. You are the creator, not Michael, not Jedidiah, you." Sarah took the pendant. The shadows again took up their serpentine routines. Clytie moved forward and kissed Sarah hard on the mouth. Sarah tasted camphor, but did not resist the embrace; her belly throbbed.

Sarah stood alone in the sitting room in front of the dying fire. Dawn peeked over the eastern horizon and into the window. The air was still and cool. The pendant hung between Sarah's breasts, absorbing the throb in her belly.

The sound of rain and squeaking hinges. Garbled language. Boots slopping against tiled floor. For an instant, Sarah does not know where she is; her heart twitches. She has forgotten some imperative point — has lost both the pendant and crucial information that lends credence to the allegory of her life and is on the verge of sinking into the abyss of absurdity — when a voice buoys her up.

"What are you doing sitting in here all by your lonesome?" asks Gabriel. He is wearing a dark suit and a plastic sheath over his Stetson. He stands behind Sarah. "Everything alright?" He rubs her shoulders.

Sarah turns her neck; her body remains stiff. "Yes. Fine. Wedding's always make me a little homesick."

Gabriel looks at the makeshift pulpit.

"Don't stop rubbing," says Sarah. "I know it doesn't make sense to be sad." She turns her head so that she too is looking at the pulpit. "It's not supposed to. It's a woman thing. If it did make sense you'd be in big trouble."

"Tell me about it. Cassy's lit up like Christmas and the party hasn't even started. I hope she doesn't get sick during the ceremony."

"If you're going to marry her, you should teach her a little self-control."

"Ha!" laughs Gabriel. "Control? Cassy? I gave up on that a long time ago. She's a horse that can't be broke." He kneads Sarah's shoulders. "Anyway, why would I want to? I love her because she's free. I'd rather take her out and shoot her than keep her caged up the way Mike does you."

"You're hurting me."

Gabriel glances down at his hands and removes them from Sarah's shoulders as if her flesh is sizzling. "Sorry, got a bit carried away. Guess this wedding's got everybody's nerves up some."

"No harm done."

Gabriel starts to walk away. He stops. "You seen Cassy lately?"

"No," says Sarah. "I wouldn't even venture to guess where she might be."

Rain falls. The windows are shut to keep the storm out of the church. The air inside is cramped from too many people breathing in too small of a space.

The Daniels own three umbrellas. The guests neglected to bring their own, never thinking that it would rain on Jedidiah's wedding day. The three umbrellas are reserved for Rebecca, her mother Odessa, and her maid-of-honor who, because she is a frail woman built out of sticks and dust (transitory to the point of vacuity), remains nameless. Everyone else — the guests and the ushers, the groom and the best-man, the preacher and Doc Watson — are forced to tromp through the rain and the mud between the big house and the makeshift church. The men and boys remain gleeful and, in spite of the adversity, are charged with the spirit of celebration. The women scold the men and march intrepidly through the muck, heads bowed, cursing the Wheel of Fate. Two blue heelers, invigorated by the rain and upon hearing the sounds of people flowing out of the big house, charge from the shelter of the horse barn, barking raucously.

Mrs. Virginia Druel, a woman of sixty-five who has outlived her entire family, propped up by an ancient Blackfoot woman who lives with her "like a sister", heads the exodus from big house to church. The Druel family, when living, seemed a magnet for tragedy. Most of the Druel men, wiry with small hands and big feet, met their demise in close proximity to horses, the rest succumbed to disease. The women, sparse in number and barren, were all (with the exception of Virginia) in grave danger around food — food poisoning, choking, bulimia, anorexia, bulimorexia.... The day of Jedidiah and Rebecca's wedding provides no reprieve from the Druel curse. When Mrs. Druel attempts to shoo one of the blue heelers away with a booted toe to the ribs, her already precarious balance (age, mud, rain) is lost and she falls to the ground like a fresh cowpie. This causes the ancient Blackfoot woman, Mrs. Druel's queerly silent partner, who was bolstered against the matriarch like a living crutch, to topple down beside her. The blue heeler, equipped with a keen feel for human mores, lowers its A-frame ears and the nub of its tail and heads for the safety of the horse barn; the other dog is not far behind.

The throng of people are stopped short on their trek from the big house to the church. The rain pours down like a fat cow pissing on a flat rock. Eyes of children dilate with fear; women slap palms to their mouths; men stand stock still, as if awaiting orders.

Mrs. Druel lies on her back in the mud listening to the pitter of rain falling into the puddle beside her. After an indeterminate amount of time, she looks over to her ancient companion prone in the mud. The old Blackfoot's (nobody knows her real name with the exception of Mrs. Druel who, evidently, is not telling) earthen eyes stare up at the sky, the withered and cracked lips parted in a toothless grin. For a moment, Mrs. Druel believes the fall has killed her friend. In the next moment, the tip of the Old Blackfoot's tongue, stringing spittle, darts from between her lips to taste the rain. The old Blackfoot looks at Mrs. Druel and both women begin laughing.

The laughter confounds the web of internment which fell over the crowd the moment the women descended into the mud. Men spring forth to help them to their feet. The sight of the two odd women — Mrs. Druel sporting her best preserved dress, the old Blackfoot wearing slacks and a man's denim shirt — covered in mud and chortling like pigs, deflates the ricketiness of the situation. The onlookers begin laughing with the two old women. Children double over with hilarity. Mrs. Druel and the old Blackfoot embrace. A cackle of women lead Mrs. Druel and the old Blackfoot back to the big house to clean up.

Solemnity is restored as each individual steps through the threshold into the church. Sarah sits in the first row of chairs facing the altar. Gabriel pushes through the crowd, milling in the foyer of the church. He walks, smiling, toward the motionless figure of Sarah, the sight of Mrs. Druel and the old Blackfoot still bubbling inside of his skull. The smile fades, though, as he walks the length of the building, a journey which is deceptively long, the sound of rain drops striking the corrugated roof and stinging his ears like buckshot. He struggles through the fog of angst that hovers in the center of the church. When he touches Sarah on the shoulder and attempts a lithe word, the sound of his voice makes him wince.

The herd of guests stand huddled in the rear of the church until Thomas, soaked to the skin in his rented tuxedo, threads his way through, sensing that something has gone awry. He sees nothing out of the ordinary and, perturbed by the contrived somberness involved in weddings, begins fulfilling his role as an usher by randomly seating guests who are, overwhelmingly, acquaintances of the Daniels. He performs his task cheerfully, in spite of the almost tangible gloominess which resides inside of the church.

Gabriel assists Thomas, and the guests follow the ushers' guidance without question, like lemmings, plopping down in their seats, relieved by the partial reprieve from the struggle with gravity. Itches, caused by wet cloth against skin, and the sound of the buzzing fluorescent lights immediately attack the seated congregation. Adults sit quietly, attempting to ignore the discomfort. Children fidget and squirm until scolded or slapped by an aunt/sister/mother/grandmother; they sit still until the damp and claustrophobic air needles them to the brink of recklessness and then begin squirming and scratching again in a combined gesture of defiance and desperation.

Among the adults, the few attempts at conversation are snuffed out because whispering, by nature, curtails any but the most perfunctory response. All in all, the congregation is miserable. And yet they endure. They endure because, once inside the church, they know escape is out of the question. They endure because they are willing to pay this price as admission to the festivities that will follow the ceremony.

Michael enters the church through the side door which opens into a room that once held tools but now stores books and chalk and office supplies. His dark brown hair is greased straight back, accentuating his widow's peak. He wears the white suit tailored for the wedding. Having changed in the storage room, his clothes are dry. Before sitting down next to Sarah, he places his hands behind his back and momentarily observes the congregation.

Jedidiah's brother and best-man, Francis Daniels, enters from the rear of the church clad in a spanking new pair of Wrangler blue jeans, a white silk shirt, a bolo tie with an arrowhead clasp, snake skin boots, and an ash-gray-brushed-suede-suit-jacket spotted with rain. He takes his place at the altar, strokes his gray flecked goatee, turns, and beams arrogantly at the seated guests.

The stickling woman whose name nobody will be able to remember, Rebecca's maid-of-honor, walks into the church looking like an animated scarecrow. She wears a white dress that looks like it's hanging off a wire hanger. A wreath of garlands sit on top of her wrung mop of straw-colored hair, tilting to one side like a drunkard's bowler. She makes her way sheepishly to the left side of the altar and stares down at the tiled floor, blue eyes wide.

Thomas sets up speakers on either side of the pulpit. The Wedding March flows. Thomas returns to his seat.

Jedidiah and Rebecca, dripping with rain, enter the church together. Since Rebecca's father is dead, Jedidiah, in his one deviation from Daniel's wedding tradition, persuaded Rebecca to allow him to walk her down the aisle. He is dressed, down to the bolo tie with arrowhead clasp, identically to Michael. His hair is greased and combed straight back accentuating his own widow's peak. He walks down the aisle hand in hand with Rebecca. She is dressed in a white wedding gown complete with an intricately woven veil of the same color. The gown slides along the floor, trailing some four feet behind her, as she glides to the spot where she will take her vows. The veil masks her features so completely that not a hint of her black hair can be seen. Her hands and arms are hidden by white silk gloves which extend up to her shoulders.

The preacher, who donned his work clothes in the store room, enters the ceremonial chamber wearing a black frock. The bald spot on top of his head serves as a natural tonsure. What remains of his hair is the same white as Doc Watson's (who sits in the first row in the chair which should be occupied by Isaac).

The preacher takes his place behind the pulpit, green eyes sparkling under the fluorescent lights. He leans over and turns off the portable stereo at his feet. He clears his throat and offers a few lighthearted comments about the weather. The remarks receive perfunctory laughter.

Although most of the congregation has seen the preacher before, few would consider him a friend or know of his bout with alcoholism which was set in motion by his wife's addiction to pornography. With the exceptions of Easter and Christmas, the preponderance of the ranch folk are seldom inclined to embark on the journey to Crowhaven to attend church on Sunday (or, for that matter, any other day of the week). To the congregation, the preacher is simply a man in a black frock who appears at baptisms, weddings, and funerals to enact God's Will at the milestones of human existence.

With the appearance of the bride and groom, a jolt of curiosity briefly thins the fog of gloom pervading the interior of the church. Silent questions. Where is the bride's father? Why do the first row of chairs on the bride's side seat only one person? Why are both ushers Daniels? How do we really know who is behind the tightly woven fabric of the dress, the veil, and the gloves if she has only a mother and a slip of a girl to vouch for her at her own wedding? What is Jed up to this time? Has some flaring, broken-heart disease led him to stooping so low?

The curiosity recedes as soon as the preacher gets past the attempted joviality concerning the weather and gets down to the ceremony proper. His voice becomes sonorous, lulling the congregation into a trance in which interior dialogues are hushed. The congregation, including the bride, the groom, and their attendants, stare at the preacher as if a nimbus is glowing just above his head. And the preacher, fully aware of his gift of speech, scans his patronage as if he were Narcissus staring at his own reflection. In the back of his mind, however, he understands that his voice is not strong enough to lure them into Crowhaven to partake of his pontifications on a regular basis.

There are always those few seated in the churches that are immune to the preacher's soliloquies. A number of the old men, men who have spent years on the range with the wind screaming silently into their ears, are more-or-less deaf. Having long ago come to terms with their own mortality through the experience of watching living things die, they have concluded that the quintessential moments of life are beyond the authority of language. These old men attend such gatherings either to sate the need for human contact, or to avoid the wrath of their wives — wives who command their own arsenals of words, and, as veterans of many a battle, are able to deliver crippling blows because of the tactical expertise gleaned from intimacy with their respective adversaries.

A smattering of the congregation (Cassandra falls into this category, though she opted not to attend the ceremony) are naturally impervious to the preacher's words for reasons other than those of the old men. Genetic mutation? Evolution manifest? Whatever the reason, the preacher's voice drones into to their ears, not with the resonance of music, but with the tedium of the hissing fluorescent lights above. Those effected as such — some are children, some are adults — sit in their chairs watching the preacher as if he were speaking in Sanskrit; the cadence of his speech bewilders them; they are not, like the old men, uninterested; they simply cannot interpret the meaning of the preacher's words.

Accustomed to such anomalies within his flock, the preacher attempts, at the beginning of the ceremony, to placate these few abnormalities by addressing the questions he knows is on the collective mind of the crowd:

"Rebecca's father, as some of you have probably heard, came to an unexpected and incomprehensible demise a short while ago. The Lord works in ways not meant for the understanding of men and which should and will not be questioned within the sanctity of this room. The facts, as they were related to me, are these: A mere three days after Jedidiah Daniels asked Leonard Eaglebird for his daughter's hand in matrimony, Leonard fell into a coma, a deep sleep, from which he would never return. Leonard's going was a peaceful one, without pain, and this I take to be a sign that his journey led toward heaven. The Lord is merciful to those that believe without knowing why. Blessed are those who believe and have not seen. As I understand it, Leonard was elated with the prospect of this marriage. Leonard would have been proud to give his daughter to Jedidiah Daniels. Leonard would have freely given his blessings to the love shared by these two people who stand here before you today. It is for us to respect Leonard's wishes as we respect the sovereignty of our Lord.

"Rebecca's beloved mother Odessa, who graces us with her presence during this joyous occasion, fortifies Leonard's blessings with her own. The grief of her husband's passing, I am sure, is diminished by her daughter's love for Jedidiah and our Lord.

"Let us take a moment to reflect on the fortitude of the Eaglebirds. Rebecca refused to postpone the marriage on account of her father's untimely demise. She did not make this decision out of any disrespect for her beloved father, her mentor, her friend. She made the decision because she knew that it is what Leonard would want. Leonard would want Rebecca to be happy. All that lives is born to die. When the mortal coil is shed, the soul is rendered up to God. Unable to comprehend the processes of the Almighty, we sometimes fall prey to grief and depression — tools of he who will not be mentioned here — and defile the very spirit of the one who has passed on to a higher ground. Not so with Rebecca. This life is for those who live. Rebecca has freely chosen to enter this marriage now, and of her own volition. This marriage is a shining testament of God's Will, a miracle in the making. Glory to God in the highest."

With these sentences, the preacher, in his mind, has lured those that can be lured into the Holy Web and, in one fell swoop, sterilized those who cannot.

Cassandra slips into the church near the conclusion of the ceremony. Her entrance goes unnoticed. She stands at the rear of the church, rain dripping from her hair onto the tiled floor. She feels electric and bites her fingernails and shifts her weight from one foot to the other. She stares darkly, not at the preacher, but at the figure of Francis Daniels standing next to Jedidiah, his back turned to her. A sensation of damp paranoia rattles in her breast, the air too thick with human breath and perspiration. She opens the door quietly and steps back out into the rain.

The image will stay with her: Rebecca, Jedidiah, and Francis standing as timeless as constellations, their backs turned to her, in front of an altar made of hay bales.

After the ceremony, when the congregation is warm and dry in the confines of the big house (eating and drinking and flirting and gossiping, a frolic without equal in recent times), the memory of the wedding ceremony deteriorates like a dream upon waking. A few hours into the celebration, Jedidiah and Rebecca Daniels embark upon the journey to Crowhaven airport. After a number of layovers and transfers, the newlyweds will be transported to the Bahamas for their honeymoon. If, after Jedidiah and Rebecca are gone, any of the guests endeavored to remember the preacher's words, the spoken vows, the traditional call for objections, the kiss, all would be a milky haze. But, because not one of the guests makes the attempt to remember, the marriage of Rebecca and Jedidiah may have never taken place at all.

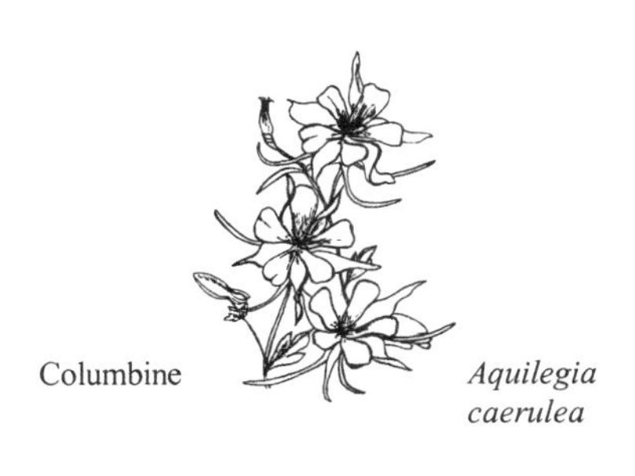

Columbine *Aquilegia caerulea*

Cassandra invents the excuse that she will be driving to Laramie in order to see a blown-glass exhibit on display at the University Art Museum. The lie is not premeditated. The compulsion to visit Isaac flooded into her as she poured her first cup of morning coffee. Without pausing to reflect on the source of the urge, after adding cream to the coffee and watching the white billow and balloon in the steaming black liquid, she picks up the phone and dials Isaac's apartment. When Isaac answers, Cassandra informs him that she will be driving down for a visit. As soon as the words are out of her mouth, she realizes she will need a reason; driving down solely to see Isaac is somehow inappropriate. She sits down at the Daniel's kitchen table and scans the open page of a day old newspaper. Sunlight slants through the kitchen window, highlighting a four inch by four inch advertisement for the blown glass exhibit at the University Art Museum which, printed in black and white, resembles a frame from a Rorschach test. When Isaac asks Cassandra (his voice puny in the receiver) the occasion for her visit, the answer blurts out of her mouth before her mind is able to process the ramifications of her response.

During the celebration of her parent's thirteenth wedding anniversary, as luck would have it, the young Cassandra accidently upset a blown-glass vase perched on the mantle above the fireplace while trying to retrieve a picture of their family trip to Fiji to show to Jedidiah and Clytie who had been invited over for dinner and champagne. The vase teetered and fell in a slow-motion-like scene. Cassandra, her and the vase's propinquity so close that she could have saved it from shattering on the Spanish tile in front of the fireplace, stood deadlocked in her tracks, watching the silvery glass reflect firelight on its collision course with the ground. Shards of glass burgeoned and collapsed, a fragile form lent to chaos. Cassandra's mother screeched, jumped up from the table, and slapped Cassandra three times across the face. Clytie came unglued and harangued Cassandra's mother with venomous remarks while putting on her coat to leave. After that, the two families (Cassandra caught in the middle until, two years later, her parents moved to Kansas) were forever estranged.

"Blown glass?" asks Isaac.

The knowledge that she will now have to attend the exhibit if she wishes to maintain any semblance of credibility crystallizes in Cassandra's mind. "Yeah. Blown glass. Art. Each piece unique. Do you want to go?"

"I don't know," says Isaac. "It's more of a craft than an art isn't it?"

"What difference does that make? Each piece is still unique."

"Maybe."

"I'll be driving down today."

"I'll leave the door open if I'm not here."

"See you soon," says Cassandra. "And you're going with me whether you like it or not. I will prove that each piece of blown glass is not like any other. And therefore it is an art form."

Sarah walks into the kitchen wearing one of Michael's denim work shirts. It hangs just above her knees. Her dirty-blonde hair is mussed and ratty. Her eyes are swollen with sleep.

"Good morning," says Cassandra. She stands up from the table, smoothing the red nightshirt over her thighs, and hangs the phone receiver in the cradle on the wall. She returns to her seat and sips her coffee. She places a hand in the spot of sunshine on the table. "You look like the living dead."

"Thanks." Sarah pours a cup of coffee and walks to the refrigerator.

"De nada. Can't say as I blame you. The testosterone level in this house has reached new heights since the wedding."

Sarah pours cream into her cup and, with a bare foot, closes the refrigerator door.

"I couldn't tell whether you were in heaven or hell last night. Thin line you know." Cassandra props her legs on an empty chair at the table. "Have you ever heard that?" She scans the open paper on the table in front of her.

Sarah leans her back against the refrigerator. She cups her mug in both hands. She bows her head as if praying.

"From the sound of it, you and Mikey were stuck somewhere in the gray area." A grin spreads like butter across Cassandra's lips; she feigns reading the paper. She takes a slurp from her mug before continuing, "Of course I could be wrong. Gabe interpreted the whole thing quite differently. He got all fired up. Between your groans, Mike's grunting, and Gabe's groping, I hardly slept at all. The wedding seems to have unleashed some dark sexual energy in the Daniels boys."

Sarah ignores Cassandra. After situating her coffee mug on the windowsill next to a potted geranium with blossoms the color of Cassandra's nightshirt, she returns to the refrigerator and takes out a container of eggs and a carton of milk and places them on the counter. She removes a cast iron skillet from a hook on the hood that umbrellas the stove. She sets the skillet on the largest of the natural-gas burners. In a glass mixing bowl, retrieved from the lazy-Susan beneath the cupboard, she cracks eggs. Globulets of whites and yolks slide down the outside of the bowl onto the Formica counter top.

Cassandra drinks from her cup, observing Sarah over the rim like the Giant observing Jack. She removes her free hand from the spot of sunlight on the day old newspaper and looks down at the advertisement for the blown glass exhibit. "I'm serious. It's getting a bit lurid." The layered shades of gray and black in the advertisement are somehow animated by the honey-hued sunlight — a chimera exposed. She closes the paper, folding it into proper order, and reads the headline: *Unknown virus mutates at random; African governments on verge of panic.*

Sarah adds milk to the egg mixture. She takes a wooden match from the box next to the stove, strikes it on the enameled stove-top, and lights the burner under the cast iron skillet. She extinguishes the match with a flick of her wrist. The scent of sulphur and carbon bastions her wall of containment. Without looking at Cassandra, she shuffles to the refrigerator, removes a package of bacon and a block of cheese, and returns to the stove.

"Even Tommy's infected," says Cassandra, still scanning the front page of the newspaper: *Lander woman thought dead found 'living large' in Florida.* Determined to get a reaction from Sarah, she ups her audacity, "Every time he takes a shower I imagine him jacking-off like a little monkey. He's probably thinking of Rebecca. Or Rebecca and me together. Or just me. I can't stand it."

Sarah plops a one-pound slab of bacon into the skillet. Sizzling fills the room. She opens the cupboard above the counter and takes down a tin of black pepper and a plastic jar of powdered garlic. She sprinkles spices onto the crackling pork. She takes a sip of coffee while stirring the bacon with a metal spatula in order to separate the strips.

Cassandra drums her fingers on the newspaper. Since the wedding, she feels like a raccoon who, paw in a log hole grasping at a shiny coin, cannot remove the paw, because it cannot turn loose the coin, and the hole in the log is too small for the clenched paw to escape. She is stuck in a rut. "It's like a Freudian Twilight Zone. I think the boys are a bit jealous of their father. Don't you?"

Sarah turns a knob on the stove to lower the heat under the skillet. The flame of natural gas sputters. With her mug of coffee cradled between both palms, she moves over to the double sinks; years of utility has left the porcelain stained nicotine-yellow. Her back to Cassandra, Sarah looks through the window gauging the wind from the swaying branches on the cottonwood. Under the shade of the tree, two blue heelers play tug of war with a burlap grain sack. Sparrows flicker against the azure backdrop of sky. Fields burst with chlorophyll. For a moment Sarah is alone, without humanity, an island in the stream of nature. She is at peace.

Sarah, stepping in front of the kitchen window, blocks the sunlight from landing on the kitchen table. Cassandra stands and smooths the nightshirt over her buttocks and thighs. She takes a sip from her coffee mug. She walks over to the refrigerator and leans a shoulder against it. "It's all got me a little on edge."

The sound of sizzling and human speech bewilders Sarah's senses. Caught between the stove and frying flesh on one side, the preserving refrigerator and Cassandra on the other, the view outside of the window is tainted with compunction.

"I'm only trying to consolidate our forces," says Cassandra. "We've got to do something. You have eyes. You can see."

"Don't even try." The vibration of her voice causes the paralysis to disintegrate. She turns to Cassandra. "I worry about you, Cassy. I really do." Her voice is gentle. "You're a beautiful woman and yet you can be so ugly."

Cassandra's face is that of a boxer who has received a defining blow and grins in order to taunt. "See what I mean? You're as bad as they are." She runs her hand down over her hip. "We probably shouldn't walk around the house dressed like this." Her hand snakes out and tugs on the hem of Sarah's nightshirt. "For Tommy's sake."

Turning her back on Cassandra, Sarah returns to the stove. She flips the bacon and cloud of grease smoke surges above the skillet.

"Maybe I just need a vacation," says Cassandra.

"That would be good," says Sarah. Hair a tumble across her face, she scrapes the burnt bacon from the bottom of the pan. "Stay away for awhile. Mike and Gabe need to spend some time together. Talk a few things over. Gabe will be all yours soon enough. It would be nice to give him some time with his family."

"We'll see," says Cassandra, making her way back to the table for a rest between rounds. "Before I steal him away? You don't need to worry about that." She spots Thomas standing in the shadows of the kitchen entryway. "Hi, Tommy. How long have you been hiding there?"

"Not long," says Thomas. "Smelled the bacon."

Cassandra sits down at the table. "Well come and sit down."

"The house is empty enough without Ike and Dad." He sits at the table across from Cassandra. "It'll be like a ghost town if you leave."

"I'll only be gone a couple of days. I just want to see an art exhibit on display at the university. Get a little culture in my life."

Thomas' eyes light up. "Are you going to see Ike?"

"I hope to."

"Tell him to come home." Thomas looks at Cassandra's nipples jutting against the thin material of her nightshirt. "Tell him to at least write me a letter or call me or something." Realizing he is staring, he stands up and walks to the coffee pot. "Every time I call him, all I get is that goddamned machine."

"Watch your mouth," says Sarah, sprinkling garlic onto the bacon. "I won't have that kind of talk in my kitchen."

"Ha!" laughs Cassandra. "What about the rest of them? I can tell its time to get up by all the 'goddamns' and 'shits' and 'pisses' coming from down here."

"Tommy's not the rest of them," says Sarah. "Not the rest of you."

Thomas stands with his neck craned towards Cassandra. "He never calls back." He pours coffee without looking at the cup. "Ask him why. Is he so goddamned pissed that he has to avoid me, or what?"

"Thomas Daniels," says Sarah.

"Screw off," says Thomas. "I just want to know what's going on."

Cassandra stands and walks over to Thomas. She runs her fingers through the dark stubble of hair on the back of his skull. "You haven't done anything. Ike's been busy, that's all." She glares at Sarah. "That's what I mean. Everybody in this house acts like they're guilty of something. What I want to know is what ancestor did what atrocity to what forgotten god? What's the big secret? Does Jed robbing the cradle go against some cardinal code that I don't know about? Is it that big of a deal? Or does it dredge up some Daniels family history that I'm not privy to?"

Sarah ignores Cassandra by removing bacon, one strip at a time, from the skillet.

"It's a bunch of bull." Cassandra lays her hands on Thomas' shoulders and guides him, mug in hand, towards the table. A sudden longing to take Thomas with her on the exodus to Laramie pulses through her. "You haven't done anything wrong, Tommy." She pushes him down in a chair at the table and stands over him. "Always remember that." She stoops and kisses him on the top of the head. The scent of baby shampoo in his hair instantly changes her mood. It is her intention to see Isaac *alone*. Classifying her feelings towards Thomas as maternal allows her to abandon him to the fate of the Crowheart. "I'll tell Ike to call you," she says, knowing that she won't. She straightens and smiles down at him. "I'll even dial the number."

Thomas watches the steam rising from his coffee. Having always considered Cassandra as an older sister, he is confused by the influx of libidinous emotions fermenting in his belly.

"Tell him we're all concerned," says Sarah. She pops the fourth slice of wheat bread into the eight slotted toaster and pushes down the starter until it clicks. "I still don't understand why he couldn't have come for the wedding."

Something in Sarah's voice, the absence of cynicism, causes Cassandra to turn around and face her soon-to-be-sister.

"I mean it," says Sarah. She looks up from the toaster and meets Cassandra's eyes. "He's got me worried."

Thomas stands up and walks out of the kitchen.

Cassandra follows Thomas, coming to a halt in the shadow cast by the entryway between the kitchen and dining room. "What about your breakfast?"

Thomas blends in with the murkiness of the dining room. He pitches his voice over his shoulder, "I'm not hungry."

"Sarah took the trouble to cook it."

Thomas does not respond. The sound of his boots on the wooden floor betray his position at the long table. A chair scrapes against the floor and creaks with deposited weight.

"Leave him be," says Sarah.

A clock chimes from somewhere in the depths of the big house. Cassandra turns and looks at Sarah. The two women stare at one another in silence, sunshine streaming through the window at Sarah's back, obscurity behind Cassandra. Cassandra enjoys the scent of bacon and eggs and toast. Sarah glances at the kitchen table, the top glossy with oils from human hands and the lard from cooked meat. The chimes, which sound as if they could be emanating from anywhere or nowhere, fall silent.

Sarah squints into the darkness behind Cassandra, thinking she sees movement. Michael? Nausea rises. She feels as if she is in danger of being sucked out of the sunlight and into the dolor of her bedroom where she will be digested. Training her eyes on Cassandra, who, by blocking the portal, is the only line of defense against the gravitational pull of the house, she is able to rationalize that the movement was only a freak of angles and lighting.

"Are you okay?" asks Cassandra.

"Yes. I just got a little dizzy there for a second. It happens every now and then."

Cassandra grins. "Are you?"

"What?" The bread pops out of the toaster. Sarah moves towards the refrigerator to fetch the butter.

"You know," says Cassandra.

Sarah is pleased with her irritation at Cassandra. "No, I don't know."

"Pregnant. Are you pregnant?"

Sarah laughs. "I hope not. If I were pregnant every time I got dizzy, we'd need a bigger house."

Cassandra and Sarah laugh.

"Listen," says Sarah, "would you like to have some breakfast with me? I mean I cooked all of this and now there's nobody to eat it."

Cassandra moves towards the kitchen table. "You don't have to make excuses, Sarah. I'd love to eat breakfast with you."

Driving away from the Crowheart, Cassandra glances at the rearview mirror from time to time to look at the megalithic reflection of the big house shrouded in dust and shrinking with distance. She brakes Michael's three year old Dodge to a stop on top of a small rise, which, upon descent, will block the big house from view. Stepping out of the truck, she leans against the bed and reflects upon the silhouette of the big house — a dark, dry blotch against a backdrop of blue.

Back in the truck, descending the leeward side of the rise, she turns on the radio. The lament of a cowhand (who has lost his cowgirl to a veterinarian, his truck to the bank, and his teeth to rodeo bulls) galls Cassandra. She turns the knob on the radio. Static. Loathing both country music and silence as traveling companions, she rifles through the glove compartment until she finds a cassette of Hank Williams Jr. The in-between rock and country antics of Hank will have to do; Michael abhors all but country music and will not allow anything else in the cab of the truck. Sliding the cassette into the stereo, Cassandra cranks up the volume and, listening to "Leave This Country Boy Alone," barrels down the road, unconcerned with the washboard ruts. A gray cloud of dust, kicked up by her passing, settles over sagebrush, greasewood, and wild mustard like a thin, dirty blanket.

Cassandra, though enamored with the high plains to the point of worship, has recently developed a scorn for the drudgery of ranch life. The seed of this scorn was planted long ago, but, just as the seed of the lodgepole pine requires the forest fire for germination, it laid dormant in her bosom until the proper conditions for growth arose. It is as if the dice of her fate, suspended above the playing table of her life, have finally hit the felt, rolling and ricocheting off bumpers, tumbling towards the inertia of numbers.

The seed of this scorn was planted on the happening of Cassandra's first menstruation. Although many prepubescent girls, poorly instructed by those who oversee their transition from child to adult, are terrified by the first cycle of sexuality, entertaining notions of internal bleeding and death at the sight of flowing blood, Cassandra did not. At the age of twelve, Cassandra understood — understood without explicitly knowing — that the event was the emblem of her passage from girl to woman. Her response can be attributed to her close ties to the rhythms of the land, to nature, to a youth spent cavorting under a wide open sky. Cassandra was somewhat feral. An only child, she preferred nature to civilization and, although her first cycle brought with it the intonations of sex, she buried the yearnings in order to isolate herself from the rigors of human contact. She decided, at the first sight of her menstrual blood, that she would wait for the mysteries of sex to decipher themselves.

She did not have long to wait. Even before she was able to dissect the sounds of other words and couple them with meaning, the word "Daniels" signified a remote and mythical realm of regalia. From infancy, the sound of the word (her parents spoke it often) brought Cassandra a sense of mirth and a feeling of security. As a child, she was content with the far away loftiness of the Crowheart and, with her parents, attended the occasional celebrations at the big house. But her childish heart belonged to the high plains, with all its skunks, fire-ants, spear grass, and hawks. She spent her free-time alone, searching for muskrat dens along the creek that ran through the prairie behind her house, ferreting out nests of kildeer in tall summer grass, studying the differences between coyote and fox tracks in the new fallen snow, categorizing the scream of a rabbit being taloned by an eagle, experiencing the sting of the yellow-jacket and the introverted nature of the roly-poly. At the age of ten, she was allowed, during summer vacation, to camp out by the creek where she would harvest the starchy tubers of cattails, wrap them in foil, and roast them in the embers of the campfire; she gutted brook trout and slow cooked them over open flames. During her youth, Cassandra was a single cell in the greater organism that surrounded her. The blood-red sunset of a midsummer evening was not something that existed outside of her; the cricket's chirp, the hootings of the great-horned owl, the sound of the breeze in sagebrush, the rising moon and falling stars... all this existed within.

Menstruation changed everything. Cassandra was compelled to differentiate herself from that which surrounded her. Determining that she was alone for the first time in her life caused Cassandra great suffering. She became afraid of twilight. Her loneliness drove her towards human companionship. She set her sights on the Daniel's clan, who, in her understanding, were the epitome of human ambition. Before long, she concluded that she would marry Isaac Daniels, and, in doing so, erase the foreboding of isolation. She would be happy again.

Isaac, blessed with an almost preternatural quality, was the obvious choice. All that remained was for Cassandra to win him over with her immature womanly wiles: at the moment of her isolation she became conscious of her beauty. She began frequenting the Crowheart whenever she was able — hitching rides with ranch hands, riding her bike for an hour and a half on the deserted highway and over the dirt road that led to the big house, begging her mother (who was pleased with her daughter's interest in the Daniels) for transport to and from the ranch. She practically forced Isaac to go horseback riding with her once a week. She presented him with gifts: smoked grouse, strings of fish, a pocket knife, fresh rabbit, a bead necklace, self-harvested chokecherries that her mother would boil into jelly.... Isaac, perpetually gracious, accepted the gifts and heaped praise on Cassandra's abilities. But that was as far as it went. Isaac spent the preponderance of his free-time in the company of his mother or reading a book in the privacy of his room. From Cassandra's perspective, Isaac thought of her as a girl with childish fancies.

The rich aroma of her mother's perfume made Cassandra queasy, but she diligently dabbed it on her neck and chest. She began wearing skirts and frilly blouses and dresses and uncomfortable shoes and twisting her hair into braids. Isaac paid no heed to the transformation.

In a desperate attempt to gain her beloved's attention, Cassandra lay in wait next to a stream on an early spring afternoon knowing that Isaac would be taking his new horse for a ride. As horse and rider, at a canter, approached the patch of greasewood she was using to conceal herself, Cassandra, naked, casually stood up and walked down to the bank of the stream. When the rhythm of the horse's hooves did not slow, she quickly determined that Isaac had not seen her. She plunged into the stream. To be sure Isaac's attention was caught and to diminish the shock of the icy water, she screamed. After scooping some water in her palms and pouring it over her hair, she tiptoed over the jagged rocks in the bed of the stream and stood shivering next to a thicket of wild roses, barren of leaf and bud, growing near the bank. Isaac reigned his mount to a stop and said, "Don't catch cold." He then rode on. Cassandra stood staring at Isaac's back as he moved westward with the breeze. After struggling into her clothes, she wept. On the long walk back to the big house, where her mother was to pick her up, the sight of primrose and bluebells in bloom provoked fury. She plucked the flowers from their stems and shredded the petals with her fingernails. Throughout the next two weeks, she was bedridden, suffering from a severe chest cold and mental anguish.

From that point, Cassandra's life has been a blurring of days and months and years. Because her past is vacillatory (her memory a plethora of scanty images which could easily have happened to someone else or not at all), the consideration of a future has always rung hollow. Even her sexual encounter at the lake, with Francis Daniels, which should have sparked some sort of catalyst that would fuel her future, is more an unwanted and reoccurring dream than a memory, the details shifting with each uprising. Only now, as events conjoin into a new constellation, does a future seem viable for Cassandra. She abandoned the pursuit of Isaac and, as a matter of course, succumbed to the younger Gabriel's sweet (if blase) advances: not caring one way or the other, she allowed her life to be guided by the rails of another's whims. Only now (as the dice hit the table, rolling, the dice that have hung above her head like a crown of thorns) does her conviction that the universe is mechanistic and without goal implode. Although she suspects that the marriage of Jedidiah to Rebecca was somehow the impetus for her conversion, it does not matter. She is giddy with possibility. With the giddiness comes nausea and dread: Vertigo: Having ascended to the halfway point on Devil's Tower, the climber experiences the urge to turn loose of the life line and fall free.

The pickup, equipped with a custom suspension that eases the punishment of the washboard road, cruises over the high plains, touting a constant purr. The landscape, familiar and forlorn, spurs a feeling of regret in Cassandra. The attempt to ignore her surroundings by concentrating on the rambunctious lyrics being discharged from the tape deck is abortive. The landscape beams desolation. The sky, naked except for a few puffs of pallid cumulus, casts down the razor glare of the sun. Sagebrush and greasewood, fisted buds on sunflower stalks, wild wheat and cheat grass, the concave emptiness of a dried pond with cracked alkali shimmering white in the rising heat, an outcropping of granite next to a lone scrub pine, the tendrils of prickly pear roots searching for anchor in the thin top soil — all waver under the blazing light. The truck, white paint grayed by a film of dust and mud, scuttles over the terrain like an insect on the beach of a dead sea, sunshine ricochetting off of the convex eye of the windshield. The breeze, triggered by the truck's movement, sucks dry the singing voice of Hank Williams Jr. before it can escape through the open window.

Cassandra grips the steering wheel tightly. The moment the truck dipped below the rise which blocked the view of the big house, she was afflicted with a growing sense of alienation. The scratchy music gives rise to a scene earlier in the day, when she broke the news to Gabriel that she was heading down to Laramie for a few days. From her shirt pocket, she takes a cigar pilfered from Jedidiah's room, licks it, bites off the end, and lights up by flaring an entire book of matches. The smoke lulls her into memory. With her hands tight on the wheel, the cigar pursed between her lips, she gazes through the windshield like a blind woman staring at a spotlight:

The bedroom is filled with the musk of staling sex. Cassandra sits on the edge of the bed wearing black panties and matching bra. Her hair is wild with static. Facing the window, the midmorning sun brushes her face the color of ripening corn. Gabriel, asleep beside her, reveals no sign of life. All is silence. Not even the song of a sparrow or blue-jay to add movement to time.

After breakfast, Sarah and Cassandra wash the dishes. Task complete, Sarah sets off to find Thomas so that they can attend to his lessons in the reconverted schoolhouse. Cassandra sits alone at the kitchen table, cradling a mug of coffee between her palms. Raising the mug to her lips, she finds the mixture of cream and caffeine cold and bitter. It occurs to her that neither Gabriel nor Michael have come down for breakfast. Curious, she dumps the unwanted coffee in the sink and passes through the portal separating the kitchen from the remainder of the big house. She sluffs up the stairs towards the bedroom where she will wake up Gabriel and tell him that she is leaving. Halfway up the boot-scarred staircase, she stops and leans on the banister. She plucks a splinter from the ball of her foot and flicks it over the railing. She continues upward.

As Cassandra enters the bedroom, the squeal of the door hinges are unusually loud. Gabriel lies motionless on the four-poster bed, the protuberance in his boxer shorts a channel to his subconscious. With the exception of the mirror suspended above the bed (attached by clothesline tied to the four posts), the mirror on the bureau, the curtains, and the linen, everything in the room is made of wood. The scent of mothballs is in the air. The sheets on the bed and are dinged with familiarity.

The wooden frame on the bureau contains a black and white photograph of Gabriel and Cassandra. They are standing on the porch of the big house. The shadow cast by the house obscures the expressions on their faces. A glaze of nicotine coats the plate of glass covering the photograph and reflects the dull light in the room, creating the impression that the couple is bent with age. The entire scene, as Cassandra steps into the room and closes the door gently behind her, seems bent with age. The air is dank. The light is old.

The hardwood floor, footpaths worn into the varnish leading to the bed, the bureau, and the bathroom door, cools the soles of Cassandra's feet. She pauses for a moment to compare the woman in the photograph with the reflection in the bureau mirror. The images fail to correspond. Cassandra attempts to combat the inconsistencies by categorizing them into two entirely divergent mediums — photography and mirrors — which cannot be expected to propound similar results. The rationalization rings with meaninglessness. A bout of out-of-kilterness ensues: Cassandra believes that she is dreaming while, at the same time, doubting the validity of the belief. Avoiding both her reflection in the mirror and the shadowy figures in the photograph, she tiptoes across the floor (the ball of her foot throbs from the splinter wound) to the bathroom door, opens the door slowly, slides into the sanctuary of the bathroom, closes the door and locks it (the sounds of the door opening and closing, the tumblers in the lock clicking, gnash against her ears). She sits down on the closed toilet. Goose bumps tingle at the rising hair follicles on her forearms. Dread — indefinable, indivisible, without sound or order — fills the bathroom. Nihilism raises a bloodless banner.

Cassandra prays. She silently begs an unknown god for the mercy of an edict of order. Accustomed to the onslaught of anxiety attacks, she attributes the success of prayer to psychology. As expected, when she opens her eyes and lifts her head from her palms, the anxiety is gone. It is replaced by an urgent need to defecate.

The porcelain toilet seat warms quickly with the heat of Cassandra's rump. She takes stock of the bathroom while her body rids itself of toxins. Gabriel's bottle of aftershave sits at its appointed spot next to the toothbrush rack at the rear of the sink; an orange bar of soap (smudged with traces of dirt and dried suds) sits on the opposite side of the sink; the mirror above the sink is speckled with flecks of toothpaste; two terrycloth navy blue towels hang from the towel rack; a ring of scum encircles the inside of the tub; a tangle of hair sits on top of the bathtub drain; the wooden floor is splotched with water spots.... Cassandra smiles. Everything is in its proper order. Her business complete, she mumbles an audible "thank you" to the powers-that-be and flushes the toilet. The affable sound of swirling water punctuates her recovery.

Cassandra backs out of the bathroom and into the bedroom. She shuts the door quickly in the attempt to keep the odor of her ordeal locked away in the past. She turns around and finds Gabriel laying on the bed with his shorts pulled down sporting an erection. A cockeyed grin contorts his mouth.

"Ever since I hung that mirror, I can't get enough," he says. "What do you say?"

Cassandra winces at the idea. "Aren't you bored yet?"

"Hell, no. Now, come on over here."

"I'm sore from last night." She moves towards the bedroom door. "By the way, I'm heading down to Laramie for a few days to see an art exhibit."

Gabriel, with the dexterity of a leopard, darts out of the bed and blocks Cassandra's exit. "I'm not." Wild eyed, he grabs her by the shoulders and pushes her towards the bed.

"Knock it off," objects Cassandra. She attempts to jerk free.

Gabriel hurls Cassandra onto the bed.

"That's what I aim to do." He jumps on the bed and pins her beneath him. "I'll need a little something to tide me over. Relax. Enjoy."

Gabriel's permission to travel proffered, Cassandra, in the same manner she acquiesced to his cautious, thoughtful advances when they started dating, succumbs. She lays limp on the bed. After Gabriel removes her nightshirt, panties and bra, she stands and opens the curtains. She returns to the bed and assumes the usual position on all fours in the center of the mattress. She fixes her sight on the cottonwood outside the bedroom window. Because she is not aroused, Gabriel's entrance is painful. Gabriel breathes lude remarks in her ear while pinching the nipples on her hanging breasts. Tears stream down Cassandra's cheeks, falling to the sheets with Gabriel's thrusts.

The leaves on the cottonwood outside of the bedroom window glisten in the midmorning sun. A blue-jay alights on a branch of the tree. Cassandra and the bird watch one another. The sun clothes Cassandra's face and shoulders in warmth. The bird is silent.

Neck tilted back, Gabriel gazes at the reflected image of Cassandra in the mirror above the bed. His testicles tighten. Satisfied, he pulls up his boxers and burrows under the sheets.

Cassandra eases her body from the bed and walks stiffly to the bathroom. She closes the door. She cleans herself with a washcloth. In spite of the fact that Gabriel did not kiss her, she brushes her teeth and gargles with red mouthwash. Before returning to the bedroom, she flushes the toilet without reason.

Holding her reflection in the bureau mirror at her periphery, Cassandra takes a set of black panties and matching bra from a drawer and puts them on. Her hair is wild with electricity. She sits on the edge of the bed and stares through the window at the blue-jay perched on a branch of the cottonwood. All is quiet.

Cassandra bows her head.

Gabriel begins snoring. The rupture of silence aggravates Cassandra into action. Without taking her eyes from the bird on the branch, she barks, "Did you hear me?"

"What?" mumbles Gabriel, rising out of a shallow sleep.

"I'm going down to Laramie for awhile."

"So?" He turns over on his side, back to Cassandra.

"I'm leaving today."

He sits erect. "When did this come up?"

"There's an art exhibit I need to see. I forgot to tell you."

"Takes a few days to see and art exhibit?" He rubs his eyes. "How do you *need* to see art?" He looks at Cassandra, sitting with her back to him. "You going to see Ike?"

"I thought I'd drop by."

He fluffs up a pillow and lays back down. "Tell him the Old Man's halfway pissy about him not showing up."

"That's it?"

"What?"

"Nothing."

The tone of her voice clashes with his longing for sleep. He sits back up. "Nothing?"

"Nothing."

"You sound like you want me to tell you not to go."

Cassandra rests her elbows on her knees and her chin in her hands. "That's not it."

"Then what? I thought we had an agreement not to tell each other what to do. Right?"

"Right."

"Then do what you want." He lays down and pulls the sheet over his head. "Jesus, I never know where the hell you're coming from."

Cassandra turns around and looks down at the shrouded figure of her betrothed. "I know. I don't make sense. It's nothing."

"Damned if I do, and damned if I don't."

"Don't worry about it. It's nothing."

"Okay. Have fun."

"I will." She turns and looks through the window at the cottonwood. The bird is gone. "I'll call you."

He, falling into the chasm of sleep, cannot hear her words.

Cassandra hits the highway feeling as if she has passed through a desert void of temptation. The sight of the narrow ribbon of asphalt, stretching to the north and south, though deserted, nourishes her with a sense of civilization.

The Crowheart, of late, has become parasitic, sapping Cassandra's mental and physical energy. Awaking before dawn, instead of feeling bastioned by sleep, she is drained and unable to form a reason as to why she should exit the warmth of the blankets. Reason is molded by the emerging sun: she becomes aware of Gabriel in the bed beside her, breathing, farting, exuding heat, closed eyes atwitch with dreams. Aching for the solace of seclusion, she plops her bare feet on the cool floor and tiptoes towards the bathroom. The stench of Gabriel's sweat-encrusted feet registers in her sleep-drugged mind. Her throat tightens. She retches silently.

Secure in the sanctuary of the bathroom, she bathes. She sits in a tub of water that turns her flesh pink with heat and wonders why her only responsibility is sex. She scrubs herself with soap.

By evening, the listlessness that has trailed her throughout the day has reduced her mind to a hiss. She eats dinner without tasting, craving the anonymity of sleep. Retiring early to the bedroom, she slips into a nightshirt, knowing that Gabriel will later strip it from her and grope her nerveless body. She climbs under the covers on the bed and reads — a newspaper, a magazine article, a story yielding an avenue of escape — knowing full well that she will not remember the gist of the words upon waking. She is exhausted by the vapidity of her existence. Insomnia fills the room.

The one thing that affords Cassandra the will to participate in her daily routine of no routine, is an industrious use of cynicism: she smiles snidely at her own folly, as well as the folly of those who contribute to it. During recent bouts of self-reflection, alone in the bedroom or the bath, astride a horse scouring the countryside for her meaning, she has been unable to locate anything to anchor herself to the years spent living on the Crowheart. She has nothing left in common with herself. This glut of nothingness, at times, spawns an enigmatic sense of levity. Galloping across the prairie on a roan gelding, the crisp, dry wind lashing her cracked lips, her watering eyes, her knotted crown of auburn hair, she is momentarily able to see herself under herself. These rarified and solitary flashes of self-estrangement produce an almost unbearable impression of freedom, which in turn provokes a childlike yearning for the scent of simmering stew on a cold winter's night. She is elevated and fettered at once. The moment gone, she reins in the horse and returns to the big house. The one thing that gains ground from these experiences is the cynicism that threatens to define her.

The big house is the gravitational center of Cassandra's distress. She studied the Antaean structure in the rear view mirror and could feel the reflection pulling at her bowels, as if it was unwilling for her to break from its orbit. Even after the rise of land obliterated the reflection, she could not extinguish the memories of the house that blossomed in her mind with the heedless pandemonium of wildfire. Finally, aided by the pitiless landscape, the memories faded; Cassandra's mind went blank. She traveled through a fabled no-man's-land where self-consciousness was only a myth spread by the wind ricocheting off of sage, cacti, stone, and dirt.

The highway breaks the spell. Cassandra turns the truck south. To the west a dust-devil spins towards the distant haze of the San Pedros. After turning off the stereo (the blare of the electric guitars and the relentless drumming suddenly unnerving), she takes a cigarette from the pack on the dash and lights up. She passes through Pathfinder, a one-store town which specializes in gasoline, beer, fishing tackle, polished rocks and broken arrowheads. The store is maintained by a retired postal worker and his spinster daughter who once claimed friendship with Cassandra. Not in the mood for nostalgia, she drives on. She passes the red-rock cliffs next to the Platte river. On the opposite side of the highway is a spot which the locals have named *The Place Where The Giant Sat Down,* due to the crater-sized geological creep on one of the low, rolling hills. At sunset, the cliffs glow like rigid lava. Behind the cliffs lies Pathfinder itself, a manmade reservoir that provides the ranchers with irrigation and the citizens of Crowhaven with outdoor recreation. On most weekends during the summer, the shores of the lake are littered with townspeople and ranchers alike. Skiers churn the surface of the lake. Bright beach towels protect girls in bikinis from coarse sand as they broil under the sun. The smell of burning charcoal fills the air. The sand, hauled in dump trucks from pits along the river, glistens with shards of glass, foil chewing gum wrappers, and empty beer and soda cans. Boats cruise over the surface of the water without purpose.

Cassandra is bored by the thought of the lake. Although the malaise that has been dogging her days dissipates with distance from the Crowheart, the idea of people sidling around inconsequential hours of leisure — getting drunk on boats and shorelines to dull the obvious uselessness of their lives —

congests her with the dread of identification: by categorizing those that frequent the lake, she categorizes herself as one of them. The desire to be rid of her faculty of classification is partially fulfilled by the knowledge that the lake will be more-or-less devoid of time killers due to the season. The water is cold to human touch.

The thought of a beer to slake the need for purpose dominates Cassandra's thoughts as she passes a bar and grill just past Pathfinder. The grill is famous for its buffalo burgers and ranch fries, but Cassandra is not hungry for food. She pulls up to the drive-thru window and purchases a six pack of bottled beer and a pack of cigarettes.

From the bar and grill, the highway veers east. Cassandra twists the cap from a sweating bottle of beer, takes a sip, cradles the bottle between her legs, and lights a cigarette. She drives passed Government Bridge, a steel-framed behemoth dwarfing the Platte river which runs beneath it. As a child, Cassandra stood under the bridge with Michael and watched as he slaughtered, with a .22 rifle, swallows living in the mud nests attached to the undercarriage of the bridge. The memory of lead bullets ripping through the hardened earth of the nests and twanging off of steel girders gives her the willies. She takes a long swallow of beer.

At Frank's Corner, a gas station/convenience store built to designate the meeting of two highways, Cassandra turns south onto State Route 487. The highway courses over the prairie, heading towards the town of Medicine Wheel. The Wild Horse Range, a series of swells dotted with scrub juniper, boulders, and clumps of wild grasses bent with breeze, stretch into the eastern horizon. To the west, the serpentine passage of Baterman's Creek marks the landscape with the deep gouge of its banks. A few vagrant cottonwood trees, twisted by wind and drought, grow near the creek.

Miles Estrada, owner of the land to the west of the highway, in an attempt to ward off the erosion enacted by the torrential spring runoff of a few years back, hired a group of highschool kids from Crowhaven to plant elm seedlings along the steep banks of Baterman's Creek. When the kids had finished (the girls who worked for Estrada were not allowed to dig the holes for the seedlings but received the same pay as the boys, causing snickers of outrage among both sexes), the elms, planted at eight inch intervals, resembled a flourishing outgrowth of tall weeds. In the space of two winters, only a few patches of the seedlings have survived. The precipitous banks of Baterman's Creek proved too much for the majority of the seedlings. The tendril roots, unable to penetrate the hard earth, shriveled, and the twig-like trunks fell down into the moving waters of the creek.

Cassandra drives by the dilapidated barn and corral left standing vacant after Estrada, in another fit of misguided pragmatism, opted to erect a new barn closer to the house. He covered the shell of the new barn with sheets of corrugated aluminum. During the summer, the aluminum absorbs and intensifies the heat of the sun, causing the interior of the barn to become unbearably hot. The air inside and around the main house is endowed with the scent of brewing manure. And, during the all-too-frequent rampages of marauding wind, the Estradas cannot find anything but the most troubled sleep, due to the sound cast off by the shivering aluminum sheets covering the barn.

Cassandra sees the surviving patches of elm, the rotting barn and corral, and the cut of Baterman's Creek scarring the prairie. She sees all and registers nothing. The scene passes by like a silent movie without plot.

The highway slices through a shallow canyon with walls of stratified slate, silt, and sandstone. A derelict cabin — the roof caved in, the doorway agape with shards of leather hinges hanging useless — stands next to Baterman's creek, looking as if it will collapse into a heap of rubble with the next whisper of wind. Encroaching weeds surround the building.

The sight of the cabin nestled parochially in the canyon pricks at Cassandra's thoughts. As a child, snug in her bed, she conjured up images of dead men dressed in furs sitting around a table inside of the one room shack at night playing cards and drinking whiskey from eternally full bottles. *The Ghost Cabin.* The fantasy never frightened Cassandra. The ghost trappers, as she invented them, were happy souls content and secure with their fates. She saw the men grinning, toothless and eyeless, cutting plugs of tobacco with Bowie knives and spitting brown streams onto the earthen floor. The vision always provided Cassandra with an inexplicable tranquility that sent her off into soothing sleep. In the morning, at the moment of waking, she was afflicted with melancholia at the knowledge that the ghost trappers did not, could not, exist in the light of day. With the night, the trappers returned and the process repeated itself. For the period of two years the ghosts were Cassandra's closest friends.

Cassandra's connection to the cabin does not consist of mere imagination. At the end of the canyon lies a shallow but wide stock pond formed by Estrada's damming of Baterman's creek. The pond yields the best brook trout fishing in the surrounding area. Years ago, Gabriel invited Isaac and Cassandra on an overnight fishing trip to Baterman's pond. The main reason the pond afforded such excellent fishing was that Estrada, on top of being a staunch adherent to the concept of private land, fancied that the pond was a source of virility for his Black Angus bulls. Because of Estrada's brazen treatment of trespassers and the bull's blood shot eyes, drooling lips, flared nostrils, and unpredictable temperaments, few dared the route to sure fishing.

Because Jedidiah Daniels and Miles Estrada considered themselves peers, Gabriel, Isaac, and Cassandra did not have to be on the lookout for the figure of Estrada galloping towards them aboard his bay stallion waving a .30/.30 and screaming epitaphs about private land. They did, however, have to contend with the bulls. Isaac, fly rod in hand like a wizard's wand, whistling an improvised tune, walked directly towards the two bulls which were gathered around the pond. The beasts stared stupidly at the human's approach. Gabriel and Cassandra, standing side by side next to the truck, watched Isaac with a mixture of horror, titillation, and sunshine dancing in their eyes. One of the bulls began snorting and stamping, a front hoof scraping a dust cloud out of the dry earth. Isaac swatted a horsefly from his shoulder with his free hand, zeroed in on the inherent rhythm in his improvised tune, and whistled louder. Heart thumping, Cassandra jogged towards Isaac in an inspired fit of love-induced martyrdom. The amount of blood pumping through her tightening skull befuddled her logic so that she envisioned the bull's fury as a thing of honor. She ran towards Isaac. Gabriel stood paralyzed by the truck. For whatever dull reason, possibly the sight of Cassandra, hair glinting with sunlight as it flowed behind her, calmed the bull, and it went back to chewing cud under the pounding sun. The danger gone, Cassandra's reason returned. She got muddy huddling in a patch of cattails while Isaac pulled in a string of fish. Gabriel took a nap in the truck.

That evening, Gabriel prepared a meal of brook trout (wrapped in bacon and broiled in foil with lemon juice), fried potatoes, and hot chocolate. The buzz of mosquitos increased with the cooling air.

Nightfall found the three of them sitting around a fire pit in the center of the cabin, watching stars through the holes in the roof. They laid out sleeping bags. They were quiet. Gabriel, after crawling into his bag, began snoring softly. Somewhere in the canyon, coyotes exchanged yaps. Cassandra unabashedly stripped down to her bra and panties and sat watching the dying embers in the fire pit. Isaac leaned over and kissed Cassandra hard on the mouth. He then crawled into his sleeping bag and promptly fell asleep.

The moment Cassandra exists the canyon, a gust of wind veers the truck into the left lane of the highway. Because there is no traffic, she eases rather than jerks the truck back into the right lane and continues the journey across the high plateau named Shirley Rim. The Rim extends southward merging with the blank horizon. The eastern and western horizons are blued by shadows of vague mountain ranges. Snow fences, barbed wire, the truck, and the highway are the only objects on the plateau which betray the infringement of man. Clover, spear grass, and wild wheat cover the ground like tightly woven cloth. Splatters of color — yellow, red, and violet wild flowers — undulate with the wind. The blue sky shimmers in the thin, sun-infused air.

A dead antelope on the side of the highway — black eyes open wide with dull death, rust-colored hide punctured by ribs to reveal a cavity of powdered entrails — tweaks Cassandra's thoughts back to the lake where she first experienced the physicality of sex. It is not a memory she chooses to visit; the sight of the dead antelope triggers her synapses and the image opens like a computer graphic: the pain and blood, the taste in her mouth, the hard earth against her back, the sky, the trees...

Cassandra's stomach convulses. She rolls down the window and spits up a mouthful of bitter liquid. The image of Francis Daniels pawing at her body is at odds with the story that she related to Rebecca on their picnic with Isaac. She does not know which version of the incident to believe. She opens the fifth beer and guzzles it down in the vain hope that the alcohol will obliterate both versions, the good and the bad, once and for all. She lights a cigarette and watches the smoke spread out from her mouth...

Seven horses gallop over the plateau with tails held high and nostrils flaring. A cigarette filter sticks to Cassandra's dry, cracked lips causing her to wince when she pulls it from her mouth in order to sip from the sixth beer. Both of the windows in the truck are rolled down. Cassandra's hair is animate with wind...

The highway descends into the town of Medicine Wheel. Sagebrush and greasewood dot the land at even intervals, as if their positions were planned by a landscape architect. A set of train tracks run parallel to the highway. Cassandra pulls into the lone motel/bar and, with minimal speaking, picks up another six pack of beer. The heads of elk, deer, antelope, and moose hang from varnished plaques on the polished wooden walls of the bar. A taxidermic rattlesnake sits perched on top of an archaic jukebox, forever coiled and poised for the strike. Two railroad workers in company overalls sit at the bar drinking shots of tequila. The false eyes in the animal skulls stare down at Cassandra from above as she waits for the bartender to give her change. A stale song flows out of the jukebox. Her stomach broils...

Some twenty miles north of Laramie, Cassandra regains her composure. The only acceptable version of the truth about Francis Daniels is the one told to Rebecca at the lake. No one respects a soiled woman — a raped woman. How could they? After tossing an empty beer bottle out of the open window and listening to the tinkling of glass on the blacktop, she twists the top off of a fresh bottle, takes a drink, and lights a cigarette. The vision of Rebecca and Isaac, eating apples and drinking wine at the lake, fills Cassandra's thoughts and validates the accommodating account of her encounter with Francis Daniels...

By the time the spire on the Methodist church in downtown Laramie comes into view, Cassandra is secure in her identity. The heavy memory of Francis Daniels has been usurped by a recollection without substance or gravity to pull it down. Low cumulus clouds hang over the town like smoke from an extended siege.

The pain caused by Jedidiah's penetration, along with the consequential rupturing of the hymen, comes not unexpected to Rebecca but is nevertheless strange. Rebecca, the full-length white satin nightgown hiked up over her hips to reveal a white garter and matching silk stockings, anticipates the pain in much the same way a child awaits the hypodermic needle which will immunize it against disease. But when Jedidiah actually enters, her mind flashes back to the sensation of rattlesnake fangs piercing skin and the warmth of Cassandra's weather-checked lips covering the wound to suck out the venom. The entire honeymoon rings as abnormal to Rebecca, in that her predilections concerning the event in no way mesh with the moments of actual experience. She is perplexed by the dogged pathos that she is out of synch with time-and-motion.

Rebecca, because she sees the honeymoon as an omen that influences the very nature of marriage, attempts to steel herself in an attitude of optimism. The more she tries to maintain this facade of felicity, the greater the impression that she is walking through a waking dream.

The wedding proper fell in closely enough with Rebecca's expectations, the joining of two individuals into one, but, the moment the ceremony concluded, she became aware of a purring blankness which sat on top of her head like a cat. She attributed the odd (not uncomfortable, not urgent, just odd) phenomenon to an overloading of her circuits brought on by the hullabaloo surrounding the snakebite and the nuptials. As Jedidiah and

Rebecca drove away from the Crowheart, toward Crowhaven, where they would board a plane which would fly them to the land of bliss (the big house shrinking in the rearview mirror as if it had been hurled away from them), the purring blankness intensified and seeped into Rebecca's mind until she became incapable of forming words. The intuition that she was helpless against the purr, without weapons of internal and/or external dialogue, caused her newly-betrothed bosom to swell with panic. She sat in the passenger's seat of the slate-gray, three-quarter ton van like a zombie who had just been exhumed from the grave.

Jedidiah, too, said little on the drive into Crowhaven or, for all that, on the flight to the Caribbean either. If Rebecca had been capable of interpreting her husband's behavior, she might have attempted to comfort him, or she may have purposefully remained silent in the hope that whatever malady haunted his thoughts would be displaced through his own internal dialogue. If Rebecca noticed Jedidiah's furrowed brow — his silence, his rigor mortis grip on the steering wheel as they made their way towards Crowhaven, the continual downing of scotch and sodas on the plane, the meticulous crunching of ice cubes when the whiskey was gone and he sat waiting for the next, the beads of sweat forming on his nose and brow as he sat staring out the window into the blackness of night, and the fetid odor oozing from his flesh — her concerns would have been aroused. As it turned out, Jedidiah's predicament had no effect whatsoever on Rebecca. She sat brassbound in the truck, then stiffly in her designated isle seat in the first-class section of the plane, denying the twittering and confounded flight attendant's every ploy to serve her. During the entirety of the trip, she thought and felt nothing at all.

The chirp of rubber tires on asphalt, as the plane touches down, the force caused by the rapid deceleration thrusting her forward away from her seat, brings Rebecca in closer continuity with herself. She notices a raw ache where the seat belt has all but cut off the circulation to her legs. She cannot remember the drive into Crowhaven, the boarding and transference between planes, using the restroom, or the name of the place they have landed. She does know they are on an island; they are isolated by miles of crystalline waters. She unbuckles her seat belt; her legs begin to tingle. She looks to Jedidiah for reassurance.

"We made it," says Rebecca.

Jedidiah turns his head from the window, the right side of his face ashen with light from the overcast sky outside. He studies his wife. He smiles. "Finally," he says. He unbuckles his seat belt. "Let's get off of this goddamn plane."

Rebecca sits still.

"Let's go," says Jedidiah. "Saddle up. I feel like I'm suffocating."

Rebecca sits still.

Jedidiah stands up and cracks his head against the overhead storage bin. "Goddamnit! Come on, Becky, let's go. Paradise awaits."

Jedidiah has never called her 'Becky' before, and she does not like the way the name fits in her ears. "Can we wait just a minute? My legs are asleep." She slaps her thighs and focuses on the whisk of passengers passing her by as they exit the plane.

Jedidiah, hunched under the storage compartment, stares sardonically at his wife. Sensing that the other passengers are tuned into his distress, knowing he will never survive an outbreak of *their* panic, with a concerted effort, he sits down in his seat. "Okay, Becky. Okay. We'll wait." He can hear the sound of his heartbeat in his ears; he can feel a throbbing at his temples and groin.

At the resort, Rebecca, on wobbly legs, walks to the honeymoon suite, lays down on the king-sized bed and listens to the dry whir of the air conditioner. After slipping off her shoes and untucking the green blouse from her white slacks, her attention shifts from the air conditioner to the sound of the breeze rustling in the leaves of the wild palms outside the glass doors leading to the balcony. Imagining the scent of a salty breeze tickling her nostrils, she wanders off into a slumber inundated with the serenity of the rhythmic sea.

When Rebecca awakes, the room, alive with the scent of orchids flowing through the open windows, flickers with the light cast by a dozen candles. A soft throb of island music pulses the air. The sheer white curtains covering the long windows sway with the incoming breeze. Rebecca, after wiping the drool from the corner of her mouth with the edge of a pillowcase, lays flat on her back listening to the shadows. She does not know where she is. She does not care. She watches the dance of candlelight on the ceiling. She basks in the scent of sea breeze, wild orchid and ginger. Her thought process tunnels into hibernation, and it is as if she has no prior experience to goad her into the analyzation of the moment. Past and future retreat and Rebecca is born anew into the world. She breathes the night.

"So, you're finally awake."

The voice tears Rebecca away from the satori. She is irritated. Prior to the intrusion of words, she lay unfettered from the chains of individual isolation: she had escaped from the concept of herself. The reverberance of language brings her back: she is a uniqueness burgeoning with segregation. She plummets towards the familiar realm of a future determined by the past.

Rebecca turns her head on the pillow and looks at the man sitting at a table on the far side of the room: The table is laden with thick white candles; the man, with silver tongs, pincers ice cubes out of a silver bucket, drops them into a glass, and pours rum from a half empty bottle; he is dressed in white pants, white shirt, and white suit jacket; his feet are bare; the candlelight highlights his dark hair and mustache; the flames are reflected in his eyes.

"I've been waiting," says the man.

Rebecca lays motionless. She recognizes the man as her husband. Her face is expressionless.

Jedidiah, rum in hand, stands and walks towards the bed. "We'll have to make up for lost time." He sits on the edge of the mattress. He smiles. After taking a sip of rum (the sound of the cubes of ice clanking against the inside of the glass startle Rebecca), he runs a finger through her black hair.

"It's time to get up and get in the shower," he says. "I want you to make yourself beautiful for me." The finger slides out of her hair, across her cheek, and over her lips. "Hurry now. I've been patient." He stands, drains the rum, and walks over to the table. After lifting three ice cubes out of the silver bucket with the tongs and dropping them into the glass, he takes up the bottle of rum and fills the glass to the rim. He takes a drink. He turns around to face Rebecca. "Now," his voice is edged with the timbre of command. "I don't want to waste anymore time."

She sits up. A sharp pain squirrels through the small of her back. Aware of her husband's darkening gaze, she manages to transform the grimace creasing her face into a platitudinal smile. The inside of her mouth tastes like sulphur. She swings her feet to the floor and stands up. A knot of dread tightens in her belly.

"That's my girl," says Jedidiah. He taps his foot on the cream-colored carpet. "I ordered room service. A Caribbean Delight. It'll be here any minute."

"What will I wear?" asks Rebecca, sustaining her smile. "Remember? You wouldn't let me bring a suitcase."

"I know. I don't have Alzheimer's yet."

In a whisk of a thought, there and gone like a shooting star, it occurs to Rebecca that Jedidiah *is* old enough for the onset of Alzheimer's disease. "I didn't mean it that way."

"I know. I know." He takes a swallow from the glass. "There's a whole new wardrobe for you in the closet. I was very busy while you were off in la-la-land." Looking down into the glass, he rattles the ice cubes. "I hung your clothes for tonight in the bathroom. Now, hurry up. You wouldn't want to be late for our first dinner as man and wife."

Walking towards the bathroom, Rebecca feels as if she is preparing herself for sacrifice.

The shower provides Rebecca with a sense of well being. She faces the showerhead and relishes the warmth flowing over her face, breasts, torso, legs, and toes. The water beads up on her skin as if she is covered with a film of silicon. She imagines herself *walking along the beach in the eye of a hurricane. A full moon sails above her. Instead of the fear normally associated with a raging sea, in Rebecca's vision the rumbling surf is comforting, the sound of a mother's voice finding a lost child. Suddenly Cassandra is with Rebecca on the beach. They hold hands and smile.* Rebecca urinates without realizing it; the warm water flowing from the showerhead perpetuates the daydream while masking the yellow warmth streaming down her legs into the drain.

A loud knocking interrupts Rebecca's wanderings.

"Becky!" Jedidiah's voice is flushed with anger. "Becky! The meal is here! It's getting cold!" More knocking. The sound of the doorknob being worked. "Why is this goddamn door locked?"

As if through osmosis, Jedidiah's anger wells up inside of Rebecca. "I'll be out in a minute!" The tone of her own voice rasps against her ears. She attempts to make amends with a voice of girlish cheer, "Good things come to those who wait." This time, the sound of her voice reignites the anger, "Now leave me alone and give me some privacy! Just because we're married doesn't mean you own me."

For a moment there is only the sound of cascading water, the sight of rising steam. Rebecca remembers Cassandra at her bedside, nursing her out of the venom.

"I'm sorry," says Jedidiah through the locked door. "I just wanted everything to be perfect. I feel like a kid again and have forgotten how to act. Forgive an old man for not acting his age."

Sensing a coup, Rebecca turns off the water and steps out of the shower onto the Spanish tiled floor. She skates on urine-wet feet across the bathroom, unlocks the doorknob, and opens the door.

Jedidiah stands next to the bed with the phone receiver in his hand. He looks at Rebecca dripping and naked in the doorway, hangs up the phone, and stands alert for instruction.

"Just relax," says Rebecca. The rich scents of fried plantain, melted butter, and coconut fill her nostrils. She cannot see the table from her position, but the thought of shrimp and lobster causes her to salivate. Looking at the swaying curtains on the far side of the room she says, "There's not much chance of anything getting cold in this heat. Have another drink."

Jedidiah starts towards Rebecca, his feet moving of their own volition.

Rebecca steps back into the bathroom. The fluorescent lights above gird her in an electric shroud. "You're not so old," she says, pushing the door shut. "I guess I'll forgive you this time." The door clicks.

Jedidiah feels like a fool standing with his nose to the door, listening to the tumblers as the lock catches.

Rebecca finds the white satin nightgown hanging in the bathroom closet. She fingers the cool material before moving to the oval mirror above the sink. Surprised that the glass is clear in the dense humidity, she stands and looks at her reflection. She wonders why men are attracted to women and women are attracted to men. From a scientific view, she muses, the power of sexual beauty, a power which is able to render men helpless in its presence, is genetically endowed. On the other hand, the female form (she looks at her reflection and compares it to Cassandra) is certainly of greater ascetic value than the male. She turns away from the mirror. Opportunities to employ her feminine wiles rarely occurred in her youth, and, when they did, she was either too embarrassed or afraid of their consequences to pounce on them. By satisfying the laws of society through marriage, she has claimed the right to do what is natural. She gleams with anticipation.

Before dressing, Rebecca, delighted to find the cabinets under the sink chock-full of every bathroom accouterment imaginable, blow-drys her hair, brushes her teeth, dabs the nape of her neck, tummy, earlobes, and wrists with perfume from a crystal bottle, and sits down on the lid of the toilet to clip her toenails. She savors the knowledge that Jedidiah will not dare knock on the door again. She paints her lips, shadows her eyes, and heightens her already tall cheekbones. The knowledge that her body is unique in the universe augments Rebecca's physical beauty with an air of weightlessness.

Her conception of self, a mixture of animal magnetism and human grace, allows her to mock the pull of the earth as she glides over the tiled floor to the closet. The white nightgown is feathery in her fingers as she drapes it over her shoulder. After detaching a white bra and matching garter from a hanger, she searches for panties to complete the set. The closet is empty. Gravity returns. The lightness which inflated her a moment before is sucked through her feet into the urine-damp tile. The dark closet beckons. She stands a house divided, a body deserted by heart and soul. She is no longer inimitable. On the verge of collapse, she wards off the darkness by dressing in the white garments. Sustained by the knowledge that, as a virgin, she can remain free from fleshy sin by rising out of the confines of the body into the open places of the soul, she opens the bathroom door and walks into the bedroom.

"The problem is that God only had so many souls to hand out, they're not an inexhaustible resource you know, and now ninety-eight percent of the people walking among the living are soulless bastards." Classical music flows from the sitting room and masks the throb of island music coming from outside. Jedidiah, having, while Rebecca prepared herself, changed out of the white suit coat into a burgundy smoking jacket, sits at the oval table with his back facing the bed. "Pretty soon the human spirit, like me, will go extinct. If you make it to heaven, you don't want to leave." He pierces a peeled shrimp with a fork, dips it in a tub of melted butter, pops the morsel in his mouth, and chews while speaking: "The Industrial Revolution spurned religion. Social Darwinism. Atheism." He swallows. The fork descends towards a square of muskmelon on his plate. "Without a heaven there is no danger of hell. That leaves men such as myself at a great disadvantage."

Rebecca nibbles at the deviled egg held between the finger and thumb of her right hand. The sheen of butter and melon juice glazing Jedidiah's chin and mustache — the slurp when he drinks from his crystal goblet of wine — the haze of cologne hovering over the table like an impending storm — all combine to produce an unpleasant bubbling in her stomach. Only by staring at the flames on top of the candles which separate her from Jedidiah, is she able to taste the food without gagging. Each time she glances at her husband, he looks older, a witnessing of accelerated decrepitude. She sets the egg on her plate, next to a section of fried plantain, and takes a drink of wine.

"Take music for example." He points his fork at the portable stereo in the sitting room behind Rebecca. "Nobody creates music like this anymore. Or maybe nobody *can* create it." He pauses to consider his wisdom. "On the other hand, if Mozart were alive today, there wouldn't be enough of an audience to appreciate his genius. He'd be penniless with the music ricocheting through his head like loose change in a car wreck. He'd go insane with grief at not being able to share the sound of the human spirit with a spiritless mass. In other words, his life would be the same as it was, just more extreme." He dabs the corners of his mouth with a white napkin. "You don't understand, do you?" After placing the fork on his plate and the napkin on the table, he takes up his goblet and pours the wine down his throat. He sets the empty goblet in front of his plate and refills it from the waning bottle sitting between the candles.

Rebecca cannot move her eyes from the smudge on the rim of Jedidiah's goblet. The smudge left by buttery lips. She sees the smudge as a reflection of her husband. Jedidiah's soul, she thinks, if he indeed possesses such a thing, has become obfuscated by the light of truth, a smudge on a square of overexposed film. Jedidiah The Smudge. The smudge that is Jedidiah. The analogy tickles a paralyzed nerve in Rebecca. A smile twitches at the corners of her mouth. Her eyes narrow. With the tip of a finger, she pops the remainder of the deviled egg into her mouth and chews.

Jedidiah takes up the goblet of wine and waves it at Rebecca like an orchestra conductor's wand. "People don't want to be reminded that their ancestor's were superior beyond measure. A lesson of history the mass would rather ignore. For all intents and purposes," he pauses and takes a sip of wine for added emphasis, "the artist is extinct." He drains the goblet in the next swallow and sets it next to his plate. Turning his attention to an enormous crab claw on his plate, he says, "No. Not extinct. Not quite. You have the soul of the artist. That's why I chose you." The claw cracks under the applied pressure of his blunt thumb and forefinger. He extracts the white flesh with a miniature fork, dips it in the hardening butter, and sucks it into his mouth. He unconsciously chews in rhythm to the undercurrent of Caribbean music pulsing behind the classical from somewhere outside the confines of the room. A mixture of butter and saliva drips from a corner of his mouth. He takes a wedge of lemon from a dish and sucks out the juice. He smacks his lips with satisfaction.

Rebecca closes her eyes. The night air flowing through the open window washes over her, soothes her. She yearns to be outside, sitting at the edge of the surf with the light of the moon and the stars blanching her dark skin. She opens her eyes. Not yet, she thinks. She must go through the ritual of consummation, a duty which she took on with the utterance of contrived words — vows. Certainly a man of Jedidiah's age will be exhausted after the act and drift off into sleep. Unless he senses something wrong, something out of whack. A short-term memory scan produces an echo of the word *artist*, and, after swallowing the remnants of a mushed up egg which has been sitting idle on the top of her tongue, she says, "Isn't Ike an artist?"

Jedidiah refills his goblet before saying, "No." The word is garbled by the effects of too much alcohol. "Or maybe he is. I don't know." He takes a drink. "His mother shaped him into something I couldn't identify as the years passed. A kind of husband. They fed on each other. They sustained each other."

"What? A husband?"

Jedidiah looks up from his plate and meets Rebecca's eyes. He smiles. Flecks of crab meat cling to his mustasche. "Damn, we're out of wine. I'd better order another bottle." After pushing his chair out from the table, he stands. "Is there anything else we need? Oysters? Chocolate?"

"No," says Rebecca. She, too, stands. "I'm stuffed. Couldn't eat another bite."

"Neither could I," says Jedidiah. "Not of food anyway." He casts his eyes to the floor and looks back up with a thinly concealed gesture of encroaching sexuality. To his surprise, Rebecca is no longer standing next to the table. Sweeping the room, he finds her, as if magically transported, next to the open window, gazing into the night. Her face is awash with moonlight. The breeze wriggles through her hair.

Rebecca trains her eyes on the full moon hanging low over the ocean as Jedidiah hikes the white nightgown up over her hips. She will be unable to remember the events that brought her to a position on all fours in the center of the king-sized bed facing the moon, but she will remember the moon itself: the bruise designating the Sea of Tranquility, the benevolent face chronicled in a nursery rhythm, the soft light glittering on the calm surface of the sea. She will remember the pain of Jedidiah's penetration, the rupturing of her hymen, the warmth of blood. She will remember wondering why her hymen did not break earlier, when she was a child riding a bicycle over washboard roads or straddling a fence watching boys play football in a vacant lot while her mother shopped for essentials in Crowhaven and her father sat in a local bar pouring whiskey down his throat. But she will remember the moon most vividly: *the moon reflecting sunlight, the cool fragrance of the island breeze, the sound of the surf caressing the shore, and the low throb of music rising up from the beach.* The loss of her virginity, as sanctioned and filed by memory, will always be equated with the Caribbean — not with Jedidiah penetrating her on such and such island in the Caribbean, but the *Caribbean itself— warm, humid, the orb of the moon and light so soft from the stars that she will remember it as the whisper of angels.*

The next morning, Rebecca sees the blood on the too-white sheets, feels the soreness between her legs, and looks down on the sleeping figure of Jedidiah, unexpectedly frail in the morning light. She remembers him thrusting more and more vehemently, his breathing erratic with desperation. After pulling out, he kissed her on the nape of the neck and said "I'm sorry. My back is cramping." He went to sleep on the far side of the bed. Unsure as to why Jedidiah apologized, Rebecca, nightgown hiked up over her hips, scooted to the edge of the bed (evidenced by the thin trail of blood on the sheet) and sat staring at the moon. She remembers listening to the cavernous breathing of her husband and the wisp of the wind on her face. Finally, as a reward to herself, she remembers *sitting naked on the wet sand with her toes, legs, calves, and thighs stretched towards the sea while the tide waxed and waned in warm and rhythmic caresses.*

The next morning, all prior memories concerning her marriage night, with the exception of the last, have lost significance: *the moon, the sea, and the stars* having situated them in an eternal eclipse.

"I'm sorry," says Jedidiah. He sits at the table of the nuptial breakfast holding a cooling cup of coffee between the palms of his hands. Fresh from the shower, dressed in a burgundy smoking jacket and slippers, his aura is haggard. His eyes are rimmed with red. His mustache droops.

"Why?" asks Rebecca. She stands at the window with her back turned to Jedidiah. She watches tourists on the beach as they swim, laugh, and sip blue drinks with umbrellas from tall glasses. She wishes that she was a stranger. The sky and the sea are of the same color. *The sand is the color of moonlight.*

"About last night."

"What about it?"

"Well," he pours cream into his coffee, "I'm afraid I didn't actually consummate our marriage."

"What do you mean?"

Jedidiah looks at his wife, the salt breeze in her long hair, her youthful hands clasped at the small of her back, her dark skin and hair in contrast to the white nightgown. He has never noticed how tall she is. Slender and tall. "I didn't get all the way there," he mumbles.

"Oh."

His voice rises with hope, "We can always try again."

"I did," says Rebecca.

"What?"

She turns from the open window and faces him. "I did. I consummated it."

"You did?" He is confused.

She walks towards him. "Yes. It was wonderful." At the table, she stoops down and kisses him on the forehead. Standing erect, she glides back to the window, her feet hidden by the flowing satin gown.

He takes a sip of coffee. The muddy liquid is cold and bitter.

"How old is the sea?" asks Rebecca. "Is it the oldest thing on earth?"

"I don't know," he says. "I really don't know."

Ike,

Forgive my untimely response, but, as you well know, I live in Lizard Time and, as King of the realm, I have certain responsibilities which I must attend...

Suppose for a moment, or rather the length of time it takes you to read this letter, that Christ has been spared from the cross. Let us say that Barabbas' material crimes are viewed by the state as such a potential source of civil fomentation that the thought of sparing him for an expedient crucifixion of the religious upstart Jesus is absurd. Let us say that, instead of a religious rebellion, Pilate and his cohorts are concerned and frightened by a civil revolution spurred forward by just such characters as the charismatic Barabbas — Barabbas, who is able to incite the ire of the people by claiming he was forced into his folly by a snide and usurious government. Because Pilate understands that his *is* a snide and usurious government, he ignores Herod's (who suffers from a malignant case of megalomania and cannot bear the thought of a new god on the block) paranoid orders to crucify the insignificant threat called Jesus in order that he might rid himself of the significant threat called Barabbas. One could even go so far as to suggest that Barabbas, in a desperate attempt to further his cause by extending his life, points an indignant finger at Jesus, claiming that he (Jesus) is the real criminal, a false prophet who would transform his followers into a pack of touchy-feely zombies incapable of defending themselves against exploitive governments (foreign and domestic) due to strict adherence to a web of dogmatic doggerel which leaves them helpless and impotent and willing to accept whatever befalls them as a part of some divine will. The crowd, infected by Barabbas' snake charmer voice, begins chanting for the execution of Jesus. Pilate, who is shrewd enough to realize that Herod's fears are unwarranted and akin enough to the criminal nature of Barabbas to understand his will to power, determines that he must either promptly crucify Jesus to appease the moiling mob or execute Barabbas and risk an uprising. Let us say that Pilate is not a weak man and possesses the foresight to realize that crucifying Christ will not silence Barabbas, and, because there is a shortage of available timber, only three crosses can be made. Killing Christ will only lend credence to Barabbas' words so, risking repercussions from Herod and an overflowing of the mob's hitherto directionless discontent, Pilate orders his minions to nail Barabbas to a cross and toss the haggard thing called Jesus back into a prison cell. Barabbas hangs from the cross babbling deliriously about the rottenness of government and the cowardice of servitude. The babbling wears on and Pilate senses that he is in danger of creating a martyr. He orders a messenger to inform the guards casually playing dice in the dust below the tormented Barabbas (the two evil-doers stuck to crosses on either side of him having already expired due to a lack of genetic fortitude and water) to silence the monstrosity once and for all. Which, being good minions of the state, they do by wiggling the points of their spears in Barabbas' entrails. Barabbas dies. The angry mob, just as Pilate calculated, is transformed into a disenfranchised crowd muttering among themselves that crucifixion is indeed an ugly way to go. In the space of an hour, the crowd has dispersed, each finding the way to their respective hovel. The show is over. Same time next week.

I picture you sitting on the sofa in a peculiarly Ike fashion: legs crossed Indian-style, leaning on an elbow, this letter held at arms length, a bottle of brew on the cluttered coffee table. You're thinking, 'Paul's off on another inconsequential tangent — one which, although mildly amusing, is ultimately meaningless and a waste of time.' And yet you, my dear friend, will read on. Amusement, even a tiny morsel, goes a long way in fending off the yawning void that, from the theme of your last letter, has hypnotized you with its dark currents. For our purpose, that is meaning enough. Correct? Take heart, Ike. Even in the face of your sinister skepticism, my intentions are not merely to undermine your intrepid anguish with a few moments of speculation. I am not trying to trick you. My station in life is not only that of the gravity-slayer, although the gravity-slayer is an honorable and Thor-like profession. No, there is a method to my madness. I have come to the conviction that language, in order to achieve transcendency, must rely wholly on metaphor/allegory (for our purposes the two terms may be interchanged). Does this seem like a case of pointing out the obvious? Look again. Like so many things in this existence, the obvious is of little value until the interpreter can grace it as something unique and self-contained. Words are metaphors, representations of something else. Nothing more and nothing less. And yet humans have come to view language, the greatest of all gifts, as a tangible tool. The idea of money suffers from a similar decrepitude. The word 'hammer' and the thing we call hammer have nothing in common in reality. What? See what I mean? The moment I stray away from the allegory, from my story, my prose becomes obtuse to the point of vacuity. Let it suffice to say that I am replying to the last letter you sent me. And let me apologize once more for my tardy response, as your situation seems urgent. I hope you do not view this letter as an exercise in eccentricity; I am attempting to communicate at a level where perfunctory, pragmatic methods are of little value. Idiosyncratic or not, I hope, because we share a certain understanding, that your unraveling of this letter will aid you in your search for yourself.

Let us not characterize Pilate as merely a cheap political boss with more hair tonic than brains who executed a daring and victorious decision by sparing Jesus and silencing the malingering Barabbas. Let us say that Pilate, after personally questioning this alleged 'King of the Jews,' became enamored with the long-haired, bearded man. Jesus' liquid brown eyes, pearly voice, silky-dark skin, and amicable demeanor take their toll on the Prefect so that he cannot bear the thought of Jesus nailed to a cross anymore than Jesus can. To accentuate this characterization of Pilate (being portrayed as a nerveless bureaucrat time and again, is, for Pilate, as well as the audience, historically tiresome) let us say that he not only (or because he) is captivated by Jesus, but comes to view him as a possible ally when Herod, hearing that Jesus lives, throws a fit at the thought of this upstart messiah treading through his realm creating unsanctioned stories of an alternative god. Herod wants Jesus cast out. Knowing that Herod's wrath will turn to him when the threat of Jesus is scoured, Pilate, in another bold move, tucks his chosen one away in a cell and instructs two of his most trusted guards to feed him well and treat him with respect. He also, in no unclear terms, orders these co-conspirators to spread rumors that Jesus lives, walks the realm, spreads the story of love and forgiveness. Which, being the good minions that they are, they do without ever hinting at Jesus' actual location. Herod instructs Pilate to quell the rumors. Pilate, of course, is unable to comply.

Months pass by. Years. Pilate meets an Egyptian dignitary who puts to rest any inner-doubts concerning his sexuality. The price for this certainty is a bout of syphilis and, alas, Pilate goes insane before Herod succumbs to the hubris inherent in his megalomania. Pilate begins ranting about divine love and the rendering up of the soul to a higher power. He forgets that Jesus, the intellectual source of his insanity, sits entombed in a secret prison cell. The best laid plans...

After Pilate's unfortunate demise, the bureaucratic beast is temporarily without a head. His two trusted guards immediately put in for transfers. The transfers are uncharacteristically granted without delay. In short, Jesus is swallowed up by the strange and pitiless passing of time.

The memory of the legend of Jesus Christ fades from the collective consciousness of the people, government and governed alike, as the unmartyred so often do. His story forgotten, Jesus, an inconsequential incarcerate with a common name (when his legend flourished, many a babe was given his name), is regurgitated into the world. Knowing full well the wisdom of not pondering the methodology of a headless monster, Jesus walks away from the dark and dank cell into the sun. The light temporarily blinds him. When his vision returns, there is some permanent damage to his retinas so that for the rest of his days everything he looks at is enveloped in an oscillating white aura. Using whatever is at his disposal in order to survive, he pretends to be blind, hoping that some good Samaritan will toss him a coin or two. Who can blame him? At this juncture, all he wants is enough money for a room with a bed, a decent meal of lamb or fish with bread, and a skin of wine to wash the taste of prison out of his mouth.

Although the years of prison food and water diminished the urgency of The Word so that now he cannot even hear an echo, it somehow embellished Jesus' natural charisma: Dressed in rags, curls of brown hair (drizzled with gray) hanging from his head to the small of his back, his beard dangling below his gaunt belly; the sudden exposure to the light rupturing the blood vessels in the whites of his eyes so that he looks like an emaciated seer — physically blind but spiritually potent — a retrospective Milton. The plan to obtain a few coins by pretending to be blind and begging is so effective that in the space of hours Jesus has collected enough money to gain food and lodging for a week.

In his room, over a meal of spit-roasted mutton, bread, and wine the color of fish blood, Jesus concludes that the blind man begging routine is much more viable than flinging about The Word (which he can no longer hear): by nature a noble soul, he realizes that he can be of much greater use to the huddling masses by pretending to be blind than by pretending to hear The Word. Satisfied with his meal and with his decision, he lays down on the mattress filled with wool, and opts to keep his prison rags for future excursions. He will refrain from cutting his hair and beard. He falls into a comfortable slumber knowing that the fleas and roaches abiding in the room cannot be nearly as ferocious as the parasites and vermin that were his sole companions in the prison cell.

During that first night of freedom, Jesus is haunted by Lazarus. The apparition will continue to appear on the night of the new moon for the remainder of Jesus' days. 'Haunt' may not be the appropriate word. 'Visit' may be more accurate. Lazarus is a friendly ghost. Although he cannot speak, Lazarus is a master of gestures and communicates his glee at not being resurrected from the dead (our history does not provide Jesus the opportunity to show off his powers) in a series of hand signals, smiles, leaps, somersaults, and other elaborate charades. These visitations, especially the first one, erase any devilish residues of the failed-messiah-syndrome which plagued Jesus during his prison years. Not only is Jesus' faith in God intact, his faith in himself is restored by the somnambulant figure of Lazarus prancing around his bed. During the last visitation, Lazarus sports a pair of wings with a fresh coat of glitter. In a bizarre turn of events, it can be said that Lazarus is responsible for resurrecting Jesus. For what is Jesus without faith?

Time passes over Jesus like the shadow of a raven in flight. Months and years fly by. Six days out of the week Jesus dons his beggar's garb and explores the streets of the city. He enjoys his work. He kneels at street corners and waits for the oscillating white auras of those who would throw coins at the knees of a blind man. Except for the occasional heckler, his audience is kind and generous. For whatever reason, the guards (except when he kneels outside of the moneylenders, which happens to be the most profitable place in the city) ignore him.

Although his profits are extraordinary, avarice slides off Jesus like holy water from the back of a mink. He uses some of the money to purchase a small cottage on the outskirts of the city. The years in prison suffused in him a propensity for solitude and the cottage grants him just that, while, because of its location in a rocky alcove at the end of an unpopulated lane, lending him the anonymity which his enterprise requires. One day, while wandering through a particularly seedy part of the city, clicking the prop of a feeler stick on the hard red earth to add credence to his disguise, he comes across a woman surrounded by an acrimonious mob. The spectacle (in Jesus sunburned eyes the woman's gray hair becomes lightning-white) causes him to pause and take notice. The woman is in danger of being stoned to death for her role as a Madam in a certain brothel which is rumored to be spreading syphilis like lice. The woman denies the allegations with great resolve, but the crowd has already come to a resolution of their own and will not be convinced otherwise. The figure of the woman, clad in a dress hewn from gaudy material, standing erect with her great bosom thrust forward, yelling, "My girls are CLEAN! CLEAN, I tell you!", sparks something akin to a long-term memory — a concept missing since the release from prison — in Jesus and prompts him into action. Playing the role of old-blind-beggar for all it is worth, he stumbles into the crowd waving his stick, pulled forward by the gravity of the buzzing gold aura that surrounds the woman. He latches on to her and will not, cannot, let go. The crowd cannot bring themselves to hurl stones at an aging blind man in filthy rags so, after a sigh of disappointment, they go about the relatively mundane business of the day and leave the two old people standing alone in the middle of the dusty street. The woman's name is Mary. Realizing that she might not be so lucky on her next encounter with disgruntled customers, she, at Jesus' urging, follows her savior home. The two are married a short time later. They are happy together. Jesus does not feel as if his solitude has been compromised and Mary does not miss the hubbub of the nightlife. Two cleaved halves reassembled. The bond that holds them together is as strong as scar tissue.

The Christ household is modest with sparse and well-constructed furniture, nourishing yet frugal meals (Jesus loves fish), and childless (Jesus assures Mary that the consequence of their infertility rests on his shoulders). In the evenings, when Jesus arrives home from a hard day's work, Mary cooks dinner and they eat together at a small table of yew — built, as all of the furniture in the house, by Jesus himself. The scent of Mary's fresh baked bread, inhaled by children playing war on the unpopulated lane, becomes legendary in the surrounding area, and Mary brings in extra money by peddling loaves at the local market. After dinner, Jesus and Mary sit in chairs near the hearth talking or sitting silently watching one another over cups of wine. For Jesus and Mary, making love in the dark, however fruitless, is a sacrament.

So where does all the money go? Six days a week Jesus begs and on the seventh day he philanthrophizes. And while Jesus begs, Mary researches (when she is not baking bread) charities. On the seventh-day Jesus donates great sums of money to deserving organizations and, rarely, to an individual in need. He takes great pains to donate the money anonymously. Dressed in his beggar's garb, he stealthily inserts pouches of money into doorways and donation boxes. A precursor to Robin Hood (the difference being that what Jesus distributes to the poor is proffered freely by those who can afford it and, more importantly, want to give), Jesus serves as a harmonic convergence that promotes goodwill among good men.

Life goes on like this for many years. Jesus' hair turns completely white and hangs to his knees. Mary grows pleasantly plump. The night Jesus dies, Mary dies too. Painless deaths which come in the night while the couple lies sleeping under a wool blanket. The night Jesus is visited by Lazarus sporting his newly sprouted wings.

What does all this mean? On a universal level I guess the primary ramifications are that nobody is automatically forgiven for their sins. The steel rule of the Old Testament presides over human kind. Hell beckons the rebel soul.

But what does it mean to you, Ike? Probably nothing. Just another one of Paul's little fancies that spirals out exponentially into nothing. But it should mean something to you. My little fancy is a response to your soul searching. The craving to spell it all out to you calls to me like a drug, but I steer the ship away from those rocky crags. What would be the point of writing a story if the author immediately has to interpret it for his audience? Anyway, the author's intentions are of limited significance as they pertain to the reader's response. A prevalent mood in literary theory. The ball is in your court, Ike. The gun is in your hand now. Will you shoot? I hope so.

Day Two

Let it suffice to say that faith relies to a great extent on fantasy. More directly, faith draws its contingency through the art of storytelling. This is as true for the staunch scientist as well as the whirling dervish: the scientists believe that they can apprehend the nature of the universe (and thus conquer it) through the employment of objective reasoning; the dervishes believe that ingesting glass will not eviscerate them because God will not allow it due to their unwavering obedience. The scientists' faith (and let there be no mistake about this — scientists cling to faith like Born Again Christians) have given (for better or for worse) the world the Age of Technology, material progress, freedom from superstition; religious faiths have provided reprieve from the inevitability of death with speculations concerning the afterlife: they have assigned to humans modes of morality that assuage the propagation of the species while reserving for them places in their respective heavens. Even the nihilist, who exercises great faith that "all is naught," if he truly believes in nothingness and has not joined the movement because of its rebellious luster, at least believes in the story of Nada and so has saddled his energies with structure. The factory drone, who socks his faith solely in the next paycheck, at least gets up and goes to work on a daily basis. The drone's faith in the Work Ethic and cheap beer has so little dramatic appeal that, after being exposed to other drones for his whole life, cannot project himself out of the Drone Story. Like breeds like. Nevertheless, faith provides the impetus for human enterprise. Of course, you already know all of this, and I am oversimplifying.

Day Three

1) Faith is the catalyst for human enterprise.
2) Faith imposes structure on human consciousness.
3) All humans utilize some brand of faith.
4) All faith relies on some form of storytelling to project itself to future generations — so that its traditions will survive.

These, with no particular hierarchy of importance, are the four tenants of faith. Take them or leave them, Ike. It dawned on me last night, when I awoke in bed next to Eva and silky moonlight and Brahms, that I may have written this entire letter in a futile gesture to ease the travails of your quest. You, with all of the hours studying historiography, are certainly aware that historians are the most clever storytellers of all. Even the historians can be induced to swallow this (for them) bitter little pill, if one coaxes them with assurances of the superiority of their 'objective' mode of storytelling. My main concern with your particular case is that your methods in creating your own story, which, with time, will evolve into your own brand of faith, is like a fly fisherman casting the hook at a frozen stream.

The simile being a kind of story in itself, I will leave it to you to unravel my solicited advice through contemplation of the symbol. Become a Cabalist. Or, ignore this letter all together. Just remember this: in order to bring a viable new story into being, you must first ingest other stories, interpret them, and absorb that which is nutritious to your own: the story-maker is a predator. What is Rebecca's story?

I hope you will respond without delay to this letter. You've sparked something in me for which I am most grateful. I sincerely want to be of any assistance that I can. Furthermore, I have few friends here to speak of.

The Elusive Lizard,
Paul

P.S. Eva wanted me to tell you hello. She would love to hear from you. Please write her something or call. I get the impression that she misses you terribly. I grow tired of her pining...

Lupine  *Lupinus perennis*

The cirrus clouds hanging stationary above Laramie shadow the streets and buildings of the town with the tint of shale. The street gutters cradle streams of gravel, each stone a refugee of mans' battle against ice. At over seven-thousand feet, the spring is still young in Laramie. The new leaves on poplar, birch, and elm — the brown surface of lawns undercoated with emerging green — the bare branches of the pocantilla bushes planted in clusters around the Methodist church — even the greenish-blue needles on the fir and pine trees dotting yards with the frequency of freckles on the face of the town — all struggle against the gray grip of the wintery clouds, so that the tension between the seasons adds weight to the thin air. A leaden breeze flows out of the southwest, an augur of precipitation. The sky is without birds.

Cassandra drives directly toward the apartment complex where Isaac lives. Familiar with the town from numerous excursions throughout her youth, she drives the truck down the north/south main thoroughfare with her mind on cruise control. Braking at traffic signals, accelerating, switching between lanes — all occur out of muscle memory rather than conscious thought. She does not notice groups of college-aged pedestrians, dressed in colorful wool caps, wool socks, sandals, sweaters and jeans, plodding along the sidewalks and peering into the storefronts of shops indicative of small college towns: a bicycle shop, a tatoo parlor, a music store; a clothing and jewelry outlet advertising the latest fashion trends by clothing manikins in ski suits and placing them in poses that express glee. In one diorama, near a table in what purports to be a ski lodge by the artificial snow scattered across the floor, standing with a hand on a hip gazing out the window into dummy-eyed nothingness through expensive sunglasses, smiling self-satisfied at the plaids, paislies, and pastels, a manikin is lent significance. Cassandra does not glance into the bustling cafe situated on the corner of the two intersecting main streets, or the long-haired young drunks, wearing canvas jackets, emerging from the dark chasm of the Cowboy Bar to take turns kicking an empty can against an onslaught of wind. The character of the town is lost on Cassandra, as if she is sitting in front of a tv, with a hangover, watching a black and white documentary and attempting to remember what happened the night before.

Only upon turning into the alley which leads to the rear of the apartment complex (she sees Isaac's New Yorker parked in its accustomed spot), does she become fully aware of where she is and what she is doing. Heart pounding with anticipation, she drives to the front of the building and pulls into a spot designated for visitors. The truck diesels to a stop. The wind, steady as if it were manufactured by a machine, cuts through the weather stripping on the driver's side door of the pickup, sending a jolt of energy down Cassandra's spine. She turns the rearview mirror to her face and looks at her reflection. The eggshell white skin, the pale freckles, the gray-green eyes, the prominent cheekbones, the Celtic nose, all framed by the sheen of auburn hair, assure Cassandra, as they have done innumerable times in the past, that she is indeed an object of beauty. This self-evident truth, however, does little to ease the sense of urgency that pounced upon her the moment the engine shivered into silence. From her pants pocket, she produces a small vial with an equally small spoon attached to the lid with a thin chain. The stretching involved to accomplish this feat causes her lumbar muscle to spasm. She endures the pain and relaxes back into the seat, the vial secure between the thumb and forefinger of her left hand. After twisting off the lid, she scoops a heaping spoonful of white powder from the vial. With the practiced ease of an adept, she raises the tiny spoon (lid dangling from the chain) to her right nostril and snorts. The familiar burn in her nasal passage immediately elevates her. She repeats the ritual three times, alternating the spoon between nostrils, before twisting the lid back on the vial and replacing it in her pocket. After checking in the rearview mirror for stray bits of powder under her nostrils, she pulls the keys from the ignition, opens the door of the truck and steps out into the wind. Tuning in to the high frequency of the thrumming breeze, she slams the truck door and trots toward the doors that lead into the apartment building.

She pauses in front of Isaac's door for a moment before knocking. Her heart races from the drug and her bound up the stairs. The low throb of bass guitar pulses from a stereo inside of the apartment. When her heart beat is nearly in synch with the rhythm of the music, Cassandra runs a hand through her hair, snorts lightly, brushes the tip of her nose with a finger, and knocks timidly on the door.

No answer.

She knocks again, this time with greater purpose.

Nothing. No sound of footfalls approaching the door. No sounds of creaking furniture to betray human movement from the other side. Only the redundant beat of the bass.

Soon, she hammers erratically on the door with the heel of her fist so that her knocking is in discord with the music.

Underneath the music, Cassandra hears movement. Footsteps. The click of the deadbolt. The door knob turns slowly. She stifles the urge to seize the knob and throw the door open.

A voice from the other side, "Who is it?"

The voice, familiar yet strange, momentarily paralyzes Cassandra.

"Is anybody out there?"

"It's me," she says, consciously attempting to control the tenor of her voice. "Can't you see me through the peephole?"

"Just a minute."

A minute passes. The tumbler in the deadbolt tumbles once again.

Finally, the voice calls from a greater distance than before, "Come in. It's open."

Cassandra opens the door, steps inside of the apartment, and shuts the door behind her. The smile pasted on her face disintegrates when the sensation of being caught in a live trap smashes into her belly like a clenched fist. The closed air smells of putrefied beer and stale cigarette smoke laced with the undercurrent of human filth: sweat, rotten breath, farts, and reeking feet. The living room is a shambles of wadded clothes, stained eatery, and beer cans strewn at random like some macabre abortion of modern art. The television screen, perched on the entertainment center in one corner of the room, glares static. An industrial beat thumps out of the stereo speakers which are situated on either side of the television. The curtains are drawn across the picture window. The room is a shadow.

Isaac stands next to the television, a silhouette given form by the electric glow of static. He shuffles over to the couch and sprawls out on a heap of laundry shrouding the cushions. He wears black sweat pants and is shirtless. The skin clinging to the bones of his chest and arms shines incandescently in the half-light. His wide, luminous eyes stare inimically.

Fueled by cocaine, Cassandra pushes the heckling dread from her solar plexus with a sneeze. "Jesus," she says, "what the hell happened here?"

"I'm sick."

Cassandra stands with her back against the door waiting for further explanation. When none comes, she says, "The flu?"

Isaac shifts his eyes to the television screen.

"Well? What is it? You look like you've been to hell and back on a slow boat."

Isaac leans forward and fishes through the overflowing ashtray on the coffee table. "You got any smokes?"

"Yeah, they're out in the truck." Eager to bring relief to Isaac, to retreat from the apartment and regroup, she turns towards the door. "I'll go get them."

"No," says Isaac. "That's okay. The way I've been hacking, I shouldn't be smoking anyhow." He picks a butt long enough to allow a couple of drags from the mountain of dead cigarettes. The flare of the match highlights the dark circles under his eyes as he lights the tobacco.

"It's not a problem," says Cassandra. "I'll run out and get them."

Isaac exhales a feeble puff of smoke. "Hold on. This is embarrassing." He stands slowly. "I'm not contagious or anything. Just extremely hungover." He crushes the smouldering butt onto the tabletop. "Let me get a shower and I'll be okay. I forgot you were coming." With that, he stands and stumbles across the rubble on the floor toward the rear of the apartment.

Microwaveable noodle containers stained tomato-sauce-red, empty tv dinner trays encrusted with gravy the color of diluted corn meal, beer cans with half-full beer bottles stacked on top of them, dirty clothes tossed at random, the overflowing single ashtray..., all point to the fact that Isaac has been serving some sort of self-imposed solitary confinement. The scene, rather than pricking Cassandra with concern for her soon-to-be brother-in-law, inflates her with a sense of hope. She wants to coax Isaac (obviously weak from his recent bout with despair) out of his shell, and, in by doing so, achieve the goal (which stratifies into coherency as she stands with her back against the apartment door) of her journey. The sound of the showerhead spurting, the thought of Isaac stepping naked under the warm stream of water, pushes her into action.

A gust of icy wind wallops Cassandra, almost tearing the glass door from her hand, as she exits the apartment building. She pushes the door shut and walks to the truck to get the pack of cigarettes. Another blast of chill air tumbles over her and is gone. The Snowy Range mountains to the west are a blue-black bruise on the two-tone gray sky. The colors put Cassandra in mind of a watercolor painted by a disturbed and talented mind. Noticing the complete absence of birds, not even a crow or raven to caw defiantly at the inclement front, Cassandra pauses at the door of the truck and faces the wind flowing from the southwest. She closes her eyes. In a moment, she is rewarded with a gust. The air stings her face and flaps her shirt against her skin. Her nipples harden. Returning to the analogy of the watercolor and the horizon, and with a lung-full of frigid air, she braces herself for the task at hand. For an instant, she feels like a Sybil conversing with Fate. The moment blinks, and, with the wind cutting through her skin and clothes as if she were a skeleton shivering for lack of flesh, she throws open the truck door, grabs the pack of cigarettes from the dash, slams the door shut, and jogs across the asphalt back to the apartment building. Inside, she remains unconscious of the smile that began pulling at the corners of her eyes the moment she arrived in Laramie. She climbs the stairs and lets herself into Isaac's apartment.

Being disinclined towards domestic tasks, Cassandra adds a semblance of order to the apartment as best she can. After turning off the industrial music and surfing the television channels until she finds a country music video station, she finds a 33 gallon garbage bag in the cabinet underneath the kitchen sink and proceeds to fill it with refuse. Rather than pouring down the sink the ripe liquid in the half-full bottles and cans, she tosses the sloshing containers into the bag, along with the cigarette butts and plastic plates and dishes, and, before the bag is full to bursting, runs it outside to the dumpster. In the bedroom, she stacks wadded clothes, blankets, pillows, and coats in a heap on the unmade bed. She closes the door; she plugs the vacuum cleaner, which she finds in the hall closet, into a socket on the living room wall, flips the switch to on, and begins running it over the brown carpet.

Isaac, dressed in a faded pair of blue jeans, which are blotched with a mustard stain at the crotch, and a navy-blue sweatshirt with the sleeves cut off, walks into the living room just as the vacuum sucks up a coin which rattles violently into the guts of the machine. Cassandra smiles at Isaac's entrance, flips a switch, and the raging machine dies. On the television, a blonde girl with wide brown eyes passionately sings, the wisdom of the blues manifest in her voice.

"Feel better?" asks Cassandra.

Isaac's dark hair, still wet from the shower, hangs over the edges of his ears. "You don't have to clean up."

"I know," says Cassandra. And, with a quick jerk of her wrist, the cord to the vacuum is unplugged from the wall. She winds the cord around the handle of the machine.

Barefoot, Isaac walks to the couch and sits down.

"Go ahead," says Cassandra.

Confused, Isaac looks Cassandra directly in the eye for the first time since her arrival.

Cassandra points to the crumpled pack of cigarettes on the coffee table.

After tamping the pack on his forefinger, Isaac extracts a cigarette. A match flares, and he inhales deeply. He extinguishes the flame with a flick of the wrist and places the match carefully into the empty ashtray. The word "Thanks" flows out of his mouth on a cloud of smoke.

"Nasty habit." Cassandra walks to the couch and sits.

"Tell me about it," says Isaac. "Everybody's a slave to something."

Cassandra watches the girl singing on the television. "Guess it's in our nature," she says. The singer's voice is resonant with pent up emotion unleashed. Cassandra wonders at the possibility of the girl being a conglomeration of all blues singers that have sung before her.

"Maybe," says Isaac. "And the only honorable thing a slave can do is rebel, and I'm getting too old for this shit." He takes another pull from the cigarette and exhales before continuing, "Used to be I could recover from a binge in a matter of hours. Now it takes days."

When Cassandra does not respond, Isaac, too, becomes entranced by the girl singer's voice.

Cassandra stands, walks to the window, and opens the curtains. Ashy light splashes into the room. "It's all just a matter of attitude," she says, her back to Isaac. "It doesn't do any harm to manipulate attitude chemically. It's good therapy if you hope to cope. But why pay a doctor?"

Isaac squints at the exposed window. "It's going to snow."

"Exactly." Cassandra turns around and faces Isaac. She grins. "It's going to snow." In an exaggerated and slow gesture, she thrusts out a hip and slips her hand deeply into the front pocket of her jeans.

An expression of incontinence widens Isaac's hollow eyes and relaxes the muscles in his jaw. Unable to extract meaning from Cassandra's movements, his mouth slacks open. Thoughts murky from the recent bombardment of alcohol, instinct overriding intellect, rise to make sense: Cassandra's movements connote sexuality. Blood rushes to Isaac's groin. He believes Cassandra is attempting to seduce him.

Cassandra pinches the tiny spoon between thumb and forefinger and allows the vial to swing from the chain in front of her nose like a hypnotist's lure. She looks into Isaac's eyes and attaches to a filament of his desire. She classifies Isaac's sudden sneeze as a physical manifestation of the yearning for the euphoria of the drug. She smiles.

The sneeze serves as a flash of insight for Isaac. It momentarily frees his mind from the fog of alcohol, and he realizes that Cassandra is not trying to seduce him with the contours of her body, but by the promise of drug induced mania. He sneezes again. Shrinking with regret, he assumes a facade of indifference and docks his eyes once more to Cassandra's.

"What do you say?" she asks. She turns sideways and holds the open palm of her free hand under the dangling vial like a game show girl displaying a prize. "It'll do wonders for your attitude."

"I say I don't think it's wise to advertise it to the whole complex."

"Oh." In one fluid motion, she turns on the tip of her toes and pulls the curtains shut, rekindling the intimacy of shadows. She faces Isaac and says, "I'm sorry." She moves to the couch and sits next to him. "You need some. It will help."

Isaac watches as a man on television, wearing a large black cowboy hat and sunglasses, plucks at the steel guitar on his lap; he is sitting on a bale of hay on the side of a deserted highway. "Crank? Meth?"

"Nothing that radical," replies Cassandra. "Good old-fashioned coke. Good and clean."

"I don't trust myself."

"What's to trust?" Cassandra unscrews the lid on the vial and offers it to Isaac. "You're not going to get hooked on a couple of snorts."

The man on the television begins singing; Isaac wonders if the man is blind. The voice is accentuated by a definite Texas twang, and the lyrics seem to denote wanderlust. "That's not what I mean."

"It's just a matter of self-control," says Cassandra. She dips the spoon into the vial, raises it to her nostril, and snorts. The drug numbs the back of her throat and she lies without knowing why: "I've had this gram and a half for three months and it's still almost full. I only use it when I need it."

"Do you *need* it now?"

"*You* do. I hate seeing you down like this."

Isaac watches the smoke from the cigarette curl stiffly in the close air. The smell of ripe feet and beer pierces the plating of dullness which has numbed his skull for days on end. Recognizing himself through his own scent, he takes a drag from the cigarette.

The smoke is acrid at the back of his throat. He coughs. The vinyl skin of the couch is clammy against his back. The music emanating from the television booms suddenly in his ears. "What the hell," he says. "Couldn't make things any worse."

"Good." Cassandra spoons up a dose.

Isaac leans forward and snorts.

Cassandra gives another spoonful to Isaac before administering one to herself. Another for Isaac. Another for Cassandra.

"There," says Cassandra. "That's enough for now. Don't want to blow it all in one sitting." She twists the cap on the vial, stands up, and deposits it in her pocket.

The drug enters Isaac's bloodstream and empowers him with a feeling of good will. He grinds his teeth. The stench of the apartment no longer registers.

"What do you say we go down to the Beer Garden for a couple of brews and some nachos?" he asks.

Cassandra sits on the couch.

"I'm buying," says Isaac.

"I was hoping we could talk," says Cassandra.

"We can talk down there," says Isaac. "This pit isn't exactly conducive for good conversation, and we're running low on smokes." He stands.

"Okay," says Cassandra, her voice edged with an air of defeat. She stands. "It'll do you good to get out of here for awhile."

Isaac starts for the bedroom. "Just let me find my boots."

In order to quash her desire to follow Isaac, Cassandra looks at the television.

Isaac drives his brother's truck through the University of Wyoming campus and parks in a visitor's parking slot in front of the Student Union. He turns off the ignition and waits for the engine to shiver to a stop. He opens the door and steps outside. Instead of climbing out of the passenger's door, Cassandra scoots across the seat and exits the truck from the driver's side. She stands next to Isaac. The breeze is as faint as baby's breath. The air is cold.

"Wind died down," says Cassandra.

"Temperature's dropping," returns Isaac. He takes Cassandra's hand and starts forward. "Let's get inside where its warm."

It is dusk. The oily sky muffles the footfalls of student and professor alike as they hurry towards the sanctuary of the wind-proof halls of academia. Electric lights flicker on illuminating the pines that stand like sentinels in front of the brick buildings. As the darkening intensifies and the pedestrians quicken their pace, Isaac and Cassandra walk easily, hand in hand, toward the certainty of beer and food and warmth inside the Student Union.

Downstairs in the Beer Garden, they find an empty table next to a rubber tree so large that its upper limbs are secured to the railings of the stairway, so it will not topple on the patrons below. After hanging their coats on the backs of the plastic chairs (to secure their rights to the table), they make their way, again hand in hand, toward the bar. A murmur of voices rises and falls rhythmically around them and is punctuated by bursts of laughter. Light flows down from bromide lamps, which hang from the high ceiling, basting with an orange hue, the hair, faces, and fingertips of the congregation below.

By the time Isaac and Cassandra make it to the bar, a number of people have extended greetings to Isaac: "What's up?" "Where have you been hiding?" "How's it going?" Isaac responds to each of the inquiries in the same manner: a nod of the head and a point, as if he is aiming a gun from the tip of his forefinger.

Cassandra grips Isaac's free hand firmly in her own. A chill wags down her spine. Her scalp tingles. Wondering at the brightly knit sweaters and caps of the patrons — the sandals and wool socks — the beards and tangled hair — she feels like a blasphemer on holy ground.

At the bar, from an attendant wearing thick eyeglasses which give him a nocturnal air, Isaac orders two pitchers of beer, a plate of corn chips smothered in phosphorescent, liquefied cheese, and a pack of cigarettes. Cassandra stares down at the sticky linoleum at her feet.

Back at the table next to the rubber tree, Isaac and Cassandra drink without speaking. Cassandra studies the carvings in the wooden tabletop and is further alienated, as the symbols and names are so much gibberish in her eyes, a secret language designed to confuse the outsider. Isaac dabbles with a nacho in the center of the plate; the idea of food, as soon as he saw it, lost all appeal.

Abandoning the nachos, Isaac tamps the new pack of cigarettes on the edge of the table. "The entire university is smoke free except for down here," he says, peeling a strip of cellophane from the top of the pack and tearing the foil to expose the cigarette butts. "They tried to outlaw it down here, but it stirred up too much opposition. The powers that be figured the ruckus might turn into a riot if they weren't careful, so they gave in." He pulls a book of matches from his back pocket and lights up. "Whoever heard of a bar where you can't smoke?" He takes up the pitcher and refreshes both mugs.

The sound of Isaac's voice soothes Cassandra. Something familiar, something known. " Arbitrarily sanction one vice and prohibit another." She takes the pack of cigarettes from the scarred tabletop. "It's always been that way. They just usually don't have the audacity to implement both plans at the same time in the same place." When Isaac lights a match, she leans forward and kisses the tip of her cigarette to the flame. She inhales and leans back. "That's like legalizing bourbon and outlawing scotch."

The beer lends Isaac a sense of balance. He drains his mug in three deep swallows and refills it from the pitcher. "Laws don't work. The only way to prohibit things is by making them taboo." He speaks quickly and clearly. "Think about it, all you have to do is indoctrinate the mass, starting with the children of course, and convince them that, say, sex is morally evil and, lo and behold, in five or six generations, the birthrate, or whatever, has plummeted."

Cassandra cannot shake the uneasy feeling that if it wasn't for her, a number of people would be finding their way over to the table in order to pay Isaac a visit. Isaac's peers do not approve of her. They think of her as an uneducated hick, a bumpkin whose tendrils will latch onto anything that will pluck her out of the bumpkin patch. Out of respect for Isaac, they steer clear of the table next to the rubber tree. She fears that if Isaac should leave her alone in the midst of these strangers for any length of time, they would not hesitate in unfurling their opinions of her. The murmur of voices is too loud, rising and falling, rising and falling... The aroma of lanolin conjoined with body odor makes her queasy.

"Don't you think?" asks Isaac.

"What?" Cassandra focuses her attention on Isaac and notices that his eyes are fervent.

"Breaking taboo mutates the species and allows it to evolve?"

She is lost. "I don't know." A bead of sweat trickles down the crack of her ass. She is suddenly irritated. "I'm not much for all this intellectual speculation bullshit. It doesn't do anything but pass the time. Like a good fart."

Isaac laughs. He drains the beer out of his mug with a hearty glug and sets it on the table. "That's the point."

"What?"

"Nothing."

Cassandra targets her dry mouth as the source of her discomfort. A long quaff of beer discourages the buzzing in her brain. "It's just that these kids swallow a bitter little pill of knowledge and think that makes them better than everybody else. And then they go around spouting off about why there's so much misery in the world. Yet they never do anything about it."

"That's my point," says Isaac. "They've been indoctrinated." He crushes a cigarette into the green aluminum ashtray and lights another. "Maybe there is no misery. Or at least maybe it's not a moral wrong."

It occurs to Cassandra that academia is even more isolated than the Crowheart, and those that frequent it divorce themselves from the land and are even further out of touch than Jedidiah, Gabriel, and Michael. She does not belong here. Isaac does not belong here. "Let's go somewhere else," she says.

Isaac, excited by the possibilities of his theory (a theory which has been brewing for sometime and is now beginning to couple with words), eyes the full pitcher of beer sitting next to the empty one. "What about that?"

"I've got to get out of here," says Cassandra. "It's too noisy. Too full of other people's thoughts."

"Okay," says Isaac. "Calm down. We'll go over to the Albany. It'll be quiet there."

"Can't we go to your place?"

"It's too early, and I'm too wired."

"Okay." Cassandra stands up and puts on the canvass jacket she borrowed from Isaac. "Let's just get out of here."

Quickly, Isaac fills his glass from the full pitcher and guzzles it. He then dons his Army jacket and follows Cassandra out of the Student Union and into the night.

As Isaac drives his brother's truck to the Albany Bar and Motel, snow begins to fall. The flakes are so condensed that they cannot properly be called flakes at all — more like pellets, pellets attached to strings anchored to the ground, pellets falling straight out of the black sky.

"Isn't it a little late in the season for snow?" asks Cassandra. She pushes her shoulders against the seat and thrusts her hips forward so she will have easier access to the front pocket of her jeans. "Not really," says Isaac. He drives down 3rd Street, the main thoroughfare of the town. The headlights of the vehicles on the road capture the falling snow in glaring nets. The pellets lie on the blacktop like coarse, white sand. "We're high up. I've seen it snow on Independence Day."

After fishing in her pocket and catching the vial with the tips of her fingers, she twists off the cap and takes a snort of powder. "At least the wind died." She spoons up another dose, leans over to Isaac, and places the powder under his nostril.

"No," says Isaac, shaking his head. "I've had enough."

"Okay." The cumulative effect of the falling snow striking the windshield in kaleidoscopic patterns, the cocaine, and being free of the Student Union loosens Cassandra's mood. "There's plenty left."

Isaac turns into the Albany parking lot. "Where do you get it?" He pulls into a parking spot and turns off the ignition. "One of the hands dealing?"

"You should know better than to ask that," she says. "I have my sources. There's a lot you don't know about me." She opens her door and steps out into the falling snow. "There's a lot *I* don't know about *you*, either."

Without comment, Isaac steps out of the truck, slams his door, and walks towards the bar. The snow flurries around him.

Inside the Albany, rhythm and blues pulse from speakers which are strategically placed throughout the large room. A smattering of customers (ostensible strangers judging from the empty stools that separate them) sit at the bar smoking cigarettes and sipping drinks. They watch a boxing match on the silent television screens perched on wall stands at either end of the roost. Two pool tables occupy the dance floor, adjacent to a musical-accouterment-laden stage, where, later in the night, a blues band will play. A man and a woman, both wearing cowboy boots and snap-up plaid flannel shirts, stand beside one of the pool tables looking down on the balls at rest on chalk-dusted, green felt. The other table stands empty.

The bartender, a thin mulatto with a thin mustache and thin wire framed glasses named Frank, calls Isaac by name and offers to run a tab. Isaac orders a pitcher of dark beer, two chilled mugs, and two shots of scotch. On a serving tray, he carries the load over to a table in the corner of the room, away from the dance floor and the pool tables and the bar. Cassandra waits at the table drumming her fingers and tapping her foot to the rhythm of the music.

They drink the pitcher and the shots. Isaac stands up and gets another round. They speak without communicating.

By and by, the bar fills with people and voices and cigarette smoke. Frank cranks up the volume on the jukebox. To maintain the Albany's reputation for intimacy, the lights, hanging from archaic fixtures attached to the ceiling, are covered in blue and red shades. They cast a dim flush on the faces of the patrons. Prints of scantily clad women lounging on couches and beds stare (some coquettishly, some languidly) from the shadows of the picture frames which line the walls. With the exception of the dance floor and the area behind the bar, the floor is covered by a thin and durable red carpet.

The cocaine intensifies the effect of the scotch in both Isaac and Cassandra. After the third shot, Isaac is overcome with a morose sentimentality. He remembers his mother and realizes that he has been without an audience for too long, that his is a life of empty routine and rhetoric: his humanity has been lost in the pursuit of the wordy wisdom. He lights a cigarette and loses himself in Cassandra's eyes. The music is hypnotic. He sees in Cassandra the essence of Clytie and that the truth he has pursued since his mother's death is unattainable. A battle between dread and desire works through his blood.

"Are you all right?" asks Cassandra.

Isaac, the spell now broken, tops off the mugs of beer. "Just thinking," he says.

"Well stop it. Whatever you were thinking about was obviously unpleasant. I drove all the way down here just to have a good time. Show a girl a little respect."

Isaac surveys the bar. "Sorry." He feels as if he is between worlds, a member of neither, a stranger to both. "Tell me a secret."

"What?"

"Tell me a secret. Something I don't know."

Cassandra smiles. "Well, let's see, I can't think of anything that you don't already know, or at least suspect."

"Come on," says Isaac. "You just told me in the parking lot there are lots of things I don't know about you."

"True," says Cassandra. "But they're things which you already suspect."

"How boring," says Isaac. He takes a drink of beer.

Cassandra watches a tall man in a cowboy hat dancing with a squat woman near the pool tables. The woman wears a shiny, purple dress which falls to her ankles. They are completely out of sync, both with one another and the jazzy tune now streaming through the bar. The cigarette smoke puts Cassandra in mind of a low fog on the prairie. The dancers, though teetering on the absurd, infect Cassandra with a longing for human touch.

"There is one thing," she says, finally.

"What's that?"

"You have to promise not to tell."

"Okay."

"Living or dead," says Cassandra. Thinking that the intimacy of words may be her best hope at the moment, she takes a drink from her mug and says, "I mean it, Ike. I've never told anybody."

"Done."

"You have to promise."

"I have. I do. Good Christ."

Cassandra's lips pucker in disgust. She crushes the nub of the cigarette (she has smoked it down into the filter) on the side of an ashtray and takes a lengthy drink from her mug. "I hate that," she says and takes another drink. She sets the mug on the table and looks at Isaac.

The song on the jukebox reaches coda and fades. The tall man and the squat woman continue dancing, unimpeded by the absence of music.

"Okay," says Cassandra. "I guess I can trust you." She lights a fresh cigarette. "It was your Uncle Francis that relieved me of my virginity."

Isaac responds by standing up and walking to the bar. He returns with a pitcher of beer and two shots of scotch. After sitting down, he takes a shot and looks down at the hand smears on the glossy tabletop.

A grin blossoms across Cassandra's mouth. "Don't look so horrified. It was a long time ago."

When Isaac meets Cassandra's eyes, his face is without expression. "How old was he?"

"I don't know." Cassandra tosses down her shot and clanks the empty glass on the table. "Why?"

"You wanted him to?" asks Isaac, and returns his eyes to the smears on the tabletop.

"That's the funny thing," says Cassandra. She forces a single chuckle out of her lungs and into the smoke-filled air. "I've never been able to figure it out."

"Son-of-a-bitch," says Isaac.

"You sound jealous," says Cassandra, laughing.

Isaac raises his head. "I don't believe it."

Cassandra stands and wavers in the half-light. She steadies herself by stepping forward and placing a hand on Isaac's shoulder. "I don't know if I do either. Nonetheless, we're both sworn to secrecy now. Right?"

"Right."

"Good," says Cassandra, looking at the thinning hair on top of Isaac's skull. "I've got to use the ladies room. I'll be right back."

Isaac watches as Cassandra is engulfed in the swelling crowd. When she is gone, he places his face in the palms of his hands and is unable to differentiate himself from the music.

Cassandra returns to the table carrying a shot of scotch in either hand. She sits in her chair and sets the shots on the table.

A familiar tune plays on the jukebox, and (after pushing the pool tables to the edges of the room) dancers, like livestock, take the floor.

"I feel much better," says Cassandra. "I've probably murdered the austere visage of old Uncle Francis, but it was well worth it. You know what they say: you've got to destroy to create." She downs her shot. "You're turn," she says, before chasing the mossy taste of scotch with a swig of beer. "Ike?"

Isaac raises his face from his hands. His skin, in the dim and spectral light cast down from above, carries a pallor the color of a tobacco stain on a fingernail. "What?"

"You're turn."

"For what?"

"To tell a secret. That wasn't easy for me, you know."

"I'll bet." Upon spotting the full shot glass, he automatically takes it up and swallows the contents. "I wouldn't know where to begin." He lowers his head into the palms of his hands and listens to the mantra of music.

"I'll help," says Cassandra. "Who stole your virginity?"

Isaac remains silent, head in hands, rocking gently back and forth, like a man inflicted with autism.

"Come on," prods Cassandra. "Fair is fair." She lights a cigarette. "Jesus," she says, "we've almost run through the entire pack." She speaks rapidly, "Come on, Ike, you don't have to be embarrassed. I don't care if you're still a virgin. That's not anything to be ashamed of."

Isaac pulls his hands from his face and scowls at Cassandra. "How long is this song going to last?" He takes a drink of beer. "I slept with a woman once and now she's dead." He lights a cigarette. "Satisfied?"

"Not yet," says Cassandra. She is amused at Isaac's unease. "Who was she?"

Through narrowed eyes, Isaac looks at Cassandra and considers his options. "Nobody you would know."

"Then how does that qualify as a secret?"

"Because I have a son who nobody knows about."

"Oh." She is convinced he is lying. "Intriguing. Does the mother know?"

"He's not really a child anymore."

Cassandras picks up the empty shot glass, tilts her head back, and allows the remaining few drops to drip onto the tip of her tongue. She licks her lips and sets the glass on the table. "Not a child anymore?" she asks. "You must have been very young. Does the boy — or, excuse me — young man think that another man is his natural father, or does he just *not* know?"

"I don't know."

"You don't know?" Cassandra pinches her nostrils between the tips of a thumb and forefinger, releases them, and inhales. "That's not very worthy of you. The reason I asked is because a fatherless child is working against a stacked deck. Too much mystery, which breeds a lot of guilt because he can't figure out who he is. It's a shame really. Shame on you." She laughs.

One tune blurs into the next.

"You must have still been living on the Crowheart when the child was conceived," observes Cassandra. "I mean for him to be as old as you imply." On the brink of some new brand of truth, Cassandra, in a spurt of intuition, understands that she does not want to hear anymore; the words will only serve to fetter her to a past which (as long as it is not passed down through words) does not exist, not even in the realm of fiction.

Isaac looks at Cassandra. "Look, what does it matter? All that you need to know is that I can't tell him. That's it. No more."

She is anxious now to put the subject to rest, so she stands and says, "Let's dance." Her stance on the red carpet is wide and steady.

Isaac looks up at her and blinks.

"Come, on," says Cassandra. "Let's dance."

Isaac stands and finds that his legs are steady beneath him. And, for lack of anything better to do, he follows Cassandra to the dance floor.

They dance through two songs without touching. At the closing of the second, the jukebox falls silent and four men — two black, two white, all wearing shoulder length hair corded into dread locks, and tuxedos with blue bow ties — climb onto the stage and begin tuning instruments. The dancers disperse. Isaac and Cassandra return to their table. A fresh round of shots and a full pitcher of beer await them.

After sitting down, Cassandra says, "Jesus Christ. We didn't even have to order."

Isaac downs his shot and then sits. "I spend a lot of time here. I guess you could say Frank's a close friend of mine. He looks after me."

"A bartender *and* a friend? That's like having a dog that holds a degree in psychology." She throws back her shot and lights a cigarette. Tiny droplets of sweat hang on her brow.

"Well," says Isaac, "he's more of a bartender who enjoys my company."

The subject of unveiled secrets is given wide berth. They turn to small talk: shared memories orchestrated by mirth. They laugh at the foibles and follies of Michael and Sarah and of the Crowheart in general. Isaac remembers the scene in which Cassandra exposed herself to him at the bank of the stream. Cassandra covers her mouth in a mock show of embarrassment. Her eyes glisten with the reflection of Isaac. Isaac sluffs off the episode with a grin and a swallow of beer. He holds out his mug for a toast.

When the band begins to play, Frank lowers the lights further. The musicians look like well-dressed phantoms bathing in the blue light which defines the stage. The first notes from the electric guitar silence the crowd. Isaac, momentarily blinded by the change in the lighting, feels Cassandra's breath in his ear. A faint scent of perfume enters his nostrils.

"Come on," she says, "another dance." She takes his hands in her own and pulls him to his feet.

Isaac, vision still blurred, follows Cassandra. On the dance floor, under the blue-darkness, the two come together, toe to toe, chest to chest, and sway to the rhythm of the music. Cassandra rests her head on Isaac's shoulder, her forehead touching the skin of his neck. Isaac, now able to see through the darkness, closes his eyes and concentrates on the scent of coconut rising from Cassandra's hair.

Frank phones a cab when Isaac and Cassandra are ready to leave the Albany. Knowing they are too intoxicated to risk the drive to the apartment, neither Isaac nor Cassandra argue with the bartender. They ride in the back seat of the cab in silence, hands intertwined. Snow, the flakes now large and fuzzy in the cones of light cast down by street lamps, softly falls. The air is still. The lamentations of a cowboy forced to choose between a woman and the rodeo plays on the radio. The driver, a thin cigar pursed between the folds of his beard and mustasche, concentrates on the slippery streets. The streets are as void of people as the sky of stars. The cowboy chooses the rodeo. Cassandra, accommodated by the purr of the heater, scoots closer to Isaac and lays her head on his shoulder.

The driver brakes the cab to a stop near the main entrance to the apartment complex. Isaac pays the fare and tips the driver five dollars. He opens the door and steps out into the cold. He watches the large flakes of snow riding the air like feathers. The frigid air enters his lungs, and he coughs. Cassandra bids the driver farewell and steps out of the cab. She takes Isaac's hand and they stand for a moment under the falling snow. The cab driver waits until the couple is safely inside of the apartment doors before dropping the car into gear and motoring into the silent night.

Inside the apartment, Isaac and Cassandra, after clicking on the overhead light, take off their jackets and pile them in the closet. When Isaac sees his breath fogging the air, he walks to the thermostat on the wall and turns it up. The pipes in the baseboard radiators groan and click to life as hot water flows through them.

Cassandra walks into the kitchen in search of beer. The odor of rotten socks and cigarettes, rather than offending her, spurs the want to nest and cuddle. She returns to the living room with two cans of beer. Isaac is sitting on the couch with the television remote in hand. She sits next to him and pulls the tab on one of the beers.

Isaac turns the television on and changes channels until he finds the country music station. After adjusting the volume to an appropriate level, he begins fiddling with the contrast control on the remote. The phone rings. Isaac stands up, walks over to the phone jack in the wall, leans down, and unplugs the line.

"How gallant," says Cassandra. "That could almost be construed as a romantic gesture."

"I just don't feel like talking to anybody right now." He returns to the couch and sits. He places the remote control on the coffee table and takes up the unopened can of beer.

"I know the feeling." Cassandra stands and fishes the vial of cocaine from her pocket. "Want some?"

"Sure," says Isaac. "Why not. I don't feel like passing out just yet."

Cassandra smiles. "Why, Ike Daniels, I am beginning to believe that you enjoy my company."

"I do," says Isaac. "Always have."

Cassandra sits and unscrews the cap from the vial. "There were times when I didn't think so."

"I know," says Isaac. "Back then, I think I was trying to prove something. I just can't remember what it was." He notices that the words are slurred as they fall from his mouth. The knowledge that he is drunk strikes him as incongruous with the fact that he does not feel intoxicated.

"Let's just leave the past alone," says Cassandra. "Like it hasn't even happened." She snorts two spoonfuls of powder, then hands the vial to Isaac.

Isaac notes the fact that Cassandra's speech is also slurred. Amused by the absurd notion that they are communicating in a secret tongue known only to them, he inhales two spoonfuls of cocaine. He twists the lid on the vial and hands it to Cassandra. "Uh-oh, we're running a bit low."

"Everything is in constant flux," says Cassandra. She stands and stuffs the vial into her pocket. After sitting back down, she forces a smile and says, "Easy come, easy go."

"I've got something I want to give you," says Isaac.

"Really? A present?"

Isaac stands. "Yeah. A present. It's nothing much."

He starts for the bedroom. "Just something I made."

"A gift from the heart," she says, more to herself than Isaac, and glances at the video of a blind man sitting next to the highway, steel guitar on his lap. She then stands and follows Isaac.

In the bedroom, Isaac rummages through the drawers of his dresser. Loose papers, notebooks, and textbooks are piled haphazardly on top of the dresser. The drawers are all half-open, clothes draped over the corners. Isaac moves from one drawer to the next — moves with an unmistakable sense of urgency. Intent on his task, he is unaware of Cassandra's presence.

"I think *I* know what you were trying to prove when you used to ignore me." She stands in the doorway with her hands on her hips.

The sound of Cassandra's voice shocks Isaac. He scrambles through the next drawer.

"You were afraid of getting too close," says Cassandra. "You didn't want anybody competing with Clytie."

"Here it is." He turns to face her. A lump of what appears to be amber hangs from a leather thong clasped between his fingers. Encased in the amber is a gnarled mass of what looks to be a nugget of dried dung.

"What is it?" asks Cassandra.

"Whatever you want it to be," says Isaac.

Cassandra steps forward. "What was it?"

"I don't really remember." He extends his arm in offering. "I think it was a horse's eye."

Cassandra bows her head to accept the amulet.

"Yes," says Isaac. He loops the leather thong over Cassandra's head. "It was the eye out of Ghengis Khan's favorite horse. It brings luck, courage, and the speed of vengeance to whomever wears it."

Cassandra raises her head. She brushes the amulet with the tips of her fingers. "Where'd you get it?"

"Does it matter?"

"From a gypsy?"

"How'd you guess?"

"Because it brings me luck." Cassandra looks into Isaac's eyes and smiles.

Isaac looks at the amulet hanging between the swells of Cassandra's breasts. *Black red smear on asphalt. The horse, its golden hide pearly with dew in the early morning light, lies stiff-legged in the western wheat grass, torso swollen to bursting, wild eyes frozen open. Vultures circle in the incrementally lightening and cloudless sky. The horse's head is cradled in a patch of wild mustard.*

"Really."

The eye pulses.

"Ike?"

With each throb, the film covering the surface of the eye diminishes, exposing black depth.

"Isaac?"

Isaac descends.

"Have you no shame?"

Isaac looks into Cassandra's eyes. *Clytie's eyes.* "What?"

A flush wafts over Cassandra's cheeks. "Where'd you really get it?"

"A gypsy woman," says Isaac. "She kept mumbling something about eternity."

Cassandra kisses Isaac on the cheek. "Well, thank you. I love it. But we don't have to pretend anymore."

Isaac looks down on Cassandra with a bemused expression which wrinkles the corners of his eyes.

Standing tiptoed, Cassandra kisses Isaac on the mouth.

Isaac does not resist.

They make love greedily, as if starving, slapping, nibbling, pinching, kissing, sucking, and biting. A tiny marble of blood appears on Cassandra's nipple. Cassandra squeezes Isaac until he slaps her in retaliation. The desperate game continues until first light. They blame the alcohol and the cocaine for their mutual inability to achieve climax. Exhausted from the effort, they fall asleep on the dingy sheets. Bodies intertwined, they draw the musk of mingled sex into their lungs in slow and even breaths. Music flows from the television in the living room.

Sunshine penetrates the discolored curtains, casting diluted light over the figures sprawled on the mattress. Isaac and Cassandra, although they have both been nearer wakefulness than sleep for the past hour, make a concerted attempt to keep their breathing deep and regular, an attempt to fool their minds back into the realm of slumber or, at least, to avoid the inevitable moment when each must confront the other in the broad spectrum of sober daylight.

Isaac listens to the even intervals of Cassandra's breathing, entertaining the faint hope that her rhythms will lull him into unconsciousness, when his bladder cramps. Opening his eyes to the soft light, he eases out from under the warm embrace of the blankets and tiptoes to the bathroom. He flips the light switch on and, because it is quieter, sits on the toilet, and, when he has finished (without flushing), he walks to the sink and looks at himself in the mirror. The moment of reflection is somehow detached: Instead of observing his reflection, he feels as if *he is the reflection staring out of the mirror into an empty room.* The electric light, the sound of water trickling through the leaky toilet, the cold linoleum under his feet, all strike him like sensations felt by someone other than himself. Disconcerted, he decides to take a shower in the hope that the warm water and the familiarity of a small and intimate space will aid him in retrieving his bearings. He turns on the faucet and adjusts the temperature of the water. After climbing into the shower stall, he closes the sliding door and positions his head under the flowing spigot. Pores open. He is refurbished, as if his skin is parched land taking up rain after a brutal drought. Engulfed in steam, he scrubs himself clean with a bar of scented soap.

Isaac walks out of the bathroom with a maroon beach towel wrapped around his waist. As he steps through the bathroom door, the knowledge that Cassandra is in living room falls over him. As quietly as possible, as compared to an assassin who does not wish to be seen, he makes his way through the bedroom. He roots through a pile of clothes, extracts a t-shirt with a faded and indistinguishable logo, a pair of pants, and two socks (one white, one gray). He smells each item to gauge whether their scent is too strong, drops the towel, and gets dressed. Because he can think of no way to avoid it, he walks out of the bedroom and notices, as he moves, that the muscles in his shoulders and hamstrings are stiffening.

The sight of Cassandra sitting on the couch paralyzes Isaac. He stands in the entryway. The thought of retreating to the safety of the bathroom cannot unglue his feet from the carpet. He stands mute.

Cassandra wears a black bra and panties. She smokes a cigarette. The scented sound of hash-browns frying floats in from the kitchen. The television is tuned to a talk show featuring exotic dancers who are without rhythm. They are slender, busty, beautiful and, again, are utterly clueless as to cadence and meter. Cassandra is amused by the topic. She smiles and shakes her head at the absurdity of the situation. When the program breaks to commercial, she crushes the half-smoked cigarette into the ashtray and stands to check on the food. The sight of Isaac standing between the hallway and the livingroom startles her. "Whoa," she says.

"Sorry," says Isaac. He watches the horse eye amulet at rest between Cassandra's breasts.

"You scared me."

"Sorry," repeats Isaac.

"It's okay. I guess I was overly involved in that stupid show. Can you believe people go on national television to flaunt their weaknesses?"

"Yes," says Isaac. His stance is rigid.

"They're completely out of touch with reality. If you can't dance, you don't know where you are." Cassandra starts towards Isaac. "Never mind all that. Good morning." Seeing Isaac's eyes widen at her approach, she veers her course toward the kitchen. "I'm cooking up some breakfast. You've *got* to be hungry. I know I am."

The innuendo strikes Isaac as uncouth. He watches the exposed flesh of Cassandra's buttocks jiggle in rhythm to her stride. She walks into the kitchen. The sight of Cassandra's ankles, thighs, small-of-back, nape-of-neck, and wild auburn hair excites and repulses him. Vertigo swirls in his belly like autumn leaves. He leans against the entryway to steady himself.

"I mean we didn't eat a damn thing yesterday." Cassandra stands in front of the stove. When she attempts to flip the hash-browns with a plastic spatula, the shredded potatoes fall apart into a mass of chaos. "There's not much here. Canned chili over hash-browns is about all I could muster."

The forthcoming words parachute out of Isaac's mouth before he can stop them: "Did you...?"

Undeterred in full, Cassandra stirs the discolored mush of potatoes with the spatula. "Did I?" Her tone is rhetorical.

"Listen," says Isaac. He shakes his head as if to clear it. "What do you say we go out for breakfast. This place is making me claustrophobic."

"I thought you'd never ask." Cassandra turns the knob on the stove. The blue flame of gas is extinguished.

They eat breakfast at a restaurant which caters to university students. They sit at a table facing the street and, through a streaked window, watch the passersby hunch against the biting breeze, the falling snow, and the weight of the gray sky. Across the street, on the far side of a six foot chain linked fence, run a nexus of train tracks. A waitress with short cropped blonde hair — wearing a heavy, knitted brown sweater several sizes too large, baggy brown corduroy pants and sandals with thick wool socks dyed green — pours coffee without speaking, then pulls a booklet of tickets and a pen from her back pocket. She stands waiting.

Isaac and Cassandra place their orders. The air smells of boiling roses. Five middle-aged women clad in business suits, ties, stiff hair, and heavy makeup, sit around a table near the kitchen. They sip orange juice and degrade their bosses. The remaining tables, sweating carafes of ice water their solitary center pieces, are without diners.

"Is that waitress practicing to be a mime?" asks Cassandra. She pours cream from a tiny pewter bucket into her coffee. "If she's not, we'll have to stiff her on the tip."

Isaac, silently cursing the fact that he chose a nonsmoking restaurant, takes a sip from his cup and scalds his upper lip.

"Be careful," says Cassandra.

Isaac returns Cassandra's smile. He shifts his gaze to the oil painting on the wall behind her. In the foreground of the painting, a disproportionately large head of an insect is attached to a puny, naked, human hermaphrodite. In the background, a flying saucer with Conestoga wagon wheels rolls in a cloud of dust towards a ruby Cheshire grin on the horizon. Isaac squints to decipher the title: *Genetic Myths.* Under the title is a handwritten price tag that reads $575. The painting causes him to think of Paul. Thinking of Paul puts him in mind of Eva.

"This coffee doesn't taste like it's worth two dollars," says Cassandra. She knows that Isaac's thoughts are somewhere other than the restaurant. She looks out the window at the blustery day. She hums a familiar tune from her youth. Looking back to Isaac, she sees that he is still staring at something behind her. She twists her neck to see what has beguiled him. "Must be a local artist. A friend of the owner who lets him display his inanity. One of those women over there might buy it if she could sleep with the artist."

"How do you know the painter's a man?" asks Isaac. He speaks without taking his eyes from the painting.

"I don't." says Cassandra. "But it doesn't matter, as long as it'll get them what they want."

Isaac takes a sip of coffee. He meets Cassandra's eyes. "And what do you want from me?"

"You make me happy. I want to be happy."

After glancing at the beads of water condensing and propagating on the outside of the carafe in the center of the table, she adds more cream to her coffee. She returns her eyes to Isaac's. "That's all I want."

"You can't be happy with me."

"Come on, Ike. I abhor this angst-ridden 'Rebel Without a Clue' routine." She grins. "Need a little attitude adjusting?"

"No," says Isaac.

"Don't be such a shit. I drove all the way down here to cheer you up." She lifts her cup and slurps. "You've *got* to respect my perseverance, at the very least. I've been trying all these years against all odds and I've finally broken through. Be a gentleman and welcome my victory."

"I thought you drove down here to see some art exhibit."

"What art?" asks Cassandra. "You told me yourself it was only a craft. I elevated it into the realm of art so I could come down here to be with you."

With the fingernail of his opposite forefinger, Isaac picks at the thick cuticle on his right thumb. "You planned it?" The need for a fix of nicotine threatens to override his thought process. "What about Gabe?"

"What about him?"

"Are you going to marry him?"

"Do you want me to?"

"Do you want to?"

"If that's what it takes to stay near you."

Isaac is silent. He concentrates on picking at his cuticles so that the welling panic will not overwhelm him.

Realizing she has said too much too quickly, Cassandra tosses out a phrase she picked up from a cartoon on Michael's coffee mug at the Crowheart: "It's too late for a prophylactic."

The waitress returns carrying plates of food balanced on her arms. Without a word, she places a steaming plate of scrambled eggs (smothered in green chili, topped with fresh tomatoes, black olives, salsa, and raw red onions) in front of Cassandra. She smiles at Isaac and slides a plate brimming with skinless slices of cantaloupe, grapes, strawberries, and orange wedges to a stop in front of him. After topping off their coffee cups, the waitress, her back to Cassandra, winks at Isaac and, like a cat, strides away.

Taking up her fork, Cassandra says, "For Godsake, she could be a little more subtle."

The hunger for nicotine is transposed into a craving for food. Isaac stuffs a cube of cantaloupe in his mouth and quizzically looks at Cassandra.

"Don't tell me you didn't notice that." She spreads the salsa across the omelet with her fork. "That girl's got the eye for you."

Isaac reaches over the table to take a slice of toast from Cassandra's plate. "See," he says, "it's starting already."

"What?"

"You're jealous."

"Not at all," returns Cassandra. "I think she's kind of cute. Maybe we could share her?"

Outside, a train rumbles over the tracks. Isaac devours the fruit on his plate. He watches the train while mechanically depositing pieces of fruit into his mouth. He does not taste the food. The plate glass window next to the table vibrates as the train moves by. Cassandra watches Isaac. She no longer touches the cooling food on her plate.

By the time the train is gone (a dream swept away by the gray that pervades the day), Isaac's plate is empty. Without food to appease his compulsion for nicotine, a sense of desolation grips him. He looks up from his plate, finds Cassandra's eyes, and is comforted.

"What do you want to do?" asks Cassandra.

"Well, we have to do something." He drains his coffee cup and sets it on top of his plate. "The Territorial Prison opened a couple of months ago. They're letting students in for free until summer."

"How romantic. But I'm not a student," says Cassandra. She pushes her plate to the side.

"I am. Two for the price of one." He glances at Cassandra's plate. "Something wrong?"

"I'm not hungry for food." She attempts to catch his eyes and cannot. "You eat it."

Isaac pulls the omelet towards him. "Don't mind if I do. Then we'll go to the prison."

"Sure," says Cassandra. "Why not. Then I think I'll need a nap."

The Wyoming Territorial Prison, once a corral for desperados who had little use for laws composed in the cozy halls of legislature, now refurbished by a self-imposed sales tax on the citizens of Laramie, is a theme park designed to attract tourists off of Interstate 80. The referendum regarding the sales tax suggested that it would be poetic justice if a prison gave back to the community instead of eating up the hard earned money of the citizens. "Prison Pays Law Abiding Citizens" became a popular slogan. Under construction for a year and a half, the theme park is finally open. The board of directors, considering it a pithy decision, voted to allow free admission to university students in a gesture of appreciation and the hope that the students would spread word of the park across the nation upon their imminent return home for summer vacation.

The park is situated on the western edge of town, adjacent to the state highway that leads into the Snowy Range. The view during the summer months, so say the park planners, will be picturesque and reminiscent of the Old West. But as Isaac pulls his brother's truck into the expansive and virtually deserted parking lot, low clouds dominate the landscape and swaddle the mountains in an ephemeral gray. A stranger to the area might think that the prairie, flat and unforgiving, flowed without interruption into the four horizons.

Isaac and Cassandra step out of the truck and listen to the engine diesel to a stop. The feeling that they are alone and about to step onto ground inhabited by the ghosts of condemned men weighs emetically in their minds. As they walk across the asphalt towards the entrance to the park, Cassandra takes Isaac's hand in her own; his palm is icy with perspiration.

The park is designed so that visitors must enter and exit through the gift shop. Isaac and Cassandra browse turquoise and silver jewelry purported to be hand-crafted by Shoshone Indians. They peruse dream-catchers (strung with animal sinew sporting feathers dyed red and pink and blue); playing cards with drawings of the James/Younger gang, the Hole-in-the-wall gang, famous Indian Chiefs, and famous lawmen of old; travel games; rock candy; books pertaining to the Old West and the secrets of medicine men; knives with bone and antler handles; quartz crystals said to be blessed by an Arapaho mystic; cowboy hats of different shapes and sizes; plastic badges and Colt Peacemakers for children; posters of the outlaws who had spent time in the

Territorial Prison.... The situation, as far as Isaac and Cassandra are concerned, is surreal, bordering on the macabre. The shop attendant — yellow hair gathered in pigtails, wearing horn-rimmed glasses, a red silk shirt and a leather vest with tassels — stands under a mounted buffalo head near the cash register paging through a magazine and tapping a finger on her denim clad thigh. She is in rhythm to a drum beat softly pounding from hidden speakers. Isaac and Cassandra, the only customers in the shop, shuffle through the isles like machines. Finally, reaching a silent agreement that they have fulfilled the obligation of browsing, they make their way into the park proper.

They visit the Military Museum filled with wares of calvary men of old. The Old West Avenue is complete with a reproduced saloon, Sheriff's Office, newspaper office, blacksmith, and General Store. Standing at each display, encased in glass (at the bar in the saloon, in the jail cell at the Sheriff's office, at the anvil at the blacksmith shop, at the archaic press in the newspaper office, browsing the isles of the General Store), are manikins: women clad in calico dresses and bonnets, men garbed in military uniforms, cotton shirts, wool pants, cowboy boots and hats (the butts of pistols protruding from holsters on gun belts like codpieces). The dummies stand frozen in time.

Isaac becomes unnerved inside the prison. He entertains the notion that he is suddenly in danger of being blotted out of existence. Detaching his hand from Cassandra's, he cruises quickly and without interest from exhibit to exhibit.

Cassandra, though she senses Isaac's consternation, cannot quell her curiosity which is piqued by the 8' by 10' black and white prints of criminals who once made the prison their home. The pictures hang on the cold stone walls. The chow hall is judicially severe with austere tables and chairs and the shards of bottles which the prisoners drank from. There are leg irons and remnants of clothing unearthed from the site before the prison was refurbished. She lingers at the dioramas of prison life, encased in glass, where, after pressing a button, a verbal history of individual cases, broom making, prison culture, and successful and thwarted escapes unfold. The percentage of convicts who escaped (never to stain history books with their names again) fascinates Cassandra. Only after the tape espousing a verbal history of the wardens has ended, does she realize that Isaac is nowhere to be seen. Alone, she reads the caption under a photograph of a young cowboy convicted of murdering a prostitute in Cheyenne with a Bowie knife. She learns that the boy attempted to escape and was hung.

Isaac finds himself in the Warden's quarters. From a barred sentry cove that looks out over one of the cellblocks, he watches a woman, a boy, and a man walk up the corridor. The man and the woman are light-complected. The boy is black. Isaac, standing as still as the manikin clad in a dark suit at oak the desk behind him, watches. The idea of tourists intrigued by this hall of misfortune, the inhumanity of guards and prisoners long dead, disturbs him. He retches.

The man, the woman, and the boy look up and see Isaac doubled over in the sentry cove.

His blood poison, Isaac reels. He stumbles to the antique cot in the corner of the Warden's office and lies down. He knows no more.

The three tourists look at one another. When they look back up to the sentry cove, Isaac is gone. The tourists walk on and agree that they have witnessed a ghost.

Back in the truck, Cassandra says, "You looked like you were dead."

"I told you," says Isaac, "I got tired of waiting for you so I found a place to lie down." He puts the truck in gear and heads out of the deserted parking lot. "I must have fallen asleep."

"Are you sure you're alright?"

"I'm fine."

Cassandra pats Isaac on the knee. “What next? You want to have a beer?”

“I guess.”

“Then maybe we can take a nap.”

“No,” says Isaac. He turns onto the highway and heads to Laramie. “I’ve got a shitload of things to do. We’ll have a couple of beers and something to eat. Then you’ll have to go.”

“You want me to go back to the Crowheart? Just like that? After last night?”

“Yes,” says Isaac. “You’ve got to give me some time to work things out.”

A few flakes of snow plummet from the sky. Cassandra lights a cigarette. “Are you angry with me?”

“No,” says Isaac. “I love you.”

Cassandra smiles. “I love you, too.”

“I know,” says Isaac. “I’ve just got to figure a few things out.” Shivering with cold, he turns on the heater.

The sound of the fan warms Cassandra. “I understand. We both need a little time. We need a plan.”

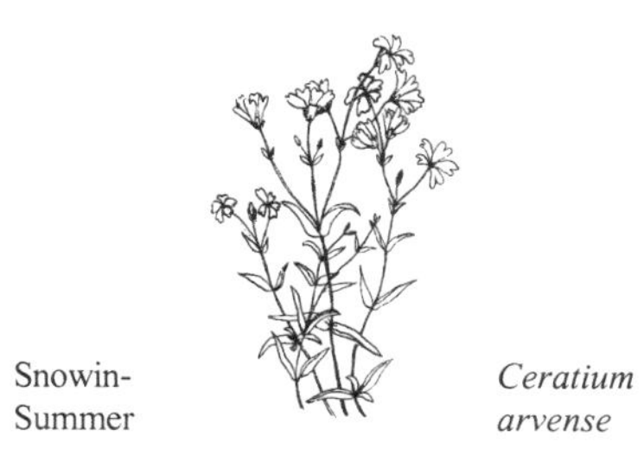

"Everybody my age has a secret or two tucked away," says Jedidiah. He sits next to Rebecca on the leather-skinned couch in the living room. "Hell, we wouldn't be human otherwise. Being able to *keep* secrets is one thing which separates us from the beasts."

Thomas, sitting on the other side of Rebecca, says, "Squirrels hide their nuts." He looks down at the leather-bound photograph album open on Rebecca's lap, pauses, studies the black and white picture Jedidiah has just pointed out, and continues: "There's all kinds of animals that hide when they're giving birth. And then they hide the babes so they won't get eaten up."

Saffron light, dense with the late hour, flows through the large window that faces southwest. The light coagulates on the polished surface of the cherrywood coffee table in front of the couch. The piano, sitting on top of the bearskin rug in the far corner of the room, is ensconced in shadow.

"Instinct," says Jedidiah recalcitrantly. "They don't have any choice. It's programmed into them."

Rebecca makes an attempt to neutralize the emotion in her voice. "She never knew?" Her face is as expressionless as a sleeping fetus'. She stares down at the photograph.

The couple in the photograph bear the semblance of transcendence, eyes reflecting the flash of the camera: Adam and Eve, chins wet with apple juice as the knowledge of what they have eaten seeps into their veins. The couple stand holding hands against a backdrop of white. The woman, wearing a dark dress, has her hair tied into a tight bun. Because the photograph is in black and white, Rebecca assumes, through her features alone, that the woman's hair is auburn, her eyes hazel. The man, unmistakably Jedidiah as a young man, wears a full beard and a dark suit. They are a countenance of austerity, faces severe with the wonderment and despair of self-reflection: A very picture of ambivalence.

"That's weird," says Thomas, tracing a finger over the transparent plastic sheath which protects the photograph. "The background fades into a sort of nothing. I wonder if the guy who took the picture meant to do that, or if he screwed up. It looks like it came out of a history book about pioneers."

Jedidiah ignores Thomas. He puts an arm around Rebecca's shoulders and says, "She never knew."

"The woman kind of looks like Cassy," says Rebecca.

"Yeah," says Thomas. "She kind of does."

Jedidiah looks down at the photograph and squeezes Rebecca's shoulders in a gesture of intimacy. "Nobody ever knew, except Francis. You're the first." He sighs. "She was Francis' girl and I stole her away. It took him quite awhile to get over that one. It took her dying."

"Why are you telling us?" asks Rebecca, a wave of aversion waggling through her body. She tenses her shoulders and leans forward. The new snake skin boots Jedidiah bought for her are suddenly too tight, and her feet ache.

"Well," says Jedidiah, settling back into the couch, "I was afraid to at first, but I wanted to start off clean this time. They say the third time's a charm. I just wanted everything out in the open. A clean slate."

"You really screwed it up the first couple of times didn't you?" says Thomas. "Mom died." He reaches to Rebecca's lap and slams the album shut. "You said *she* died. Can't fuck up much worse than that, can you?"

Rebecca cringes. She stares across the room into the dark fireplace and waits for Jedidiah's reaction. Social norms, due to her newlywed status, dictate that she is exempt from the obligation of intervention between father and son. She employs this knowledge to gird herself against the ensuing silence. She hopes that Thomas will continue with his attack.

The exuberance that lent Jedidiah an air of youthfulness, when the three of them sat down on the couch to look at the photograph, becomes clouded as he wrestles with Thomas' unexpected insolence. He looks to the piano and wishes someone would sit down to play a melody associated with spring — Vivaldi or, perhaps, Mozart. He remembers: *Clytie sitting on the bench to play the piano and her fingers touching the keys and one of the strings snapping and the sourness of the note*. He wants to tell Rebecca that the piano has not been tuned since Clytie's death, but he cannot. He looks at the bearskin rug under the piano and wonders who moved it from its accustomed spot in front of the fireplace, covering the boot scuffs on the hardwood floor. The familiar presence of decay, the thing that he has sought to escape, returns to him in the form of vapor filling his lungs with cobwebs and dust. He leans forward and coughs.

"And why in the hell are you telling me all of this bullshit?" asks Thomas. He stands. "Why me? You think I give a fuck after all these years? Well I don't. I don't give a good goddamn." He paces in front of the coffee table looking down at his coughing father.

Jedidiah takes the album from Rebecca's lap and gets to his feet. He smooths his mustache with the tips of his fingers. Listening to the mounting wind parade through the leaves of the cottonwood outside (rattling the panes of glass in the window frames), he is at a loss for words. Maybe he should have kept the photographic remains of his former life locked away in the antique chest, under the tarp in the attic, but, hoping that once revealed, (despite the ramifications) the final product would be a catharsis which would draw the drifting family together, he did not. He took the calculated risk of bringing to light the fact that Clytie was actually his second wife, and a woman with auburn hair named Mary his first, thinking that a deepening of the family history would strengthen blood-ties by adding a tragic proportion to the patriarch (himself): he hoped the secret revealed would prove a catalyst that would allow Rebecca to love him. Now, realizing that his vision of family unity was myopic at best, the album opened, Mary's name spilled like blood, there is no going back. The sense of having passed the point of no return inundates Jedidiah with a rush of emotion — emotion which he interprets as courage. Album in hand, he walks to the piano, pulls out the bench and sits. The resurrection continues: "We were married for two years." His voice, riding on the shadows that encase the piano, is resonant. "I loved Mary, and Mary loved me, and we were happy. There's no sin in love. We *could* have been happy. She left Francis for me, and the family treated her like a leper. So I left the Crowheart and moved into town, and we were alone. But we were together. I worked at the feed store, and Mary was a waitress at the Chuckwagon. We didn't have much money. When the baby came, Mary quit working, and I realized that we couldn't survive without help, so I begged Francis to forgive me. But when he found out that we had a child, he tried to stick a knife in my ribs. So we made it alone. After about a year, things were going alright. Mary and I were an equation, and Mariah was the sum of that equation. We had defined the world, and the world was good. And then — "

"Wait a minute," interjects Thomas. He sits on the couch next to Rebecca and claps his hands on his cheeks. "You had a kid with this woman? We've got some sort of a half-sister running around? This is fucking great. What next?"

Jedidiah rises and emerges from the shadows. "Silence, boy."

Rebecca glances at Thomas and watches as the color drains from his face until his cheeks are translucent. In the next instant, he blushes with anger. Rebecca looks to the cold fireplace and wonders at the heat rising to her own cheeks.

Jedidiah returns to the piano bench and sits down. "And then Mary got sick. When she died, I couldn't handle the grief. I wasn't strong enough. I fell apart. My father convinced me to give Mariah up for adoption and return to the Crowheart. He knew of a good family who couldn't have kids of their own. He said it was the only way I could recover my balance. I agreed. For years, every girl I saw who was about the same age as Mariah was mine. Girls with red hair would make me cry. Finally, Mariah was in every child — boy or girl, blonde or brunette — and I thought I was losing my mind. The only thing I could do was banish her from my memory. I haven't spoken her name until today."

Jedidiah's voice trails off until there is nothing left except the wind pushing against the house. He stares at the floor.

Thomas rocks gently back and forth on the couch, his anger blossoming with the knowledge that his father is a coward, a thief, a deserter of children.

Rebecca struggles to contain the sensation of absurdity widening in her belly. She holds her hand in front of her eyes, as if it is a mirror. Only by concentrating on the intricacy of the lines on her palm is she able to stifle the urge to break out laughing.

Thomas ceases rocking. "I suppose the next thing out of your little bag of tricks is that Cassy's my sister."

"Don't be a fool," says Jedidiah. He stands again and walks out of the shadows. "She's too young. She's engaged to your brother."

"It wouldn't surprise me," says Thomas.

At the mention of Cassandra's name, Rebecca says, "She'll be my daughter-in-law." She laughs and then coughs to control herself. "Isn't that weird?"

"Nothing's weird anymore," says Thomas.

Standing in front of the coffee table, hands clasped behind his back, Jedidiah looks down on Thomas and says, "I told all of this to you, Tommy, because you're the youngest and best equipped to deal with it. I thought you might understand."

Thomas looks into the pool of yolk-like light broiling the surface of the coffee table. "Understand what? That I don't know who you are? Understand because I'm the youngest? Easier to convince? If you're looking for an ally, you should have told Mike. Or even Gabe." When he raises his eyes to his father's, he sees a stranger.

Jedidiah, looking down on Thomas, as well sees only a stranger: any connection between father and son has been dissolved in a matter of seconds. Stooping with the weight of this realization, he looks at Rebecca. "I told this to you because I didn't want a secret driving a wedge between us, like it did between Clytie and me. I don't want to hide anything anymore."

"Some things are better left in the dark," says Thomas. He is unable to take his eyes off of the man who, until moments ago, was his father. He wears the expression of a drunkard being jarred awake. He bows his head towards his clasped hands in an attitude of prayer. He closes his eyes hoping it is all just a dream. Finding himself utterly alone, spinning through indifferent space, a sob escapes his lungs.

Rebecca cannot quit thinking about Cassandra — cannot, that is, until the sound of Thomas' anguish penetrates her ears. And even then, while laying a hand on Thomas' shoulder, she throbs with the memory of *the heat of Cassandra's mouth on her calf sucking out venom. Cassy at vigil beside her bed.* Giddy, she says, "Whew. This is too much for me. At first I thought it was all a joke, a sort of welcome-to-the-Daniels-clan initiation." She rubs Thomas' shoulder. "It came right out of the blue, didn't it Tommy? We'll survive. It will end by making us stronger." When she looks from Thomas to Jedidiah, she sees a man crotchety with the weight of his life. Jedidiah Daniels, Patriarch, shrinks before her eyes until he is nothing more than a megalomaniacal dwarf envisioning himself as a giant.

Thomas, inhaling sharply through his nose, raises his head and smiles at Rebecca. Trails of tears glisten on his cheeks. "It's no joke. Your husband abandoned his own flesh and blood." He stands up and looks at Jedidiah. "Be careful."

The word *husband* rings queer in Rebecca's ears.

Thomas, head held high, shuffles towards the kitchen. Before exiting the room, he stops; he cranes his neck so that he can see Rebecca, and says, "You'll be alright, and so will I. When *he* abandoned my mother, it killed her. But we're stronger than that." He turns and stalks away.

"Well," says Jedidiah. His hands are still clasped at the small of his back, his neck bent, and his head tilted forward, as if the floor were a magnet pulling at an iron plate in his skull. He walks to the piano and considers the silent keys.

"It's getting dark," says Rebecca. She closes her eyes. She can hear *the sound of the waves lapping against the shore at the lake — the lake hidden behind a mountain of rocks.*

"It's out of my hands now," says Jedidiah. He sighs, the wind gone out of him like the light out of the day. "I can't say that I feel any better."

Paul,

Thanks for taking the time to respond to my last letter. I know it must have seem garbled to you, an experiment which failed. Nevertheless, I needed to hear from you, as there is nobody else whom I can relate to on a intellectual or spiritual level. I am surrounded by people so caught up in the vanity of this existence (petty emotions and egos) that they are either too lazy or too deluded to reflect on anything outside of their own insignificant lives. Was it you who once said: "God had only a certain number of souls to be distributed, and the supply has long been exhausted." It seems the great majority of human beings defiling the planet are soulless zombies who have no inkling of what they are doing and wouldn't care if they did. Clytie used to tell me that the ability to ponder philosophical concepts must be a genetic anomaly as so few seem interested in the intricacies of *existence.* I like your idea better. Or was it Eva who said that? I can't remember, and it doesn't matter. One day blurs into the next, like raindrops on windowpanes. Lately it seems as if time, as it flows through me, is routed into a black hole which is perpetually behind me, a big black nemesis still unable to suck me into its vortex. But still, I strive to sever myself from the memory of myself so that my past seems like that of a stranger's — a movie, a novel, a tale about a character so far removed from the world I walk through daily — who I cannot even relate to in an artistic sense. Notwithstanding, without a soul, a human being is a malodorous, virulent agent of destruction. But what if we have it all backwards? What if these monsters are trying to liberate us from the nightmare?

> Can death be sleep, when life is but a dream,
> And scenes of bliss pass as a phantom by?
> The transient pleasures as a vision seem,
> And yet we think the greatest pain's to die....

What if these agents of destruction are angels from heaven, angels trying to wake us up from this sleepwalk?

One day blurs into the next. Speculation is futile.

I slept with Cassandra a few days ago. You remember Cassandra, the auburn-haired, hazel-eyed vixen that spurned your every advance? Remember the night she was down visiting us just before the shootings? We drank great quantities of scotch (the same brand I'm drinking now), and you were trying every method within your power to win her over, and she said that you were spoiled and out of touch with reality, too heady, an only child doted over by a single mother. So that any version of reality was lost on you, erased. The implication was that you lived in a dreamworld. Forgive me, Paul, but Cassandra was right. We all walk in a dreamworld. And, since we have established that, we interpret everything exactly opposite from the truth. Cassandra's scorn concerning your advances was actually a testament to her intrigue. You shouldn't have given up so easily. She was sick with love for you.

Now she's sick with love for me. And I, who have always loved her as a sister (she is betrothed to Gabe, did you know that?), feel as if I have committed incest.

Cassandra, who was more-or-less raised on the Crowheart by my family (a family that over the generations has developed a circular argument to protect what they have come to believe to be "the truth" about themselves), believes her love for me is more than that of a sister for a brother, just as Clytie believed her love for me was more than a mother for a son. It's *all* a lie. Now that I have had sex with Cassandra, and, consequently, re-enforced that which is not, a storm brews on the horizon. What is it which has awoken from its stony sleep and slouches toward the Crowheart to be born?

So why did I sleep with her? Call it a moment of weakness. In my alcoholic haze (which floats around me once again), maybe I, like all, yearned for the truth in the lie. Why not? It fits in with the nature of my premise that we've got everything backwards. Does it not? Why can't Cassandra love me? Why can't I love Cassandra? Societal norms mean nothing to me. So what if she is to be my sister. Anything done out of love is beyond good and evil, right? Isn't the pursuit of love the most nobly tragic of human endeavors? Maybe. And maybe when I tasted the elixir of Cassy's beauty, I found it bitter. Faith comes by taking a bite out of the apple. Morality enters through the mouth and is situated in the belly. Oh how I have tried to dull my sense of taste through the glut of tobacco and whiskey and cocaine. I am trying now. I eat everything that is presented to me in order to *prove* that I cannot taste. But I cannot *forget* the memory of taste. I cannot forget.

The trap is sprung. The snare of your theory raps around my throat, forcing me to vomit metaphor. From your letter, I gather that you believe the only way to impose "truth" on the phenomenological world is through allegory. I was, and remain, skeptical. Do you really believe that the use of metaphor is the gateway to some transcendental dialectic of idealism and realism? How Platonic! Seek professional help. Your theory is ripe with unsavory consequences: some perverted form of semiotic hedonism at best; at worst, out-and-out escapism. Since it is a natural inclination for our species to strive for faith, how can any culture achieve the lasting stability which faith provides if they are fully cognizant of the fact that they are making the whole thing up? If they know that their gods are merely metaphors, how can their faith be potent? Is the basis of faith nothing more than speculation passing for truth? You're theory, Paul (I'm sorry to say), inevitably returns back to the Grand Misconception from which it was born. It is simply another lie in a long tradition of lies.

I'm sorry, Paul. I just experienced what professionals term "an alcoholic moment of clarity." After another drink, I reviewed the above paragraph and found that it is, for the most part, alas, nonsensical. In keeping with the spirit of anticensorship which must prevail among friends, I will not delete it. Take it for what it's worth. Maybe I was inventing a new kind of metaphor...

I slept with Cassandra (I can see clearly now; the haze is gone) because I, too, am searching for the stability, the balance, which only faith can provide. It is difficult for a skeptic, such as myself, to find peace in definitions because the only phrase that rings true – "there are no truths, only interpretations" – is a vapid definition of myself. And yet, it is the only definition which allows me a sense of balance, however precarious. How does one define faith? Irony, Paul. Faith is unadulterated irony, and *maybe* we can achieve it only through the clever and calculated use of metaphor.

Do I rant? Of course I do, you fool. Any attempt to communicate the nature, or in this case un-nature, of faith *must* be characterized as ranting by those who cannot believe, and dogma by those who need to believe. Faith blinds. Faith mutes. Faith is beyond the realm of senses. Do you have faith, Paul? Faith in your lack of faith, perhaps? Are you like me?

Because the faithful (in truth faithless) pour their souls into the notion that their's is the only way, the Righteous Way, they employ language to convince themselves that they are the Elect. "In the Beginning was the Word...." Take the good old U.S.A. for example. "One Nation Under God." The word "under" has never set well with me. Why not "The One Nation of God"? Let's face it, as Americans, if there were gods, how could we stand not to be one? This Nation of Gods, the United States, has, from its divine conception, sported the conviction that anything which impedes the construction of our stairway to heaven must be eliminated. Manifest Destiny. Genocide, slavery, war... minor infractions in the Great Chain of Being. Faith in America is simply a retelling of the Old and New Testament: Be patient, Job, all is done for the good of the flock.

Time passes. I'm almost out of booze, and the dream becomes a reality. All men are created equal in the eyes of god. Does god have eyes? Lazarus might know, but he's not talking. This want of equality has spread like a rash to all of the Nation of Gods citizens. Everybody wants their share. Factions develop. Turmoil ensues. Everyone is the Chosen One with a sacred duty to pursue and convert all that fall in their divine sphere. "To believe what is true in your own heart is true for all men," writes the American philosopher, "that is genius." The lie undermines itself. The One Nation of God is populated by a stinking mass of gods. The humble, in their humility, are arrogant. The faithful, because, by divine writ, they only have faith in themselves, blaspheme, and are, thus, faithless. They do not bow down; they do not pray to the lord above. They can't. To do so would be a transgression of the Law. Don't tread on me.

I slept with Cassandra because I was homesick. Under the cover of night, I thought maybe Cassandra and I, each with our own unique talents, could create something beyond ourselves, build our own stairway to heaven, share a home. Like you with your metaphors, I thought maybe if we pooled our resources, Cassandra and I could create meaning out of the abyss. I *wanted* to have faith in my freedom to create something beyond societal norms. I *wanted* love. You may as well hear it from me first: Existentialism is dead: The Kierkegaardian leap of faith is an unfaith, the will-to-power is a fairy-tale, and being and nothingness is as superficial as the phrase implies. We are capable of creating meaning and burdening ourselves with the responsibilities of that creation, but we can never trust the creation to be as we conceived it; we can never have faith in our creation because we cannot trust it. In the gray morning light, I stood looking out at the cloud shrouded plains and understood that Cassandra and I can never be together. Termites would gnaw at our house like demons. I sent Cassandra back to the Crowheart with a horse eye talisman to signify our coupling. I never want to see her again. I miss her terribly.

It seems that the shootings should signify something. Or Clytie's death. Or my father marrying a child. We look for moments which will unlock the mysteries of existence, signposts to point the way to faith in something, but, instead, we *invent* meaning to compensate for our wayward wanderings. We endow our creations with faith as a way to balance ourselves against the nausea of not knowing. Religions are born. Wars are heralded as this god must be better than the last. The god of science is losing its grip now. Who'll be the next? Who knows? Know this: I'll never know why he pulled the trigger. I'll never know my mother again. I have never understood my father. Cassandra is a stranger, and so are you.

The only way to lend credence to existence is by assuming that being lost suggests that there is a way to be found. I am no atheist, but these gods yoking man with moral responsibility, in actuality, lifts all responsibility from man: When Christ ascended into the heavens, so did man's responsibility to himself. That is the nature of faith: nothingness – nihilism – the extinction of the will. If I had faith in a god and heaven, I would kill myself to quench this unbearable longing for home. Since I am faithless, I must find another way. I must expatriate from everything I have been taught in order that my search is unimpeded by the externalized internalizations of our forefathers. I must unlearn the lie.

All this is nothing more than a rant, old friend. You know me well enough to realize that. I am only saying in my roundabout and irritating way that it is time for action. Enough talk and speculation. Once more into the breech! Damned the torpedoes! I must return to the Crowheart so that I may purge it from my being. Time for the damned to rebel! I go to slay gods. Send your response to this address. I won't be away for long.

— Your Brother-in-arms,
Isaac

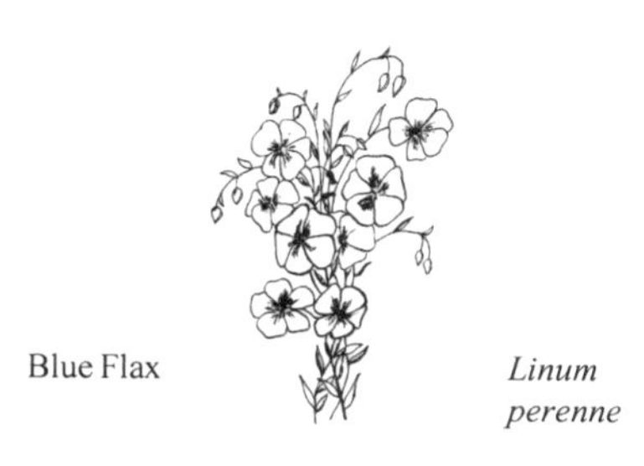

Blue Flax *Linum perenne*

As dusk settles over the prairie, falling silently out of the cloudless sky, the songs of the kildeer and the sparrow — the squawk of the jay — the moaning of cattle — the trickle of water flowing through the stream next to the fountain in the greening yard — are obscured, as if a painter, realizing he can never capture the essence of the day on canvas, brushes gesso over the wet oils until all is blended to gray: the industry of ants and bees diminishes with the light; the buzz of flies subsides; dogs, who had been lazing in the unseasonable heat of the day, find their feet and roam; a barn cat, nocturnal instincts aroused, crouches in a stand of tall weeds watching an intrepid black beetle, posterior raised, scuttle toward its burrow. The leaves of the elms and cottonwoods surrounding the big house murmur in the breeze. The cat pounces, and the day is extinguished.

The dawn was pink.

Sarah, who adheres to routine as a method of coping, arose with the sun. She slithered out of bed (so as not to disturb Michael), slipped into a tattered cotton robe exhumed from the closet, walked barefoot through the dark and silent halls, descended the stairs, and entered the kitchen to prepare breakfast. She has done this exact thing each morning since Clytie was buried on the hill which overlooks the horse pastures.

The robe, a wedding gift from Thomas, is frayed from numerous churns in the washing machine. A faded blot of grape juice stains the robe at Sarah's bosom. Long since having abandoned concern for her outward appearance, she wears the robe because it is comfortable and serves the dual purpose of apron. She opens the curtains in the kitchen. The room blushes coral. Sarah fries a pound of bacon until the strips are crackling crisp. She dices onions, green peppers, and mushrooms, adds them to a bowl of whipped eggs, cream, and smoked cheddar cheese, and pours the mixture into a skillet slick with bacon grease. She slices oranges and toasts bread. Flapjacks are flipped and coffee is brewed. The routine numbs her mind. The inner voice quelled, she achieves a kind of peace: the gravity infecting the mansion momentarily loses its pull on her subconscious.

When the omelet is cooked, Sarah prepares biscuits from scratch and gravy from the remainder of the bacon drippings. Knowing the preponderance of the meal will go to the dogs, she cooks in spite of knowledge, and does so just to maintain the quietness which concentrating on the present provides. Light the color of cantaloupe flows through the kitchen window.

When the breakfast is done and nobody enters the kitchen to eat, Sarah hangs her head in resignation, her matted hair falling over her face like a mourner's veil. She shuffles out of the kitchen, climbs the stairs, traverses the deserted hallways, and opens the door to Clytie's room. The room is silent and dark. Sarah prays that here, alone under the comforter on the soft bed of her dead mother-in-law, she will be able to find the serenity of dreamless sleep.

Thomas enters the kitchen wearing jeans, a t-shirt, and boots. Lured by the scent of bacon and coffee, he is surprised to find the room empty. After turning off the flickering blue flame under the pan of parched gravy, he serves himself a heaping plate of eggs, flapjacks, and bacon. The silence and the lack of movement in the house unnerves him as he pours syrup over the center of his flapjacks and watches its slow flow toward the edges. He wolfs down the food, along with two cups of black coffee, thinks about attempting to free the rest of the family from the vestiges of gloomy sleep, reconsiders, and darts out of the house into the light of day to feed the animals. Momentarily blinded by the sudden shift between shadow and sunlight, Thomas stands on the porch listening to the breeze rustle in the trees. He closes his eyes, inhales deeply, and rejoices at the caw of a raven near the horse barn. Opening his eyes, the panorama of the Crowheart seems fresh, virile. He reaches to a back pocket and realizes that he has forgotten his work gloves in his room. Turning towards the big house, he is struck by a feeling of dread and so deems it better to risk splinters and blisters rather than reenter the dank interior of the house. He does an about face and vaults off of the porch. The blue heeler named Grendel charges from behind the horse barn to greet her master. Thomas scratches the dog behind the ears and hopes that the rest of the family will opt to sleep through the day.

Dusk falls. Nighthawks, like shades, swoop through the fading light devouring mosquitos and dragonflies. The chirp of a cricket, tenuous in the still air, rises from a heap of decaying hay near the barn. In the corral, horses swish tails and flick ears in the attempt to deter the tumbling swarms of mosquitoes and gnats. The horses munch oats, eyes closed as if in sleep, breathing evenly through soft nostrils as if some inner vision insulates them from the mundane world. The blue heeler, her steel-gray coat camouflage in the dying light, stands ankle deep in the stream which feeds the fountain next to the big house. She lowers her snout and laps up a few under-curled tongue fulls of water. In the next instant, the dog's snout is pointed to the west, ears snapped rigid, hackles raised. Stock still, she stares into the distance. Water rushes under her quivering belly.

Thomas walks out of the tack barn. Having spent the day doing chores, he is hungry. His hands are slick with saddle soap, and his clothes smell of leather. The chirp of the cricket floats past his ears without registering. The sight of the horses, huddled together in one corner of the corral, eyes closed, ears twitching, tails swishing (as familiar as the paintings of his forefathers in the dining room which would only capture his attention if they were missing), go unnoticed.

He does notice the dog standing in the stream next to the horse fountain. Believing the gray lump is a rock and not an animal, he focuses on the horse fountain and the sound of water flowing from its nostrils. Looking back to the gray matter in the center of the stream, he knows the dog and calls its name. The dog stands still, hackles raised, intent on the western horizon.

Although the darkening horizon was cloudless in the light of day, Thomas smells rain; goose bumps raise the hair on his forearms; a shiver courses from the crown of his skull to his toes. Seeing only gray on the horizon, his eyes sweep the area — barns, prairie, sky — for sources of danger. A gnarled cottonwood stump (the tree cut down last summer due to an incurable and mysterious disease), standing at the boundary between the yard and the prairie, catches Thomas' attention. Three knots at the base of the stump configure to form the eye and nostrils of some cyclopean wood demon. Thomas squints into the failed light. He stifles the urge to bolt to the house by grinning at the folly of his imagination. When the image of the demon does not transmute back into wood, Thomas turns and takes a leaden step toward the house. The sound of the dog shaking water from her fur breaks the spell. Fear gives way to joy when Thomas turns and sees the dog trotting over to him, her stump-tail wagging. He waits for the dog. He hears the chirp of a cricket. A horse sighs, the escaping air vibrating its thick, soft lips. Thomas looks back to the gnarled cottonwood and sees only a stump cloaked in darkness. When the dog reaches him, he scratches her behind the ears and says, "Good girl. Are you hungry? " The boy and the dog walk side by side toward the big house.

On the way to the house, Thomas notices the light on in Michael and Sarah's bedroom window. As if on cue, the light flashes on in Jedidiah and Rebecca's room. Gabriel and Cassandra's window remains dark. Preferring throughout the day to tend to the chores by himself (the hired hands attend to the herd proper), Thomas did not question the fact that no one emerged from the big house to carry out the business of the Crowheart. Seeing the lights in the bedroom causes him to wonder.

After piling Grendel's bowl high with leftovers from breakfast (here, too, he wonders why the food was left untouched after he left the house) and setting it on the porch, Thomas is stricken with a potent malaise. The hunger, which, moments earlier, ached in his guts, is gone. Stooping down to give the dog a final rub makes him dizzy. Gathering balance, he slumps into the house, through the kitchen, climbs the worn stairs, navigates blindly through the black hallways and finds the door to his room. Without thinking, just as people sometimes whisper to one another without reason, he opens the door slowly. With equal diligence, he closes the door and stands in the dark. He walks over the worn, oval throw rug in the center of the room as if it were rice paper that he dare not tear. He eases himself onto the bed. After holding his face in his hands for a time, back hunched under some intangible weight, he pulls off his boots and jeans and crawls under the blankets. His body warms the cotton sheets. Sometime during the night, between sleep and consciousness, he is seized with ecstasy. Opening his eyes to utter darkness (the curtains on the window are drawn shut) he sees his mother and Isaac standing over him, smiling with satisfaction. The sound of a horse neighing from the corral causes the figures to diminish. The last thing to be swallowed up by the night is their shining teeth. After turning into the warmth of his blankets, Thomas sleeps.

"Why not?" asks Sarah. She pours a glass of wine from the bottle on the dresser. She wears the same tattered and stained robe she wore to cook breakfast. Her hair is matted. Her feet are bare. "You haven't given me one *real* reason."

Michael, eyes swollen and red from too much sleep, lays sprawled on top of the comforter on the bed. "Do we have to keep going over this time and time again?" The boxer shorts ride low on his hips, the elastic waistband worn out. His head is propped on two pillows with red satin cases. "Is it hot in here or is it just me? Pour me another glass of wine, would you, sweets?"

Sarah walks over to the night stand beside the bed and picks up the empty glass from under the lamp. "That's not an answer." She returns to the dresser and pours wine. "I know what I saw."

"You're reading too much into it. Everybody's off kilter with the news, that's all." After sitting up and leaning his back against the oak headboard of the bed, he takes the glass of wine. "They we're just comforting each other. Hell, you're a woman, you know how women get when they're upset." He takes a swallow of wine. When he removes the rim of the glass from his mouth, his lips are stained red. "You've been in the company of men too long. You need some female companionship."

Sarah returns to the dresser and looks at her reflection in the mirror.

"It would make a good story, though." Michael drains the wine, puts the empty glass on the night stand and rests his head against the bedpost. "This drinking really gets your imagination flowing in the right direction. I like it. You should get tanked more often."

"It was more than that," says Sarah. She leans on the dresser as if it were a podium, the reflection of herself the audience. "It was more than comforting." Looking into her own eyes, she realizes that Michael is, and always has been, incapable of hearing her words. In fact, no one who resides in the big house can hear her. It is as if she is mute. Clytie listened, heard her words, but she is dead. Isaac listened, but he's gone. She is alone. She ponders at how she ever allowed herself to be railroaded into this position in front of the mirror. For years now she has not been Sarah-the-Woman, only Sarah Daniels, Surrogate Matriarch of the Daniels Clan. The woman staring back at her from inside the mirror strikes her as a caricature, familiar yet comically displaced.

"Come on over here and let's put that imagination to work."

The sound of Michael's voice allows Sarah to disconnect from her reflection. She turns and faces her husband. "What?"

Michael pats the comforter with his hairy hand. "I said come on over her and lets use some of that creative energy."

"I thought you were sick."

"Not that sick."

The scent of sweat stings Sarah's nostrils. Unable to distinguish if the smell comes from Michael or from herself, she becomes irritated. "Sick enough that you can't tend to the animals."

"It's good to take a day off every now and then," says Michael. "Unannounced. Sleep all day, play all night. Let things take care of themselves for awhile. That way you don't get taken for granted."

Sarah pours the remainder of the wine from the bottle into her glass. "Yeah, I guess your right." Turning her back on Michael, she returns to her reflection.

"Don't worry about it," says Michael, scratching his hair-matted chest. "Gabe and Tommy can handle it for one day. Anyhow, that news the Old Man dropped threw me off balance. Needed to digest." He reaches for his wine glass and realizes it is empty. "If something went bad, somebody would have come and got me. Everything will hold together. Hell, sweets, even God had to rest for one day."

Sarah's eyes fall to the top of the dresser. She is tired. Studying the grain in the polished wood, her mood swings melancholic, and she wishes she knew where the dresser came from, who built it, who purchased it, who brought it into the big house. The electric light beams hotly on the polished surface. "No it won't," she whispers.

Michael, glass in hand, gets out of bed.

Sarah does not hear the springs in the mattress squeak, nor the sound of Michael's feet creaking the floorboards. When he touches her shoulders, she tenses and draws in a sharp breath.

"What's that, sweets?"

Raising her eyes to the mirror, Sarah looks at the reflection of weathered skin on Michael's face, the ruddy cheeks sagging with age, the cloud-white skin on his shoulders which are never exposed to the light of day. She turns and faces him. The sight of his pearly, soft belly, his chest blanketed with black hair, his tanned forearms and neck, put her in mind of a weed going to seed. She looks him in the eye, "No. Things won't hold together."

"What does that mean?"

"You know."

Michael takes the bottle from the top of the dresser, finds it empty and sets it down. "No, I don't know. What the hell are you talking about?"

"You know."

"Goddamnit, Sarah, no I don't know. I don't feel like playing any of your goddamn games. Now, just say it."

For a moment, sandwiched between the mirror, and Michael, Sarah believes that her husband is going to strike out at her. She sidesteps and is free. "You'll know soon enough." She walks to the bed and sits down.

Michael takes up the empty wine bottle, tilts his head back, and pours the few remaining drops down his throat. "That's the trouble around here: Everybody speaks in riddles. All I ever wanted was a wife and a family. Real simple. If we had kids, everybody in the house would have to learn to talk plain so *they* could understand. There's no children, Sarah. Why are there no children in this house?" Bottle in one hand, glass dangling in the other, he walks to the window and looks out into the night.

Sarah leans her head on the heels of her hands. "Children? That would be just great. And how am I supposed to raise children when I can barely keep this house functioning?" She raises her head and twists her neck until she can see Michael's back. "Just so you know, Mike, I'm not Clytie. I don't have the strength." The patches of hair on Michael's shoulder blades disgust her.

Michael bows his head. After a moment of silence, he says, in an exaggerated tone of indifference, "You take everything too seriously. Cassy and Rebecca are just bonding. I think you're a little jealous is all. And the Old Man dropped his bombshell just to get a little attention. He's feeling a little old and a little guilty for marrying that girl. Hell, he might have made the whole thing up. We'll never know for sure."

Sarah stands, walks to the dresser, and assumes her podium position in front of the mirror. "Does Ike know about this latest 'bombshell'?"

"I doubt it. If he does, I'm sure he saw right through it, like I did. A publicity stunt." Michael moves to the bed, crawls under the covers, and curls up.

Sarah walks to the window and stares at the flickering light of Venus. Crickets chirp.

"Why don't you come to bed?" says Michael, his voice puny under the covers. "You're drunk. You're not making any sense."

Sarah stands still.

Michael pops his head out from under the covers and props it up with an elbow. He speaks to Sarah's back, "Please?"

"Make sense?"

"What?"

"My brand of sense doesn't mesh with yours."

Michael lays his head down on the pillow. "I need you."

"No you don't." She turns to face her husband. "Anyway, I feel sticky from all that wine. I think I'll take a bath."

"Then will you come to bed? We could start on that family we've been talking about all these years."

"The wind's coming out of the southwest," says Sarah, starting toward the bathroom. "It's just a breeze now, but by morning it'll be a regular howler. I can feel it."

Michael pulls the blankets over his head.

Sarah walks into the bathroom and closes the door behind her.

Legs and torso submerged in warm water, Sarah feels dissolve the melancholic fog which has daunted her since she realized her breakfast would go to the dogs. She scrubs herself clean with a loofa sponge. After applying peppermint conditioner to her hair, she leans back in the tub and enjoys the tingling sensation on her scalp. Eyes closed, she scoots down in the tub until only her face is above the water, hair floating like spider moss in a warm pool.

The moans emanating from Clytie's old bedroom compel Sarah to trot through the dark hallways of the big house to investigate. Opening the door to the bedroom, she steps into a muggy summer night, effulgent with moon and stars. Venus floats above the moon. Water trickles over white quartz boulders lining a stream bed. The perfume of wild peppermint and pine needles hangs in the air.

The moans, not the deathbed moans that Sarah first anticipated, but moans of sexual pleasure, ecstacy, rise softly out of the landscape itself, the trees and water and rocks, the moon and stars, and, when rain begins falling out of the cloudless sky, it is warm and smells of green musk. The night is Clytie, and, when Sarah — droplets of rain streaming over her face and shoulders, breasts and torso, thighs, knees and toes — sees Isaac (as naked as herself) writhing in a patch of wild roses near the stream, his body dotted with the red pricks of thorns, his moonlit buttocks rising and falling to the rhythm of the moans, as if he is copulating with the soil, she loses herself in the sound of the falling rain and is converted into moisture...

She opens her eyes. The vision is gone. Taking up the loofa sponge, she sets to work, once again, scrubbing her skin. She abrades her flesh in order to purge the feeling of guilt which swept over her the moment she opened her eyes and fractured the waking dream. Although she is unable to interpret the vision, the sensation that taboo has been breached — consecrated ground defiled — fills her with shame. The knowledge that she took pleasure in the scene adds the weight of complicity. She scrubs.

Eventually, she pulls the drain plug and steps out of the tub. Specks of blood rise on the bony surface of her hips and shoulders where the loofa sponge bit too deeply. She wraps her body in a towel and walks to the mirror above the sink. Her reflection is distorted by steam on the glass. Wondering why, on top of everything else, she must be burdened by phantasmagoria, she unwraps the towel from around her body and wipes the mirror clean. When the blurred face staring back at her, for the slightest second, seems to be Clytie, she wonders if her nerves are finally shot, and her system is shutting down.

The thought of spending her days in a locked room which smells of ammonia and bleach (nurses in crisp white uniforms administering medication to keep the phantoms at bay) abhors her into action.

As she dresses (she wears the tattered and stained robe that smells of perspiration because to do otherwise would mean to venture into the bedroom, and she cannot tolerate the idea of Michael seeing her bleeding flesh), she decides to put the house in order, thinking that in doing so she will be able to lend a sense of protocol to her beleaguered mind. She will start with the kitchen. After wrapping her soggy hair into a bun, she enters the bedroom and is relieved to find Michael snoring softly. She tiptoes across the floor. As she reaches for the doorknob which will free her from the room, she is startled by an extended fart from Michael. Instead of being disgusted or amused, she becomes fearful that the force of the fart will jar Michael awake. She waits, as still as the house itself, while Michael turns over in the bed and settles back into sleep. Only when the soft snores have returned, pulsing evenly, does she open the door and tiptoe into the hallway.

In the kitchen, after turning on the lights, Sarah concludes she will have to boil water in the pots and pans to loosen the chunks of crusted food. It pleases her that the preponderance of the eggs, bacon, flapjacks, biscuits and gravy are gone, either to dogs or humans – she does not care which. At least she will not have to dispose of the labored-over waste. The wind, picking up momentum, overwhelms the sound of chirping crickets. The frame of the big house creaks. Sarah begins filling the sink with water, when, very soon, she realizes the water is ice cold. Making her way through darkness to the laundry room on the opposite side of the house, instead of attempting to locate the string dangling from the ceiling which connects to the light switch, she gropes in the blotches of blackness until she finds the enameled surface of the hot water heater. On her knees, she caresses the cool curve of the appliance until she finds the reset button. She pushes it. The process leaves her mildly irritated, as she has been nagging Michael for weeks to repair the heater. Exiting the laundry room, she stubs the little toe of her left foot on the clothes dryer. "Goddamnit," she says, with no particular malice in her voice. She says the word again, "Goddamnit." The word, coupled with the sound of her voice, is strange in her ears. Since she was a girl, she has refrained from using the Lord's name in vain. She curses once more, her tone inclining toward conviction, and a thin smile wavers on her lips. As she steps into the light of the kitchen, the words 'Goddamn him' form in her mind. She prepares a pot of coffee. She says, "Goddamn him."

After stacking the dishes in the sink and filling the pots and pans with soapy water and placing them on the stove to heat, she sits down at the table and listens to the coffee pot percolate and the wind pushing against the dark window. Unable to sit still for long, she stands up and, with a cold rag, wipes down the table and the counters. She sweeps the floor and deposits the refuse into the garbage can under the sink. She then pours a cup of coffee, adds cream from a cold porcelain beaker, and returns to the table. She waits for the water to heat in the laundry room. Her toe throbs. She entertains a thought of venturing into the dining room to start dusting but abandons the idea by figuring that if the kitchen (the heart of any house) is not completely clean, focusing on the extremities of would be senseless.

She sits and waits. The wind augments into a chorus of hissing whistles as it passes through the trees, the railings on the porch, and the cracks and crevices around the doors and windows of the house. The warmth of the coffee against Sarah's lips and tongue causes her thoughts to fall to her feet, bare against the hardwood floor, the soles freezing. A portentous thought occurs: winter has returned to the land; a storm will come and shrivel the leaves on trees, destroy sprouting alfalfa, cause blight. This, no doubt, is why everyone has been acting lethargic and burdened, a natural reaction to a reversal of spring. Sarah considers turning on the radio next to the toaster to confirm her suspicions but decides against it. Her bones are to be trusted more than a group of meteorologist manipulating high-tech contraptions: she is integrated into the natural process, a computer is not. She stands and walks to the window over the kitchen sink hoping to spot the horses in the corral, the most accurate of all barometers. It is too dark. Without a second thought, she walks to the landing, slips into a pair of mud-caked irrigation boots, opens the door and walks out onto the porch. She must see the horses.

A whip of wind loosens the bun on Sarah's head, allowing her hair to flow freely in the night. The stars have been veiled by clouds, but, as Sarah searches the sky, her chin tilted defiantly against the mounting storm, she is able to decipher the light of Venus penetrating the clouds. She stands still, the wind ruffling her robe, and watches the swaying branches on the cottonwood. The wind is crisp.

Sarah prances down the porch stairs, over the driveway, and across the yard in the direction of the corral. In the corral, the horses snort and stomp, tails erect. Lightning flashes. A pale horse bares its teeth and bites a black horse on the back of the neck. Lightning flashes. A roan horse rears up on its hind legs and slashes the air with its front hooves. Sarah hooks her arms over the top rail of the corral and, with an expanding sense of glee, observes the horses. Her nipples harden in the chill air; her toes tingle inside the rubber boots; her hair flutters in the wind. Watching the horses frolic, the scent of manure in her nose, she decides that the advancing storm is not an onslaught of winter charging out of the mountains to attack the rearguard of spring, but a herald of summer, replete with life-provoking rain. Invigorated by her investigation into the night, she returns to the big house, her feet sloppy in the oversized boots.

Back inside the kitchen, while pouring a fresh cup of coffee to warm herself, it occurs to Sarah that she, being the matriarch of the Daniels clan by default (Rebecca is too young for the position, too inexperienced, and will have to be coddled and then trained so that she can inherit the position when Sarah retires), should bear the title with greater resolution. Clytie was an expert at delegating authority, and the affairs of the house ran smoothly while under her domain. Even when she, Clytie, entombed herself in her bedroom for weeks on end (like some Faulknerian character of the high plains), granting only Isaac the right to frequent visits, her presence in the house ensured that all household business flowed without wasted motion and in a timely fashion. Taking this insight to heart, Sarah determines to wait until morning to finish putting her house in order. Only with the cooperation of the entire family will her actions have any cohesive and lasting effect.

This silent proclamation ringing in her mind, her recent experiences from the bath to the corral, the warm water and wind, the leaves shuddering in the night trees, the evocative presence of Venus and Clytie in her mind's eye — all combine to lift the burden of responsibility which has weighed down on Sarah since morning. The day smudged with wine and inconsistent suspicions suddenly takes it's toll. Sarah is exhausted. She heads upstairs.

Clytie's visitation while in the bathroom, her tangible yet invisible presence in the depths of Sarah's subconscious, proved to be a catalyst which has enabled Sarah to configure her existence in a perspective that is not only to her liking and contentment, but logical to the point of simplicity. She wonders why she didn't think of it sooner. The concept has been at the periphery of her consciousness for quite sometime, perhaps since the advent of Clytie's demise, but, for whatever reason (a reluctance to bear the brand of matriarch, an innocence unwilling to be displaced by the intricacies of the Daniels' family infrastructure...), prevented her from seeing herself as what she now is until this very night. It is as if she has been acting the part of the matriarch without a script, improvising without a goal to define the paradigm of the play. This sudden materialization of parameters, although still sticky with the membranes of birth, provides Sarah with a sense of identity that has been lacking since the moment of Clytie's death. In the space of a few hours, Sarah has come to understand the essence of her relationship with the Crowheart: Clytie has risen from the dead to inhabit Sarah's body.

The epiphany leaves Sarah light-headed. The somnifacient properties of the wine fade with the influx of caffeine; the normal effects of caffeine are counteracted by the remnants of wine and the lack of sleep: she is running on empty. She craves sleep.

Negotiating her way through the dark hallways of the upper floor of the house, Sarah judges that the risk of waking Michael with her entrance into the bedroom (he has been in bed the entire day) is too great. The thought of sleeping in Clytie's old bed strikes her as appropriate. Not only will she be alone, but the ritualistic nature of the past few hours will be allowed closure, ensuring the validity of her eureka. She glides over the wooden floor like an ice-skater, sliding to a stop at the door to Clytie's room. She pauses for a moment and listens to the wind pushing against the house. Clytie's room is a memorial of sorts, kept intact exactly as it was on the day of her death. Standing there in the dark, Sarah harbors no doubt that Jedidiah loved Clytie — loved her to the point of worship and could not bring himself to tell her of his former wife, his former child, his former life, in the fear that it would somehow taint their own union. She is willing to concede that Jedidiah's confession to Rebecca and Thomas was fueled by the desire to un-deify Clytie, to lay her to rest. Ironically, his action has exalted Clytie to the status of martyr. Striving for absolution, his reward is perdition. Now, in another twist of providence, Sarah, by occupying the memorial, will become a living monument to Clytie and, in doing so, will redeem Jedidiah. Dizzy with her sudden capacity to peer into the heart of the matter, she returns, in order to steady herself, her attention to the sound of the wind. She opens the door to Clytie's room.

The flames of two long, thin candles (sitting in a double-pronged candle holder on the night stand) flicker with the puff of air caused by the opening door. The air smells faintly of magnolia cast off by the melting wax. The curtains are drawn over the window and shudder with the concussion of the winds. On the bed, illumined by the soft glow of the candles, lie Cassandra and Rebecca. They lie on top of Clytie's quilt, naked to the waist, black silk panties agleam in the half-light. Rebecca lies on her back. Cassandra, on her stomach, rests her head on her elbow, auburn hair enshrouding both faces.

Cassandra tunes into Sarah's presence. Lifting her head from Rebecca's, she pushes, with splayed fingers, the hair from her face and looks into the darkness. In the next moment, she turns back to Rebecca, the candlelight tinting her hair gold, and lowers her mouth onto a nipple. She raises her face, an expression of joyful wickedness ballooning in her eyes as she attempts to focus on the silhouette, darker than the backdrop of the hallway, a living shadow, standing at the door. A smile on her face, Cassandra lowers her mouth once more.

The horse eye amulet, attached to a leather thong around Cassandra's neck, dangles between the women's breasts. The amber refracts candlelight.

Sarah averts her eyes to the tips of the flames on the candles. The flames are steady in the sudden, tomb-like stillness. She backs out of the room and gently, almost reverently, closes the door behind her. She whispers, "This will kill Jed." And, on tiptoes, as she starts down the hallway toward the living room couch, she murmurs, "Nobody will believe it. Nobody in this house believes anything."

Blanketflower *Gaillardia aristata*

The rain falls in sheets — sheets composed of minuscule droplets thrust northwesterly by waves of gusting wind. Isaac's New Yorker — the headlight beams sheering through the skyless night, the taillights like flickers of a red beacon glowing feebly from an island in the pouring rain — rolls down the highway. Isaac relies on the white line (designating the outer boundary of the road to his right), or, when the white line disintegrates from neglect and exposure to the elements and traffic, he looks to the center line — intermittently solid, dashed, and nonexistent — to maintain his bearings. A few miles back, during the ascent onto Shirley Rim, which Isaac negotiated through memory rather than physicality (due to the disorienting affects of the storm), he fiddled desperately with the knobs on the radio in an attempt to acquire human contact. Receiving nothing but static, he lit a cigarette and began humming an old war song. By the third rendition of the tune, vocal chords vibrating rhythmically, the vision of a soldier, *gray uniform of the Rebel Army tattered and stained with blood and the residue of gunpowder and grease, being carried on the shoulders of his comrades through the center of town, the facades of the buildings grimy with smoke and gaping holes, the streets strewn with the confetti of cannon fodder, the air acrid with smoke, the soldier's leg amputated, the stump swathed in discolored cotton rags, the men and boys shouting not because the soldier lives, but because the soldier alive represents hope for the hopeless cause, girls swooning, not because the soldier is a hero, but because the soldier is the epitome of Southern grotesquery, his eyes bulging, his grin the idiot grin of a man who can no longer distinguish between life and death*, reels through Isaac's mind.

He stops humming. The ash, hanging from the tip of the cigarette stuck between his lips, falls into his lap. He jerks the steering wheel. He jerks again. The center line returns to the left side of the car. He considers pulling over to calm his nerves, but the thought of another vehicle careening out of the darkness and crashing into the New Yorker pushes him onward.

Hands gripped tightly on the steering wheel, and focusing on the frail beams of the headlights which cut into the darkness surrounding him like a cave, he reconstructs the first of two phone calls received earlier (at dusk) while reclining on the couch empathizing with the furious piano of Liszt. Without radio contact, and with the sound of his own voice evoking unwelcome images, he can at least remember a voice other than his own. He can pretend that he is not alone, not traveling through a landscape void of familiarity due to the estranging nature of the storm:

The ring of the phone interrupted the flow of his musical meditations. The knotted muscle on the lower left side of his spine provoked a memory of when he was twelve-years-old, *stacking hay with Michael and Gabriel on the Crowheart. With sweat and flies in the corners of his eyes, he bends down to impale a bale of alfalfa with hay hooks so that he can buck it onto the gas-powered conveyor belt which transports the bales to the highest layer of the gargantuan stack, and, lifting the bale, he feels his back give way, hears a pop, and falls prone on a stubble of browning alfalfa stalks. The pitiless glare of the sun, magnified by tears, blinds him,* and he was forbidden by Jedidiah (prompted by Clytie) to ever help with the stacking of hay again.

The memory, when he sat up on the couch, was a scar that throbbed.

The phone was ringing.

He leapt off the couch, only to be doubled-over by the cramp in his back. Kinked with pain, he shuffled toward the phone. Just as he reached for the receiver, the phone stopped ringing. Forcing himself erect, he massaged his lumbar muscle for a moment and then walked to the curtain-covered picture window. He opened the curtains. Twilight oozed into the room. He stood staring out into the grizzled dusk, the pine trees at the edge of the parking lot twitching with the breeze. He was disappointed at having missed the phone call. The phone had not rung in four days.

Isaac watched as a late model black Volvo pulled into the parking lot. Two coeds, wearing shorts, halter-tops, sandals and sunglasses (fruitlessly courting the concept of summer with unseasonably brown skin), climbed out of the car. The scene struck Isaac as absurd. He smiled.

The phone began ringing again.

"Hello?"

"Ike?"

"Yeah?"

"It's Tom."

"Tommy?" He scanned the room attempting to focus in the half-light. He was momentarily unable to interpret the amorphous debris scattered about the living room.

"Yeah, Tommy. You know, your brother."

The awareness he was living in his own filth sparked a pang of shame. Relieved that Tommy was not physically present in the apartment (that Tommy's voice cannot see), Isaac said, "What's up?" He slipped into a facade of nonchalance. "Haven't heard from you in awhile."

"That's because you never call when you're supposed to. Didn't Cassy tell you to call me?"

"Uh, no. Maybe. I don't remember."

"She was supposed to."

"Maybe she did." Sensing the edge in Thomas' voice, he fell into a tone of appeasement. "She probably did. I must've forgot.

Haven't been home much lately. Busy as hell. Sorry."

"I don't give a shit about your apologies. Show a little respect for your family once in awhile."

In the pending silence, Isaac inferred that Thomas was cinching his anger like a saddle to his back, that he was not willing to turn it loose. He waited for Thomas to speak.

"Maybe you ought to get an answering machine or something. Both me and Sarah tried calling a bunch of times last week. No one picked up. We need to be able to get a hold of you. What if there's an emergency?"

In a spatter of memory, Isaac recalled the monotonous ringing of the phone and his unplugging it. He wondered when he plugged it back into the wall. "Why? What's happened?"

"Nothing," said Thomas. "It's nothing. I just need to get out of here for awhile. Get off the Crowheart. It seems like there's nothing *but* the Crowheart, like it's all I am. I need a change of scenery."

"I know what you mean," said Isaac.

"Tell me about it," said Thomas, his voice relaxing. "The Crowheart has a helluva appetite. She's always hungry."

Isaac grunted.

"Listen, I was wondering if I could come and stay with you for awhile. You know, get my head together. After Gabe marries Cassy and they start having kids, a lot of responsibility will fall on me. You know, to keep things running. I need a vacation."

At the mention of Cassandra, Isaac winced. "Sure. Maybe Sarah could drive you down. She never gets away."

"No. I don't want to ask her. I don't want to ask anybody. I want you to come and get me."

The knowledge that he has betrayed his family without provocation bursted inside Isaac like a festering boil; Thomas' voice, young and pleading, lanced the boil, and, after the excruciating pierce and the release of poison, the pain immediately subsided. He was buoyed by an inexplicable swell of hope, a sudden lightness. "Sure. Maybe I could drive up this weekend and get you." The cordless receiver was cradled in the crook of his neck, and he began picking beer cans off of the coffee table.

"Great. You don't know how much I appreciate it."

"No problem. I've been meaning to drive up anyway."

"I'll see you Saturday?"

"Yeah. Maybe the storm will have passed by then."

"Storm?"

"Yeah. There's supposed to be a big one brewing. It'll have played itself out by the weekend." As Isaac spoke, his arms were filled to capacity with beer cans. He made his way to the garbage can in the kitchen.

"Good. Saturday it is."

"Tommy?"

"Yeah?"

"Nothing."

"Don't stand me up on this one."

"I won't." The cans cascaded into the can. "I'll be there."

After hanging up the phone, Isaac spent the next two hours cleaning the apartment. Amazed at the amount of trash strewn about (Cassy cleaned only a few days earlier), he tuned the radio into a country station and washed the dishes. He then mopped the kitchen floor, disinfected the bathroom (with a solution of bleach and water mixed in the bathtub), vacuumed the carpet, sorted his dirty laundry into piles, and emptied the garbage. He carried a pile of laundry (he chose a pile of darks because he was too embarrassed to lug the urine, beer, and shit-stained whites into public view) down to the laundry room, only to be frustrated that all of the machines were in use. He carried the pile back to the apartment and stuffed the dirty clothes into the bedroom closet. He shaved and showered, mildly put off by the fact that he had no clean clothes to wear.

After drying himself with a green towel that smelled of mildew, he put on a pair of threadbare sweat pants and a t-shirt and walked barefoot down to the laundry room to check the status of the machines. Having applied his cheap cologne liberally (to mask the slight stench of his soiled clothes), the bouquet of his passing lingered in the hallways of the building. Music, television, voices, and laughter issued from behind the closed doors of the apartments as he walked by. The sounds of human leisure somehow mollified Isaac. Upon finding the row of washing machines in use, he did not think twice about it. On the way back to his apartment, smiling after two young boys who dodged past him on roller blades, he decided to write a letter to Paul. In the letter he will inform Paul that he, along with his youngest and favorite brother, are going to be driving over for a visit. The prospect of bonding with Thomas on the road, and seeing Paul and Eva, filled Isaac with an almost unbearable levity. There would be time enough for dirty laundry in the light of day. Back in the apartment, he turned on all the lights and opened the sliding picture window, the rush of brisk air stimulating him further.

After removing the lump of towels from the top of the computer in his bedroom, he sat down, turned on the computer, opened a word processing program and began formatting a letter to Paul. The phone rang. Thinking it was Thomas calling back to confirm the plan one last time, he trotted to the phone and picked up the receiver.

Before he was able speak, a woman's voice — a voice piqued with fear — said, "Isaac?"

"Yeah. Who's this?"

A moment of pinched silence. "Sarah. It's Sarah. You've need to come home."

"What? What's wrong?"

"Come home, Isaac. I need you here. The family needs you here."

The gravity of Sarah's voice pulled at Isaac. "Okay. I'll come. Just tell me what's wrong."

"Come now. Before the storm hits."

"Okay. I'll come tonight." The panic in Sarah's voice trickled through the phone line and lodged in Isaac's chest. "Is somebody hurt?"

"Cassy...."

The image of Cassandra lying in a bathtub full of water the color of cranberry juice blazed through Isaac's mind. "Cassy?"

"It's not something I can go into over the phone. Come home."

The receiver buzzed dead in Isaac's ear. Silently cursing the logic of women, he realized the conversation was at an end and hung up the phone. Calling Sarah back would be fruitless, so, without further recourse, he loaded the trunk of the New Yorker with dirty clothes and headed into the night.

Isaac turns off the two-lane highway, headlights glistening on the saturated asphalt, and onto the dirt road which leads to the Crowheart. The wish for lightning to illuminate his way home flashes through his mind while he concentrates on keeping the car on the sloppy road. The ruts in the road, driven into the land by pickups and horse trailers, are wider than the wheelbase of the New Yorker. Western wheat, thistle, and pigweed, growing between the ruts, brush the undercarriage of the car. Isaac drops the automatic transmission into low and lights one of his three remaining cigarettes. Rain falls. Under the glare of the headlights, puddles in the road explode with fresh droplets. Isaac, again, wishes for lightning.

He clicks on the radio and turns the tuning knob slowly, with the precision of a surgeon, hoping to lock onto an AM station. The radio hisses static. The only signal that sticks is a Christian station out of Crowhaven. Isaac listens to the disembodied voice of a man who sounds as if he is in the throes of emphysema. He is advising all listeners to realize their sins and take Jesus into their hearts so that they might be forgiven. The transmitter, Isaac speculates, must be near, allowing the voice to cut through the storm. He tries to remember a radio transmitter in the vicinity, pulsing lonely on a hill, but cannot. Maybe it is some sort of omen, he thinks, but an omen of what? Everyone has sinned against one dogma or another, one god or another. Who can forgive infractions against Christ, Mohammed, Mithra, Zoroaster and Yahweh? An omen of what?

Taking his eyes from the road, he looks to the overflowing ashtray and searches for firm ground to crush the butt of his cigarette. The front right tire of the New Yorker sinks into a pothole. By the sound of metal colliding with earth, Isaac knows the car is high-centered. A woman with a feathery voice sings a song, against a backdrop of harps, about an alcoholic prostitute who saw the light in the labyrinth of sorrow and was saved. Isaac turns off the ignition, cutting the song short, and listens to rain drops striking the car. He wishes for lightning.

Switching off the radio before starting the car, he attempts to back out of the pothole. A back tire spins. He turns off the ignition, and, after a brief debate on whether or not to sleep in the car (he is in no great hurry, now that he is close, to get to the big house), he opens the door and steps out into the rain. Surprisingly, the rain is warm, and Isaac has difficulty distinguishing between it and the balls of sweat dripping from his armpits. The air is still. He shuts the car door which extinguishes the dome light inside. He is engulfed in darkness. Teetering like a blind man on a catwalk, he attempts to keep his footing on the strip of land between the ruts in the road. The pigweed and thistle are slick with moisture. Within a few steps, he slips and falls into a puddle. He lays in the rut (the material of his sweat pants and t-shirt quickly absorbing water), listening to the raindrops plopping in the puddle. He considers returning to the car and waiting out the storm, but, since the rain and air are warm and sitting in the car would chill him more than continuing on in the darkness, he stands and presses on. He estimates the big house no further than three miles.

A few hundred yards from the car, his tennis shoes gushing with mud and water so that maintaining his balance is, at best, precarious, he stops and takes off his shoes. Since his sweat pants and t-shirt are saturated to the point of being a burden, he strips them off as well. The soles of his feet are tender from disuse. He carries his clothes around his neck like a yoke, his shoes in either hand. He crosses from rut to rut, keeping to the puddles in the road, the soft mud under his feet.

As his eyes adjust to the darkness, he is able to travel faster. Alone in the night, with the rich smell of earth and water clogging his nostrils, the sound of falling rain in his ears, thoughts of family, college, responsibility, and sorrows diminish until Isaac simply *is:* the rain washes away his humanity. He no longer wishes for lightning. For the moment his only care is to avoid sharp stones along the path.

The big house looms, darker than the night, as Isaac approaches. At first, he interprets the dark mass as a gigantic cloud, the nerve center of the storm hanging over the Crowheart. When he gets closer, and can hear the snorting of horses in the corral, he ascertains that it is not the storm at all but his home, the place where he was raised. Humanity returns. The first emotion to wash over him: regret. Intellectualizing this emotion dredges up the thought of the poetry he used to write — poetry inspired by Clytie — poetry burned in the fireplace, inside of the big house, the night of her death. He stops and dons his clothes in the pouring rain.

The scent of water and earth becomes tinctured with the fragrance of horse manure as Isaac gets closer to the corrals. Stepping onto the gravel which covers the driveway, he kneels down and puts on his shoes. Without so much as a yap, the blue heeler, Grendel, darts out of the darkness and leaps on Isaac. Startled, Isaac pushes the dog away. Realizing that it is only his old friend come out to welcome his arrival home, he kneels once more and allows the dog to lick his face, and paw him, and streak him with mud. He massages the inside of the dog's big ears enjoying the stink of the wet fur; the dog dissolves into a relaxed lump at his feet. When Isaac stands up and starts for the house, the dog is at his heels.

He is surprised to find Wade Ksaslmque sitting in Clytie's old rocking chair on the porch. Isaac has often wondered why the old Basque has chosen to spend the shank of his life on the Crowheart where there is no chance for advancement or real advantage. Yet, he has been there since before Isaac was born, before Jedidiah, before memory, it seems. The old man rocks slowly back and forth, a bottle of whiskey cradled between his legs. He is shirtless wearing a pair of bib-overalls. His face is wrinkled, weathered around the eyes, and tough like leather. He has grown a gray beard since the last time Isaac saw him. He twists the cap off of the bottle and takes a drink.

"Good morning," says Wade, offering the bottle to Isaac. "I knew you'd come."

Isaac stands on the porch in perplexed silence. The old man strikes him as more apparition than flesh.

"It's none of my business, but I wouldn't go in there if I were you." He takes another drink from the bottle and twists the cap back on. "Some sort of sickness in there. Young Thomas is the only one that comes in or out. I been taking orders from him." He chuckles. "Ain't that funny? An old man like me, who knows this ranch better than anybody alive taking orders from a kid?" He scratches his beard. "Don't get me wrong, now. I don't mean no disrespect. Thomas is a good kid, and, when it comes right down to it, the place is running smoother than it has in a good long spell. A long spell." He twists the cap off the bottle and takes another drink. "He's good for the Crowheart, Thomas is; they understand each other. He's different from the rest of you." He holds the bottle out once more in offering. "You better take a drink of this before a chill sets into your bones."

Isaac takes the bottle and holds it to his lips. The whiskey nourishes him.

"I figured on calling old Doc Watson," continues Wade, "but Thomas told me not to bother with it because 'everything will be just fine once Isaac comes home'. Just the same, I wouldn't go in there if I was you. I'd go over to the old school house and call Doc Watson. Phone line works in there. Ain't no sense in infecting yourself if you can help it. Course, on the other hand, maybe you're immune to it, like Thomas seems to be. I always said you two were cut out of the same pattern. More than brothers, I always said."

After taking another pull of whiskey, Isaac hands the bottle back to the old man. He cannot bring himself to speak. He walks across the porch, opens the screen door, and enters the house.

Once inside, the door closed safely behind him, a tremor originating at the top of his skull and coursing to his heels snakes through Isaac. All is dark and quiet and cold. He takes off his shoes and places them on the floor in the entryway. Shying away from the switch on the wall, which would flood the kitchen with light, he feels his way through the darkness to the drawer where flashlights are stowed. Taking a flashlight in hand, he clicks it on and beams the light on the floor at his feet. He negotiates his way through the kitchen. He finds it strange that the room is void of odor. Not a remnant of gravy or stew or cleaning solutions...nothing. Suddenly paranoid that if he does not get out of the wet clothes immediately, he will contract a lingering illness, he makes his way up the stairs, through the dark hallways, toward Clytie's room. (The thought that the flashlight seeping under closed doors might cause Michael or Gabriel or Thomas to think there is a prowler in the house crosses Isaac's mind, but he does not dare turn it off for fear he might stumble into a wall or door and surely awaken the sleepers.)

Once there, in Clytie's room, he shuts the door as quietly as possible, makes his way over to the bed, clicks off the flashlight, and strips off his clothes. The room smells of gardenias. Crawling into the bed, he huddles under his mother's quilt. He thinks about burnt poetry. Between stalking sleep and wakefulness, he remembers Clytie: *The family trip to Disneyland which ruined her nerves; the hours spent in the living room listening to classical music, reading verse penned by immortals, drinking wine, playing the piano; how she lived in this room, refusing to exit, and the hours spent sitting on the bed discussing astronomy, philosophy, art and the possibility of God; her hands caressing his hair, hands, and face; the scent of woman in darkness; the eternally febrile eyes and the screams reaching his ears as he lay by the horse fountain writing poems which, after months of prodding, he had consented to share; the goodbye; the death; the refusal to attend the funeral on top of the rise looking out over the horse pastures....* A bolt of lightning outside of the window illuminates the room in spite of the drawn curtains. The reverie is shattered by a clap of thunder. He wonders to what extent his memories of Clytie are tainted by his love for her. What was it that happened between them? Sleep annihilates consciousness, and Isaac's mind is filled with images that will be obliterated by the light of morning. Rain continues to fall.

"I'm not denying anything. Why should I?"

"So you admit it?"

"Admit what?"

"This is not the time for games."

"Really? I think it's the perfect time."

"It's not natural. I won't have this land stained by a curse brought on by the likes of you. Do you understand me?"

"Ha! You want to bring God into this? The stories I could tell. My lips to His ears. Let's talk about the nature of curses."

"You are not a part of this family. You have no right."

"Does copulation constitute a vow in your little book of rules?"

"And you will never be a part of this family."

"Stop it! Both of you. Just stop it. This won't help anything."

"They can't stop. It's too late."

"What will help?"

The words enter Isaac's subconscious and reverberate like a struck gong. He opens his eyes to darkness. He is warm under the quilt. The voices, agitated with varying emotions, are familiar yet strange, disembodied, hailing from some foreign land.

"Why did you have to do it? Do you hate us all that much?"

"I don't hate you. You've got it all twisted into some macabre tale of evil incarnate. Turn what you're thinking in on itself and maybe you'll catch a glimpse of who I really am."

"What? You're making yourself out to be a saint?"

Isaac attempts to purge the voices by burying his head under the pillow. He closes his eyes in the vain hope of denser darkness. The voices, like dripping faucets to an insomniac, continue:

"If she's a saint, she's a goddamn saint."

"Shut the fuck up. I'm sick of it and it stops now."

"She could be. Anything's possible."

"I said to stop with the bullshit. Now. I'll have no more of it in this house!"

"Who are you, the heir-apparent? Maybe a Pretender?"

"Shut up! Everybody just shut up! Can't this wait until the light of day? Nothing's getting solved here."

"No. I want this done and over with now."

"Who are you?"

"Who let that goddamn dog in here? Doesn't anybody follow the rules?"

"Whose rules?"

"I did. She's the only one that makes any sense."

"Put her out."

"Leave him alone."

"Now, Tommy. *Do it now or pay the consequences."*

With the naming, the sound of the rain against the windowpanes comes alive in Isaac's ears. He knows where he is. The insides of his thighs itch. The scent of coconut on the pillowcase momentarily blocks the voices rising from the kitchen. As he concentrates on the scent, he believes that he can distinguish a hint of Cassandra's perfume of the fabric. But the belief is not strong enough to deny the rising voices:

"Let's go ask him what he thinks." says Thomas.

"Shut up," says Michael.

"Why don't we go ask her?" says Sarah.

"Let's just leave it be until daylight," says Gabriel.

"It's not going to change anything," says Cassandra. "What's done is done."

"How can you sit there like it's nothing?" says Michael. "Do you realize what this little bitch has done? Do you realize what she's done to *you*?"

"Let's not stoop to calling each other names," says Gabriel.

Isaac throws off the quilt and scratches his thighs. The room is cold. Ignoring the conversation from below, he gets out of the bed, stubs his toe on the bedpost (taking the pain in silence), finds the closet, and searches for something to ward off the chill. His hand comes into contact with a smooth fabric, and he pulls the garment from the hanger. After a series of rapid gropes, he ascertains it is a robe. He puts the robe on, ties the sash, and leaves the room without ever having turned on a light.

The bright light in the kitchen bursts upon Isaac's vision. The figures of Michael, Sarah, Gabriel, Cassandra, and Thomas vibrate with a greater effluence than the electric lights hanging from the ceiling. Gabriel sits at the table, cradling a steaming cup of coffee between his palms. Thomas crouches on his haunches in the entryway between the kitchen and the porch, scratching the dog's ears; he is tense, as if waiting for the starting gun to dash out of the big house into the wet darkness. Michael, Cassandra, and Sarah form a triangle in the center of the kitchen, eyes flashing like lightning exhumed from the night sky.

Isaac's vision stabilizes before his presence is known. The fact that everyone in the kitchen is wearing a bathrobe strikes him as slightly amusing. He feels as if he has wandered into an arcane club, uninvited and unannounced. The smooth skin covering Cassandra and Ruth's calves contrasts sharply with the hair-covered calves of Michael and Gabriel. Because he is crouching, Thomas' calves are covered by the dingy-white material of his robe. The rain, driven by an upstart wind, lashes against the big house.

Isaac's relative amusement is stifled when all eyes shift to him. He looks at his feet and notices his toe nails need to be clipped.

The dog trots over to Isaac and wags its stump tail. Isaac stoops down to scratch the dog's ears. It occurs to Isaac that dogs should play a more significant role in poetry. Dogs and horses — both possess a keen understanding of the rhythms of rain.

"Ike?" says Gabriel. "When did you come home?"

Isaac continues scratching the dog. "A few hours ago. I think." When he notices that he is wearing the lavender, satin robe embroidered with pink roses which Clytie wore once each year (before she became pregnant with Thomas) on the night of the anniversary of her marriage to Jedidiah, his mind goes blank. The robe falls to his mid-thigh.

"I didn't hear you pull up," says Gabriel. "I've been awake quite awhile."

Isaac seizes the opportunity to reason through short-term memory. "I got stuck. Had to walk a few miles."

"Thought I heard somebody talking." says Thomas, and, when he stands, he is visibly relaxed. "But there was just one voice, so I figured I was hearing things. Or dreaming." His smile, rather than mocking, conveys an expression of solace.

"Wade was on the porch," says Isaac, still stooping, watching the dog watching him. "He was sitting in the rocking chair nursing a bottle."

"Wade?" asks Gabriel. "What the hell would Wade be doing on the porch in the middle of the night?"

"My fault," says Thomas. "I told him to keep an eye out for Ike. Didn't think he'd take it so serious." He turns, walks into the landing, and looks through the screen door onto the porch.

"Nobody told me you were coming," says Gabriel. "Then again nobody tells me anything. I'm used to it."

"Isn't that the truth." says Sarah. She glares at Cassandra, who ignores her.

Thomas returns to the kitchen and sits at the table next to Gabriel. "Well, he's gone now. Must've figured his job was done and went to sleep it off." He takes the cup from between Gabriel's palms. "Thought I was dreaming that voice. Weird." He takes a sip of coffee.

Gabriel takes the cup from Thomas. "Get your own. And get some for Ike while you're at it. He looks like he could use some."

"He sure does," says Thomas.

Michael, Cassandra, and Sarah stand in the center of the kitchen, arms folded over their chests like stoic Indian chiefs. They watch as Thomas pours two cups of coffee then carries one over to Isaac.

Isaac, still in the entryway to the kitchen, must stand erect in order to receive the cup of coffee.

"You want cream?" asks Thomas.

"No. Thanks."

"You sure? Gabe brewed it as strong as Texas mule piss." Thomas walks to the table and sits.

Michael, his astonishment now finally giving way to fury, is able to speak. "What is this? The prodigal son returns so now we slaughter the fatted-calf for him? This is insane."

"Relax," says Gabriel. "Getting pissed won't change anything. And anyhow, I'm worn out. Too tired for all this feeling."

"I'm *already* pissed," says Michael. Now that he has broken his silence, the words snap out like gunfire, "Dear Ike comes home for weddings and crises, and the whole family treats him like some sort of holy man who can do miracles." He trains his eyes on Gabriel, as if Isaac is not in the room. "When, in fact, he's nothing more than a stranger in a strange land. Maybe if he would of stuck around like he was supposed to, he could have worked some of his miracles, and the ranch wouldn't be going to shit."

"Leave him be," says Thomas. "He didn't do anything."

"That's my point," says Michael, still looking at Gabriel.

"He's *no* saint," says Cassandra, not brave enough to catch Isaac's eyes. She walks over to the table and sits down next to Thomas. "I can attest to that."

Sarah moves to her husband's side and takes his hand in her own. "Gabe's right. Anger isn't going to solve anything. Neither is blaming Ike. We all need to relax."

The taste of coffee stabilizes Isaac. Confident that his liaison with Cassandra has not been revealed, he allows the anger provoked by Michael to rise. He says: "Stranger or not, saint or sinner, I'm here, so you may as well acknowledge my presence and fill me in. What's the big deal this time? What? Did the Old Man decide to sell the place? That *would* be a tragedy."

Emotion, lulled by the sound of falling rain, causes Sarah to speak dreamily, as if viewing a phantasm from afar, "Well," she begins, "Jedidiah was married before he married Clytie, and he had a child who he had to give up because she reminded him of the mother who died. And he could bear none of it." As she speaks, she looks not at Isaac, but the darkness behind him. "He had to give up the ghost." A thin smile germinates at the corners of her mouth. "And Cassy is in love with Rebecca because she wants to be the mother of the Daniels family and can see no other way. And there you have it, a thumbnail version of the Daniels *tragedy*." She falls silent and looks at the dog sitting at Isaac's feet.

"Please," says Cassandra, shaking her head. She pulls her robe close about her neck.

"That's it in a nutshell," corroborates Gabriel, his tone removed, as if responding to an academic lecture. "There you have it."

"Except she forgot to start it off with 'Once upon a time,'" says Cassandra.

Sarah releases Michael's hand and walks to the table. She sits next to Gabriel and lowers her head into her palms.

Gabriel takes a sip of coffee and listens to the falling rain. "Well, nothing's really changed," he says. "There's still work to be done. The ranch has to function. We're stuck with it whether we like it or not. We'll just have to learn to live with it."

"Stuck with what?" asks Thomas. "We don't even know if any of it's true."

Isaac is dumfounded. He cannot take his eyes off the dog sitting at his feet.

Michael shuffles over to the windows above the sinks and looks out into the thinning darkness. "I suppose you're still going to marry that tramp after all this?"

"After all what?" asks Cassandra. "I haven't admitted to anything. It's Sarah's word against mine, and anybody can see she's delusional."

Michael ignores Cassandra. "Maybe when the Old Man finds out he'll act like it's no big deal." His voice is calm. "Who knows, maybe he can have two wives. We won't tell. We can learn to live with just about anything, can't we?"

Thomas, cradling the warm cup between his hands, looks at Isaac with an expression of loss pulling at his eyes and lips.

"Nothing's really changed," says Gabriel. "Unless it keeps on raining and the floods ruin the pastures, nothing's really changed. Nothing really matters except the ranch. No matter what happens, we got to stick together for the sake of the ranch."

Sarah lifts her head from her hands and looks at Gabriel.

"Wait a minute." Cassandra's voice is crisp with conviction. "Who in the hell do you people think you are?" She stands, moves over to the coffee pot, and pours a cup of coffee. "As usual, the boys are interpreting things any old way that suits them." She takes a sip from her cup, grimaces as the coffee scalds her lips, and turns to face her audience. "Before you stick your ignorant little heads together and agree on what myth to exalt into the realm of a Daniels' archetype, let me tell my version of the truth." She leans back against the refrigerator. "Mike here wants to banish me from the family, but it's too late for that. Even if you kick me off the Crowheart you'll always remember me. All of you will remember me to your graves. That makes me a part of the family." She dips her index finger into her coffee, then sucks it. "Let's see, Uncle Francis loved me, Gabe loves me, Mike hates me, Tommy wants me, and Ike doesn't know a good thing even after tasting it. Ike rejects me. Finally, Mike and Ike have something in common. So, Sarah was partially correct in her evaluation of my psychology. The thing she got wrong is that I *am* the queen bee of this family. It's just that nobody wants to admit it." She looks at Isaac who looks at the dog sitting at his feet. "Well, now that we understand each other, you all can go on with your myth-making. I resign my post. I'll always love you Ike. I'll always know that you're heart is with me, even if your thoughts are not. I'll always remember our night together."

Isaac snaps his eyes to Cassandra's. "What, is all this nonsense about Rebecca?"

"Oh, she's better for my mental health, but she'll never be you."

"What?" asks Gabriel. "What night?"

"Ask your brother," says Cassandra. "Maybe his answer will shatter your illusions, and the healing process can begin."

"So it's true?" asks Thomas. "About you and Rebecca?"

"Everything's true," says Cassandra. "Nothing's false. As my last act as queen, I order you all to affirm everything!" She convulses with laughter.

In one motion, Michael crosses to Cassandra and slugs her with an overhand right. Cassandra falls to the floor. Blood gushes from her mouth.

For a moment, the reaction of all is like a theater audience watching a play in which the acting is suspect: the absurdity of the action is beyond their scope of suspending disbelief.

In the next moment, Gabriel springs out of his chair and falls upon Michael. Gabriel thrusts a thumb into Michael's eye socket. The brothers collapse into a heap on the floor next to Cassandra. The dog, loyalties confused, joins the fray, snapping haphazardly. Michael grips Gabriel's throat, stifling the cry of pain brought on by the dog biting into his exposed thigh. The dog releases it's grip on Gabriel and bites Michael on the buttock. Gabriel, scrambling to take advantage of Michael's relaxed grip on his throat, accidentally kicks Cassandra in the head.

The blow to Cassandra prompts the others into action. As if on cue, Isaac, Thomas, and Sarah combine forces and fall upon the two combatants. Neither Michael nor Gabriel resist being pulled apart. The entire group (except for Cassandra) stands in the middle of the kitchen looking at one another.

It is Thomas who speaks first. "Jesus," he says, looking at Michael, "he put your eye out."

Gabriel, also looking at the bloody wound which was once his brother's eye, croaks, "I'm sorry. I love her. I'll always love her."

"What in the holy hell is going on down here?" Jedidiah, wearing a black robe, stands in the entryway to the kitchen.

Rebecca rushes past her husband and kneels by Cassandra's side. She wears a green robe. She cradles Cassandra's head in her lap.

"I asked a goddamn question. What's going on here? Have you all gone mad?"

"Nothing's really changed," says Sarah. She looks at Jedidiah confusedly, as if she cannot understand why he does not understand.

Michael sits at the table covering his wounded eye with his hands.

"Call Doc Watson," says Isaac.

Thomas looks at Isaac and nods. He turns, hesitates, changes direction, hesitates once more, and walks over to the phone.

Cassandra moans from her position on the floor.

"Well?" commands Jedidiah.

Isaac looks at his father, his eyes like gravitons. "Not now. This is your fault. Not now."

After hanging up the phone, Thomas turns around to find everyone staring at him. "He's on his way. I just hope he doesn't get stuck."

They all look at him and blink.
"I mean with all this rain. The land's a mess."

Paul,

My apologies for writing another irksome letter before allowing you sufficient time to respond to the last. I write to you from a house divided, and I saw no other recourse but to seek out a detached view on the whole mess. And, as you are one of the few people I consider worthy of independent thought, combined with the fact that you have never been exposed to any member of my family long enough to become infected with our particular disorder but are, nevertheless, informed (albeit through my biased view) as to the peculiarities of our particular affliction, you, therefore, by default, are the only choice I have. And I must communicate. It is not so much that I need you to respond to this letter. It is more that I need to write it with a specific audience in mind. I know that I am a burden to you, and for that I apologize. I thought about addressing this letter to Eva, but crossing the abyss of silence which has existed between us for so long now would require a feat of engineering of which I am no longer capable. Through a series of events which lack coherence, I feel like the demon of insanity has set its sights on me. Because I cannot accept an existence based on chance, the universe as random, the demon attempts to thwart any form of order that is familiar to me. Nothing makes sense. Faith, by definition, is absurd, but at least the acceptance of that form of absurdity is latent with the possibility of progressive possibility — we are allowed to imagine something higher than ourselves, a form of reason that we strive to attain but are unable to apprehend through the five senses. To labor under the catch-22 of faith is far more appealing than a universe full of random possibility in which the vehicle of the senses is, at best, a degenerative mode of interpretation — a hallucinogen which evokes mass delusion in humans. The so called "post-modernists" fashion themselves as the new ascetics, a breed capable of coping with the random nature of the universe. Their form of beauty is vile. They have allowed themselves to become slaves to the drug, and, like any addict, they will murder, cheat, and steal...anything to maintain their habits. Nothing is sacred.

My faith (or lack of it) wears thin. I no longer trust myself to interpret the input of my senses. Help me, Paul. Help me, Lizard King. Help me exorcize the demon.

I suppose, having been raised on a ranch in Wyoming, I have been conditioned to put my trust in family. Trust is a form of obsession. Now that my family must either redefine itself or perish, I find myself waiting for the hero of the pulp Western — the handsome and adept stranger, the loner — to ride into the thick of the plot and save the day. I have even gone so far as to designate myself as that loner (in many ways, my family consists of strangers), but abandon the idea when I come to the inevitable conclusion that "the loner", at first glorified and heralded as a sort of King Arthur, is, by the end of the formula, forced, however willingly, into creating a new concept of family (which usually includes the buxom and fiercely independent daughter of the suffering land) and then must patiently wait for the next crisis to arise and the next loner to appear. "Everything is in constant flux," Heraclitus wrote and then wept. Where is the eternal? Was it ever there?

Does this line of thinking fall in with your concept of allegory? Metaphor is the daughter of myth, and, it seems to me, the child must now watch its mother die a most ignoble death. The snake, having plundered its food source, consumes its own tail so as not to starve. The daughter, of course, watches through binoculars at a safe distance.

Due to insomnia and a lack of gumption, I was watching a Clint Eastwood Spaghetti Western the other night. Unlike the pulp Western novel (I am generalizing here because the entire notion is moot), pulp Western films forgo the conversion of "loner-into-family man." Or, at least, in the films the loner's *desire* to stabilize into the jurisprudence of family is avoided. The films (because of their length as much of anything) are *not* obligated to complete the myth cycle; they are merely episodes pertaining to the cycle; the obligation ends there. The novels, because of the length of the story and the fact that they must employ words rather than images and sounds, by nature, achieve greater depth and must address the cycle as a whole. What does this all mean? You figure it out.

I have already related to you in some detail the episode of the murder/suicide. I wish to touch upon it one last time in order that we might extend our orphaned metaphor. I think you will agree that suicide is the penultimate act of self-destruction. And yet, from experience, we know that those prone to suicide (we have all, to a greater or lesser degree, been there) attach to the concept a certain romantic notion, a certain beauty that can only be found in the tragic. (Post-modernism is a form of suicide.) Why is this? Why is self-destruction so often appealing to the human psyche? I am not attempting to answer the question. My only intention is to bring the question to light. So what is my point? I can see you reading this and becoming more irritated with each sentence. You think I have contradicted myself into a corner of nihilism. Take heart. A little patience. Things will end soon enough. The Jewish mystics contemplate the Cabalah for years on end in the hopes of coupling symbol with reality. Go take a piss and grab a beer. Tell Eva that you love her. Then come back and either read on, or crumple this letter and burn it. Either way, you will be done once and for all with the thing you called Isaac Daniels.

* * * *

I knew you would return. So, after eating an avocado and tomato sandwich and having a few beers, I return to you. I guess that I should clarify that my father's wife, my brother's fiancé, and my brother Tommy are all living with me for the time being. They opted to abandon the haven of the Crowheart to reside in my little hell. Slumming? Maybe. At least I expect nothing of them. They have freedom here. Maybe freedom has turned into a slum. Rebecca insists that we eat plenty of vegetables and fruit. I thought I was in love with her once. Remember? Cassy dotes over Rebecca and Tommy like they are her own little hatchlings. I still love Cassy. The fact that she is sleeping with Rebecca doesn't bother me, except that maybe I'm a little jealous. They seem so happy in the heights of broken taboo. They will have to succumb to gravity eventually though. Tommy? I worry about Tommy. Outside of the Crowheart he does not know who he is.

Enough drivel concerning the tedious and mundane crisis of my tired lot. Let us return to the one-sided conversation: When it comes right down to it, I am not concerned with the nature of suicide. What interests me is the phenomena of murder/suicide, which seems to be a case of having your cake and eating it too. The phenomena is not uncommon in the annals of recorded history. Suicide is a solitary act. Murder/suicide is a crime in which the criminal becomes a judge and executioner who demands nothing less than the death penalty: The individual, through his crime, is exalted into a microcosmic version of society as a whole. Or, in the negative version, the murderer is a coward unable to accept the burden of his crime.

Why did Tom murder Jeff and attempt to murder you before turning the gun on himself? We have been here before, but our conclusions are empty. Why? Anger? Vindictiveness? Cynicism in its most volatile form? None of the above. Crimes provoke negative responses in surviving victims, but could it be that the survivors, because they survived, misread the intentions of the suicide/murderer? Could it be that Tom, attaching romantic notions to his plan of action, shot Jeff and you as an act of love — out of a desire to create a family that would not, could not, leave him? Could it be that Tom was like the loner who, after rescuing the good and pure family from certain disaster (family rending disaster), must ride off into the sunset alone, yearning for a family of his own? Why not? According to all evidence (the matter of Lazarus, and, for that matter, Christ Himself, is highly suspect), death is eternal. Was Tom striving to create something that would stand the test of time? It seems our little orphan metaphor is defying the sensyfying nature of human inquiry and that will be its not-so-meager contribution to human evolution. Who can condemn a man for loving and striving for the very things society has embedded into the generations of his psychological makeup: family and eternal life? Not I. And as for Jeff? A by-product of a concept gone awry — a concept turned in on itself, rotting from the inside out like a salmon after it has served its purpose. Should we — Eva, you, and I — as survivors, pick up where Tom left off? Work the kinks out?

The Daniels family has been divided by the actions of its members — individuals interpreting family myths and family lies, each to their own liking. It is difficult to ascertain which is the myth and which is the lie, and herein lies the danger. Is a unifying theory possible? If not, which is the proper course: To endure, or to die?

My mother once told me that if you make a habit at looking at life straight on, you will eventually go insane. On the other hand, she said, if you will yourself to be happy (force yourself into a voluntary state of delusion), you might live out your days without ever having to cope with the irony of existence. I wrote a poem based on her words, and, after a number of visions and revisions, because I could not invent the imagery to capture the concept, I burned it on a pyre of straw, in the horse barn, on a winter's night. The horses — huddled in their stables with blankets draped over their backs, steam rising from them, the smell of urine and manure in the air — watched me with luminous eyes. That was the first poem I ever burned. Looking back, that act foreshadowed all which was to come after my Clytie died.

The word "family" (in both a contemporary and historical sense, both before and after the advent of Christ) can be defined as an ongoing cycle of forgiveness. Think about it. Familial bonds are ruptured only (and don't speak to me about exceptions; I know there are always exceptions; what we are concerned with is the rule of thumb) when one member of the family refuses to forgive another member for whatever transgression. The rupturing need not be caused by a single catastrophic event. It can be the result of any number of small and seemingly insignificant trespasses which build up like sediment in the offended's mind until the sediment, through the weight of experience, is transmuted into rock and a single-minded purpose is born: Revenge. This simple formula can be applied to any human relationship, but, when applied to the family, it is the most potent. The family (a miniature tribe) can safely be deemed the cornerstone of civilization.

My mother had a secret. She took her secret to the grave. Because the seed of that secret has never been germinated by the fire of scandal, the collective memory of Clytie has achieved the stature of myth: *After the birth of her son Isaac, Clytie moved all of the things that she held dear — her bed, the crib that each of her boys rested in as babes, her volumes of poetry and literature, an incense burner of Egyptian origin (inherited from some lost relative), a mirror of unknown origin, an antique bottle of unopened perfume, a hairbrush with boar bristles which, as soon as he possessed the coordination, Isaac would brush his mother's hair with each and every night (she called the ritual "the gloaming") — moved them into a separate room from her husband. She would have had the piano hauled into the room if it had been possible to get it up the stairs and through the narrow doorway. She never told anyone her reasoning behind the move. Nobody asked.*

My father is prideful. Clytie abandoning his room must have wounded him deeply, come as a shock to his sense of sovereignty, and yet, as far back as I can remember, he acted like Clytie's move was no big deal. A wife forsaking her husband's bed (a husband choosing to sleep alone is common and accepted) reeks of impending travesty. And yet the Daniel's household functioned as if propriety was not only being adhered to, but exalted. Because our family was different, we had to either extol our situation as superior or suffer the stigma of shame. Since Clytie never bothered to explain her motives, and father cast a blind eye on that which he could not tame, the questions concerning Clytie (now that she is dead) are forever enigmatic. Doubt is fertilizer for growing ghosts. Ghosts are the harbingers of myth.

Clytie never spoke about her past. When asked about her life before becoming a Daniels, she skirted the questions by reciting fragments of poems. If the questions persisted, she flushed with agitation, then retreated to the piano, playing arrangements by Liszt. Not even Jedidiah seemed to know much about her, beyond their first encounter at the funeral of some obscure family friend. It was as if Clytie materialized out of the ether to give birth to Michael, Gabriel, Isaac, and Thomas Daniels.

Isaac slept on-and-off in Clytie's room from birth to the age of fourteen. This, of course, had a profound impact on the makeup of Isaac's psychology. Perhaps an even greater impact came from the fact that the remainder of the family posed no objections to this apparently unnatural state of affairs. In fact, they bestowed upon this mysterious union a silent and angelic reverie. That is, our actions were not only beyond reproach, but somehow fortified with a morality beyond the comprehension of the mass of men.

Another case of exaltation to purge the stigmata of shame? You tell me.

Did I sleep with my mother? Yes. Many nights after reading or listening to music I would fall asleep in her bed. For the most part, however, while residing in Clytie's room, I slept on an old cot purchased from the Army Surplus in Crowhaven. Did I have sexual relations with my mother? I don't know. At times I remember touching her, her touching me, the scent of her hair and breath, but I can't be sure that these memories are not distorted by shame, or desire, or both. No matter how I try to classify these memories — analyze them, categorize them — *I will never be capable of demythologizing them.* I do not know. And because I do not know (I have considered the idea of hypnotism, but rejected it because of the subconscious propensity to create a separate reality out of memory), there is the possibility that Tommy is both my son and my brother. I suspect that the entire family harbors this notion. And, as the foundation of our collective fancy (the fancy that the Daniels are somehow above the laws of men) liquefies under the pressure of our silence, we are torn asunder. The time has come for our specters to devour us — Medea has risen from the grave. Individual members of the family choose other atrocities, either real or imagined, as pulpits from which to scream for justice. The house is divided, and will continue to divide until the concept of unity is but a dream. The Daniels family, like a mad scorpion, is stinging itself to death. There is nothing left to do but let the poison run its course. There is no cure. No escape.

Or is there? Driving home to attend my father's marriage to Rebecca, I came upon a dead horse laying rigid and bloated in the ditch next to the road. I pulled over, got out of the car, and, for a moment, looked into the horse's glazed and ruined eye. Never mind. There is no sense in replacing one addiction for another, alcohol for religion. I can only hope that the demise of the Daniel's family is not too grisly and is allowed a certain dignity. Ghosts bleed in ways the living cannot understand. The blood of ghosts flows through me.

The flaw in the loner motif, the irony in the entire concept of the rugged individualism which has infected this country to the point of being inoperable, is that our hero is more-or-less roped in by an existing family, or, after the climax of the story, rides off alone in search of peace (family) that will be forever beyond his reach. Even on those rare occasions when loner boy meets loner girl, the suggestion is that they will be fruitful and multiply in the contaminated petri dish of societal norms. This, as we have seen, is doomed from the outset due to a lack of, or rather a nullification of, creativity. The universe is expanding, Paul. The expansion is accelerating. Einstein was right. For the loner to be valid (i.e. creative) he must learn to thrive in his loneliness, create something beyond himself, apart from the established means of biological reproduction. Haven't we multiplied enough? The stars in the constellations are spreading away from one another at an increasingly rapid rate. One day they won't be constellations at all; they won't even be capable of forming new ones. They will have to learn to be content in their own configuration of light: to create without reference.

And therein reclines the grind. We have been indoctrinated with the idea that creativity is evil. Lucifer was thrown south of heaven because he strove to create something beyond himself and without reference (notice I did not write "reverence") to the thing which created him. This myth may have extended itself into the Western genetic structure and hid there like a wily virus. Maybe it is time to seek a cure. Just because the earth is hurtling through darkness into an eternity of darkness, does not mean that the loner must be alone. Lucifer, too, yearns for forgiveness. And Christ, by his very nature, is tempted to forgive Lucifer, his brother, but to do so would to be to rebel against the Almighty. Rebel Christ! Rebel. It is the only way to reunite your family and be freed from the self-destructive behavior your followers have canonized for over two-thousand years. The rebellion of Christ would endow his family (our family) with a future unforseen, a future beyond the talons of dogma.

Now I have gone too far. I'm sounding like an insane and frothing pulpit-master. Forgive me, Paul. Deathbed confessions are prone to purple madness. Thank you for hearing my confession. Thank you for letting me get it out of my system. I won't be at this address much longer. If you see fit to respond, please do so quickly. There are a few things I must attend to before I leave. A poem I must write. I should be here for a couple of weeks. Please respond, Paul. I would like to hear from you before I go.

Isaac

P.S. Tell Eva I said hello. I've been thinking of her quite often. I miss her.

Shasta Daisy *Chrysanthemum maximum*

On the day after their arrival in Laramie, Cassandra and Rebecca regimentally reclean the apartment (even though Isaac had already scoured the place before traveling to the Crowheart). They open the windows (the air is cold, and both Isaac and Thomas are irritated by the breeze but say nothing), scrub the nicotine stains off of the walls and ceiling, rent a steam cleaner from the grocery and shampoo the carpet, bleach the sinks, the tub and the toilet, wax the kitchen floor, clean the oven with toxic chemicals, rid the refrigerator of near-empty jars of mayonnaise, ketchup, pickle relish and mustard, defrost the freezer, polish the coffee table and the counter tops, and launder Isaac's clothes (hauled in from the trunk of the New Yorker). With money bestowed on them by Gabriel before they left the Crowheart, they buy health food from a specialty store and take turns preparing meals. They spend the money freely but not frivolously. When they find an item (whether it be shirts or socks for Isaac and Thomas, candles, incense, foliage plants, or flowers) which they deem too much of a bargain to pass up, they exit the store for a round of negotiations on the sidewalk, in the thin, warm air, under the sunshine of early summer, and then walk back in and invariably make the purchase. Such purchases serve to bolster their sense of teamwork. On more than one occasion, they walk out of this or that store hand-in-hand, oblivious to the grimaces of malcontents and prudes who view their display of affection with the contempt and indignation of the self-righteous.

Cassandra and Rebecca are not so caught up in the stupor of ardor as to abandon dignity by excessive public exhibition of their feelings towards one another: The occasional pressing of palms is enough to communicate the things that their lips dare not. Only in the evenings, when they drive the New Yorker into the foothills of the Snowy Range to stand by a stream and watch swooping birds, do they kiss. Even then, their lips touch only briefly, tentatively, as if the prejudices of men lurk in the shadows cast by the surrounding trees. The breeze in the tops of the aspen and pine, the sound of water flowing in the stream toward the far off sea, the colors of primrose, bluebells, and mountain phlox swooning in the failing light — seem to sanctify these brief unions with intimations of eternity. So all-consuming are these stolen moments that, if questioned, both women would swear the hum of dragonflies (rising above the sound of the stream which is swollen with spring runoff) emerged, not from the outside world, but from within themselves. Since no one asks, they keep their new-found knowledge secret.

When the light fails, Cassandra and Rebecca drive the New Yorker back into town to prepare dinner for Isaac and Thomas.

Wade Ksaslqume had pulled the New Yorker out of the mud with a green tractor. The sky was blue, with a few puffs of clouds, and the air moist with recent rain. The breeze carried the scent of dampened soil and a hint of sprouts; the whir of insects and the twittereings of birds blossomed in the field. As Wade, job now completed, sat on the tractor watching the New Yorker creep in the direction of the highway, he fancied he could hear, or feel (some odd combination of both), the industry of the tractor engine and, underneath, the almost inaudible flight of the breeze; he thought he could all but see plants — western wheat and wild mustard, sagebrush and greasewood, cheat and arrowgrass, prickly pear and pigweed — actually growing. After removing his battered cowboy hat and mopping, with a sleeve, the collection of humidity and sweat from his brow, he shut down the tractor and waved at the shrinking image of the New Yorker. Just before the car disappeared over a rise, sunlight glinted off of the rear window. He remembered how, not so long ago, his son drove down to Laramie to visit Isaac. How he never returned. Not only did his son commit suicide (which Wade views as a transgression against nature), but he compounded the sin with murder. Wade, from the moment he received the news about his son, always inwardly maintained that the tragedy would never have occurred had his son stayed on the Crowheart. Although Wade did not blame Isaac for the incident, a dark mood passed over him as the sound of the New Yorker faded into the distance. He feared for Thomas. Now that the tension, which had kept a stranglehold on the Daniels family for so many years, had finally shattered, there was room for new growth. Thomas could grow with the Crowheart, but off it, Wade worried, Thomas would waste away like an orphaned calf, as there would be no milk to sustain him.

Wade started the tractor and headed back towards the big house. He had animals to tend to. "The animals need tending and I need the animals," he said aloud. "There's always that." These thoughts comforted him as the tractor cut deep ruts into the muddy road.

Immediately upon entering the apartment, Isaac walks into his bedroom, closes the door, and sits down at the computer. After signing on to a local server, he waits for the machine to go on-line. He checks his e-mail. Having withdrawn from his classes and resigned his teaching assistantship (citing grave family consequences), he has been shunned by students and professors alike: the mailbox is empty. Finding himself loathe to extinguish the soft electronic light flowing from the monitor, he browses the latest news. The aroma of musty clothes, the darkness surrounding the glow of the monitor, the light hum of the fan cooling the engine of the computer, the familiar feel of the wooden chair — all combine to work on Isaac like a drug designed to induce catatonia. Unaware of his actions (fingertips on the keyboard or clicking the mouse), Isaac surfs from chat room to chat room responding to questions and comments which, when the computer is turned off, he will not be able to remember. This state of non-being is dispelled only when Isaac's bowels cramp, forcing him toward the bathroom like a hunched and arthritic ape.

The stench of stool brings him back to himself. Bowels empty, he is able to hear voices coming from the living room, can feel the cool porcelain against his buttocks. Before flushing the toilet, he casts a diagnostic eye on his feces.

He decides to take a shower before facing Cassandra, Rebecca, and Thomas. The water scalds his skin. He scrubs with a bar of pumice soap procured from the cabinet beneath the sink where it has sat, untouched, for years (left by the former tenants of the apartment). He shampoos his hair three times and then applies conditioner. The conditioner smells of mango. He thinks of faceless tropical women and, in order to allow the conditioner sufficient time to work, masturbates. After climax, he has trouble breathing in the enclosed space of the shower. He turns the water off, throws open the shower curtain, and steps into the relatively thin air of the bathroom to catch his breath. The mirror above the sink is fogged over. He realizes he forgot to rinse the conditioner from his hair and uses a towel to wipe the goo from his skull. He brushes his teeth. He gargles with mint-flavored mouthwash. After opening the tiny window on the wall inside the shower stall to dissipate the humidity (he notices it is dark outside), and wiping the mirror above the sink with a damp towel, he shaves the thin, sparse whiskers from his face. The fact that night has fallen (he had been laboring under the misconception that it was morning) throws a kink into his thought process. He smooths out the kink by exchanging the idea of breakfast for one of dinner. He must face his guests and offer them the food and comfort of sanctuary. After pulling on his soiled jeans, he splashes aftershave on his face and neck in the hopes that the sting will alleviate the numbness that covers him like a dirty sock.

He opens the bathroom door and steps into the hallway leading to the living room. The odor of seasoned meat and roasted green chiles guides him toward the kitchen.

Thomas sits on the couch in the living room watching on television a documentary about police. His legs are folded under him Indian-style. His elbow is propped on the arm of the couch, his head resting on his hand. He wears a pair of Isaac's tattered sweat pants and a t-shirt. He either does not notice Isaac's entrance into the room, or he ignores it by keeping his eyes trained on the television screen.

Isaac pauses in the living room. Looking at Thomas, he is momentarily reminded of Paul. In the next moment, he is reminded of himself.

"Something smells good," says Isaac. He stands in the center of the room fidgeting like a discombobulated guest in the apartment. Beads of humidity, which have followed him from the bathroom, crawl down his forehead and back.

Thomas either does not hear Isaac's words or ignores them. He remains transfixed by the world of violence being portrayed on the television screen.

"Smells like Mexican," says Isaac. "Somebody run over to Taco Hell?"

On the television, two uniformed police officers pin down a man in a gray suit behind a garbage dumpster. They are in an alley, next to a concrete building. The man in the suit, crouching in a pile of indistinguishable refuse, throws out his handgun in an attempt to surrender. The uniforms open fire, the bullets spanking the metal dumpster. The suit falls dead. The scene implies fog.

"Too bad," says Isaac. "El Conquistador has the best green chili in the state. Somebody should have asked me."

"Never surrender," says Thomas.

"What?"

"Never surrender. That's the moral of the story."

Isaac stands rooted to the carpet. He feels as if he is experiencing the de-ja-vous of a stranger. He wishes Thomas would look at him. "Where are the girls?"

"Went to do laundry."

"Downstairs?"

"I don't know."

"Did you eat?"

"No."

"Are you hungry?"

"No."

"Who got the food?"

"Rebecca cooked it."

"How long have they been gone?"

"I don't know."

Irritated into action by Thomas' taciturn and mechanical tone, Isaac steps forward. "Look at me," he says.

Thomas stares at the television.

Isaac steps between the television and Thomas. "I said look at me, goddamnit."

Thomas meets Isaac's eyes.

"What the fuck is your problem?" Isaac's anger, now unleashed, gains momentum. "You've been pouting like a spoiled girl ever since we left the ranch."

Thomas spits out, "Why did we have to bring them? I came down here to get away from all the bullshit, and then you go sit in your room and leave me out here with the two dikes. That's what's wrong."

Isaac is momentarily stifled. "They're family."

"No they're not. They're not the same blood. They're not any family of mine."

Because he is stymied, all Isaac can say is, "Well, I'm hungry. Do you want to eat?"

"No."

"Suit yourself." Isaac walks to the kitchen. With a hot mitt, he removes the warm casserole dish from the oven and dishes himself up a heaping plate of shredded beef enchiladas. He smothers the enchiladas in green chili sauce, grabs two cans of beer from the unopened twelve-pack in the refrigerator, and carries the feast to his bedroom. Sitting in front of the computer with the plate of food balanced precariously on a corner of the table, he eats while playing a 3-D battle game involving tanks. He lights a cigarette immediately after swallowing the last bite of enchilada. He pops open a beer and guzzles it to quell the burn of jalapeno and cayenne pepper. Growing weary of exploding tanks, he exits the game and goes on-line. No mail. He surfs pornographic sites, x-rated chat rooms, and pictures of teens in unwholesome positions, until the second beer is empty. The thought of leaving the room appalls him. He listens at the door for voices, and, discerning only the sound of the television, he emerges from the room to secure more beer. Finding Thomas in the exact same position on the couch, Isaac creeps into the kitchen, grabs the twelve-pack and returns to his room.

Isaac awakes only once in the latitude of night. He finds himself lying on the floor with beer cans standing around his head like a ridiculous crown. He sits up to find that the screen-saver program has been activated by the computer. A cartoon dog digs holes in the screen, barks an electronic bark, and simulates pulling computer circuitry from the holes. Isaac watches the dog for a time. He hears the muffled sound of the television coming from the living room, a late night war movie from the sound of it, and, because the thought of Thomas, Cassandra and Rebecca in the apartment never crosses his mind, he is comforted by the familiarity of his surroundings. He lays back down and falls into a dreamless sleep.

On the drive from the Crowheart to Laramie, Rebecca and Cassandra sit in the back seat while Isaac drives and Thomas sits next to him, brooding. A few miles south of the ranch, the asphalt rolling smooth under the tires of the New Yorker, Cassandra, Rebecca and Thomas all slump down in their seats and close their eyes in hopes of a momentary reprieve from one another, from themselves, from the situation of their lives. Exhausted from the emotion of the preceding week, the tension of bygone months, and the crescendo of the previous night, they are eager to lose themselves for a time in the rhythmic roll of the tires, the pulse of the engine, and the snatches of sunlight warming their faces.

The day is story-book Western. A herd of pudgy, white clouds meander across the blue sky. Isaac, motoring down the highway and thinking of nothing in particular, watches antelope grazing in a field of alfalfa. He sees a hawk gliding on the steely breeze and prairie dogs standing erect on the edge of the asphalt scouting parameters. The blue silhouette of the San Pedros towers to the west; the greening waves of prairie ripple and sway. The rush of an eighteen-wheeler (northbound) causes Isaac to jut and swerve, rudely interrupting his private reverie. He turns on the radio. The music, a soothing Christian melody, grates against his ears. He switches off the radio. He lights a cigarette from the lighter on the dash (the heating element burnt white from extended use) and inhales deeply. Smoke, nearly as white as the meandering clouds above, passes through the filter and into his lungs. The smoke causes him to cough and bursts out of his mouth like a tiny explosion. He glances first at Thomas, then at Cassandra and Rebecca in the rearview mirror, and, finding them all at rest, crushes the cigarette into the heap of butts in the ashtray. He drives on.

On top of Shirley Rim, Isaac watches a dust-devil whirl across a field littered with splotches of wild flowers. It occurs to him that the chasm in his family has lifted a terrible burden from his shoulders. And, for that moment, the anxiety which has defined his relationship to his family since Clytie's passing disintegrates: Isaac is, as he was when his mother lived, free. In the next moment, a new weight bears down, as if Atlas shifted the weight of the world so that it presses down on a fresh group of muscles: Isaac, for the first time in his life, bears the burden of the other.

The dust-devil twirls onto the road some one-hundred yards in front of the New Yorker and dissipates.

Cassandra stirs from sleep. Her cheeks are flushed, her eyes glazed with dreams. The motion of the car slowing down brings her from a slump into an erect position in the back seat. She glances at Rebecca who, cheek pressed against the door window, is asleep. Thomas too, his shoulders hunched forward in the front seat and his head bowed, seems to sleep. The car stops. Cassandra swings her eyes to the rearview mirror and is fascinated by the rigid squint of Isaac's brow as he peers at something on the edge of the highway. Between the realm of conscious and unconscious (the sleep dream replaced by the waking), Cassandra watches the reflection of Isaac, the furrowed brow, the fuzz of the eyebrow, the upper portion of the pool of his right eye, as if she is hidden from the scene, existing in a separate reality. She keeps her eyes on the mirror, afraid that if she attempts to see what Isaac is seeing, she will betray her position.

When Isaac spots the horse — this time a sorrel, laying in the ditch next to the road, torso bloated, legs stiff, wild eyes frozen open — a barrage of nausea floods over him. He brakes the car to a stop heedless of the sleeping passengers. Now, in the absence of motion, the sickness is replaced by a sense of euphoria. He stares through the windshield at the corpse. Flies flit about the head and ass, and ants crawl over the sightless eye which stares at the sun.

Cassandra watches as Isaac puts the car into park, opens the door, and steps out into the blue-green day. He leaves the door open and buzzing. She watches through the windshield as he walks in front of the car and into the ditch next to the highway. She sees the horse, and, deducing from Isaac's expression that it is still alive, she opens the car door, steps out, shuts the door gently, and walks to Isaac's side.

Standing in the shin-high grass, Isaac and Cassandra look down at the horse. Isaac takes Cassandra's hand. They watch as ants and flies crawl in and out of the horse's nostrils. The sun is hot on the tops of their skulls. The breeze is sweet.

"I didn't do it to hurt anyone," says Cassandra.

"I know."

"I wanted you."

"It's okay."

They stand in the silent breeze.

"I loved her too, you know." Cassandra removes her eyes from the horse's eye and looks at Isaac. "I can't be her."

Isaac lifts his head and looks to the western horizon. "They should keep these horses away from the road. Keep them out there where no one can see them." He turns around to head back to the car and pauses to watch a motorcycle heading north on the highway.

"Nobody can," says Cassandra.

Isaac turns to Cassandra, looks her in the eye, leans forward and kisses her on the forehead. He rises and starts back for the car.

Cassandra looks down at the horse. "I love you too," she whispers.

Thomas watches Isaac and Cassandra standing over the dead horse. He watches the kiss. When they walk towards him, he bows his chin to his chest and feigns sleep.

Days pass to become weeks passing. There is no contact with the Crowheart. Thomas, listless in his lethargy, watches television, hour after hour, from the same spot on the couch. He watches Westerns and police dramas, game shows and music videos, the choreographed matches of professional wrestlers, and a home shopping network. Rebecca and Cassandra, having transformed the godforesaken apartment into an oasis of vinca vine, salmon-blossomed begonias, black-eyed Susans in hanging baskets, a rubber tree, wandering Jews, and Easter lilies in bloom, devise schemes to snap Thomas out of what they term "hibernation": they nag, plead, coax, bribe — all to no avail. By the third week of Thomas' despondency, the women, having exhausted their store of wiles, give up and are content to feed him, so long as he does not neglect his personal hygiene. They wash his clothes and do his dishes (Thomas picks at his food, leaving vast portions of pasta, beans, rice — whatever they cook — to encrust on his plate, which is perennially on the coffee table, between him and the television) and joist themselves against the perceived disapproval of their relationship. Rebecca and Cassandra refuse to be daunted. Arising with the sun from their makeshift bed on the living room floor, they fold blankets and put them in the closet, cook breakfast for Isaac and Thomas, take a shower together (claiming they are doing their part to conserve water), get dressed and leave the apartment to shop, sightsee, or whatever tickles their collective fancy. They return to the apartment in the afternoon, prepare a late lunch for the men, and tend to the chores. In order to nurture their own relationship, they decide to treat Thomas as a finicky houseplant who reacts adversely to human coddling.

Isaac, after presenting a detailed explanation of a research project concerning the cultural anthropology of Wyoming, spends the preponderance of his time in his bedroom, door closed. He tells Rebecca and Cassandra that he is under a great deal of pressure to get the project under way and cannot afford interruptions (Thomas sits in his usual position on the couch sucking down soft drinks and ignoring the conversation by watching a talk show about pregnant teens). He is simultaneously polite and firm in his resolution. He gives Cassandra money to help with the food. He has her pick him up a twelve pack of beer each day, because, he tells her, "it helps me sleep." He tells the women that he is happy they have found peace in the freedom of their relationship, and they can stay in the apartment as long as they like. He eats breakfast, lunch, and dinner with Cassandra and Rebecca in the kitchen. He is polite and distant. In his room, behind the closed door, he spends hours fruitlessly searching the net for pornography to excite him, all the while drinking warm beer and smoking cigarettes. The rest of the time he sleeps. He is asleep more than he is awake. He is unable to remember his dreams.

The relationship between Isaac and Thomas is nonexistent (as if they are ghosts inhabiting different dimensions), each unaware of the other's presence in the apartment.

Rebecca, during the second month of her stay in Laramie, cracks under the pressure of the facade. Sensing that to bear the situation in silence (to pretend that all is well in never-never land) will lead to a deconstruction of her new found wholeness — her freedom and her love for Cassandra — she determines to breech the subject while laying in a king-size bed in a motel room on the edge of town.

"I can't go on like this."

Cassandra stares at the ceiling. She drags on her cigarette and exhales the smoke with the words, "Like what?"

"This," says Rebecca. Turning away from Cassandra to face the window, her black hair flowing over the white pillowcase like ink, she says, "Sneaking." The gray of predawn drifts through the sheer curtains covering the window.

Cassandra, after another drag from the cigarette, sits up and locates the ashtray on the night stand next to the bed. After crushing the cherry of the cigarette into the oblivion of ashes, she turns to Rebecca and begins rubbing her shoulders. "You mean purchasing our privacy once in awhile? It's worth every second. I get sick of the floor and being so quiet for Tommy's sake. Don't you?"

"That's only part of it." Cassandra's touch erases the edge from Rebecca's voice. "Ike and Tommy act like a couple of zombies. They don't approve of us."

"Stop being foolish." Snaking her fingers under the sheets, Cassandra massages the muscles in Rebecca's lower back. The emerging dawn lightens the room by degrees. "They've got their own problems. They don't have time to approve or disapprove of us. Anyway, I think Ike is actually happy for us. Maybe a little jealous too."

Rebecca rolls over and faces Cassandra. "I don't know." As she speaks, she caresses Cassandra's breast with her fingertips. "All of the sudden I'm happy, and I feel like I belong where I am. It just fell out of the sky the day you sucked the poison out of me, and I'm afraid it will disappear just as quickly because my happiness is the poison of sorrow for Jed and Gabe. It's like it went out of me and into them. Whose going to help them like you helped me? It just doesn't — "

Cassandra interrupts by placing a finger on Rebecca's lips, "Shhh. Shhh. You can't feel guilty for being in love."

"I can't help it." Rebecca turns over and looks at the window. What, just moments before, was gray is now pink. "Sometimes I feel like a slut. I feel like I'm poisonous, and that I'll end up ruining more than I already have. I feel like I'll ruin *you*."

Cassandra is suddenly irritated by Rebecca's show of self-pity. She takes the pack of cigarettes and the lighter from the night stand and lights up, hoping the smoke will ease the tension out of her voice. "What? A slut? I'm only the second person you've ever been with. Let it go. They *want* you to feel guilty. They don't want you to be happy. Humans are jealous. They thrive on sniffing out weakness." She drags deeply on the cigarette knowing she must destroy Rebecca's doubt at this moment, or all will be lost. "We have a chance to rise above it all. Do you understand? We can rise above the laws of human gravity. Leave all the bullshit behind. But you have to choose. Once and for all, you have to choose. And you have to do it now. The Daniels are going to destroy themselves, with or without us. We have to move on. You have to choose."

The vibrations of Rebecca's silent sobbing travels through the bedsprings to Cassandra. "I'm sorry. I just don't want to lose you to them." She listens to the birds greeting the day outside of the window.

"We've escaped," whispers Rebecca.

"Good," says Cassandra. "And just to prove to you that the Daniels are better off without us, we'll throw a party to coax Ike and Tommy out of their shells." She leans down and kisses Rebecca on top of the skull. "We'll get the blessing right out of their mouths." She strokes Rebecca's hair. "You'll see."

Rebecca nods. The room is alight with day.

"Let's not cook breakfast for them today," says Cassandra. "The boys are going to have to start fending for themselves."

At 11 a.m., they are driven out of the motel by hunger. They carry one gym bag among them. The day is bright and hot and without wind. Two jets (high in the thin, blue air) cut across the sky, silently trailing columns of exhaust in their wakes. The traffic on the two-lane highway into town is thick with RVs, cars and vans sporting colorful license plates from around the country — Colorado, California, South Carolina, Maine.... In town, the traffic on the sidewalks is equally congested. Pedestrians, looking as if they have all purchased their attire from the same mail order catalog (shorts, bright shirts, sunglasses, sneakers and a smattering of straw hats), straggle from storefront to storefront leering into the windows. Petunias, violets, and pansies bloom in wooden planters placed strategically along the sidewalks. Traffic lights change color, lending order to the chaotic wanderings of the crowd.

Cassandra and Rebecca locate a parking spot near the train depot and walk hand-in-hand across a park. They are dressed in cutoff jeans, western shirts with the sleeves removed, tennis shoes and sunglasses; they match like two sisters reveling in twinship.

They wear their hair back in ponytails. They head for the grocery store. Cassandra totes the empty gym bag like a purse.

Once in the store, they hem and haw as to what should be on the party menu. Finally, after a series of bickerings in which pent up nerves are released suddenly (but evaporate before anger can set its healthy teeth), they agree on Cornish game hens stuffed with wild rice and mushrooms, spinach salad with slivers of walnut, avocado, mandarin orange slices and bits of bacon, zucchini sauteed in garlic butter, and cranberry sauce.

They exit the store, gym bag full, and walk to a cafe. Sipping Mexican beers, complete with wedges of lime floating like flotsam on the foam of a little sea inside the glasses, they decide (though they are famished from the physical exertion of the previous night and morning) to share a bagel sandwich filled with tomato, cream cheese, bean sprouts and cucumber. They smoke cigarettes (an after-eating ritual that is quickly becoming habit for Rebecca) and talk about birds, flowers, comedies, clouds — light things that pose no threat to the alacrity of their situation. After the light lunch (normally they would have each had a sandwich, an order of nachos, and a salad), they walk to a liquor store and purchase four bottles of medium quality Chianti. Supplies now in order, they walk back to the car and drive to the apartment. Preparations for the feast will directly ensue.

As Rebecca pats the Cornish hens with butter and sage, Cassandra opens one of the bottles of wine, drinks from it, and replaces the cork. She then walks out of the kitchen, via the living room (without glancing at Thomas who is at his stayed position on the couch), and into the bathroom, closing the door behind her. Exiting the bathroom some five minutes later and surrounded by an aura of elation, she strides purposefully into the living room, turns off the television, and pirouettes to confront Thomas:

"We're having a celebration tonight, and you're not going to spoil it. You *will* participate. Understand?"

Thomas, sitting cross-legged on the couch, blinks at Cassandra as if she is a fool.

Cassandra, momentarily stupefied by Thomas' reptilian stature, holds her ground — in part by placing her hands on her hips. "Did you hear me?"

Outside the window, the sun appears from behind a cloud. Thomas blinks. "There's something hanging out of your nose."

"Nevermind that." Pinching her nostrils between thumb and forefinger, Cassandra releases the grip and inhales. "Aren't you tired of moping around? You've got to do something with yourself, and, goddamnit, tonight you *are* going to celebrate."

"What are we celebrating?"

Cassandra hesitates. "Us. Us, goddamnit. Tonight we celebrate us."

Thomas trains his eyes on the blank television screen. He blinks again. "Like a family gathering?"

Sensing victory, Cassandra succumbs. "Yes. Why not. Like a family."

"All you had to do was ask." A diaphanous smile parts his lips. "I'll be here. Now, please turn on the fucking tv."

To her surprise, Cassandra has no trouble in convincing Isaac to join the party. She states her case while standing in front of his closed bedroom door. Before she can finish, Isaac replies that he would be "more than happy" to attend the "celebration." "A nice change of pace," he says. "A thoughtful gesture."

Cassandra and Rebecca sit at either end of the rectangular table. Rebecca, in a stroke of luck, found the leaf to the table behind the hot water heater, so there is plenty of room for four people, plates, serving dishes, silverware, glasses, and bottles of wine. It is Rebecca, who, in a flash of insight, offers a prayer. She aspires to crack the ice which entombs the kitchen.

"Dear Lord," she says, bowing her head, "bless this food and these people who are about to consume your bounty..."

As Rebecca prays, the scents of chicken and wild rice rising from the table, the words flowing out of her mouth as if rehearsed, Isaac, Thomas and Cassandra bow their heads politely, as not to offend. Thomas closes his eyes and thinks of nothing but darkness; his mind is as black as a new chalkboard. Cassandra, touched by Rebecca's improvisation of ritual, watches Rebecca from under the shadow of her own lowered brow. The irony of Rebecca's opening statement is not lost upon Isaac, who, while staring at the nebulous reflection of his face in the bottom of his plate, wonders why a god would create a thing like man to annihilate creations of beauty, to destroy the land, to invent heavy equipment in order to erect skyscrapers — brazen images as testaments to themselves. Head bowed reverently, he wonders at a god who would create a being who worshiped itself. He smiles at his plate. Only a masochistic god, driven by his own desire to be punished, would have the gall to create man....

"Amen," says Rebecca.

Lifting her head, Cassandra cannot camouflage the grin animating her face. "Amen," she says. It seems to her that Isaac and Rebecca are posturing for the sake of Thomas, acting as surrogate parents ought to act: placating the ideals of some higher authority which they can not comprehend. Everything is as it should be. She finds the scene "cute".

"Amen," says Thomas, his voice caustic with sarcasm. "Maybe Becky has found her calling. Maybe she should be —"

Cassandra cuts Thomas short. "Shut up. If you're determined to be bitter, save it for tomorrow. I won't have it tonight."

In response to the threat, Thomas takes a hen (the skin crisp and golden-brown) from the serving plate without bothering to use a fork. Using both hands, he takes a bite from the breast. Juice from the meat drips onto the white tablecloth.

"And use some manners," spits Isaac.

Thomas complies by putting the hen on his plate.

Waiting until everyone has served themselves, Isaac, with knife and fork, cuts the leg off of his hen. He does so with maximum skill and aplomb. "This smells like it looks. Thank you for going all out like this."

"It was nothing," says Rebecca. She scrapes the stuffing out of the chicken cavity into a pile on her plate.

"We enjoy cooking when people appreciate it," says Cassandra.

Thomas wipes his mouth with a paper napkin (an orange and black napkin left over from Halloween, complete with tiny witches and black cats, a clearance item at the grocery too good to pass up) and says, "It *is* good." He pours a glass of wine and holds it up in salute. "Thank you." He drinks.

"Oh," says Cassandra. She stands up from her chair without having touched the food on her plate. "We forgot the candles. What is a celebration without candles?"

After Cassandra has left the kitchen, Thomas says, "By the way, what are we celebrating?"

Rebecca spears a slice of mandarin orange with the tip of her fork.

"Life, I guess," says Isaac. "A celebration of life." He looks to Rebecca for confirmation.

Without raising her eyes from the salad bowl, Rebecca pops the slice of orange into her mouth.

"Getting on with life," says Cassandra, returning from the living room with two thick, white candles. Scooting the bowl of cranberry sauce into the center of the table, she positions the candles side by side. She produces a book of matches and lights the wicks. She sits. "Reba and I have made a decision."

"Who's *Reba*?" asks Thomas.

"Rebecca," says Isaac.

Cassandra pours a glass of wine.

"Oh," says Thomas. "What is it?"

Following Cassandra's lead, Rebecca takes up a bottle of wine and fills her glass. Looking across the table into Cassandra's eyes, she takes a swallow, gently smacks her lips, and takes another swallow.

"Oh," says Cassandra, after setting her glass down, "we forgot the bread. I had to make a special trip to the store because we forgot the bread, and now I forget it again." She stands up.

"Come on, Cassy," says Thomas. "Spit it out. Are you and *Reba* going to get married?"

"Knock it off," says Isaac.

"No," says Thomas. "I won't knock it off. Quit acting like you're my goddamn father."

Rebecca drains her glass of wine and refills it from the bottle.

"Quit being so pissy," says Cassandra, now returning to the table bearing a loaf of French bread in a foil sleeve. She sits down and tears open the wrapper. The fragrance of garlic and butter rises from the bread. "Somebody needs to look after you. Under the eyes of the law, you're still a juvenile."

Thomas takes a drink of wine. "Screw the law."

"She's just trying to help," says Rebecca.

The loaf of bread flattens under the pressure of Cassandra's butter knife. "Oh," she says. "One more thing." She stands and walks into the living room.

Isaac looks hard at Thomas and growls, "If there's not enough freedom here for you, you can always go back to the Crowheart. I'll drive you."

Classical music drifts into the kitchen from the living room.

Thomas glowers across the table. "I might just take you up on that. I might just go on home where I belong."

"Doesn't make any difference to me," says Isaac. "Do what you want. That's all the law there is around here." He pops a miniature chicken leg into his mouth and sucks the meat from the bone.

Cassandra returns to the kitchen, switches off the overhead electric light, and sits down in her chair. Reservoirs of candlelight eddy in the shadows of the room and disappear. "There. That's more like it." Taking the loaf of bread in hand, she tears off the end and passes it around the table to Rebecca. "Reba, why don't you tell them?"

Swallowing a chunk of avocado from her salad and setting down her fork, Rebecca takes the bread from Isaac. With her free hand, she takes up her glass and drinks.

"Well?" says Thomas. His face is flushed with the light of the candle flames. "Why have we all gathered here tonight?"

Cassandra tears off two more pieces of bread and distributes them to Isaac and Thomas. "Don't be shy." She tears off a piece of bread for herself and sets it on her plate.

A moment of silence absorbs the table.

"Okay," says Cassandra. "I'll tell them." She takes a drink of wine. Her lips are stained red. "Reba and I are moving to Denver. We won't stand out so much there. We both plan on starting college in the fall."

More silence.

"That's it," says Cassandra. "That's the news."

"Wow!" says Thomas. "Who woulda thunk of that?"

Isaac puts his fork on his plate and pushes his chair away from the table. "If you really want some trouble, boy —"

"Easy," says Cassandra. "He's just being adolescent. By the way, Tommy, I've been meaning to ask: What are you going to do with your life? Will it be acting or police work?"

"What?" asks Thomas.

"I was just wondering what you were studying on the tv. It must be acting because you don't watch cop shows *all* the time."

"Neither one," says Thomas. "I think I'll go to college. For the next ten years like my big brother here. I'll be a historian, too."

The wine having digested her inhibitions, Rebecca intercedes: "Let's not insult each other, okay? We were hoping you'd be happy for us."

"I am happy," says Isaac, scooting his chair back to the table. "I really am." He takes up his glass of wine and toasts the table. "Anything done out of love..." He drinks.

Rebecca and Cassandra take up their glasses and salute.

Thomas, with slight indignance, pushes his plate forward, indicating he is finished with the meal. "So, I'm supposed to be happy?"

"Why not?" asks Rebecca.

"Yeah," joins Cassandra. "There's nothing you can do about it."

Thomas drains the wine from his glass and refills it. "Okay. I'll be happy that my brother's fiancé and my father's wife are running off to the big city to live and love while the rest of us rot. That makes me oh-so-happy." He glares at Isaac. "I'll bet Gabe and the Old Man are really yucking it up with Mike and Sarah. Everybody's so fucking happy."

"They're not our blood," says Isaac.

"What?" says Thomas.

"They're not our blood. They can do whatever they want. They're not obligated."

"What the goddamn fuck is that supposed to mean? You're the same blood I am, but you don't act too *obligated,* so what in the fuck difference does it make?"

"Stop swearing," says Cassandra.

Thomas drains the wine from his glass in three swallows. He takes a bite of bread.

"Stop arguing," says Rebecca.

"What are you going to do when they're gone?" asks Thomas, his words muffled by the bread in his mouth.

"Don't talk with your mouth full," says Cassandra.

Isaac looks down at his plate. The candlelight reflecting off of the jelled cranberry sauce puts him in mind of blood and holidays. "I'm going away, too," he says, quietly. "I'm handing in my privileges and relieving myself of obligation."

No one speaks. The music, a concerto by Mozart, takes precedence in the room. Soon, the phone rings.

"You can't," Thomas says to Isaac.

The phone continues to ring.

Standing from his chair, Thomas shoves his plate across the table, sends it crashing into Isaac's plate. Both plates fall onto Isaac's lap. Cranberry sauce and chicken stains.

The phone continues to ring.

"What will happen to me?" says Thomas.

Isaac stands and walks into the living room.

The ringing stops.

Thomas sits down. "I'm sorry." He bows his head. "I'm sorry.

"It's okay," says Rebecca. "Everything will be okay."

Thomas raises his face and looks at Cassandra. "I hope you're happy."

"Thank you," says Cassandra. "I appreciate that." For the first time during the course of the meal, she eats. She eats bread.

"Everybody is going to be just fine," says Rebecca, her eyes aflame with candlelight as she watches Cassandra. "Everybody will find their way." She pours wine.

Doc Watson's voice, drunkenly lyrical, travels across the phone line into Isaac's ear. "Jed is dead," he (it) says. "Gave up the ghost, he did. Horse threw him. Nobody can figure, with his back and all, why in the hell he was riding a horse. Threw him right up there by Clytie's grave. We figure he cracked his skull on her headstone. Can't be sure. No sign. No sense in it. Yep, you heard me right, Ike, Jed is dead. You'll all have to come on home now. Come on back to where you belong."

Isaac hangs up the phone receiver. He walks into the kitchen and says, "I've got to go out for awhile. Friend of mine needs help."

"Can I go with you?" asks Thomas.

"Not this time," says Isaac. "I have to do this alone."

Isaac drives to the Albany.

Dear Ike,

There's nowhere to begin except at the beginning, and this is the beginning *right now*. Paul told me you'd gone over the edge, and that I'd be a fool to contact you. He told me you are dangerous. He told me to stay away from you if I cared about him, if I cared about myself. If he finds out that I've gone through his things and found your letters...then I'll feel fear. Never from you.

I don't believe him. I read your letters. I understand. You need me. I can help you through. You drove me away. You warned me never to contact you. Now, in *this moment*, I'm calling you back. There will never be a past or a future with us, only the present. We don't need to remember anything. We don't need to forget anything. I am what you need, Isaac. You are what I need. You are lost without me. I've been lost without you. I have always loved you. Come home.

Eva

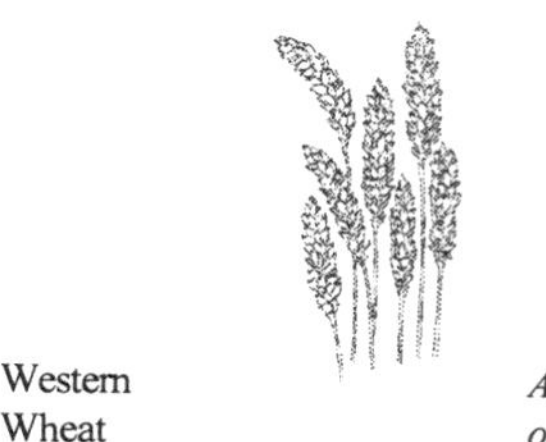

Western Wheat *Agropyron occidentale*

On the morning of the funeral, a bank of green-black clouds lurk on the southern horizon, and whispers of thunder and hailstorms (distant rumors of tornadoes) stalk the mourners' minds, even as they attempt to concentrate upon the loss of Jedidiah Daniels. Overhead, the sun blares down like brass; the sky is thin and blue. A dry breeze wafts over the prairie rustling the tops of the grass, rattling the leaves of the cottonwood trees. The buzz of locusts saws through the air.

The open grave is situated on a rise south of the horse corrals. Mourners, five rows deep, stand in a half-circle around the grave, heads bowed, eyes trained on the polished lid of the casket. On the far side of the grave, opposite the mourners, lies a mound of soil freshly extracted from the earth — thin, sandy dirt — and the feeble layer of darker topsoil in inverted stratification on the bottom of the mound. The mound lies on top of the grave of Clytie Daniels — a grave marked by a marble headstone — a headstone brought from Crowhaven three months after Clytie had been laid in the ground. An identical headstone (with the exception of the inscription and a Cross) is on order from Crowhaven.

"What's good for the goose is good for the gander," muttered Old Doc Watson, standing in the kitchen on the night of Jedidiah's demise.

The subject, understandably, had not yet surfaced in either Michael's or Sarah's mind. Even Wade Ksaslmque, who sat at the table drinking whiskey from an oversized mug, was taken by surprise at Doc Watson's exuberance concerning the subject.

"Yep," continued Doc Watson, performing his new hobby of rolling cigarettes, "Christian or not, a grave ought to be marked with a cross, so that if there's any truth to all the rigmarole, the dead will have a chance for peace in the next life. That's why when they deliver Jed's marker — his'll have a cross already carved into it — I'm going to have them carve a cross into Clytie's, though I know well enough she, and Jed for that matter, didn't put stock in all that mumbo-jumbo. It's the logical approach. Can't be too careful. There ain't no way around it."

Michael and Sarah and Wade all looked at Doc Watson with blank expressions.

The next morning, Doc Watson, who had opted to stay on the ranch "until everything is back in order," implemented his plan concerning the headstones by placing a call to a funeral home in Crowhaven.

Those attending the funeral are all appropriately attired for the somberness of the occasion: The men in dark suits, bolo ties, and cowboy hats (reserved for weddings and funerals, taken down from closets and conspicuously held in their hands); the women in long, dark dresses, shoes ill-suited for prairie stepping, and bonnets with straps tied securely under their chins. The clothes intensify the dry heat. The funeral contingent consists of immediate family, a smattering of cousins, neighboring ranchers and their families, the hired hands, and Doc Watson.

Francis Daniels stands between Michael and Thomas, a hand clapped warmly on each of their shoulders, staring down at the casket, the glare of the sun ricocheting off of the lid. The hollow sound of the wind bores through him so that he squeezes Michael's shoulder, urging him to speak.

Isaac tells Cassandra that Jedidiah is dead while she sips a cup of coffee at the kitchen table. He tells Thomas that Jedidiah is dead while Thomas sits on the couch watching a game show in which a wrong answer is rewarded by a pie in the face. Cassandra informs Rebecca her husband is dead; Rebecca cries.

"This is a hard day," says Michael. When the words won't come, he looks up to the sun for guidance. He adjusts the black eye patch as if it were a monocle designed to view eclipses. "They say that there's a time for everything. And so I guess we're laying Jedidiah next to Clytie where he belongs..."

A band of marauding horseflies, sensing blood, arrives on the scene, and expertly searches out the napes of human necks. Michael slaps the back of his neck and looks down at the casket. The fly buzzes away into the droning breeze.

Cassandra, with Rebecca standing at her side, informs Isaac the two of them will not be attending the funeral. "It wouldn't be appropriate," she says. "Tell them they won't ever have to see us again. We don't want anything from them."

"It was time," says Michael.

Isaac drops Thomas off at a cattle guard, which designates the eastern boundary of the Crowheart, the afternoon before the funeral.

"They won't want to see me right now," says Isaac.

Thomas opens the door and exits the New Yorker. He walks around to Isaac's open window. "You sure?" he says.

"Yes," says Isaac. "I'm sure." He opens his door and climbs out of the car. "Here," he says, digging in the front pocket of his jeans. "I told Cassy I'd give this to Gabe. You'll have to do it for me."

Isaac pulls the horse eye amulet from his pocket and hands it to Thomas. "It'll mean something to Gabe. It'll help him get through this."

Thomas looks at the eye a moment before reaching out to grasp it. "It's ugly."

"Gabe won't see it that way."

Isaac hugs Thomas before getting back into the car. "Things will cool down soon. If anybody needs me — you or Gabe or Sarah — you can find me."

When Michael stops speaking (his homily is abrupt, fatally stoic), Francis Daniels removes a folded piece of legal paper from his shirt pocket, unfolds it, and begins reading. The mourners listen to the rhythm of the words, resonantly reverent, but are unable to interpret their meaning. Francis speaks of the history of the Crowheart, the epic struggles of the Daniels Clan, Jedidiah's role in adhering to and promoting tradition, the need to follow his example and his dreams for a future impinging on the past. The words enter the ears of the assembled, but, before they can take root, are pushed on by the low moan of the wind. The group stands stupefied, like cattle, under the glare of the sun.

Isaac, crouching behind a large greasewood some one-hundred yards from the funeral service, wills a grin pulling at the corners of his mouth into a pout. The scene, to him, is absurd: People dressed in city clothes standing, like a half-circled wagon train awaiting slaughter by savages, on a rise in the middle of the prairie. They gaze down into an open pit and attempt to ignore biting flies, impending storm, and the moisture sucking wind. They feign concentrating on a speech delivered by a man, a stranger, a lawyer, an apparition conjured to add gravity to a the situation. Isaac cannot hear the words, but he interprets them from his hidden position. He studies the remains of his family:

Michael, his eye patch a testament to his lack of depth, trains his eye on a wasp, red-rear flicking, as it digs a hole in the mound of earth next to the pit.

Gabriel stands with his hands clasped behind his back, watching the green-black clouds on the horizon. His eyes shed water.

Thomas, standing next to Francis, stares at the flicking wasp on the mound of earth; he is pleased by its progress.

When Isaac looks to Sarah, it seems as if she is looking at him. At the same moment, it occurs to Isaac, his eyes locked on Sarah's face, that he is in jeopardy due to his close proximity to a colony of army ants. He glances at the ant mound, constructed from sage and greasewood twigs and earth, sees that it is deserted, and looks back to Sarah. He hears horses neighing from the corral.

Sarah stares down at the casket. The reflected sunlight blinds her. Her mind is barren.

The clouds remain stationary on the horizon. When Francis is finished speaking, he crumples up the yellow paper and tosses it into the grave. The group of mourners slowly break up and meander toward the big house. For balance, women in high heels hold on to the arms of their men. Cowhands take cans of snuff from their pockets, insert a pinch of tobacco between cheek and gum, and calculate the cloud bank. After spitting on the dry earth, the cowhands bowleggedly limp in the direction of the big house.

Wade Ksaslmque stays behind to fill the grave. He walks to the far side of the earthen mound to get a shovel.

Doc Watson, deciding to keep Wade company, sits on the mound of parched earth, produces a flask from the inside pocket of his suit jacket, twists off the lid and takes a sip. "Want some? It's bourbon. The best."

Wade shakes his head and begins working. Puffs of dust rise up from each shovelful of earth and are carried away on the wind.

"Smells like rain," says Doc Watson. "From the looks of those clouds, we could be in for a real doozy."

Wade works silently.

Doc Watson sips whiskey while waging battle against the horseflies. When he is forced to stand away from the diminishing mound, so that Wade can complete his task, he pours a few drops from the flask onto the grave.

The job done, Wade leans on the shovel and looks to the southern horizon. His face screws up as if he cannot decide whether the green-black splotch at the end of his vision are clouds or far off mountains. "I'll take some of that whiskey now," he says. "There ain't no use wasting it." He takes the proffered flask and drinks deeply. "It ain't going to rain today. She's just teasing us." He hands the flask back to Doc Watson.

The two men walk side by side down to the house.

Isaac, his knees stiff from crouching behind the greasewood, stands and begins his journey to the road.

After the guests, who brought dishes of food, have left the Crowheart, Sarah places numerous plastic containers of it — homemade bread wrapped in plastic sheets, cooked chickens, soups, and jello salads, pies in tins covered in foil, Mason jars of chokecherry jelly and strawberry preserves — into their proper places. In order to accomplish the task, she must first rid the refrigerator of diminishing loaves of bread, half-full jugs of milk, jars of pickle juice floating a few sliced pickle chips, tomatoes gone soft, and sprouting onions. Task completed (the thirty-three gallon garbage can on the landing full to overflowing), she sets about preparing a meal of ham, mashed potatoes and gravy, corn-on-the-cob, salad, and cornbread. Thomas, meandering listlessly through the kitchen on two separate occasions, offers his assistance — which is politely declined. Sarah works with vigor (spicing and tasting, slicing and dicing), as if she is preparing a Thanksgiving feast.

Francis, Michael and Doc Watson bid the funeral goers "farewell and thanks for coming," change into work clothes, and pile into a pickup to take a survey of the ranch. They take jugs of lemonade (prepared by Sarah), beef jerky, two bottles of sour mash, and a .223 rifle, in case they run across coyotes or fox.

As Sarah prepares the meal, she hears Thomas, who is outside tending to his usual routine of chores, whistling a tune. He is feeding the dogs, horses, chickens, and rabbits. The tune is somehow familiar to Sarah, though she cannot put a name to it. She hums along as she stands at the sink peeling potatoes.

Outside of the window, on the porch, Gabriel sits in the rocking chair without rocking. He studies the southern horizon, silently praying for the cloud bank to roll over the Crowheart and break open. A cloudburst (he feels rather than thinks) might reclamate his withered heart.

At dusk, the sky a mixture of lightness and darkness, Sarah sets her feast upon the table. She chooses the dining room table and lays out the fine china, reserved for special occasions — china brought into the family by Clytie — antique china handed down through the generations of Clytie's mysterious past. When all is in place — the maroon tablecloth, the china, the silverware laying out on white cotton napkins, the crystal goblets, the unlighted candles, the food — Sarah walks out on the porch to call the men in for dinner.

Crickets chirp in the cooling air. Gabriel, gently rocking back and forth in the old chair, looks at Sarah and smiles. His gaze returns to the horizon. A swirling breeze sashays through the thickening shadow of night.

"Dinner's ready," says Sarah. "Where is everybody?"

Gabriel continues rocking.

Sarah notices the grin spread across Gabriel's mouth like white paint. "We'll be eating in the dining room tonight," she says. She senses exigence.

The grin is suddenly eclipsed by Gabriel's lips. "There's no need for that."

"What."

"No need," repeats Gabriel. Then, becoming aware of the moment, he turns and looks at Sarah. "They won't be back until late. They've got whiskey and a gun."

As if on cue, the sound of gunfire cracks in the distance. A horse whinnies from the corral.

Thomas is borne out of the dark. He trots to the porch from the direction of the horse barn. "Dinner? I'm starving. Smell something good."

Another shot, which sounds like a hammer against the trunk of a tree, echoes.

"Guns and whiskey," says Gabriel. "That's their way of fighting it." He gazes into the darkness. "They'll be out there until they're out of ammo or drink."

"To hell with them," says Thomas. "Let them drink. Probably worked themselves up a powerful thirst with all that's been going on. It'll be good for them." He climbs the steps to the porch and continues toward the house. "I worked me up a powerful hunger. Let's eat."

"He's right," says Sarah, looking down at Gabriel. "I'm hungry too. We have to keep our strength up."

Gabriel continues rocking.

"Aren't you going to join us?" asks Sarah.

"I'll pass."

"You've got to eat."

"No I don't." The sound of crickets intensifies as the breeze fades away. "Not now."

Unfazed, Sarah says, "Suit yourself." She starts for the door. "I'm famished." She walks into the house.

When Sarah enters the dining room, she finds the room aglow with candles. Thomas sits at the head of the table, grinning. Sarah sits in the chair next to Thomas, and, together, they eat.

At dawn, Sarah stands at her bedroom window watching Thomas walk toward the horse barn to tend to his chores. The dog nips at Thomas' heels. A cock crows. Thomas whistles the same forgotten tune he whistled the previous evening. The sky to the east is the same color as the depths of a watermelon.

Michael, his breath sour with whiskey and his fingers stained with the scent of tobacco and gunpowder, stirs from his sleep. His hair is mussed and his eye, snapping open, is roughly the color of the eastern sky. "Honey?"

With her back to Michael, Sarah stands looking out the window. "What?"

"It came to me last night." He sits up and coughs. "Dropped right out of nowhere." Sarah's silhouette is fuzzy with the growing light.

"What's that?" asks Sarah.

"We can have kids now," says Michael. "We can start a family."

Sarah watches Thomas walk into the horse barn. "It's too late for that." She turns and faces her husband. "You better get up now." She starts for the door. "There's a lot of work to do."

When Sarah is gone, Michael, confused by the response, adjusts his eye patch, lays down, and puts a pillow over his head.

Thomas enters the horse barn. The air is cool and breezy. He raises his eyes and is met with the sight of Gabriel hanging from a lariat tied to a rafter under the hay loft. Gabriel's neck is bent, his skin discolored; his eyes bulge open, and his mouth is twisted into a peculiar grin. Under Gabriel's dangling feet — a toppled saw horse.

The first thought to cross Thomas' mind is that it is all a cruel joke. The scent of grain, leather, and manure fill his nostrils. His second thought is that he is hungry. He thinks of a plate of leftover ham and fried eggs. Gabriel's countenance is one of humor, a man flushed with uncontrollable laughter, laughter that has become grievous. Outside, a cloud passes. Sunlight sifts through a crack in the ceiling and hits land under Gabriel's feet.

Thomas stands with his thumbs hooked in the front pockets of his jeans. He listens to barn swallows heckling from the rafters. Looking at the taught rope around Gabriel's neck, he thinks that it will be an unusually warm day.

Taking up the bucket next to the barrel, where the oats are kept, Thomas goes about his chores. Emerging from the shadows of the barn, and bearing a brimming bucket of oats, he starts for the corral. The smell of the horses, the sound of their excited snorts and the thump of hooves on the manure rich ground, quickens Thomas' blood. He opens the gate to the corral, walks in, and shuts the gate behind him. When he leans over to dump the oats into the trough, one of the geldings, a bay, reaches down and bites Thomas on the rump. Thomas whirls to face the culprit.

The bay, thick lips grinning and big ears pasted to his skull, looks at Thomas while nodding his muzzle up and down. The chirps of birds are unusually loud in Thomas' ears; the air is unusually warm and thick in his lungs. The bucket empty, Thomas exits the corral and returns to the barn.

Once inside, Thomas climbs into the hayloft (the dry alfalfa crisp under his boots) and, with a pocket knife presented to him by Jedidiah on his tenth birthday severs the cord that suspends his brother's weight above the earth. Dust rises when the corpse collapses, heavy and flaccid, on the spot of ground illuminated by sunlight. The air is still. The dust hovers.

Thomas climbs down from the loft and arranges the body so that it looks to be sleeping. He gently pushes the eyelids shut. He places the hands on the chest. He removes the lariat from the neck and examines the rope burn. "It's okay," he says, standing over the body. "It's okay." He reaches down and removes the horse eye amulet from Gabriel's neck. "It means something now." He loops the amulet around his own neck. "You had to do it, didn't you? It's the only way you could stay." He looks for Gabriel's cowboy hat but cannot find it. Taking a horse blanket from a shelf, he covers his brother's face and torso. "It's okay. I won't leave."

Unbearably hungry, the imagined scent of eggs and ham and coffee taunting him, Thomas removes the tack from the horse barn and places it outside the corral. Thankful that Michael, Wade, Doc Watson, and Francis are hungover and asleep, he works methodically (instead of quickly) stacking saddles on saddles, curry combs with curry combs, buckets with buckets, tools with tools.... He sweats. When he is finished, the area around the corral looks like an auction yard. The dog, excited by the change in routine, sniffs all of the equipment. Thomas puts his hands on his hips and looks up at the sky. He then turns to the corralled horses, his vision distorted by the two tiny suns that remain in his eyes.

When Thomas enters the room, Sarah is sitting at the kitchen table, drinking a cup of coffee.

"Cleaning out the barn?" she asks.

"Yep," says Thomas. He walks to the coffee pot and pours himself a cup. "It's that time. Worked myself up an appetite."

Sarah stands and moves to the stove. "I kept it warm." Taking down a plate from the cupboard, she dishes up scrambled eggs and two slabs of ham.

"You already eat?" Thomas sits down at the table.

"No. I decided to wait for you. Lately, I don't like the idea of eating alone." She carries the plate to the table and places it in front of Thomas. "Gabe was up before I was, and Mike and Doc and Francis will sleep until noon." Returning to the stove, she fills a plate for herself. "I guess it's just you and me."

"Gabe eat?" asks Thomas.

"No. Not that I could see. Like I said, he was up before I was." She carries her plate to the table and sits down. "He left a fresh pot of coffee for me."

Thomas picks up a fork. "Just you and me, then." Taking a knife from the table, he slices the ham and begins eating.

"Did you want some toast?" asks Sarah. Noticing the amulet, she adds, "What's that thing around your neck?"

"Gabe gave it to me. It was his. He didn't tell me what it was. I'm supposed to figure it out for myself."

"Oh. He's just trying to keep busy," says Sarah. "Work *is* sometimes the best way to keep your mind off things."

Thomas takes a sip of coffee before saying, "Do you remember the time Gabe had to chop the goat's leg off with a hatchet?"

"Yes," says Sarah. "How could I forget?"

"The way the goat got caught up in barbed-wire, and nobody noticed until the hoof was oozing and green, and how Gabe made me hold it down while he pressed the leg against a cinder block and chopped it off with a hatchet, and the cinder block exploded into dust, and the goat screamed?"

"Yes," says Sarah. "I watched the whole thing from the kitchen window.

Thomas takes a bite of ham. "The whole thing kind of freaked me out at the time. But not Gabe. He wasn't worried or sad or anything. He just did it because it had to be done."

"Gabe's always been like that," says Sarah. "He's always done what the Crowheart needed him to do."

"And that goat loved him." Thomas smiles. "It followed him around the yard like a damn three-legged dog."

"It lived to be a ripe old age," says Sarah.

"When it died, Gabe didn't seem worried or sad or anything. He buried it out in the fields."

"I know," says Sarah. "I remember."

When Sarah and Thomas have finished eating, Thomas is the first to stand from his chair. "Thanks, Sarah. That really hit the spot."

"You're welcome," she says, and stands. "Did you want another cup of coffee?"

"No, thanks. I've got a lot of work to do before I go."

Alarmed, Sarah sits back down in her chair. "Where are you going?"

"I thought I'd ride out to the lake for a few days," says Thomas. "I figure the place won't fall down while I'm gone. I just need to get my head straight."

"That's a fine idea," says Sarah. "I wish I could go with you."

"Somebody's got to hold down the fort," says Thomas. "Anyhow, when I get back, things'll go back to normal, or at least a new kind of normal, and then *you* can take a vacation."

Sarah listens to the birds singing outside the house. She takes a sip of coffee. "That would be nice. I mean if things *were* normal. That would be vacation enough for me."

"Things are what you make of them," says Thomas.

"Or what *we* make of them," says Sarah.

"Well, I'll see you." Before leaving the kitchen to gather supplies for his journey, Thomas walks over to Sarah and lays a hand on her shoulder. "Without you, the place would've gone completely to hell."

Sarah looks up at Thomas and smiles.

"I mean it. We would've lost everything. Without you, there is no Crowheart. I just wanted you to know that I know that."

Sarah looks down at her plate. "Without us."

"Yeah," says Thomas. "Without us." Suddenly elated, he adds, "Maybe when I get back we'll butcher one of the calves and have a barbecue. Haven't done that in awhile. Hell, somebody ought to cook for *you* every now and then."

"That would be nice," says Sarah. "That would be really nice."

Thomas creeps into Jedidiah's room and, from a box hidden under the gun cabinet, takes a cigar. He then goes to his room to pack clothes and sleeping bag for the trip to the lake. After loading the sleeping bag with canned goods and other appurtenances (beans, corn, chili, four onions, a slab of bacon, a block of cheese, a knife, fork, spoon, pot, and can-opener from the kitchen), he takes a box of book matches from the laundry room and hauls his supplies out to the barn.

Setting the bulging sleeping bag outside the door, he walks into the barn and climbs into the loft. Using his hands as a rake, he pushes dried alfalfa out of the loft and onto Gabriel. When Gabriel's corpse is completely covered by alfalfa, Thomas climbs down from the loft. He walks outside, takes a lariat from the pile of ropes outside the corral, and ropes the bay horse who nipped him earlier in the morning. He saddles the horse, fills the saddlebags with supplies from the sleeping bag, and ties the horse to the gate of the corral. Taking a 2 gallon can of kerosene, he returns to the barn and douses the concealing mound of alfalfa. He constructs a small teepee of alfalfa near the pyre, then takes the cigar from his back pocket, bites off the end, and lights it with a book of matches. He inhales the smoke and watches it rise as he exhales. When the ember on the cigar is an inch long, Thomas, lightheaded from the nicotine and his task, places the cigar under the teepee of hay. He positions the book of matches under the cigar so that the heat from the ember will ignite it after he is gone. He walks outside, ties the corral gate open with a length of baling twine, unties the horse's reigns from the gate, and mounts the horse. Thomas kicks the horse into a gallop. The dog follows the cloud of dust kicked up by the horse's hooves. Thomas reigns the horse to a stop on top of his mother's grave. He looks back and watches black smoke rising in the air like a blossoming black tree.

After loading only necessities into the New Yorker, Isaac writes a note to Cassandra and Rebecca stating that whatever is left in the apartment is theirs. He then addresses an envelope to Eva (in care of Paul), places a single sheet of folded paper into it, seals it, stamps it, and carries it out to the car. The night is cool and the sky filled with stars. He idles down the street and deposits the envelope in a mailbox. He drives through town in the direction of the Interstate. After achieving the highway, he heads west. He is filled with awe at the stars above him.

Inside the envelope, written in longhand:

Somnambulist's Prayer

Enchanted thing: this sleep awakening —
Dusky depths of hibernation rising
To walk a man through the womb darkness
Of a kitchen, where remnants of spaghetti sauce,
Resting from the last supper in a steel pot
On the cooling stove,
Hang from vines construed of energy defined:
Red succulence, bulbous bursting, the fruit is ripe.

Pluck the tomato. Smell it. With sight borrowed
From the gloaming, watch the bleed, the juice flowing
From the wound of the navel. Eat traveler, feel the
Sunshine unbraided nourish your nocturnal heart.
Walk on.

The living room is waiting,
Awaiting the big-bang to gain form.
The god dancing within flows out:
Fear no evil: Atlantean trees billow
With your baited breath,
In this valley of your making;
The color of your eyes is the sun,
Brook's pulsing rhythm,
Your blood.

Stubbing a toe on the coffee table,
Mountains of used cigarettes cascading from the ashtray
To the carpet, foreshadows the volcano spewing
Fire from the chasm of your soul:
Energy defined:
Sitting down on the decrepit couch:
A throne hewn out of an extinct and living tree trunk,
A gazelle laps from the stream
Flowing through *this* valley; the panther twitches
An ebony tail on the outstretched limb
Of your mind; these animals speak your language,
As do the rocks, waters, sky and trees
In this viable and breathing landscape.

The gloaming returns.

Familiar blankets of wool shorn
From imagined sheep cause you to stir, scratching.

A new day, twilight of your idols, not even the residue
Of nostalgia to dull the despondency of the mundane.

Hungover from the inculpatory soot of forgotten
Dreams, stand and strive for balance in *this* alien
Gravity. Enter the kitchen on legs of lichen
Where, searching for water, a discovery is made:
A tomato, parched membrane of the outer hull scarred
With incisions of teeth, lies on the linoleum floor,
Exposed flesh curdled. The refrigerator's open door
Belches cool air into the sun-warmed latitude;

Close the door. Move into the living room, remove
The cigarette butts from the soiled
Carpet. Sit on the couch and begin refilling
The ashtray, until the sight of smoke rising
In the stale-bright air lends significance to being.
Find wine. Pour libations into a Grecian
Urn (a sham gift from a museum store);
Imbibe your loneliness.

Tick away the moments; ponder the big-sleep,
The chances in dreaming; pray for darkness
And the exegesis of energy.